We, The Fallen

David A Dunlop

Copyright (c) 2018 David A Dunlop
All rights reserved
ISBN: 9781726328111

DEDICATION

For Gerry Moore and all the staff and students involved in the 'My Adopted Soldier' Project, 2015 & 2017

and

*with special appreciation of Gerry's son,
David Moore,
whose beautiful rendition of several of the songs which appear in the text of the novel may be listened to on the Soundcloud accounts of 'dadunlop', 'DavidMoore' or of 'Patrick McAleese'.*

We, The Fallen

Chapter 1

Bernie Doherty

This is the story of how I lost my son.
Actually, now I think about it, it is also the story of how he found himself, but that is for him to explain to you.
It all started with some scheme called "Find The Fallen". Why, in heaven's name, would you apply for some random history project, right in the middle of your final year in school? You'd think he might have had a bit of sense, been more focussed on his A levels. Not my Patrick.
Isn't it the weirdest thing that a decision like that can change the course of a life? An air-headed, out-of-character call made on some brainless whim!
Who am I to be talking? I have the gold-embroidered T-shirt for that one myself; I just didn't write poems or songs about it, like he does.
Where he got his creative gene from I haven't a clue but it has been there from when he was a nipper. It used to drive his Philistine father mad but I sort of liked that side he had to him; 'the Derry Air' in him, I always thought. The number of scribbled verses on wee bits of paper that I would find lying around his room; I could've papered a wall with them.
This is the latest one.
He sent it to me from the hospital.
Make of it what you will; myself, I wonder if he's on some drug or other but maybe that's unkind. It all sounds very grand. Maybe some of those poems he was reading for his A Level English are fizzing around in the haze of his poor concussed brain. Maybe the ghosts of Hopkins and Yeats are communicating with him at some level that I will never understand.
Maybe he will explain it all to me some day, please God.

If I had known..

If I had known when I saw her first,
Her perfect beauty darkening my screen
The hidden girl behind those fallen eyes
The sorrow and the pain of where she'd been
If in a horoscope or sacred text
I'd heard a warning bell of coming fire
Or had a nightmare vision where I saw
Two flaming spirits dance a spinning gyre
Till in a blaze of fury we'd be burned
Down to the naked marrow of our souls
But we - the fallen innocents - arise
Like Phoenix, shaking off the dusty coals

Patrick McAleese
(September 2017)

Chapter 2

(Patrick McAleese)

So this is how I filled in the application form. Why I did is another question, one that I'm not sure I understand the answer to myself.
I hate forms like this; I hate having to commit myself to paper in this way, forced in between the lines like some new type of 'you-might-be-right, you-might-be-wrong' crossword puzzle.
I was in two minds about it from the start. The 'Somme trip' part sounded interesting enough but there were a couple of down-sides. The timing, first week in July...not good. What about the wee summer job that I had been angling for in the Port? How would Moran's feel about me asking if I could start a week late? I could not see them jumping up and down in delight about it. Maybe have to look elsewhere; there's no way I can afford to miss out on the cash at the minute, not with needing fifteen hundred smackers for the Suzuki 125 of my dreams.
Then there's the 'Research-a-local-soldier-who-fell-at-the-Somme' bit. I have to be honest about this; my first reaction was, 'No way! I've sort of had my fill of 'local soldiers'. That's another story and it's hardly a fair reaction. Even the idea of 'research', extra work like, in the year when I'm supposed to be studying for my A Levels...it did not seem like a plan to me. I was pretty sure that my mum would not be happy. She'd have a hundred and ten objections, at least one of them to do with my future and the vital importance of this vital year of this vital little life of mine. I had no notion of how much work it would mean. Would there be info online? What sites are there to help find out about particular soldiers, their regiment, where they served, how they died? Would there be local sources I could contact...like the British Legion? (And, did I really want to get mixed up with them, given my own connections?)
So why did I bow to the pressure, imaginary, of-course, and stick my hand up, like some thirteen-year-old teacher's lick? No idea.
It wasn't as if Donaldson even looked at me or anything. He rambled on about the thing for ten minutes and not once did he squint in my general direction. A few people in the class asked questions, maybe as much to keep him talking and delay the sand-blast of detail about Russia's Cold War Policy that he hits us with. Most of us sat quietly, happy to let him ramble on behind his whacky black beard; (why this

hang-in-there hipster look? So pathetic. But he's a History teacher, of-course! Is he trying to look like Parnell or something?)
Then he asked the hook question.
"Some of you must have ancient relatives who fought in the first World War, I'm quite sure. Do any of you have any knowledge of such a family history? Come on, some of you must?"
There was a bit of looking around in the class; one or two mumbled 'could-be' sort of responses. Nobody was coming out and saying anything definite. At this point I was hoping he would not fix that famous stare on me and sense the increased thump of my heart, like the echo of marching feet as a whole line of my ancestors paraded off into battle.
Anyhow, the thing would not leave my head and, after forty minutes of distracted imagining when I should have been concentrating, I found myself queueing up at Donaldson's desk with about a dozen others. They were mainly girls but my mate Barry waited to get an application form as well. He was well surprised to see me standing there beside him. Not any more so than Donaldson though.
"Real-ly Patrick?" my teacher said, still holding suspiciously to the form as I tried to take it out of his hand. "I wouldn't have thought this was your cup of tea....but there you go. You might as well try your luck. Nothing ventured... Now girls, when you are filling it in read the rubric carefully. Like I said earlier, they are looking for someone with a commitment to research, so try to show that in your entry. And try to demonstrate some kind of connection to history....connection! That's what it's all about. We all have a connection to the past, whether we know it or not. You leaving Patrick?"
I was edging away towards the door. He was not showing any sign of giving up. Nor was he showing any sign of really knowing anything about me, after all this time in his stupid class. How could he though? It's not as if I myself have much of a handle on my own internal conflicts...why should he? Something about his skepticism bugged me inside. I did not like to be rude or ungrateful, but I was out of there. The smell of the canteen chip-pans was calling.
"And don't forget what I said about an interest in the Arts. Are you a fan of Owen or Sassoon or Thomas Kettle maybe? Or have you studied the paintings of Paul Nash or Otto Dix? Can you sing 'It's a long, long way to Tipperary'? Maybe not though. Or do you have an interest in photography or early war movies or...."
I slithered around the open door and headed to the dining hall leaving Barry to fill me in on anything I missed.

Find the Fallen Project 2016

Entry Form

Please complete the form below by filling in all your relevant details.

Your Full Name   Patrick Gordon McAleese.

Address   72 Bannview Close.
Coleraine.
Co. Derry
BT 65 32 HY

Email address   pgmcaleese97@yahoo.com

Date of Birth   27th September 1997

School   The Academy, Ballymoney

Name of Teacher who will be your Referee   Mr D Donaldson

Current stage in school   Year 14. Doing A Levels this year

Subjects currently being studied
History
Music
English Literature

Special skills/talents which you would bring to the project
Music; I enjoy writing, both lyrics and tunes. Also photography and IT. I get on well with most people and enjoy working in a group.

County you wish to represent   I could represent my own county, Derry, or I could represent Antrim because my school is in Co Antrim.

In the space provided below you must explain in less than 500 words why you believe you should be the student chosen to represent your county in the Find The Fallen Project.

I feel I should be chosen because my ancestors call me, that is the simple answer. I will explain. My life is complicated; so is my family history.

I come from a long line of soldiers. My father, (ex-father, in my mother's view), was…is…in the British army. He fought in Kosova, then in Iraq and Afghanistan; may still do, for all I know. Then there was my Grandfather; he was full of stories about his exploits in World War Two.

Before him, my Great-Grandad fought at the Somme with the famous Ulster Division. I never met him of-course. He is one man I would love to have talked to.

With this background you might expect that I would be marching in their footsteps sometime soon. Unlikely!

Maybe there is a contrary family gene in me but I cannot imagine myself in any conflict situation, much less those 'kill-or-be-killed' war-zone scenes that my father terrorised me with in his stories. Give me a guitar please and I will sing a Dylan song to douse your flame-throwers. (I've written a few of my own; please find attached the one about my fighting fathers which you can listen to on my Soundcloud page if you like.)

I think it is a brilliant idea that this project involves meeting with a group of students from Germany who will be doing the same kind of research. I can imagine some interesting conversations with them when we meet. "Don't mention the war" will be out the window for once.

I have always loved History as a subject and have been studying it for A Level. I will probably make it my main subject at University if I get the grades. I would be so proud to represent my county and my country in this project; to research a local soldier who was not so lucky as my Great-Grandad and who lies there in a Somme Cemetery, long separated in time and in place from the family who should have come after him. Perhaps beside his grave I will find the answer to the big question; why is fighting a war more important than raising a family? More important to be killing enemies than to make peace with your wife? Perhaps not though.

Signature Patrick McAleese.   **Date**   14th Nov 2015

My Warring Family

1. Daddy was a soldier man
   Bedtime stories, gun in hand
   How he fought the Taliban
   Tales beyond belief
   'And did you shoot men over there?'
   'Of-course I did! Now say your prayers.'
   I lay and hugged my Teddy Bear
   And cried myself to sleep.

2. His father was a soldier too
   He joined up in Forty Two
   His blood was red and white and blue
   A loyal Ulster-man
   He fought the Nazis all through France
   To Bergen-Belsen he advanced
   Survived the war but not by chance
   'It was God's master-plan'

3. Great-Granda fought in World War One
   Gallipoli and then the Somme
   He saw his mate fall near Bapaume
   I can't recall his name
   His splintered bones were never found
   They rotted in the chalky ground
   Where up above the bugles sound
   The Last Post yet again.

4. So why not me? I ask myself
   A Théoden or just an elf?
   I'll have no medals on my shelf
   For killing fellow-man
   No signing up for rich-men's cause
   No mad heroics, no applause
   No glory breaking moral laws
   Just do the best I can.

Patrick McAleese July 2015

Chapter 3

(Patrick McAleese)

It is several weeks later.
Donaldson fusses at his desk, digging in his briefcase. The class is slowly settling down but he seems to be ignoring us, distracted.
Is he looking for his sandwiches, maybe feeling a twinge of hunger this close to lunchtime? Eventually the bag-rummaging slows and we get the vacant look, like he's forgotten where he is and what he's supposed to be doing.
"Right....ah, just looking for a letter here....from...from whatever-you-call-them, the...ah, the project thing. Here it is; thought I'd left it in the staff room. I was reading it to a...to a few colleagues at break."
'What's he on about?' I am thinking. I have pretty much forgotten the application letter. I'm guessing I am not alone in that.
"Right. Listen up! Josh! Sit yourself down and be quiet. Now....you will recall last month, I invited you to submit an application to take part in the...the 'Find The Fallen Project'; remember that? Trip to the Somme? Research type thing?"
Most of the class look blankly at him and each other. I remember though; so do the others who had filled in the form. I start wondering if somebody in our class has been chosen; hardly likely, given the stacks of applications they'd have gotten from all the schools in the county.
Donaldson is taking an age here; seems to be staring at the page like he's trying to decide whether to read it out or just bin it and jump straight into Russia.
"Right, I'd better read this out; I will give you the gist of it anyhow."
He goes into quick-read-whatever-mode. "'Dear Mr Donaldson, thank you for your interest in the Find the Fallen Project. It was such a pleasure to receive so many wonderful entries, from your students and from young people all over the county, indeed the country.'"
Wordy, this writer. Get to the point. Donaldson clears his sinuses with a sickening snort, swallows and continues. He starts to get more animated as he reaches the crux of the thing.
"It gives me great pleasure to inform you that one of your students has been chosen as the Find the Fallen representative for your county."

He looks up at us, a clever little pause for effect. Who will this be? Likely Ellen as usual.

Why is he doing the reluctant half-smile? Why the wee glance over in this direction?

"Believe it or not folks, we have a winner, right here in this class. I am not sure how he managed to do this, but the person chosen to represent us in this project is none other than.... Mr Patrick McAleese!"

Cue wild whooping and cheering from the rest of the class. Most of them anyway. Possibly a sprinkling of giggles and at least two uncontrolled belly-laughs. A couple of sideways glares of disbelief from Julie and Olivia. Ellen looks slightly sick. Can't believe she has been beaten by me. Neither can I. Neither can Sir.

"How you managed that, Patrick, I will never know, but congratulations anyhow. Our new Principal is delighted, or at least she is now, after she got over her annoyance!"

I mutter embarrassed thanks, head down.

"Yo-ho! Maca's got a reddner!"

Thanks Josh.

"You will have to go and speak to Mrs Ramsey," Donaldson continues. "Explain what this is all about. She will have plenty of advice for you. I mean, you'll be representing the school as well as the whole county."

I nod. Talk to the new Head? This will be a first. At least we don't have any track record.

Ross has a question though.

"What do you mean that she was annoyed Sir? Sure she wouldn't know Maca yet?"

"Never you mind, never you mind. I didn't say anything about her being annoyed, did I? Now, let's make a start on today's...."

A stirring of protest. You don't get away with a slip of the tongue quite so easily with our class. We didn't pass the transfer test by being a bunch of dumb-asses, did we?

"Ah come on Sir; you said she was annoyed."

"No I did not. Now open your..."

"Aye, you did Sir, you said she was livid. We all heard you."

I join in. Anything to hold back the flow of Russia's revolutionary politics.

"How come she was annoyed Sir? What did you tell her about me? I mean, that's hardly fair if you are...."

"I did not say she was annoyed at you, Patrick. I said..." He tails off, bait taken.

"Yeah, you said she was annoyed....you just admitted it Sir." Ross is rubbing home our advantage. "I don't think it's very fair of you to be telling the new boss your opinion of Patrick....him just after winning this thing."

A bit of back-story here. Mr Donaldson has never had a great opinion of me. I could never work out why. I seemed to get on well with Miss Craig when I had her for GCSE history; I did well in it too, an 'A' grade, just a few marks short of 'A*' I was told. That's why I chose history for A Level. I'm guessing his dislike of me goes back to Third Year when I was a far-too-cocky fourteen year old and he was new teacher on the block. I made a habit of totally bugging him back then. I remember one particular class, last period on a Friday; my crowd, 10A3, was giving him a run for his money that was going to take him the whole weekend to recover from. He did not enjoy the banter at all but the thing was, he always seemed to reserve his most abusive rant for yours truly. I was no more guilty than any of the others in the class, in fact I was mild in my rascality compared to some. I was simply talking, joking with my mate Jojo in the back corner. Donaldson zoned in on me but it was nearly half past three, bell time, and it was always going to be water off a duck's back.

"You little twerp, Patrick McAleese. You have been messing around there all period, keeping everybody back, just pushing, pushing, pushing your luck with me all the time," I think he said....something like that anyway.

I did the innocent face, arms and eyes wide.

"Me Sir?"

"Yes you, McAleese. Do not try to play the innocent with me. You have been deliberately trying to wind me up ever since we began this lesson. And you have succeeded, so now I am going to put you in double detention next week! You hear me? Double detention. I am determined to teach you a lesson, even if your parents can't!"

That was a low blow. I did not like it but I covered my annoyance by a piece of pure cheek that I had been saving up for such a time as this. I took the chance of playing to the gallery, if that's not too grand a term for 10A3.

I put on my best Jamaican drawl.

"Why yo aw-ways a-pickin' on me Suur? Is it 'cos I'se is ginger?"

The class erupted. The bell went a few seconds after but nobody heard it. 10A3 had their hero and Mr Donaldson went down like a spent firework.

"Get outa my sight," he muttered, his slightly pompous pronunciation deserting him for once. As we had always suspected, when the chips were down he sounded just as north-Antrim-Ulster-Scots-working-class as the rest of us.

Mind you I still had to do the double detention; my mother was not impressed with me when the 'behaviour letter' arrived... just like she was not impressed by my Year 10 History Report back then.

School Report Summer 2012.

Subject <u>HISTORY</u>

Name <u>Patrick McAleese</u>   Class <u>10A3</u>

Percentage <u>63%</u>   Attainment Grade <u>C</u>   Grade for Effort <u>E</u>

Patrick has undoubted ability in this subject. It is highly regrettable, therefore, that he seems intent on making a minimum of effort. He shows only the faintest hint of interest and, in the end, scores a below average grade. He should be ashamed of this; I doubt if he will be though and I would value a parental intervention to persuade him to change his attitude. He needs to settle himself next year, abandon his attempts to be the classroom joker and take more seriously the rigorous task of obtaining a pass grade in GCSE History.

Teacher's Signature   <u>A J Donaldson</u>

Pass Grade indeed; I got a frickin' 'A', no thanks to him either!

"Alright, alright. Let me explain. It was nothing to do with Patrick. I did not say a thing about you, Patrick. The...ah...the small bit of annoyance came due to the simple fact that our new Principal did not know anything about the project, this competition. I had omitted to inform her that we were encouraging some of you to enter. I suppose I was guilty of not anticipating that we would be successful..."

"Ah, Sir?" comes a little mumble of fake hurt pride and protest. "You never imagined any of us would win? That's terrible."

"No, that's not what I am trying to say, Emily. Of-course not. I'm sure all of your entries were top notch. But it is just....I suppose in previous years we were just allowed to get on with it, do our own thing and so on. But Mrs Ramsey is much more hands on, if you know what I mean. It's a good thing, don't get me wrong. We all appreciate her interest but it just takes a bit of getting used to. Anyhow, once we had had a discussion about it she seems entirely in favour of the project and is delighted that we have been successful and that Patrick here will be representing us at the Somme centenary next June. Really that was all there was to it. She is most enthusiastic. Puts our school up front on the county map and all that PR stuff."

James cannot let things lie. "Hey Maca, what county will you be representing? Sure you don't even live in this county?"

He has a point. I said something similar on my entry form.

"I can represent Co Derry or Co Antrim," I say, disinterested, no agenda.

"County Londonderry, you mean." Never miss a chance, Josh . I give him the look. "Just sayin' like," he says.

I am fairly sure though that I am chosen to represent County Antrim, where my school is. I'll have to work on the oul accent.

Twenty minutes later I take my phone out and text my mum, keeping it under the desk of-course.

> Got some good news 4 u!
> Later

I press send and pocket the phone. The Donaldson drawl drags on; he stands at the White Board reading text to us, like we can't read for ourselves. Next we'll get a handout...I can feel it coming. Sheer excitement. I wish I could concentrate but I'm torn between staring over at Madison Morrow's legs, (far too long and shapely for a history classroom...art room maybe), and imagining what I have let myself in for in this project thing. Should I just pull out now, good and early, so they can get somebody else? Naaw, it might be good craic. And it's a bit of an honour to be chosen, puts me one-up on some of the rest of these swots in my class. Let's face it, I am more than delighted to be clambering up over the low expectations that people like Donaldson have of me.

I feel my phone vibrate in my blazer pocket and slip it out. He won't see me anyhow, the way his eyes are glued to the board, his back to us like he can't bear to look at us any longer.

I squint down at the screen. It's my mum. She must be on a break.

> Good news? Who is this?

> Haha Mum! Ok now I'm not 4 teln u!

> Ah go on. U no u want to. Meant to tell u a strange letter came 4 u this am. I have it in my bag. U want me 2 open it?

> No way ma. Just le

"Patrick!"
Scramble to stick the phone under my crotch.
"What Sir?"
"Are you using your phone in my class?"
"No Sir!"
"Come on, Patrick..."

"Not any more, Sir."
The silent treatment; disbelieving, disappointed, offended. He can say so much with that dull-eyed-puppy look. More or less every face in the class is ogling me now, glad of the interruption.
"I am disappointed in you Patrick. Using your mobile in my class! What does that say about my lesson, my studious preparation last night? What does it say about your attitude, more like? And you only after being chosen to represent the school on..."
I interrupt him. No point in prolonging this. I am in the wrong.
"Sorry Sir," I say ...like I mean it.
"And just who were you texting that was so important, that couldn't wait until the bell...hmm? Who Patrick? Who or what was so vital that it could not wait?"
I sit in the silence on the other end of his mocking grin, not unpleasantly so, just a sort of fake-sycophantic smile. He knows he has back-footed me here, and I am going to have to fess up. When I can wait no longer and the faint giggles of anticipation begin to bubble around the room I put my hand over my mouth and mutter into my fingers.
"It was just my mother, Sir."
I hate this. I can never handle feelings of embarrassment without my face going red; it's just my skin type, susceptible to sun and emotional change. (How often have I regretted this curse...the DNA of my ancestors that has denied me the ability to stop these adolescent colour-surges.)
I get no sympathy from anybody in the class...every single person laughing like eejits at me. All I can do is wait it out.
"His mother, God bless the child," says Donaldson in his glorious moment of triumph. "Well now Patrick...just send her another wee text there and tell her that she can call at the school tomorrow, at her own convenience, to pick up her son's very valuable and much over-used phone, alright!"
"Agh Sir," I say, "that's ridiculous. I was only telling her about getting selected for the project thing...you can understand that Sir."
Piss-taking laughter from my 'mates'. Donaldson seems to be considering this, either that or he is having a blank moment.
"Tell you what, Patrick," he says in a compromising tone as he comes down the aisle between the tables to me. "You give me the phone now and I'll keep it until half past three. Then, if you come round to me and beg nicely and say three Hail Marys to

demonstrate your penitence I might just give it back to you....alright?"

No choice here; I don't want my mother having to drive the seven miles up here simply to get it back. I lock the phone and give it to him, really slowly to show how this is hurting me, my eyes fixed on it until he pops it in his pocket. As he turns back to the lesson I remember that this is Wednesday.

"Sir, I can't come at half three. Could I come to you at three o'clock instead?"

He ignores me until he reaches his table. He glares a bit, then, in a bored voice, "And why not three thirty Patrick?"

"It's complicated Sir. I do guitar at ten past three, you see...for an hour; then I have to run to get the quarter past..."

He interrupts...tones of consternation and disbelief.

"You get out of class early to learn to play guitar? What is this school coming to since we..."

My turn to interrupt him.

"No Sir, I'm not learning the guitar. I'm teaching it, to a wee group of first and second years."

"You are teaching guitar ...during school time? I don't believe you Patrick? You have a part-time job when you should be...And who lets you out of class for this little side-line?"

"It's only Games anyway Sir, and I don't do PE this term, since I hurt my back. Mrs Kelly fixed it up for me to help out in the music department, just voluntary like, till the back gets better."

"So you do an hour of unpaid music tuition during timetabled classes, all to help out Mrs Kelly and some..."

"Only twenty minutes of it is during school, Sir. The rest is after."

"You amaze me Patrick. How about you stay after school on Thursday and help me teach a bunch of boisterous third years about The Great Famine? Would you fancy that, would you? Another little random act of kindness? Good for your CV and all that, eh?"

I notice he is smiling. That's nice. I smile back.

"Not really Sir. I practice with the orchestra on Thursdays."

"The orchestra on Thursdays? Tell me Patrick, what has Mrs Kelly got that I seem to be missing? And I suppose you play the church organ in Morning Worship every Sunday, do you?" he mocks.

Everybody enjoys this; in the twittering laughter I hear Josh's voice chirp, "Just for info Sir, Maca goes to Mass."

I give him a black look, even if he is only riding quietly on the back of the teacher's ignorance. I don't think Donaldson heard him.

"OK, OK Patrick. Come whenever you can fit me in, with your busy schedule and all. Let's get back to this lesson. Goodness, you wouldn't think you crowd are supposed to be doing A Level exams in five or six months!"

I knock Donaldson's door at exactly 3.00pm. I see through the glass panel that he does not have a class; he is bent over his desk like an evening drinker after too many pints...and I should know that pose. He raises his head off his hand and his eyes from his pile of books, looks at the door and waves me in with his marking pen.
"Come for my phone, Mr Donaldson," I bluster. 'I am in a hurry', my body language says.
He rummages in his desk drawer. I reach out my hand. He holds the phone close to his chest. This is awkward for a second...then he gives it to me with a half-grin.
"I shouldn't be doing this but there you go. Put it away and keep it away in future, will you!"
I turn to go.
"I will Sir."
"Hang on a second."
I do as he asks and half turn round to him, sort of poised like I'm about to start an 800m race.
"I wanted to say...right, look, I was surprised, I have to admit it, that you were chosen for this...whatever-it's-called. But I just want to say well done and good luck with it. If you need any help with the research, please come and ask. I'll be only too glad to help, alright?"
"Thanks Sir."
"I wouldn't mind having a read at your application form, if you still have a copy, just to see what..."
I smile.
"You still can't believe it Sir? Do you want to check if I stapled a twenty pound note to the back of it or what?"
Good, a broad grin.
"No, no! I believe you won on your merits. I'm just fascinated to know what you wrote that caught their attention. I mean, let's face it, Paddy, you don't always produce any hugely memorable work for me in your home-works, do you?"
('Paddy'? Jeez, that's the first time he's ever called me 'Paddy'! What's he after?) I scratch my ear, thinking.

"The only thing I can think is the song; like, I am as surprised as you are."
"The song?"
"Yeah. I included a song I had written."
"A song? You mean a recording of..."
"No, just the lyrics. It was about my father and grand-father and all."
"Really? I don't...what was the relevance?"
"Well, you see, my granda was in the War. He was in the D-Day landings."
"Really?"
"Yeah; and his father was at the Somme. So like, maybe it was that. I wrote a song about the three..."
"Interesting!" He's beaming now. "That is fascinating; why did I not know this before? You never mentioned it when we were doing World War One in third year; you never really seemed to engage much at all in third year, if I remember correctly."
He remembers correctly, alright; so do I. Time for a bit of resolution.
"I was just a messer in third year Sir. I was going through a bad time at home and all that war stuff just bored me to death at the time. Probably embarrassed me too a bit, if I'm honest."
"Tell me about that," he says.
I must show some sign of impatience in the way I'm standing, or shifting from one foot to the other, to be exact, for he suddenly changes his mood a bit and waves his pen again, dismissing me.
"Sorry. I forgot; you are on your way to show some twelve year old how to play G-minor-seventh. Go on, away you go."
He has me on the end of his line with that.
"You play yourself Sir?"
"Used to. I was in a Dire Straights wanna-be-band back in the day. Hard to beat Mr Knopfler...you ever listen to him?"
"Aye, of-course. 'Brothers in Arms'! Love it. Just never saw you as a guitarist."
He looks back at his pile of essays, slightly reluctantly I am thinking. "Ah well, all our yesterdays, eh? The older I get the better I was. Go on with you now. You're keeping me back here."
I turn and make for the door, with a mumbled, "Thanks Sir."
That was a weird conversation, I am thinking; could never have imagined that happening when I was younger. Funny how teachers change towards you as you get older; or maybe it was just the one-on-one context of the thing. I wonder will I ever run into him in Sailors or somewhere, and will he buy me a pint if I do?

As I'm turning the door handle he says, "And bring me a copy of that song, alright. Maybe get you singing it to the class as a Christmas treat."
"Don't think so Sir," I say into the corridor as I pull the door behind me.

Chapter 4

Bernie Doherty

I am home from work, it's coming up to seven and I still have not set eyes on him. I know he is home, I hear the odd shuffle from his bedroom above, but there's no sign that he has been in the kitchen...the chicken and ham pie is still sitting where I left it out to defrost this morning. He might have had the forethought to put it in the oven, the lazy wee bugger, the least he could have done. Wains!
I am dying to know what that text was all about. It's only once in a blue moon that he would be texting me, unless it's for a lift or something else that he needs.
I climb the stairs and rap his door.
"Patrick? Are you alive or dead?"
Nothing.
I open the door. He has headphones on, umbilically attached to his Mac. He does not even sense me coming into the room. Quick glance at the screen...Instagram. The smell in here is terrible...reeking of rotten socks, and worse.
"Good to see you taking your studies so seriously."
No response except to quickly change the screen.
I go past him and open the window. This interrupts his concentration.
"Ma! I'm foundered. Close that! It's frickin' December baltic out there."
"Aye, and the chips were baltic when I arrived in. They won't cook in the freezer will they? 'Oven-ready', eh? That's the clue you know."
"Sorry, I was busy, I forgot. What time is it anyway?"
"Tea-time! Come on down...you never know your luck. You might find some warm food on the table, no thanks to you," I say as I pick up a few bits of discarded clothing and head back downstairs.
He follows me after a bit.
"Well, what's the bars?" I ask as he arrives in the kitchen and perches by the worktop.

"The bars?" he laughs. "You can take the woman out of Derry but you can't take Derry..."

"Give me your plate. The text message, the 'good news'? What was all that about?"

"Ah, nothing...nothing much anyway."

"Come on, spill the beans! It wasn't just a rush of blood to the head, was it? Or did Madison what's-her-face finally agree to go out with you?"

"Give over Ma. How'd you know about her anyway? You in my phone again?"

"Give me a break son. You want any corn? There'll be something badly wrong when I have to start snooping in your phone for my social stimulation," I say, just a little bit dishonestly. I bet he will change his passcode after this.

"How do you know Madison then?"

He is fishing here, or is it 'phishing', as they spell it now?

"I don't know Madison. Maybe I saw her name on the back of an envelope on your desk, one of your song scribble note things."

"Well, just keep your nose out of my business," he grumps.

"How was it you described her?" I say, faking an attempt to remember his lyric. I can recall it so clearly; learned it off for a moment like this. "Oh yeah. 'Madison, a poor boy's Taylor Swift, she feeds my eyes and gives my heart a lift'. That was pretty good..."

"That is low of you!" he shouts. "I'm going to get a lock for my door." He does look very angry to be fair, flaring red, turkey faced. I have gone too far.

"Alright, I apologise."

Silence for a while.

"Are you going to tell me what the text was about or not?" I say.

He stuffs a huge bite of pie in his mouth and proceeds to speak through it.

"I won a thing," he says and wipes the pastry flake off his chin.

"You won what thing?" I ask, mimicking the stuffed mouth mumble.

"Never told you about this 'cause I never expected it would come to anything," he says and proceeds to explain about this war project. As he talks I am surprised at how enthusiastic he already seems to be about it all, quite shocked actually. I feel a surge of fear rising in me, like indigestion after a feed of cucumber. He rambles on about it but I have stopped listening. My brain is short-circuiting as unbidden associations arc unexpectedly in my head. He eventually notices the glazed look and fades to a stop.

"What?" he says, genuinely puzzled.

"Let me get this straight," I say. "You have been selected... from all the students in County Antrim? You, Patrick? How did that happen?"

"I just filled in the application form," he says. "No big deal. I did it as best I could but I never expected to win, not in a hundred years. I thought Donaldson was joking when he read out my name...and the whole class laughed like it was..."
"And you have to find out all about some British soldier who has been dead for a hundred years?"
"Yeah...except he is an Irish soldier."
"He is a British soldier son. They are all British soldiers. 'Irish soldiers' were the boys fighting the Brits in the streets of Dublin. This year is the centenary of the Easter Rising you know, or do they not teach you about that in your history class in the Academy? Is it too embarrassing for them to be telling yous how a few brave men took on the mighty British Empire? Sacrificed themselves for their own nation, instead of away abroad fighting working class Germans that they had no quarrel with."
"You're so wrong Mum," he says. "Aye of-course Irishmen were fighting in the Rising but you can't deny that long before it even started there were thousands of Irishmen joining the British army; they were from here, this island; they were Irish soldiers."
"Where I came from they were all Brits," I say, surprised at my own tone.
He looked at me sadly. "Didn't stop you marrying one," he says, a low blow and a fairly obvious one.
"Yeah, and look how that turned out!"
"Don't look at me," he said back to my glare. "Wasn't my fault."
"Wasn't Josie's fault either, so don't you go blaming her. I made a mistake..."
"Yeah, you made a mistake. You got pregnant to a UDR soldier. In Norn Ireland! At the height of the troubles! That was a great life choice..."
"RIR, not UDR," I interrupt him.
"Yeah, whatever! Same difference," he says. "You married a British soldier and I am one of the results so..."
I want this conversation to end once and for all. We don't often talk like this; it is such a minefield. I don't want to hurt him unnecessarily with bitter aggro about his father. He had enough emotional scarring from our rows when he was a wee lad before I finally threw his father out for good.
"Stop Patrick," I say.
He doesn't hear me.
"You don't have a clue how it feels to know that your da was...that he walked out when I was a wee lad. Other people still have fathers, or at least they see their fathers."
"You do see your father."

"Yeah, like once in a blue moon."

"I didn't think you were in much of a bother about that," I say.

"And I'm not; it's just...I don't even have a photograph of him; sometimes I can hardly even remember what he looks like. I can understand that you burned the pictures and all trace of him but can you not see? You had a good man for a father; Granda Doherty was a good kind man, and even though you and him didn't speak for years you are still proud of him. Who can I be proud of, eh? Who?"

I am a bit stunned by this. I say nothing. He grabs the remote and turns up the TV sound just as Chrissie Sugden off-loads angrily to someone in Emmerdale. It does nothing to improve the atmosphere in our kitchen. I let it rest for a minute, then mute the sound so I can talk to him. God love him, he's all I've got now.

"Patrick," I say.

Head down, he pushes pie around his plate.

"Patrick, listen to me please. You can be proud of yourself. You can be proud of Josie. I hope you can be proud of me, but above all, and most important of all, you can be proud of yourself."

I touch his hand across the table. He pulls it away.

"I am very proud of you son, you know that..."

"Yeah, and the first time I succeed in anything, the first time I've done anything off my own bat and managed to beat everybody else in the class, in the whole bloody county, for God's sake...you can't be pleased for me. You can't see past your own grubby wee history, your own...prejudices."

He has a point.

"I suppose it's just that anything to do with soldiers or armies just triggers stuff off in me; but you're right. I am sorry. I don't even know much about this 'Find the Fallen' thing and I am scared for you."

"What are you scared of? It is a history project; it's not like they're trying to recruit me or something."

"Yeah, I know, and I know it is probably a lovely idea and all, trying to find out about some fellow who went to war without a clue what he was getting into, and got killed for his innocence, but all that poppy stuff and the hero worship, the British Legion; all that glorification of killing and...".

"This won't be glorification of killing. It will be about remembering the ones who were killed and forgotten about. For all you know I might be the first person ever to go from here and visit this man's grave."

"And what do you do when you get there, to his grave like?"

"I don't know. Probably...I don't know, just stand there, say a poem or a prayer or something."

"That won't come easy, saying a prayer. You haven't been to Mass in yonks."

His eyebrows lift and his mouth twists up to one side, as if to say, 'Who is in a bother about that?' But all I can see is Robbie's face. He has the exact same expression as his father, even though I pride myself that he takes after the Dohertys in so many other ways. So 'the grimace' is in the DNA, is it? Nature 1 Nurture 0 yet again. I hate it, this genetic-inheritance thing. I bury the memory and ask another sensible question.

"And who else is going? Who is behind it all?"

"I don't know; the detail is likely in that letter you are keeping from me," he says.

Of-course. The letter. It had gone totally out of my head.

"Sorry, forgot about the letter. I met the postman at the gate and..."

I take my handbag from the work-top and find the white envelope inside.

"Here you go."

I watch him read the contents in silence, just a half smile at one point.

"Here, read it yourself," he says.

Find The Fallen Project 2016

5th Jan 2016

Dear Patrick,

Thank you for your recent application to be a part of the 'Find The Fallen' Project. We are delighted to confirm that you have been successful and have been chosen, from a large number of entries, to represent your county in this Project. Many congratulations.

The committee has requested me to underline that it was the uniqueness of your application and the depth of emotional input which led us to select you as our County Antrim student. In particular, I have been asked to thank you for the very brave decision to include a piece of your own creative writing, a very mature and evocative lyric indeed. You may have opportunity to contribute further in this vein as the project unfolds and in particular as we visit the cemeteries of the Somme battlefield area.

It will interest you to know that you will be one of thirty two students from each county on the island of Ireland who will be part of this experience. In addition, we will be joined by a class of students of a similar age from a school in southern Germany. It is envisaged that the two groups will integrate and exchange information and perspectives during this unique educational experience. We look forward to having you on board.

Information concerning the official launch of the project will be sent to you soon; you will be required to attend this launch with a parent/guardian so as to receive information regarding the following;
~ The costs of the trip
~ The name of and some details regarding the soldier allocated to you
~ The project website
~ The exact details of events before, during and after the actual trip
Should you or your parent/guardian have any further questions, please feel free to contact us using the contact details provided overleaf.
We look forward to seeing you at the launch which will probably be in early March. We wish you well in your research and your ongoing studies in the meantime.
Yours sincerely,
James C Quinn
(Secretary)

"Wow," I say, "the boy really did good."
"Yeah," he says, "I thought so too."
"And what is this 'mature and evocative lyric' that seems to have taken their fancy?"
"Just a song I wrote."
He looks a bit vague about this. My antennae immediately pick up a defensive vibe.
"What's it about? Can I see it?"
"Don't know why I stuck it in; I wasn't going to, then I did, just for the craic, like. Can't believe it swung it for me."
"Can I read it?" I try again. "Please?"
He is definitely hesitating here. What is he hiding?
"Don't know if I still have a copy," he says reaching for the remote again. I grab it first.
"Please Patrick. Go on, I am curious. Is it in your computer somewhere?"
"Aye, likely," he says reluctantly.
"Print me out a copy."
"Like now?"
"Yeah, like now; why not?"
He says nothing but drags himself upstairs for a few minutes. I read the project letter again. Goodness, my Patrick involved in an all-Ireland project like this, chosen over all those uppity Presbyterians in The Academy? I wonder if he had chosen to go to St Martin's, like Josie did and like I wanted him to, would he

have had this opportunity? By the time he was eleven he had so turned against religion and the church, especially with all the abuse stuff in the media, that all he needed was to feel uncomfortable with the atmosphere when I took him to the open night in St Martin's and his mind was made up against the place straight away. That and the fact that The Academy let him play guitar and drums and a pile of other musical instruments during their open night; their pretty wee music teacher had him eating out of the palm of her hand. I could hardly get him out of the music room. There was no talking to him after that.
"Sure it's a mixed school anyway; they said so," he kept arguing back at me.
'As long as they don't have any army cadets,' I remember thinking.
Down the stairs he comes and hands me the sheet of lyrics. 'My warring fathers.' I read it, and my eyes widen with every line.
"How do you know all this stuff?" I ask him, amazed.
"All what stuff?"
"About your father? The Taliban and all?"
"Sure he told me, like I say in it. He half scared the living day lights out of me sometimes with his stories. I didn't like to say anything, 'cause it was his thing. He likely thought he was bonding with me or something."
"You never told me either, you wee...I'd have sorted him and his stories. But all this stuff about D Day and this Bergen place? Did he tell you that?"
"Sure did."
"How'd you remember it, for God's sake? You were only six or seven."
"I was older than that ma," he says. "Must've been eight or nine. Wasn't I nine when he left us for that soldier doll? I was in Mrs McBride's class, P6."
"You have a great memory...unfortunately."
I look back at the third verse. I read it aloud to him.
"'Great-Granda fought in World War One, Gallipoli and then the Somme, He saw his mate fall near Bapaume, I can't recall his name.'"
I look at him for an explanation.
"What?" he says.
"How do you know all this? I never even heard of these places."
"My dad had some kind of diary that he had been given by his granda. I saw it often enough, and he read it often enough...so the names stuck in my head. Then we did about Gallipoli in school when I was in third year...it sort of came back to me; it felt that I had...like, I actually had a connection to these places, to history."
This is the sort of thing I have dreaded. I have tried so hard to draw a line under the past, to cut my children off from any legacy of their Belfast father, their hard-wee-loyalist-da and all of those associations. I even moved house, away from the

other side of the River Bann to this estate where we would be surrounded by people more like ourselves, where I can meet folk in the street without wondering what they are saying about me behind my back. And all the time Patrick has had this rancid residue slopping around in him, this throwback, like a cursèd heirloom that he can't escape from.

"You know how I feel about all this?" I say.

"I know you would rather I had a different father, if that's what you mean."

I scratch my forehead a bit, as I often do when I am stressed. He reads it.

"Mother," he says gently, "I can't help it if he is my father. I can't help it if I remind you of him. We've talked about this before. I have enough struggles in my own head without having to worry about protecting you from yours. You've got to let me be myself. I have to deal with who I am. Writing a stupid song is..."

He tails off.

"Is what you do, I know," I say.

"Anyway, you are missing the point. The point of it all is in the last verse."

I read it again. "'So why not me? I ask myself. A Théoden or just an elf?' What's a Théoden when it's at home?"

"Just a character in Lord of the Rings. Read on," he says.

"'I'll have no medals on my shelf, For killing fellow-man, No signing up for rich-men's cause, No mad heroics, no applause, No glory breaking moral laws, Just do the best I can.' Yeah," I say, "that sounds more like my Patrick."

"You see?" he says, a sort of 'told-you-so' in his voice. "Chill ma. I'm me. I'm not my da."

Later I go upstairs and open a vanity case that I only open once in a very blue moon. I have a secret myself.

From under the various bits and pieces of old jewellery, stuff I will never wear again, I find a folded buff envelope, open it and take out a Polaroid photograph, square, slightly creased, faded colours...not unlike myself, I suppose.

Yes, when Robbie left me I did destroy every trace of him about the house, the wedding pictures, the wall photographs, the plaques, every last thing that he had not taken with him on this 'vitally strategic tour' of some place in the Middle East. On a gale-ridden March afternoon I had even opened every door and window in the place and let the storm suck the very smell of him from the house, the roar of it drowning out the sounds of my manic screaming. But there was one photograph that was so special to me that I had hidden it away in a secret place. I have it in my hand now. I sort of steel myself into numbness to stare at it again.

The original selfie, long before the modern craze was ever invented. He had held the camera high above us as we lay on the summer grass on top of Benevenagh Mountain. In the background you could just about see Magilligan Flats and the Foyle, and beyond that the bulky shape of Inishowen where the sun was just about to disappear below those grey-blue hills. You could see the glint of it on my head, bringing up the orangey colour in my long hair. He looked so happy, so handsome in that photo. Our heads were right up close to the edge of the cliff. It was a bit risky, but not as big a risk as what we had just done, done for the first time, my first time anyhow. Who knows, that might even have been when Josie was conceived....I used to like to think that it was. It made it all seem more right, not such a sinful and disastrous thing to do.

Why take this illicit memory from its hiding place, at this particular time?

Patrick says that he hasn't got a single picture of his father from back then. Is this the time to be giving him my only photograph? Not that his father looks anything like that now, with the start of his beer belly and a comb-over up top.

I have always known that, at some stage, (and I would know when), I would pass the picture on to...well, actually I had thought it would be to Josie. My guess is that she could handle its history better than Patrick. I stare at it for a few minutes, my mind doing its best to float painlessly back to those happier times; the self-induced concussion that blocks out the hurting years does not last, however, and I suddenly find myself shaking with emotion. I hold it together and stuff the picture back into the exile of the envelope, stick it back in the box and sharply close the lid. He can stay in the darkness there for another while before he has served his time, before I restore him to either one of his offspring.

Chapter 5

(Patrick McAleese)

> Hiya Madison- wot u up to?
> Will u b in Sailors on Sat night?

Time crawls past. Jeez, she might have answered, stuck up bitch. I can see she's online at the minute, still online, and it's twenty minutes since I messaged her. It's not like she hasn't messaged me back in the past, but she is so moody. All smiley and nice and chatty and so flippin' hot when we are in school and there's nobody else around, until one of the rugby guys comes in; then it's a whole different ball game. I don't have a six-pack, nor broad shoulders, nor a bull-head on me, nor a couple of cauliflower ears like hard-man Jonny Morrison. When those guys are around I don't exist.

Still, I thought she might get back to me if I asked her, casually like, about Saturday night; it is not as if I am asking her out or something. And I have seen her in Sailors before; it was the usual open-mic night, a few months ago. I think she was with a couple of older blokes, one of them from school. I remember how nervous I was when I got up to do my two songs; the nerves were wasted though, 'cos when I got up to perform I had a good look around while I was pretending to tune my guitar and she was nowhere to be seen; must have left with those Upper Sixth fellows. I sang anyhow but it all felt a bit pointless; singing about *'Facebook flamingo, my long-legged angel with a flower in her hair'* when the bird had already flown. The barman said to me afterwards, "Maca son, no harm to you but you sounded wile flat the night." I blamed the monitor mix but I knew he was spot on. I had sounded as I felt.

I wrote 'Facebook Flamingo' kind of with her in mind but with enough cloudy anonymous sort of lyrics that she would never have guessed. After it I sang Ed Sheeran's 'Photograph'...so love that song;

> *"We keep this love in a photograph,*
> *we made these memories for ourselves,*
> *where our eyes are never closing,*
> *hearts are never broken and time's forever frozen still."*

One of my favourite songs to perform and it always goes down great; maybe it's the red-haired-look-alike thing but when I sing Ed Sheeran I just know something clicks, it works so authentically and I get a real buzz out of it. But this time I was just shit and I couldn't wait to get off stage. The barman was right. I was pathetic, all for want of her staying in the audience for another half hour.

I close down Messenger and go on GarageBand for a while, listening to the makings of a song I started recording a fortnight ago. It's called 'Serendipity'...about Sara, a fictional girl who

> *'comes into my life with perfect timing, perfect babe, perfect smile,*
> *the missing piece in the puzzle of my life'.*

As the song develops you realise that this girl is not actually real, she is a 'virtual girl', a sort of X-box development where I put on a 3D head-set and she is there, in my room, beautifully scented, dressed in whatever way I want, ready to hold, just the perfect date. (The 'scented' bit is hyper-fantasy...it all is of-course.)
I listen for a while. The guitar sound is nice and meaty with a fair bit of delay, the keyboard sound spacily futuristic and the tune works fine but oh my Lord...what was I thinking with those lyrics? My English teacher had used this word 'serendipity' in class; it was new to me and it rang a bell of curiosity, so I googled it. Neat word, neat idea...just terrible lyrics!
As I am dumping this page I see a message appear at the top of my screen. It is Madison...woo hoo! She's gotten back. I open it up, my heart doing a bit of gentle arrhythmia.

> Hardly; Kelly's with Sam. Nite.

> Ah ok, nite

Only manners to reply but I go down like a child's helium balloon that somebody has stuck a pin in. What a torture that girl is; what a fool I am, more like, for ever imagining she would have any interest in me. Dah, ginger-nut; get back in your box.
Used to be that after I would see her with another guy I would sing in my head, "*Let me be the next to be with you*", sort of like a pop-mantra. So hard core, wasn't I? Now I don't bother. There is no point, just let it go, Patrick. But she is so fabulously attractive, the style, the classiness of her features, those eyelashes, the blonde-ness, those model-standard legs. Damn Sam. Damn all the others.
What if she tells her mates about my message? What do I mean....'if'? Of-course she will tell them. They will all be laughing about it right now probably. I just hope Barry doesn't find out; he will give me another wild ribbing if he does. I can just hear him.
"Who do you think you are, Maca? Just because you look like Domhnall Gleeson's wee brother doesn't mean you should try to pull

a dame like her, you ginger-knob ejit! You're punching way above your weight man."
He'd be right too. Time to get back in my virtual world, I think.
Aloud I say, 'Come back Sara, all is forgiven!'

Chapter 6

Patrick McAleese is at **Dublin Bay Hotel** with **Bernie Doherty**

Friday 4th March- A diary blog that turned into an essay!
Interesting day @ project launch. Met some others, mainly ones in Ulster group, (cos 4 of us travelled down together with our parents in a beat-up old minibus), but met some from Republic too. 1 or 2 gave talks re what they hope to get from the experience. Class accents all over the place, especially the Cork girl (who 'sang' her speech). Welcome talk from the boss man, James; seems dead on. Also speech from German embassy lady; met her afterwards with mum...very chatty & warm...which blew my stereotype a bit.
In my group I got on well with Pearse from Armagh & Katie from Tyrone. (Cutie, more like; cool smile and eyes). Mainly girls overall, mostly nice but one or two a bit up themselves. A bit of GAA rivalry going on, which is ok unless you are a 'non-believer', like Simon from Co Down. (I was kinda sorry for him when one of the southern teachers said something jokey, like 'Up Down for Sam'...Might as well have been speaking Hindi as far as Simon was concerned and he took a real beamer, thinking people were laughing at him).
We were all taken outside to the garden for a group photograph, a press release, we were told. Mum took one too; it looked pretty impressive on her phone, 32 students from all over Ireland posing together like county mascots.
My mum...so cocky in situations like this, talking to other parents from all over like she knows them, like she's Derry's special ambassador to Dublin. Introduced me to family from Roscommon, O'Malley I think. Never met anyone from most of these counties before. Like, where the hell is Roscommon anyway? This is a learning curve. No doubt by the time it's over I'll know what most of them eat for breakfast.

The main man, James, came looking for me, staring at my name tag and then saying, "So you're the song-maker then? I'll be expecting some inspired lyrics from you during the trip." Sounds like I have a role to play.
Got my soldier's name & some details. Cpl Hugh McLaughlin from some place near Ballymoney called Scot's Hill. I'll have to find out where that is and go see if I can trace anybody there who might know of the family. Also info about online databases, 'Forces War Records' & the 'Commonwealth War Graves Commission'; apparently there will be info in there. I can also contact local British Legion to see if they can help. My account will go online with all the others. I'm thinking that this sort of thing is very 'individual' in a way; suits me fine; I am probably better at working on my own than in a team, despite what I said in my application form.
High-light of the day? A FaceTime call from the teacher in Germany, (Bavaria, he insists!) who is the one leading the group of German students. Came across as a cool guy, very funny, brilliant English, a real enthusiastic character. He explained why he is involved in this project; his motives seem different from the ideas behind our trip...less to do with honouring dead soldiers and more to do with the present state of Germany in the modern Europe, with all the immigration issues and the rise of the new extreme right-wing parties there. ("What does it mean to be a European Citizen?" he asks. I don't know; never thought about it before.) He is a teacher of English and wants his students to meet and learn from students from another European country, not just to practise their English but to learn about attitudes, prejudices, healing past conflicts and so on. Wow, this is going to be something, this trip!
These Germans are all from the same school, not like our 'All-Ireland-All-Stars' selection thing. I was thinking this might be a disadvantage; we are a very loose group but they will all know each other and maybe be cliquish. No sooner had I had these thoughts when this Oskar, (the teacher, Herr Oskar Fischer), made that very point. He said he wants to make sure that this does not happen, so he has this idea to prevent it, if our leaders agree. (This was all happening live in front of us, Oskar's face blue-toothed on to a massive TV screen, James Quinn chatting to him and sort of planning bits of the event with us watching and being asked for our opinions there and then. Made us feel very involved and important.)
So his idea was to get us all communicating before the trip to France even begins.

"Hang on," I was thinking, "not a 'German-pen-pal' sort of thing surely?" But I was wrong.

"You all have access to FaceTime, don't you?" said Oskar, the innovator. "Or, if not FaceTime, then Skype?"

There was a chorus of "Yeahs" and "Yips and "Sures" around the hall...and a few relieved smiles.

"Why don't we get you all paired up with one of my students and get you talking, what do you think, James? Then they can work together in small groups when we meet up at the Somme?"

I could see that this had taken James completely by surprise but, to be fair to him, he didn't let it phase him a bit.

"Ah, yeah; sounds like a great idea. How would we do that? Do all your kids have access to..."

"I'm ahead of you there, my friend," said Oskar. "I have a list of all my students' handy numbers and email addresses? Why don't I send it to you right now? I have the list here on my screen."

"Handy numbers? You mean..."

"Sorry James, ja...'handies'; that is our word for mobile phone."

"Ah, of-course; yeah, why don't you send a list of your students and their numbers and we will see how our students feel about that," said our leader.

"I will do that right now," said Oskar and we watched him on screen as he turned to his desktop and forwarded the list. "One little difference James. What I am sending you here is just a list of 32 contact details, no names attached, ok? So you can allocate one to each of your Irish students, without knowing names, is that OK? How do your young people feel about that?"

James turned to us but he didn't even have to ask the question; we were all instantly chatting and laughing, our imaginations running away with us in an instant.

"I think you can see the reaction, Oskar!" James laughed.

"Good, I am glad they like it," he said. "We should perhaps arrange a time for these FaceTime or Skype calls to take place?"

But the buzz of our conversations sort of overwhelmed the poor man's attempt to have this all organised down to a German T!

Around me I heard the guys reactions.

"How random is this going to be?"

"Totally! Very weird....I'm up for it though."

"Sort of like a cold call version of 'Take Me Out'."

"Depends on who you get to talk to though...like you could get some real oddball and have to talk to him."

"Meet 'The Undate-ables', German style!"
"Yeah, or some Neo-Nazi freak."
"What if you get a girl and she's kinda like....you know...?"
"'Sorry, wrong number mein Fräulein! I'm outa here!'"
"Ah no, it'll be grand. I'm game for it anyway; it's only a conversation; could be a laugh."
That was only the lads; I have no idea how the girls were responding to this random plan.
Mr Quinn, James as he insisted we call him, interrupted us, a bit of a smile behind his eyes.
"Come on now folks; try to get those hormones under control. We are not interested at this point in time in some Euro-style 'Blind Date'! Let Oskar finish what he was going to say here."
"Ja, ja," he said, not making much of an effort to conceal his amusement at our reaction. "I am seeing already that there are many similarities with my German students. What I was going to suggest is that we will arrange a set time for the first contact to be made between you guys and my guys, is that OK? We can arrange such a time when we think about it, alright James?"
"Yeah, we can do that and I will email the details to all our representatives."
A guy with a really strong Dublin accent, (Darragh I think), spoke up.
"Why don't we set up a Facebook page so we can get information whenever you want to tell us things; both sets of students can have access to it?"
"Yeah, and we can share how we are getting on researching our soldiers and stuff."
('Jeez, I can't believe I just said that,' I thought. 'Our soldiers!' Both ideas went down well though.)
"Let's do that. Great idea," said James...then, with a sly look at me, he added, "Maybe even have a song or two on there."
I got a few stares at that point, curious.
"Never know your luck," I said.
I caught a quick glimpse of my mother among all the mums and dads at the back of the hall; she was wearing her semi-smile of proud mother-hen-ness.
"'Don't wave now, mother," I begged inside myself.

Chapter 7

(Patrick McAleese)

So it is that I am sitting in my bedroom, looking at my iPad screen; I am frozen in some mixture of mouth-drying dread and nervous anticipation. Three weeks since the Dublin meeting and this is the date, the very hour, when we are all supposed to be FaceTiming our 'partners' in Germany and I am horrified by my own shyness, my lack of self-confidence. Why this irrational fear?

I suppose it's the unknown aspect of it all. I am supposed to call this stranger; I have the number. This number identifies some person, some anonymous human being; no name, just a number. No identity, neither male nor female, a 'nothing' person. For some inexplicable reason the whole practice of tattooing a number on the arms of inmates of those infamous concentration camps flashes into my head. It's the non-person thing. I have the fantastical thought that if I insert this list of digits into my device and touch 'Connect' I might be dialling back in time and see some emaciated body, dull eyes looking out of hollow sockets through the barbed wire of Belsen into my grandfather's shocked face.

I know this is way too irrational but I have to admit to a scarring that goes back to those early bedtime horror stories of my fathers. Although I class myself as a modern young man, Irish and atheist, non-political and fair-minded, I suspect that I am still haunted by a sludge of anti-German feeling which lies deep in my psyche. I frequently have to dredge it up and consciously put it out of my thinking. I totally get that it is some kind of primeval prejudice thing, a dragon that probably all of us have to keep slaying over and over again.

Slowly I type in the long string of digits. But there I stop. I stare at the number. What if this person is some tall, handsome, Teutonic, firm-jawed, body-building super-sportsman? I would feel so inferior talking to such a person. What if it is...

I need a drink. I leave the iPad and run downstairs for a glass of orange.

"What's wrong with you? You look like you've seen a ghost."

"Not yet, mother," I mumble into the fridge.

"Dinner is ready in ten minutes."

"I might need longer. I'm in the middle of something."

"In the middle of what?"
"Never you mind. Just don't disturb me. I'll come down in my own time," I say as I close the hall door behind me.
I've wasted fifteen minutes of this allocated half hour already. I sit down at the desk again and stretch out to the iPad....and stop. Again.
What if it is a girl? The image of a buxom bar-maid clutching litre-jugs of lager comes into my mind from I don't know where. Maybe it will be some classically round peasant type like you might see in an old cartoon? Braces on her teeth, greasy fair hair in lob-sided bunches above her two big ears, a liberal coating of pimples, thick glasses and even thicker legs?
'Agh, catch yourself on, Patrick,' I counsel myself. 'How will you know what he or she is like if you don't click on this number and connect?'
My finger hovers above the screen, like the finger of God in a Michaelangelo painting.
Touch!
Ring tone...ring tone...ring tone...ring tone...
Connecting!
'Oh frick NO,' I think, my finger going to the screen again to cancel the thing when suddenly, too suddenly...
A face appears...a girl's face.
Oh my God.
Oh my God. I have the face of a German girl onscreen and it is the kind of face that drives from my mind everything that I was planning to say.
I stare at the screen and for seconds; I can't speak. I have no voice. It seems I have no breath.
Yeah, she is a girl and she is really...actually I am surprised by how young she looks; my first impression is that she looks more like a fifteen year old; a fifteen year old with lovely fine features and beautiful skin which, and this is my biggest surprise...beautiful skin which isn't exactly white. How silly of me to just presume my Bavarian contact would be the stereotypical fair-skinned German. This girl, I am guessing immediately, is of Mediterranean background, maybe even middle eastern, like Syrian or Turkish or possibly even further east. The surprise, once I deal severely with my own preconceived expectations, is a pleasant one.
She's pretty, that's for sure, what I can see of her anyway...her features are kind of hidden; well, half of her face is concealed from

me behind a rich shock of curling black hair...it's a very modern asymmetrical style, swept over her head so that it's short on one side and long and lush, on the other. So I can only see her left eye, beautifully made up but dark and apprehensive, focussed on my image on her screen. An eye that is the colour of a dark beer....'What a stupid thought,' I think. 'Stop gawking at her. Say something.'

I speak....No, actually I squeak. "Hi," I say but it comes out as a high-pitched whisper. I wet my mouth and clear my throat and go again, trying for a more baritone effect.

"Hi; what's up? My name is Patrick."

Silence; not a flicker of a move from her, her one visible eye staring off to the left, not engaging with mine. ('Of-course it's not engaging with mine', I think. 'That's how FaceTime works; we watch the image on the screen, we tend to not stare straight at the camera.')

I can feel her fear through the screen; she is like a scared little deer caught in someone's headlights, petrified to the spot.

Oh God...I want to ....she looks so scared. I am instantly moved by her in a way that I cannot comprehend. I want to hold her. I can feel something like tears at the back of my eyes; no, not tears, just a sensation of identification or something, something I don't understand. She is so....so lovely, but she looks desperately vulnerable. I can sense that straight away. She is finding this even more difficult than I am. How stupid I was to try to imagine what this person would be like and to dream up all sorts of identities which would intimidate me; she is the one feeling most inadequate here, from what I can see. It is almost like she is trying to camouflage herself, using her mop of hair to protect herself from my view.

'Help her; give her some mercy,' is my instinct.

"Can you hear me ok? Is my microphone working?" I ask.

"I can hear you," she says; then after a pause she gets the courage to ask, "How are you?"

Was that, 'How are you?' Or 'Who are you?' I'm not sure and I delay for a second. She has much less of an accent than I had imagined, not a typically German one anyhow; quite soft and musical in this her first practiced question, even if I couldn't be sure which question it was. I make a choice.

"I'm great, thanks. Yourself?"

"Sorry?"

"How are you yourself?"

"Ah, I see. I am also... great."

"Great," I say.

She flicks her hair back a bit from her right eye so I see more of both sides of her face. Her complexion... I am not good at quick descriptions but the first thing her skin colour makes me think of is the cedar wood top of my guitar. That or the kind of colour I used to get if I tea-stained a piece of paper for an aged effect, like for a history project or in GCSE art class.

"And you are in this project to visit France with us?"

"I am," she said after a pause.

"What a stupid question," I say, laughing at myself. "Why else would we be talking to each other at the minute?"

I see a flicker of confusion cross her eyes at this observation. I decide to keep it more simple, at least until she gets to understand my accent.

"I'm sorry," I say. "Maybe my accent is difficult for you to pick up. We have a strange way of talking in Northern Ireland."

"No. Well, yes, yes you do," she says, "but I understand you ok."

"Ah, that's good."

"Yes, it is. And you are Northern Ireland?" she asks.

"I am. Even though we are a small island we are divided into two different parts, politically anyhow," I tell her.

"Ja, I know about that, a little. I want to ask about it when we meet. But not now...it is too complicated for this..."

She runs out of how to say what she means but I get it.

"Your English is very good," I say.

"Thank you. I have been practicing...for this moment," she says.

"Me too," I joke...but she just looks puzzled.

"By the way," I continue. "You haven't told me your name yet."

"Ok, I am sorry," she says. "I mean to start with my name but I get nervous and it tied my tongue. Is that how you say it, it tied my..."

I grin for the first time.

"You were tongue-tied, I think you mean. I was too, to be honest. It seemed such a strange thing to be doing, FaceTiming someone I have never met before. I didn't even know whether you would be a boy or a girl."

"And I did not know what you are," she says. The first hint of a smile, a very faint hint. Jezz, what a sweet face this girl has; those eyes could melt a statue.

"Well," I say, "I'm a boy as you can see and I hope you are not..."

Stop; what were you about to say? 'Not too disappointed'? Wise up Patrick...keep this sort of normal.

"No, I am ok," she says, totally sincere, with not a hint of coyness. Just a statement of fact.

"Good," I say. "So you were about to tell me your name."

"I am sorry, yes. My name is Magdalena Rosenthal."

"Magdalena Rosenthal," I repeat carefully, thinking, 'That's a mouthful and a half'. Instead I repeat, slowly, "Magdalena...that's an epic name; unusual, I must confess, for me anyhow, I mean. Is it..."

I stopped, unsure of what I was going to ask. Is it German? Or is it Turkish or whatever country her people originally come from? She helps me out this time.

"You don't have to call me Magdalena," she says. "It is too long for many people. So I am called Lena by everybody. Everyone except my parents. To them I am always Magdalena. To you I can be Lena."

"Ah good, that's easier. 'Lena' I can get my tongue around. Can't say I have ever heard of anyone called Magdalena."

"And what is your name...again please?"

"I am Patrick, Patrick McAleese."

"Patrick...I do not say the second name. You are called after your special saint?"

My special Saint? Oh yes, of-course.

"I suppose I am," I say. "How did you know that?"

"All the world knows about Saint Patrick and Ireland," she tells me. "And most Irish men are called Patrick, yes?"

"Not quite," I say. "It's not such a popular name now as..."

"Patrick!" I hear my mother's voice from the foot of the stairs. "Your dinner is on the table."

Jeez mum! I react as if I'd been caught making out with somebody in the dark of my bedroom. I jump in embarrassment and annoyance. Lena notices.

"What happened?" she asks. "Did someone call?"

"Yeah, just my mother wanting me for dinner. Never worry about it."

She looks a bit bemused by this.

"How do you mean? Is she upset that you are talking to me..."

"No, no!" I interrupt. "I mean, it's ok, it can wait for me. She doesn't know I am talking to you. Just keep talking."

Oh Lord, why do I sound so desperate?

"Ok, I have more things to ask you. I have a list here."

I smile at this. A German with a list... figures.

"Fire away, " I say.

"Sorry?"

"Go ahead, ask me something."
"Ok. Let me see. What do you like to do best?"
This time I do laugh...out loud, a kind of surprised snigger. Her eyebrow arches; she is confused by my giggle and she clarifies.
"Your hobbies and things you do when you are not studying, I mean."
"Yeah, I know what you mean," I smile. A question straight from her English classroom, no doubt. 'Today we will be learning how to have a conversation about past-times and hobbies!'
"Ok, let me see..." I begin.
What would impress her the most, I am thinking if I'm honest.
"Well, I suppose the big thing in my life is music," I tell her. "Are you on Facebook? I have some of my songs on there...well, links to Soundcloud mainly."
"I am not on Facebook, not now. I have been, but my parents..."
"Snapchat? Instagram?"
"Sorry...I am not permitted."
"Patrick, are you coming now or next week?"
My mother is to international diplomatic relations what Bob Dylan is to tuneful singing.
"Hel-lo! I'm busy here. I'll be down in a minute," I call at the door.
"Sorry, I should let you go," Lena tells me. "It seems like you are going to have trouble by your parents for talking to me too long."
"No, definitely not. It's just my ma anyhow. She gets impatient."
"It's ok, we can talk again... if you like? I have more questions..."
"Absolutely. Yeah, sure. When do you want me to..."
"Only if you want to?"
"I want to."
"You are sure?"
"Of-course I am sure...we are supposed to get to know each other, aren't we? I mean, just for this project like."
Oh damn....that was not how I meant that to come across, and I can see in her reaction that she doubts me. I am hopelessly stupid at times. She hesitates, thinking, looking down, presumably at her list of questions.
"It is ok if you don't want to..."
"No, no, listen. I ... I want to chat, honestly."
"When is good for you?"
"Tomorrow, same time? Six o'clock?"
"Ok. Seven for me. And I will ask more questions. You can ask me too if you like?"

"Great, thanks; ok, chat later?"
"Ja, goodbye for now."
"Sure, bye...bye."
Wow...This is a good feeling; she's really nice; different, for sure, but nice. Thank you 'Find the Fallen Project'!
I stare at the screen. I want to see her face again. Can I find her online? Ah damn...she said she's not on social media. Why the heck did I not take a screenshot when I had the chance? I won't miss it tomorrow.
Tomorrow!
I feel a song coming on. I can't claim the idea as an original though.

Chapter 8

Bernie Doherty

I am so tempted to open this letter. Actually, my first inclination is to throw it in the fire and say nothing about it but I know that would be the wrong thing to do. If ever he found out, which he definitely would, he would never forgive me.

This is not a mystery letter, like before; I know this handwriting all too well.

I tell myself that it is none of my business. His father has every right to communicate with his son any time he wants. It was part of the settlement. It should not concern me at all, but my God how it does. Why is he writing to Patrick now? It's not Christmas, it's not near his birthday. What special gem of wisdom or advice is he offering him? My curiosity is nearly fit to burn a hole in the paper. Oh for a set of laser eyes. The chances are that Patrick will tell me nothing. I look at the seal, trying to work out if I could steam it open. No chance; the mistrusting bastard has it well cello-taped and I haven't a hope. Nothing to do but trust my mother ability to suss out from her 'darling boy' what's going on.

I decide to hit him with the letter the minute he comes in the door from football; that way he might open it before he has a shower, read it and leave it lying behind him. I even say a quick prayer for the intervention of whatever Saint might be interested in helping a mum keep tabs on her teenage son.

So that is what I do, failing to notice that he is walking quite gingerly as he comes in the kitchen door.

"There's a letter for you," I say sticking the thing under his nose. This is different from the usual, "Stop. Get back out and take off those filthy boots," but he doesn't notice.
"Leave it there and get me a couple of Ibuprofen."
"Why? What have you done now?"
"Ricked my back a bit," he says as he carefully sets his backside down on a stool and uses his hands to lever his leg into the air, presenting me with the task of untying his football boots.
"Please," he says dully.
I oblige. Then I get him his drugs and a glass of water. As he downs these I try again.
"You and this back! Here, lie down flat on the sofa and I'll read this letter to you."
"What letter?"
I fuss around helping him get stretched out. This has become a fairly regular occurrence; as he has grown in the last couple of years he seems to have developed a weakness in his lower back; physio and regular stretching exercises have helped a bit but a quick jerk at the wrong angle in sport can tear whatever ligaments are weak and leave him stiff for a day or two.
I pick up the letter and open it. He is sore enough, distracted enough not to be in a bother about it. He even closes his eyes.
"It's from your father," I say, like as if I had only just realised that. The eyes pop open again but he says nothing. 'Goodness, he must be in pain,' I think.
"Do you want me to read it to you?"
"Whatever," he grunts.
I notice the address; some Army Barracks in England, but I don't bother to read that.
"'Dear Patrick, I hope this finds you fit and well. It's not often I write to you and I am sorry for that. I hope you are working hard at your GCSEs and not giving your mother any bother.'"
"My GCSEs? For God's sake! What age does he think I am?"
"I think he likely just means your exams; he knows you are eighteen alright; he just gets confused about what exams come where," I say.
"Not like you to be defending him."
"You can say that again."
I read on.
"'I am delighted to hear that you have been chosen for some World War One project....'" I tail off. "How in the hell did he hear about that? Isn't that just like

him...he doesn't know what stage you are at at school but somehow he knows you are involved in this war thing!"

Patrick is fully alert now, pain or no pain. "How did he find out? I never wanted him to know about it. Read on."

"'...some World War One project and I wanted to say that I am proud as punch of you getting chosen for a great cause like this. I would never have known a thing about it, (your ma would never dream of letting me know anything about you), except that your aunt Ina in Lisburn saw your picture in the Belfast Telegraph. She couldn't believe her eyes but she read the article and discovered that yes it was you and that you were one of a company of young ones from Northern Ireland selected to go on this trip to the Somme in June. She posted the clipping to me. I am more proud of you than I can tell you. You have a good dose of your father's blood in you, aye and your grandfather's too, no matter what your mother might hope. So when you go there you **MUST** find the name of your great-grandfather's old mate who fell in the battle. His name was Pte John Patterson and the name is up on the Thiepval Tower for his body was never found. And when you find his name give it a good old sacred salute, from me and and your grandad and my grandad. I have been there myself. A crowd of us from the Ballymacarret Somme Association went to the Ulster Tower a lot of years ago. It's a marvellous place, you will love it. Such sacrifice and heroism. The Ulstermen who fought there were the finest in the whole of the British Army; still are, in my humble opinion, but then I would say that, wouldn't....'"

"Stop mum, for God's sake stop!"

I stop and sit in silence, staring at him. His temper is up and his face is the colour of tomato soup. After a bit he calms down and speaks.

"I don't want to hear any more. Burn it!"

Slowly I fold the page and stuff it back in the envelope.

"I know what you are going to say," he says.

"What am I going to say?"

"'Told you so.'"

"It had crossed my mind," I agree.

"Look mum, I can still pull out of this thing."

I wait, giving the impression that I am considering this. We both know I'm not.

"What do you think yourself?" I ask.

He takes a long drink of water and wipes his mouth. Oh the echoes!

"I don't want to...to pull out, I mean. Two reasons; I want to be able to go through the whole thing to prove to myself that war disgusts me...and no amount of so-called honour and sacrifice can water-down that disgust. Do you see that? I *have to be able to survive all that...that appeal to glory. I have to be able to stay true to myself, cut loose that part of me that my dad thinks I should have inherited. Prove to myself that it's not hiding somewhere in my DNA. Can you understand that?"*

"I think I can. You know what? I am actually proud of you for wanting to do it, but..."

"But what? You can't trust me to see that through, is that it?"

"It is not going to be as easy as you think son....like when you are with a bunch of other kids and the whole emotion of it all when you see the memorials and the hundreds of graves and you hear the Last Post and all..."

"But look, it's always been like this for you and me. You've always lived with the worry that I will turn into my dad, and I have always had to live to prove that I won't. You can't be putting a firewall around me for ever, protecting me from the military virus or the Brit virus or whatever other viruses you think I am vulnerable to. You gotta trust me in this one like you have had to trust me all along."

"You are right, and I do trust you, honestly I do."

"Good. Now go and get on with the dinner."

"Certainly, mi Lord. Whatever you say, mi Lord," I say getting up from beside him. "But tell me first, what is your second reason."

"What are you on about?"

"You said you had two reasons for not pulling out."

"Did I?"

"You did....so?"

He turns away again, closes his eyes. Just the faintest wee smile around the corners of his mouth and I know instinctively that I will not be able to prise this secret out of him. I also know instinctively that it has a lot less to do with his father, with the research of a fallen soldier, with the honour of representing his county abroad...and a heck of a lot more to do with a certain young German Fräulein who has been tantalising him across cyber-space for the past few days.

Oh to be a fly on his wall during those conversations, rather than just a shameless eavesdropper at his door. Oh to be a swarm of flies on the walls of his fantasies. I just want a glimpse of her. Is that so wrong?

Chapter 9

(Patrick McAleese)

Way too exciting! We are having a 'class discussion' in English class; topic...the up-coming vote in June on whether to leave the European Union or stay in.
"To Wrexit or not to Brexit? That is the question," as Mr O'Brien puts it. 'Deccie' O'Brien is one of my A Level English teachers and he loves these debates; so do I, if I'm being honest, though it is not like him to take time out from 'Farewell to Arms' to be chatting about anything less important than Hemingway's 'depressing disillusionment', especially now, six weeks out from the exams. Now there's confidence for you. Respect, Sir! Just hope for his sake that Mrs Ramsey doesn't choose this moment to do a check-up visit to this class, as she's reported to be doing around the school.
Last week in History class it was the Easter Rising centenary celebrations that got us talking...nearly caused a riot. It really divided the class down the middle; actually there was only a handful of us who saw the commemorations in Dublin as relevant to us as young people in Northern Ireland; the bulk of the class had barely noticed them. It's as if the whole thing was happening on another continent, which for some of them I suppose, just about sums up their attitude. Mr Donaldson cut the debate early and went back to the syllabus.
Now 'Deccie' fires out a stack of newspapers, sort of as a kick-start. We flock around the centre table, reading headlines aloud.
"Remember, these are newspapers; look out for lies and bias," he shouts.
"Lies in a newspaper Sir? Surely not?"
I am hearing...
'Britain faces migrant crisis. Daily Express.'
'Boris: It's mad to stay in the EU.'
'The Mail says 'EU Vote: now PM warns of war and genocide.'
'EU opens door to 79 million from Turkey'...that's more from the Express. Jeez, the Express doesn't half ramp it up.
And a lot more. The discussion develops. Plenty of shouting and laughing at each other as we seem to be naturally falling into two camps. To be fair, in the class of 21 there are only about six who were pro Brexit; the rest are for remaining in the EU though some couldn't care one way or the other.

O'Brien is enjoying this squabble but he gets us settled down. A lot of the chat has to do with the actual newspaper coverage.

"We are so susceptible to what is in the tabloids and social media drip-feeding us this 'island-Britain' stuff," Barry says.

"Will it make a difference though," O'Brien asks, "when it comes to the privacy of the voting booth? Surely not? People have more sense, don't you think?"

This annoys a couple of the Vote-leavers. Sharon, who would be a DUP type, and Paul who is a farmer to the core, speak up.

"You shouldn't be trying to influence us with your political opinions, Sir. My parents are voting 'Out' and they wouldn't be happy with what you just said."

"I'm sorry Sharon, you're right of-course, but we are only having a harmless debate here."

"Ah, naw Sur," chips in Paul. "Just because we are younger than you, just because we are your students doesn't mean you can put us down for having an opinion different from yours."

"Did I do that Paul? Did I put you down for..."

"You did Sir. You started off by calling it Wrexit. That was your word and it was a put-down. Then you said people like me and my oul boy should have more sense than to vote out, didn't you?"

"Sorry, maybe I did Paul. But you don't have to think the way your parents think, do you? Surely you can have views of your own?"

"Aye, I have Sir. Look, Europe has made it nearly impossible for farmers to make a decent living, with all their red tape. So many daft laws about things we used to do as a matter of course."

"You have a point there," says the teacher. "But what about all the subsidies you get from the EU?"

"No problem. Our government will look after us, so it will."

"I hope you are right," says O'Brien. "What do you all feel about these headlines about migrants, terror threats and so on? You all comfortable with immigration?"

First to speak is Kasia, the one Polish girl in the class. She is very clever, a real swot, always gets top marks in whatever subjects she picked for GCSE and AS; generally she is so quiet in class; now she is talking and I sense that we are all delighted that she has opened up to join in this argument. 'Go on girl,' I am thinking.

"What will happen to me and my family if the vote is to leave? Will we have to go back to Poland? Think about all of your relatives who have left Ireland to go to work in America or Australia; imagine if those governments suddenly had told them to go home because they are not welcome any more. How would they feel?"

"Yeah, I know, but...like, no harm to you Kasia, and I hope you never have to leave this country, but you would have to admit that there are too many foreigners here now, especially in England, but even Belfast and places like Dungannon. It dilutes the culture of the place. Walk around parts of Belfast and all you hear is foreign accents." This from one of my former friends who will be nameless. He is immediately set upon verbally by the rest of the class.

"You're kidding ____. 'All you hear is foreign accents'? Bollocks!"

"How does it dilute the culture, for God's sake?"

"They're all doing jobs that our people don't want to do. Gutting chickens and all that stuff."

"Totally. Most of them fit in and mix the way Kasia does. What's your problem?"

The teacher settles the thing down a bit.

"Kasia, thanks for sharing your point there. Would you like to tell us about your family, or even what your folks work at here, what they did back in Poland before you came...when was it?"

"We came in 2006; I was just eight. In Radom, where we lived, my father told me that the unemployment rate was 20%. My mother worked in a cafe but my father stayed home for the children, yet he is a very good engineer. Some friends told him about a recruitment site for jobs in UK. He saw online that an engineering works in Ballymoney was expanding and needed engineers. So he applied, sent all his qualifications and they interviewed him on Skype and he got the job. We all came the next summer and we love it here. I can hardly remember what life was like in Radom any more. If we had to return it would be impossible."

"Don't worry; it's not going to happen anyway," O'Brien comforts. He gets up off his perch on the front desk and heads towards his computer.

"Now, I think it's time we got back into the mind of a certain Lieutenant Frederic Henry because, let's face it, understanding his complicated thoughts will be more useful to you in a few weeks than understanding the mind of Michael Gove or his ilk, yes?"

I am walking down the corridor after English Lit, arguing with Barry, when we bump into Mr Donaldson.

"Patrick; just the fellow I was looking for. Have you got a minute? Pop up to my room and make yourself at home till I fetch a cup of coffee from the staffroom, would you?"
I hesitate; I have time alright but...
"Would you fancy a cup yourself?" he asks.
"No, no; no worries. I'll wait for you sure."
He rounds the corner and disappears.
"Woo hoo," Barry laughs as he leaves me. "Coffee with the enemy, eh? You blackmailing him or something?"
I stand in the Humanities corridor studying ancient photographs of the various musicals and plays that the school has done over the years. Some famous faces in there apparently, staring out in sepia concentration at the present crop of navy-blazered pupils as they crush along the narrow passages of the old part of the school. Funny how life was in black and white back in the day; I'm thinking that kids must have been midgets back then if they were able to survive in the tightness of these corridors.
Donaldson arrives with coffee spills on his hands and a wet splodge on his jacket. I follow him into the room as he mumbles something about a gang of third year boys running over him at the corner, 'boys of questionable parentage', to use his expression. Never use one simple word where a flowery expression will do if you are a teacher.
"So, I just wanted to ask you how you are getting on in your research, your fallen-soldier project? Any progress?"
"Yip, it's going well," I say as I park myself on a desk. "There's far more information available than I had imagined."
"Good. So what sources have you used?"
"All the ones you suggested. I even got a picture of him in his uniform and all; got it in some random book; 'Stories of the Fallen Heroes'.
"Yeah, great source, that. And you used the online sites?"
"Yeah. And my mother took me to a church over in Scot's Hill, the one that Hugh McLaughlin would have been at when he was a kid. The minister didn't seem to know very much but an old man working in the graveyard came and talked to us and he was great. He even knew about my soldier's relatives; some of them still have a farm over there."
"Brilliant. Did you go to talk to any of them?"
"Not yet, but...this is the best bit...he told us about a lady who is still alive who is an actual niece of the guy, the soldier like."
"You're kidding?" He looks genuinely pleased for me.

"She's ancient like; she's in some care home near Antrim. So my mother is going to take me up at the weekend so I can talk to her."

"Excellent. Just be aware though that she may not be totally compos mentis, if she is that age. It may be a wasted journey."

"Not according to him; she's still alright...anyway, even to talk to her and shake her hand will be great; it will feel like I am reaching out across history, touching someone who knew him like."

He frowns at me.

"Wait now Patrick. You may be a maestro of guitar but you're not so hot on the Maths."

"Meaning?" Oops, I realise I haven't figured out when she might have been born; how naive of me, and my face must show it.

"Yeah, now you're counting. If she is...say 86, that means she was born in 1930ish. But he was killed in 1916, fourteen years earlier."

"Aye, of-course...I knew that!" I lie but with a smile of admission of my stupidity. "Still, she's a blood relation and her father or mother was Hugh's sibling, so the chances are she would have heard it talked about in the family, maybe have more details about him, like pictures before he was a soldier and all."

"My word lad! You are really into this, aren't you? I'm impressed. I hope you are going to write the whole thing up for us?"

"Write it up? What for? We have to post our findings on the project website but..."

"Yes, but for the school magazine, for example. Maybe even the local press. You'll do that, won't you?"

"Could do I suppose, but I'm kinda busy with this exam thing that I keep hearing rumours about."

He drains the rest of his coffee and stands up.

"I understand that Paddy; you have a lot on your plate, with your music and your studies and....and now with you trying to learn to speak German."

I feel instant scarlet rise in me from the neck up!

"Whaaat?"

He grins at me, like I'm some comical meme.

"Ah now. I won't mention this in front of the class of-course, but I've been hearing things."

"That's big of you," I say. "I only asked her how to say a couple of things."

"Well, Miss Gillan was all delighted. It's not everyday a sixth form fellow comes up to her in the playground and asks her for a stack of

German phrases. She was just curious about why you had developed a sudden interest in the language."

"I didn't ask her for a stack of...I just wanted to know how to say a few things, that's all."

"Sure. Like, 'It has been nice to talk to you again' and...."

I follow my red face to the door in a rush.

"Ah that's not fair Sir. Two teachers talking about me behind my back. There should be a rule about that. Freedom of information or something."

He's smirking away here, enjoying this.

"Ah come on. This teaching can be boring enough, you know. We have to keep ourselves amused somehow, Paddy boy. Auf Wiedersehen, mein Freund."

The hound.

Still, at least he is interested. How long though before he tries to take the micky out of me in front of the rest of the class?

I flee to the Music Suite for some respite, for some music therapy with the beautifully gentle and non-invasive Mrs Kelly who will allow me to self-heal on whatever instrument I fancy. As I sit down at the clavinova in one of her rehearsal rooms and play a slow arpeggio on a D Major-Seventh chord I have a really random thought, a thought that quickly turns into the most impetuous decision I've ever made, but one that feels so right. When it comes to finally choosing what to study at Uni in September maybe I should turn down my first choice offer, (History at Queen's) and go with my second option instead...Music at Magee in Derry. I don't even know if this kind of change is possible or how I go about switching but I think I am going to try. It's got nothing to do with Magee being a lower ask in terms of grades either. No. It's because I am coming more and more to realise that music is who I am in the bit of me that is most me.

Stranger still is the immediate thought that the first person I will tell about this decision is a certain German girl that I have never even met, unless you count three kinda stilted FaceTime conversations in the last couple of weeks.

I haven't actually thought much about the fact that my time at school is almost over; only a few weeks to go to freedom. This is transition-time for me and my mates. None of us has actually mentioned the subject; it's like we are in denial that this phase of life is ending, that the cliques we have been jigsawed into for the past seven years are going to be broken up and scattered. I am not sentimental about it really, not yet anyhow. Too busy thinking about exams; that's the lie I tell myself anyhow. Maybe my lack of engagement with this 'death of childhood' thing has more to do with the trip to France and all my innocent speculation about Lena. If so, that is no bad thing; way better than having to deal with the disappearing comfort-blanket of school; better too than worrying about the coming period of uncertainty as I wait for the results that will determine my future, a future which I am starting to look forward to, now that I've made the call to switch to music.

I need to run this past Mrs Kelly. I'm sure she'll have an opinion; hopefully she will be pleased. I can just imagine her fighting my corner when my history teachers find out.

Actually, now I think about it, I might just need her to call round at the house for whenever I pick up the courage to inform Bernie.

Chapter 10

Bernie Doherty is at **Rushybeg Residential Home** with **Patrick McAleese**
Saturday 14th May 2016

I watch Patrick as we sit in the waiting room. The place is pleasant, lots of natural sunlight from big bay windows, beautifully decorated, prints of nostalgic country scenes on the walls, castles by loughs and sheepdogs patiently studying stray lambs. Lovely except for the faint sick odour of sick and worse that betrays a disinfectant response to some recent little accident.

Patrick lies back lazily in the armchair and stares out the window across the breadth of Lough Neagh; he seems miles away. No matter how I tried to start a conversation with him on the way up today he just blanked me off. Short grunted answers, his eyes glued to his phone. Not nice, considering I gave up my Saturday to drive him up here, like I gave up my Saturday a couple of weeks ago to take him to Scot's Hill.

Kids! Well...sons, to be more accurate.

"Will you take a photo of this old lady?" I ask.

"Why would I do that?"

"Don't know. Just asking. You might want it for your website."

"Maybe; but I'd have to get parental permission though; that might be difficult."

I'm confused as to why he is being like this, so sarcastic, so negative. I start to tell him that I am not appreciating his attitude but he is spared by the arrival of one of the staff, a very tall blonde girl in a blue uniform, holding the door open for us to follow. She is brusque, obviously busy, overworked.
"You are wanting to see Miss Barclay, yes?" she says in an east European accent. "Please follow me."
We do. At the end of a long passageway we turn into a private bed-sitting room and there on her armchair sits Miss Adeline Barclay. Her beady bright eyes squint out from a potato-grey face that looks well and truly squished under the weight of her years.
"Hello," she says reaching up to shake Patrick's hand. "You must be the young man who is interested in my uncle Hughie? Well come and sit down and I'll see what I can do for you. Ask me anything you like but just remember it's a long time since anyone has talked to me about those times past and I may not have much detail to give you. The memory isn't as good nowadays as it used to be but we can't help that, can we?"
"We can not indeed," *I say as Patrick struggles for the right response. He sits as she rises stiffly and shuffles across the room to a sideboard to bring a biscuit tin, a very old one with a stag's head painted on the lid and which had once contained "All Butter Scottish Shortbread", if the label is to be believed. I wonder for a second if she is going to share some 1950ies cookies with us but I needn't have worried.*
"I got this all ready for you when I heard you were coming today. You know that poor uncle Hughie's body was never found? I think that must have been one of the hardest things, for my grandparents I mean, and for my mother, never to be able to go to an actual grave to lay a flower for him or anything."
Patrick speaks for the first time. I am pleased by his whole tone of voice. Suddenly the grumpy youth from the car journey is replaced by a mannerly, well-spoken young man and I am proud of him.
"Miss Barclay, you know that..."
"Adeline son, call me Adeline. I'm not one of your teachers."
"You know that I am going to France with this project and that I am intending to try to find his name on the Thiepval Memorial and lay some flowers there. You don't have any objection to that do you?"
"Oh goodness no," she says. "I am delighted. I should have tried to go; it's too late now. No, no, I am delighted that you are going to honour him. Tell me, have you any relatives yourself who were lost over there?"

It is an awkward moment; I sense a hesitation in Patrick, just the ghost of a glance across at me, before he replies.
"No, but my great-grandfather fought there in 1916. He was injured and sent home so he survived."
He pauses, then...
"I'm sorry your uncle didn't," he says.
"Well," she says, "that's nice of you to say. It was just one of those things. There were hundreds of thousands of them that perished in that war. And what was it all for? Sure they had to go and do it all again in the Second World War and beat the Germans for a second time. Aye, and look at it all now. The Germans are the richest country in Europe and are virtually ruling the whole place now. They did really well out of losing two wars, didn't they?"
'Oops,' I think, 'I hope Patrick won't rise to this bait. Let's get back to the subject, to this Hugh soldier fellow.'
"So what can you tell Patrick about Hugh, Miss Barclay? Did your mother talk much about him?" I say.
"Not very much. The war was just the war and Hugh was never coming back home to the family, I suppose. The only time he was ever mentioned when I was small was at Christmas when we would all gather in front of the tree for the King's speech on the radio. We'd stand to sing the anthem and then hold hands and wait on for a minute's silence for uncle Hughie. Mother would shed a few tears. Once or twice I remember she would bring out the letters he had sent home from the front and read them out to us. We would all have to sit and listen without a sound. Then she'd read the letter that had come to tell his parents that he was missing in action at the Somme. And we'd pass around the death penny, as if it was some sort of sacred object...we'd all hold it in our hands for a second or two. It was always very sad to think that that was the only reminder of him, that and those letters."
"Do you know what became of those letters and the penny thing?"
"Of-course son," she smiles. "I have them here for you. They're all in this box. I looked them out for you. There's a couple of pictures of him as well. Look...wasn't he the handsome fellow. Never got to marry though. He had a girlfriend too before he went, so my mother told me. She was heartbroken, but it didn't stop her marrying the young clergyman that arrived soon after."
Patrick's attitude changed perceptibly at this. The historian in him sat up and stared as these items were spread out in front of him on the table.

"This is brilliant," he says, the eyes lighting up. "Primary sources. Would you mind if I take close-up pictures of all these? And the death penny....here, you hold it, no, lift it up closer to your face, like as if you were kissing it....that's it."

And he spends the next few minutes using his phone to photograph all this evidence like an excited school-child, which is, I suppose, what he still is, despite all his sophistication.

On the way home we have a row and it has nothing to do with dead soldiers or world wars or mysterious Germans.

We are having coffee in the new service station café on the A26. Out of the blue he tells me he has changed his mind about university.

"I'm going to Magee to do music."

I am dumbfounded by this. I know he loves his songs and his guitar but he has always been good at history, probably his best subject in recent years. And with his success in getting into this project...I just can't fathom it. We argue along those lines for a bit. He is adamant that music is what he wants to do. I had imagined that when he put it down as his second choice it was simply because the grades being asked for were a lot lower than Queen's were demanding for history. I had suspected that he was just covering his back.

"I wasn't playing safe," he argues. "I was just never sure whether I wanted to do history or music. Now I have made up my mind."

"Is this Miss Kelly's influence?"

"Not really. And she's Mrs. She hasn't ever talked to me about it."

"This close to your A levels you tell me this. And why Magee, might I ask? What would have been wrong with Queen's? Is it because they don't ask for a couple of 'A's?"

"Magee is better for performance," he says. "Anyway, sure you're from Derry. What would be wrong with me going there? I can take the train until I get my bike."

"Your bike? You are talking about thirty miles son; you can't ride a bike to Derry, don't be daft."

He looks away out the window in disgust at my naivety, his mouth twisted up in disdain, just like his father's mouth used to do. After a bit he speaks again.

"I am buying a motor bike. That's why I am saving up."

"A motor bike? Over my dead body, Patrick. Are you out of your mind?"

"I am serious mum. I need a bike. I can't be always relying on you to take me around, like today. And when I get my driving test I can't expect you to let me have the car when I need it. It's not like we can afford to buy one for me...so...I need a bike."

"You'll get yourself killed on a motor bike! That road to Derry is crazy in the mornings. A bike in the middle of winter, in snow and ice...no way, Patrick."

"If the weather is bad I can take the train or the bus; I'm not stupid ma and I have thought this all out. If I have a bike it means I can stay at home and travel up when I need to, rather than have to pay to stay up at uni, which we couldn't afford. The other thing is... it means you won't be left on your own."

So clever, this son of mine...subtle as a bin lorry. Still, I have to confess that the way he said it, the wee quick look of affection in his eyes, does really affect me and I take my turn at the silent stare at the passing traffic.

"How do you think you are going to be able to afford to buy a motor bike?"

"I have been saving; gig money, Christmas and birthday money...plus I have some in the savings account, haven't I? And if I work all summer, that'll bring me in a good pile. Plus I can use some of my student loan."

"You have it all worked out, haven't you? And I suppose you have already lined up a deal?"

"Not quite but Barry's da is into bikes and he says he'll help me. He has a couple of bikes himself. He has a Suzuki 125 he might sell me; gave me a spin on it a few weeks back. It's class you know. The wind flying through your hair going up the Limavady mountain...so fast that you nearly take off when you reach the top; you feel like a bird, total freedom, massive G-force, 120 miles an hour..."

I can't help smile at his attempt to wind me up.

"Yeah, you're a right wee rebel, aren't you? Planning to buy a motor bike so you can stay at home with your mummy!"

Touché, my little one!

He does the lip-curl-of-defeat thing and turns away to stare at a waitress' backside as she wipes a table opposite.

"Eyes front!" I say emphatically.

"Sorry...sergeant," he smirks.

One all.

Chapter 11

(Patrick McAleese)

Sunday 12th June-   Another mega diary entry

Played in Sailors last night. Went well. Forty quid. Three covers and three of my own. Barry came with me for the first time in a while. He can be such a swot at times, like the only thing in life that matters is his 2 'A's and a 'B'. I noticed a few other people from school there, Madison included. Ah well, good luck to her and whoever is her next victim. She is starting to collect guys like she's playing Pokemon.

I sort of scored myself actually, though it might be more of an 'own-goal', now that I think about it. There was a gang of girls out for a birthday party and a couple of them came up after I finished the set, wanting selfies with me. One of them was all up for a bit of action, hanging around me like she was a scarf for a while. She'd had a few too many bottles of WKD though, a good few too many by the sound of her, so when it came to exchanging phone numbers at the end of the night I gave her a false one and slipped out the backdoor. No doubt she'll try to track me down on Facebook if she can remember my name but I can always ignore it. She was no Lena Rosenthal.

New song in my head but it's not quite coming together. I hope I have it ready for this France trip in two weeks time, not for public consumption, for her ears only, if I have the chance and the courage to share it with her...with Lena of-course. Lyrics are a bit clumsy still and the tune changes every time I play it but it will get there, hopefully. Theme? Just this weird idea of two lives spinning around in their own little orbits, independent and totally oblivious of each other, until something interrupts, some external force-field intervenes and pulls the two into a random connection that neither of them have consciously looked for or anticipated.

Angles
To this point of our existence,
Each with our own almanac
Vapour trails across a blue sky
Two lives lived on separate tracks
Yet now we seem to touch each other,
Staring through this cyber space
Searching for the clues of meaning
With eyes that never quite engage

So when I walk around the corner,
See her first in face to face
Will I stand in sheer amazement,
Will I be able to meet her gaze

This song may never be sung, never see the light of day; depends. She is one strange girl, that one. Strange and beautiful; not beautiful in a Madison sort of way but...Actually, I don't even know why I think she is beautiful. I am not even sure what she looks like; it's not as if I have even had a good full look at her. She seems to be always half-hidden. Her hair seems to blur her face somehow, like it's out of focus half the time, and half an hour after I come offline I can't quite get the picture of what she looks like. Nor can I remember much of what she told me. One thing I do remember is that she is only 16, will be 17 this summer. She is into music as well, she says, and she likes cycling and skiing. She never stands up or moves about when we are FaceTiming so I don't know if she is short or tall, thin or fat or whatever. I have to admit I find her totally intriguing, in the sense that I cannot work her out at all.
She had laughed at me when I tried to show off a few German phrases that I picked up from Miss Gillan and on the Duolingo app; that was when she was at her most animated actually, and the wide-mouthed grin was magical, even if it was at my expense.

"Good that you try to speak my language," she says, "but that is not how we say in Bavaria. We say..." And she spoofs off a whole rigmarole that I have no hope of remembering.
This morning is only the fourth time I have FaceTimed her. Well actually, it is more like the eighth or ninth time but she only answered four of them. Even this morning she didn't connect at first. I left it an hour and tried again and this time she does respond; she says she had been out at church. Even that is a bit odd; I'm not sure why I am surprised that she should be at church but I am. I suppose that in my stereotype of a modern German girl there has never been any possibility that she might be religious. It just seems strange. What happens next is even more of a shock.
We are chatting away; well, I am chatting, she is listening, to be fair, when I see her look up behind her as somebody comes into her bedroom. She speaks over her shoulder, in German, just a bit

sharply, I think. Suddenly two other faces appear on screen, two older faces, a man and a woman. Her parents, I presume. What I find a bit rare is that they are much older than I expected, like middle-aged, and that the man has a strange white collar on, sort of back to front. It takes me a second to realise that he must be a priest or a minister of some sort. Never would have imagined that, but then an even more interesting thing dawns on me.

Both faces are clearly German, white German, Aryan German if it is politically correct to use that phrase in this context.

Lena's face is anything but. Not sure what her ethnic background is but these two are clearly not her biological parents, not unless there has been some freaky genetic throwback.

I am well shocked by what I am seeing, not to mention kind of scared that, here I am, having to confront two very curious foreign strangers across cyberspace and 'do' some sort of conversation.

To be fair to them they are both trying to smile; Lena seems to have disappeared for the minute. I'm sorely tempted to quit the connection and go back to my previous life, unencumbered by these international complications. Only one thing keeps me in the loop; my fascination with Lena, my growing curiosity about her backstory.

The man, 'father', speaks; his English is pretty good; he does all the talking while his wife just smiles in that way that you know she's trying hard to make a good impression. He asks me a bunch of questions; it becomes kind of like a GCSE Language oral, but in reverse, the adult practising his English.

"What is your name?"

"What do you study?"

"What do you like to do?" (And when I do not respond with the classic, "I like to play football with my friends," he actually asks me, "Do you not like to be playing football?")

He asks me if I go to church, what I am intending to become after school, am I looking forward to the 'exchange programme' and some other things I can't remember. I think I'd better explain that it isn't an exchange programme, that he needn't be concerned that some random Irish boy is going to be coming to stay in his house anytime soon, that the trip is simply a joint visit to the Somme.

"Ah ja, the Somme," he says. "We Germans have a problem with remembering and honouring the innocent victims of our nation's aggression, innocents on all sides. I am very glad that Magdalena is having chance to go and to see the scale of those...how do you say...places of burials?"

"Cemeteries," I say.

"Ja, those cemeteries. I have been myself to such places. There are some in Bavaria also, from the second war. It is sad, so many graves."

I find this very interesting but I'm not going to be trying to develop the conversation in the circumstances. I want them to just go and let me talk to Lena again but I can't very well say, "OK, bye folks! Let me see your enigmatic daughter again," can I? Thankfully the enigmatic daughter herself arrives back in the picture, speaks quite firmly to her folks and waits for them to say their goodbyes to me. They do, again in a very pleasant manner...I can't complain. Lena can though, and does! I watch her, (standing up for the first time), as she ushers them out of the room with a few German words which, if they are in tune with her body language, are not exactly in appreciation of their interference.

She sits down again, her mood even more closed than usual.

"Hey, it's ok," I say as I wait in vain for her to speak again.

"No, it is not ok!" she says, still obviously bugged by the interruption.

"Are you alright?"

"Not really," she says. "I wish they would leave me to be."

"They seem nice," I try to console her. "I never imagined that your father..."

She sits forward to the screen and interrupts me. "Can we talk about something else?"

"Sure," I say, "what do you want to talk about?"

"I don't know," she says. "It was you called me."

A little silence of doubt. Her mood is not good.

"It's ok, I'm sorry... I can go if you don't want to talk."

More silence. My hand goes up to the disconnect icon but I hesitate, thankfully.

"Patrick, wait. I am sorry; it is annoying for them to do this to you, to ask you all the questions."

"It's ok. They are just curious who their daughter is going to be with in a few weeks time on the trip."

"Yes but your parents are not so...how do you say...?"

"Curious?" I offer.

"Yes, but...more like having bad manners. They do not want to know me, they leave you alone as a person of individual...yes?"

I smile, thinking about how totally curious my mother is about the mysterious cyber-friend I am talking to; more than likely she is listening with her ear to my door right now.

"Why are you laughing at me?" Lena says suspiciously.
"I am not laughing at you; I am laughing at the idea that my mother isn't curious about you."
"Why? She is?"
"Absolutely. She would be in the middle of every FaceTime call if I didn't keep my door locked. She can barely wait for me to come downstairs to attack me with questions," I tell her.
"And do you answer these questions? What do you say?"
The tease-instinct in me is too much to resist and I temporarily forget about the dangers of cross-cultural humour, especially when the 'foreigner' is in a grump.
"Of-course I do," I say. "I tell her that you are in a reality TV show and that you are a Turkish princess who is in exile in Bavaria while you wait for your handsome...your fairy godmother to restore you to your kingdom."
There is a short pause while she processes this; then, to her credit, a half-smile crosses her face.
"You are so funny," she says. "I am looking forward to meeting you."
"That makes two of us".
She sits back, a puzzled expression on her face.
"Two of you? I do not understand this."
"Sorry...no, there's just one of me. I mean...I am looking forward to meeting you as well. It should be good fun, this trip, I mean. I have finished my soldier project; just have to write up the whole thing and post it on our webpage, once I get the last couple of exams out of the way. How about you? You done anything like that?"
"Not like that. Our ideas are a lot different in our school. Some of my friends have found out about a soldier, perhaps a soldier who was killed from their community but...for me, my teacher...you saw him? Herr Fischer, yes? He told me not to worry about that. You see, because I am not of here...it is different. I have no... no meaning to the big wars of Europe. So I will just find out...find what I can about the people and...I suppose I will watch everything and learn. Learn from friends like you...if that is permitted?"
"Absolutely. Of-course. My pleasure. And I will learn from you too."
A slight raising of the one eyebrow I can see, then a hand across her face to flick her hair, defensively, I think.
"You may not want to learn from me when you..."
She stops, and I sense again that vulnerability in her, that lack of self-assurance. I wait but she just continues to stare off side-screen and rub her fingers up and down her forehead in that idiosyncratic

way she does. I don't know what to say; I don't know her well enough yet to be making a clumsy effort to cheer her up, certainly not in this kind of situation. I actually consider lifting my guitar and playing something to her, just to ease her tension, but I don't of-course...it would seem too random. I think of reading her the words of this last song but maybe she would struggle with the complicated concepts in it, or think I was being very pretentious. Instead I just watch her in silence; instinctively that seems to be the right thing to do, just wait her out, let her think her private thoughts. I'm starting to wonder if she's forgotten I'm here, but she turns back to the screen.

"Thank you for calling again but you do not have to call back before the trip, if you don't want to. It's ok. I am not good company for you sometimes, for any person. I am too...too complicated, I think."

"You certainly know how to make a fellow curious," is all I could think to say.

A tiny smile and then, "That makes...how did you say? That makes two of us, yes?"

I go straight back to the song after we disconnect. I have no idea why but this stranger is starting to get under my skin. Curiosity, yes, but definitely spiced with something way more fascinating.

Will I find the chords to play her, Choose the key, unpick the lock
Therapy or mere seduction, Are my motives in the dock?
I must find a way to reach her, A vocation laid on me
Light a flame within her darkness,
Save her from her mystery

Chapter 12

Bernie Doherty travelling from **Coleraine** to **Dublin Airport** with **Patrick McAleese**
Friday 24th June 2016

Hard to believe; when I woke up today my wee baby boy stood by my bed and said, "You need to be getting up!" And when I opened my eyes and looked at him he was eighteen and tall and with a coppery fuzz on his face that he believes is the start of a beard.

First time in the history of the world that he has been the one to waken me. If I had a pound for all the other times I could have told him to go waken the chauffeur and let me sleep. Bloody four o'clock in the morning and he was straining at the bit to be on his journey, his journey away from me, away on this expedition to 'Find the Fallen', away to her, whoever she is, 'the faceless one'.

Why could they not have chosen to fly later in the day and not have people all over Ireland getting up at this unearthly hour? And a drive of 300 miles there and back when I could still be in dreamland, all so my pacifist Patrick can stand by the grave of some Protestant soldier and say a prayer for him to a God that neither of them likely believe in? It's all pretty daft to me, but what do I know? I'm just a bitter wee Derry woman, as I was often reminded.

I did try to persuade Josie to drive him down. She was half-asleep on the couch, laid out like a fish supper, as my mother would have said.

"Josie," I asked her nicely, "would you ever be able to drive Patrick to this meeting in Dublin if I pay your petrol?"

All I got was, "Wise up ma!"

Apparently she is "exhausted" after finishing her finals...yeah, yeah! More like after her week of celebratory boozing around Leeds, blowing what was left of her student loan. Well, she will be ready for a job now but where is she going to find work with a degree in Health Informatics, our NHS being what it is? She tells me she will likely have to go back to England for work, maybe even further afield.

Isn't it funny how you remember where you were when you hear of certain big shocks on the news? Like, older people say, "I remember where I was when Kennedy was shot." Myself, I can still remember where I was when I heard of Diana's death. I had gone for milk and people were standing crying in the corner shop, crying and hugging each other. And I know exactly where I heard about Nine-Eleven; I had to come out of work to go to get Patrick; he had been sick in playgroup. As I walked out the path to the car park this stranger came up to me and said, "This could be the start of World War 3." I must have looked a bit blank for then he went on to explain about the twin towers and these planes flying into them. "This could be the beginning of the end," he said with a wild look in his eyes. He put his hand in his pocket and I thought he was going to hand me one of those gospel tracts, as has happened, but all he did was take out a bottle of tablets and pop one in his mouth.

It is a bit the same this morning. We had had our breakfast, far too quickly but Patrick was so impatient. He had the car sitting ready, engine running, his suitcase in the boot and his precious guitar safely on the back seat where he could keep an eye on it in case it spontaneously combusted in anxiety or something. Now we are driving on the motorway around Ballymena; little traffic at this time of the morning; it will be good to get through the West Link before the rush hour; the traffic can be pure mental then. I switch the stereo from his Hozier album to listen to the radio. Good call and good timing, in spite of his drowsy protests.

"Britain has voted out!" says the slightly distressed voice of a Radio Four presenter. "Brexit is a reality!"

Patrick seems to suddenly rouse himself. "What was that?" he says.

"Sounds like we are out of Europe."

"Oh my God!"

We listen to the programme all the way from Ballymena to the south; he is hanging on to every last sentence; I had no idea he was so politically minded.

A few miles south of Newry I say to him, "I should let you out here, Patrick."

He looks at me.

"What do you mean?"

"You could hitch a lift. I would need to turn now before I go over into the Republic, just in case they close the border before I get back up again."

He doesn't even bother to try to see the joke.

"What are you talking about mum? This is a serious issue for people like me."

"Of-course it is. It's a serious issue for all of us. And I am serious about the border. You see, the thing is, and you can't remember this of-course but back in the day it could have taken half an hour to drive across here, right here. There were police checkpoints, army checkpoints, customs posts, Garda posts. If Britain leaves Europe that could all come back. This will be an international border. Keep the immigrants out of Britain."

"I doubt it," he says. "The people wouldn't stand for it. The border only exists in some people's minds."

"Don't you believe it son," I tell him. "There will be stacks of them crawling out of the woodwork now; they'll be delighted to see hard lines on the map and even harder faces manning the checkpoints. Some of them will be demanding a ten-foot high wall again. Once Trump's boys are finished in Mexico there'll be a job for them here, just wait till you see."

"You're talking crap mother. Trump hasn't a snowball's chance. Anyway, why do you always have to reduce it to a rant about Ireland? It's far bigger than 'our wee country'. What about all the people who work here, like from Poland and all? And all the Brits working in Europe? And our right to travel anywhere we want? It's crazy."

"Of-course it's crazy. Well, at least you are getting the chance to go on a trip like this now, before they clamp down on such things," I tell him.

We drive on in silence for a good twenty miles; silence except that every so often there is a string of obscenities from him, mainly about bloody Boris Johnston and frickin' Farage.

"What are people thinking? This is madness," he says.

"You wouldn't be all that into politics then?" I say, faintly sarcastic. "Sure I had to persuade you to come to vote yesterday, if I remember correctly."

"You did not. I was always going to vote...."

"Ah come on Patrick. I had to coax you downstairs to come with me."

"Well, sure I did go and vote but I really did think it was a foregone conclusion. All the polls and all. Like everybody, near enough every one of my friends were voting 'Remain'. How did this happen?"

"Must be a lot of very angry people in England," I say. "Especially up north. Josie was saying that there's a lot of racism around the whole Leeds area; a lot of ordinary folk there voting out, wanting the Government to do something about immigration."

"Taking a hammer to crack an egg," he says.

This is the most serious chat I've had with my son in ages, maybe ever, on this kind of subject. It's nice, but I find myself wondering if his father had still been on the scene would he be holding these same views or might he have been influenced by that more instinctively hard-line that would have been his dad's default position. I'll never know, of-course, but I am quietly satisfied that, whatever has shaped his opinions, they are ones that I can understand and agree with. His values coincide with mine on most things and I feel blessed that this is so. Yes we have our differences and our rows but Patrick has been an easy son to rear and for that I am more than thankful.

True he doesn't have a massive circle of friends but the few he does have seem decent and unlikely to be the type of fellows who will lead him into trouble. Only two or three times has there been any issue with drink and, so far as I know, he has never shown any sign of dabbling in drugs. Maybe I am naive in that; possibly he has tried some stuff but I have never noticed any ill effects. Then again, how would any mother ever know? He does 'inhabit his own space', as they say, pretty much all the time now but, all in all, I haven't much to be complaining about.

True he has given up on Mass but he has time yet to make up his own mind about religion. As long as he is a decent human being; that is all that counts to me.

True he can be expensive to run at times. The guitar, (which was far too dear, but it had to be the best), the amplifier, the recording mic and his iPad...it all added up and ate a few holes in my alimony; but at least it was money going after healthy pastimes. He could be doing worse than recording songs or singing in Sailors. He did fail his driving test the first time and hasn't bothered about getting more lessons or re-sitting it; at least it means I don't have to put him on the insurance of the car. I am not sure how that will work when it comes to this motor bike idea of his but we will see.

True I am a bit worried that whatever girl relationships he has had, (reportedly...I have my spies), never seem to last very long. Frequently I can sense an annoyance in him that some plan or some connection has not worked out the way he had fantasised that it would; sometimes I find a screwed up bit of notepaper in his waste-paper basket and the words, (or lyrics, as he might want me to call them), are quite revealing...also quite sad at times. I have to admit that he does have a real talent for expressing himself and his inner frustrations in these lyrics. Whether it will ever amount to anything in terms of a career I very much doubt but, like I say, he could be doing worse things.

Maybe this trip away will help him find a sense of meaning and purpose, over and above the whole palaver of commemorating these long-dead fighting men. I have come to rest in the anticipation that when he witnesses the multitude of white tombstones in cemetery after cemetery and the thousands of names on their towers of remembrance he will be convinced once and for all, (if he needs any more convincing), of the madness and futility of these wars; not just the ones a hundred years ago, or seventy years ago, but the ones still raging wherever you look in the world.

We reach the airport, park in the short-stay park, (on his orders), and I start to walk with him towards the terminal.

"You don't have to come in you know," he tells me.

"You kiddin'?" I say. "I have to meet all these lovely Irish 'coleens' that you are going away with."

"No you don't. Just say 'Goodbye' here."

"And miss the chance to give you a big slobbery kiss in front of your team-mates? Like it's not every day you get the chance to play for Ireland! I'm proud of you, you know...and I feel that it is time I showed that to the watching world."

"Jeez mother! Will you for God's sake turn and let me go in on my own," he pleads.

I laugh at him.

"I'm winding you, son. I promise I won't even give you a hug, if you don't want me to, alright?"

He is still doubtful, walking on ahead, guitar case over his shoulder, trailing his case so quickly that I have to skip along to catch up with him.

"Promise?"
"Of-course. You know me," I tell him.
"Yeah, I do! That's the trouble," he says.
I glance at his face and notice the tension in his eyes.
"I'm sorry son; I shouldn't be stressing you. You're tense enough, so you are."
"I'm not tense. Just...just don't say any more."
So I don't. Not until he has been standing looking around Terminal 1 for several minutes. I'm not surprised; there are literally hundreds of green-topped football fans in the place, all heading to France to support either Northern Ireland or the Republic in the Euros at the weekend. I can't help noticing that they all seemed to be getting on well together. There is plenty of singing and banter but I don't see a single face that has anything other than a broad smile on it. Wouldn't it be great if it could always be like this? Where have I heard that before now?
Patrick is still gawking at the football 'flash-mob'.
"Where did it say you were all to meet up?" I ask.
Out comes a crumpled envelope and he skim reads it again.
"Just to the side of the Information Desk in Departures, second floor," he says.
"Ah, that's good to know," I say and wait for the penny to drop with him. He looks around for a further couple of seconds and takes off towards the elevator, mother in tow, silent again.
No bother this time. There they are, a whole regiment of them, pulling on purple T-shirts like they're going out of fashion...which they look as if they did a few years ago, but I'm saying nothing. 'Find The Fallen Project 2016' is emblazoned in gold on the back, within a silhouette outline of a soldier, head bowed, leaning on his rifle.
Well at least these kids won't get mixed up with the hordes of footie fans, I'm thinking, though if either of the Irish teams get knocked out of the tournament maybe this 'Find The Fallen' logo will have a cross-over meaning.
The leader of the thing, James somebody if I remember correctly, notices Patrick and comes across; a quick shake hands and he guides him to the Ulster group who are gathered with one particular teacher. Little fear of a goodbye hug, as my son is quickly submerged in the purple sea. James returns to me for a quick word.
"And I see he has his guitar with him. That's great. We have a flute player too, a very good one I hear, Caoimhe from Clare...and a banjo player from Wexford who has unfortunately forgotten to bring his banjo."
"Why 'unfortunately'?" I ask facetiously but James doesn't quite pick up on my Derry humour...at least not immediately.

"Ah ha," he says, "you are not a fan of the banjo? That's a shame. I play one myself."

Oh Lord, I think; open your mouth and put your big foot in it without even looking.

"Oh, I'm sorry," I begin. "I didn't really mean..."

"Just kidding," he laughs. "I can't play a note."

Right. That will 'larn' me. Trust a man to want to get the last word at my expense. I've got quite a few of that particular T-shirt myself.

Chapter 13

Patrick McAleese is at **Hotel Ibis, Albert, France** with (God knows who)
Friday 24th June 2016

We arrive in Albert, our base, by coach. All very smooth. The Germans don't get here until this evening; it's a very long journey apparently. They'll be some craic after nine hours cooped up in a coach.

This gives us time to visit the local WW1 museum which seems to be in the basement of Albert's main church, at the end of a very long underground tunnel. Having looked around at all the memorabilia I am sort of half glad that we are on our own for this experience; I wonder how the German students would take this place, with its distinctly Allied flavour; red, white and blue everywhere. I also have a feeling that Lena might have been a bit bored by it all, maybe I'm wrong. I stare at the cabinets of rifles but I am finding it difficult to concentrate on what I'm supposed to be learning. The girl hasn't even arrived yet and the adrenaline of expectation is running through me like I've popped a couple of 'Happy Pills'.

In my head I have been rehearsing how this first meeting will be; what I will say, what I will do, how I will greet her. Actually I have been imagining it for a good few weeks, so much so that I am a bit of a nervous wreck about the whole thing. My main worry is that she will ignore me altogether. She will be with all her school mates, she'll be part of an 'in-group', her clique, likely surrounded by a pack of good-looking skier-types and I will be looking in from outside. She will be gabbling away to them in German and I will be stuck out on the fringes, isolated and feeling utterly useless and self-conscious. This is a feeling I am well accustomed to but it never gets any easier to handle. Do I try to break into the circle, chat to her in front of all her friends, be the centre of her attention? No way! She would be totally embarrassed and anyway that is just not how I am; I will stay apart from that sort of group. I am too much the individual, the shy observer. I will not make any great fuss of greeting her when she arrives; I think I will wait for the right moment when I can talk to her on her own.

It has not really struck me until now that we Irish are all in the same boat here; each of us has made contact with our German counterparts, some with more warmth than others I'm sure, but all are about to meet these FaceTime friends for the first time. Same for the Germans, of-course. Even worse for them as they will be exhausted from their travels and probably too grumpy to be making a great attempt at initial conversation. It could be a bit awkward.

James makes this very point to us when we are all gathered in the foyer. I am at the back, half-watching TV with one or two of the Irish lads; Northern Ireland v Wales in the Euros; I'm not really all that interested but it is a useful distraction while we wait. Then there is a bit of excitement behind us. The coach from Bavaria is pulling into the car park. I turn to watch through the window as the German students get off and hang around, waiting to collect their baggage. I suspect that we are all caught in a strange mix of excitement and apprehension. You wouldn't guess that to look at us though as we pretend to be totally chilled.

I stare at the silhouettes milling about out there in the gloominess of the car park, tall angular shadows projected up by the low pedestrian lights, reminding me of a shot from some old black and white Hitchcock movie. I look for Lena but I struggle to see her; maybe I just don't recognise her among all these gangly figures. Eventually they start to wander into the foyer, some of them looking kind of dazed and pretty tired. There aren't many smiles among them. My fellow students go forward to shake hands and a queue develops around the door. My eyes scan the faces.

I cannot see her.

She is not here.

My heart gives an irregular lurch. She must have chickened out at the last minute. Oh my God, after all that anticipation. The disappointment rises in me like sick. I can almost taste it. I am left alone by the TV, everyone else doing the warm-greeting thing.

Behind me Wales are celebrating a goal but I am not bothered. In something like despair I turn and glance back outside to the coach and...

There she is...at least I think it's her.

She is walking slowly toward the entrance and she seems to be talking to a much taller figure. He is bending over a bit to listen to her. I recognise him as the teacher, Herr Fischer. She follows him into the foyer, reluctantly, it seems to me. She stands apart from the other Germans, her head down as she fiddles with her case...no attempt to look around at our group. I am a bit taken aback by this; it is not quite the fantasy coming together that I had imagined and, to my shame, I am slow to make a move to her to say hello. The clamour of greetings, conversations and laughter fills the room but I am in a silent cocoon of my own and I am hearing nothing, nothing but the thud of my heart in my ears. Eventually her eyes flick up for a very fleeting scan of the room, then back down to her case, but only for a second.

She has seen me and she raises her gaze to meet mine across the space of the foyer. It's a blank sort of a stare; you could write anything into that look, but I choose to think that there is the ghost of a smile of relief in it. She holds my stare and I move across the foyer towards her, only to make an eejit of myself by tripping over a German rucksack as I am not watching where I'm stepping, ending up draped over the back of a chair. Thankfully nobody else has been paying any attention to me and my ungainly stumble goes unnoticed, except by Lena of-course. When I look back up her hand is over her mouth to hide a giggle but I see it in her eyes anyway. What a first impression to make, clumsy fool that I am! I feel another crimson tide rise from my neck.

I try to smile it off as I rise and finally reach her.

Now, here is the awkward issue. Do I give her a red-faced hug as I have seen a few do in the last couple of minutes, (all girls, it must be said), or do I play safe and shake hands?

I chicken out and go with the formal hand-shake. And, of-course, being me, I over-analyse her reaction. The wee semi-scared smile is still there but do I read relief or do I see a little disappointment in her eyes? Forget it Patrick; be natural, normal.

"Hi," she says.

"Welcome Lena," I say, like I am in training to be a hotel maître. "You must be very tired after..."

"Yes," she says.

"Good," I say after a little pause, thinking 'Why am I saying "Good", as if it's good that she's tired? Excellent! You're tired out!'
"I mean...it's good you made it."
"Ja, it is good," she says.
"No problems...like on the journey?"
"No, no problems."
"It must be a long way..."
"It is, very long."
'Jeez, this is going great,' I think to myself. 'It's going to be a long week if it goes on like this.'
"And your folks?" I ask. "They are well?"
Oh cringe, I am starting to sound like some stuffy novel from the 1800s.
"Yes, they are good also. And how are your parents?"
Hmm...we'll talk about this later but in the meantime I keep it simple.
"Yeah, dead on, thanks," I say.
Immediately I regret the thoughtless use of Norn Iron idiom. I can see the question in her eyes before she asks it.
"They are... they are dead?"
"No, no, they are fine. It's just something we say when we mean that something is fine...it's 'dead on' like. Sorry, I shouldn't have confused you. We have a lot of daft sayings in Ireland that aren't exactly what you would read in an English text book. Don't worry, I'll explain them as we go along."
She looks a bit anxious about this but I change the subject. The others are starting to move towards the lifts and the stairs and I don't want Lena to be last again.
"I think we're going to have a bite soon so maybe you should follow...I mean a bite to eat, like, our evening meal... in a wee while, so you'd better find your room with the others," I tell her.
"Ja, I think I need to have a shower now."
"Yeah, sure, go ahead," I say.
As she picks up her case and follows the others I am struck by the realisation that I am sort of looking out for her, in a big-brotherly kind of way. That's what I tell myself anyhow.
I have no more conversation with her this evening. The Germans all head to bed after the grub and I sit down with the others in the foyer for a while, before going up to my own room. As usual there seems to be a lyric beginning to form in my mind and I want to write it down before I forget it. Guitar on my knee, I start on the iPad, just a rough first draft.

I catch her glance across the crowded room
Her eyes wide open like a harvest moon
I see the underside of her disguise
A special something that I recognise
She gives me feelings that I can't explain
I'm like a moth drawn to the flame

Next morning we are all gathered for a 'workshop', so we are divided up into small groups. My group, four Irish and four Germans, is one German light though, as Lena is in a different group.
'Come on, Patrick; concentrate.'
James and Oskar speak for a bit and tell us that this had been intended to be a discussion on the subject, 'What it means to be a European'.
"However, in light of the UK's decision yesterday to leave the European Union, this Brexit thing," says James, his tone like a priest at a wake, "maybe in your groups you could just reflect on this momentous decision and what it might mean for Europe as a whole."
Oskar is equally grave. "Already in Germany our media is expressing the feeling that this is like the unexpected break-up of a happy marriage. So please talk together, make some notes for feedback at the end."
Goodness, that is going to be some task, I am thinking. I look around at my group. The other three Irish are all from the Republic so they are hardly going to be in much of a bother about it; the German students look a bit bemused by the topic; I am the only one who will be directly affected, as a Northern Ireland person.
Anyhow, we have a bit of a chat about it, nothing too earth-shattering or deeply interesting. Maybe because I am the only northerner I get nominated to do the feedback. I make some notes and, when it comes my turn towards the end of the session, I spoof for a couple of minutes, keen for this to be over.
"Yeah, we wouldn't be too happy about Brexit. We're all pretty surprised about it, like the rest of you, but I am actually the only one in our group to be directly affected by it...and blah, blah, blah."
As I sit down I hear a dismissive southern accent.

"I don't see that it has much to do with us. Ireland will still be in Europe; let them ones go whatever way they want. Doesn't affect us, just the north."

"No way," says the Longford girl. "It's not just the north. We are going to be seriously damaged by this if our businesses and farms can't export to Britain. Think of the jobs that will go. It's a disaster."

Martin from Dundalk joins in. "Look," he says, "where I live, we are near the border but we are back and forward into Co Down all the time, maybe three or four times a week, like shopping in Newry or up to Belfast and we never even think of it as crossing a border; the border thing is only politicians' talk but now with Brexit they will have to put up checkpoints and have border guards and all."

James steps into a lull in the debate.

"Can I ask you all something, the students who live in the Republic. How many of you have actually ever been in Belfast? Show of hands please."

There's a bit of muttering.

"Does Enniskillen count?" someone asks.

Dah!

"Just Belfast."

Hands go up slowly, heads look around. He does a quick count.

"Eight," he says. "Only eight of you out of the twenty six counties have been to Ireland's second city. That's amazing. You must try and get up to the Titanic Centre...it's brilliant, great day out."

"Too risky! Watch that iceberg!" quips Dublin Darragh. He gets a ripple of laughter but the Germans are lost. Oskar talks them through it, in German. Not a smile though.

James resumes his survey. "Now can I ask the Northern Irish students, hands up if you have ever been to Dublin?"

All six hands go up.

"I went to Dublin yesterday," quips Tyrone Katie. "Had to catch a plane!"

"Ok, apart from yesterday?"

Still six hands but Simon looks a bit unsure.

"Does going to see Ulster playing Leinster at the RDS count?" he asks.

"I think it does," James laughs, "and I hope you enjoyed the hammering. So just the once then Simon?"

"Yip, just once."

"And what is your opinion about Brexit, may I ask?"

I kind of feel for Simon at this; it is putting him on the spot a bit and he is a fairly quiet big fellow. I needn't worry about him though. He pauses for a second or two, then what he says brings a really warm response from everybody.

"I can see why some people would want to leave but I think it's a bad sign. Look, there are sixty something of us here, half from Germany, half from Ireland, north and south, and we are all here together to sort of pay our respects to all these soldiers who were slaughtered in a war between our countries, a hundred years ago. But people didn't learn anything from it, they blamed each other, so it all happened again, in the Second World War. So, in my opinion, anything that pulls countries apart and splits people up can't be a good thing. It might just be the start of a slippery slope to more conflict. And who knows where that might end up. We'd have been better to stick together."

'Good for him,' I think as everybody gives him a clap. 'Well said.'

༄

We are all standing in a big circle in Fricourt German Military Cemetery. This place is darkly morbid. The surrounding trees, tall and sombre, seem to want to deny entry to any hint of sunlight. I find the atmosphere oppressively dull as we wander between endless rows of small black crosses. We are meant to be having moments of reflection here, according to Oskar, but all I can reflect on is the fact that Lena is ignoring me.

"Seventeen thousand soldiers buried here," he tells us solemnly. "Almost twelve thousand in this communal grave alone."

These are massive numbers. It's all so different from the graveyard we visited earlier today. There, only two hundred Allied soldiers lie in pristine symmetry in a tiny Commonwealth Cemetery called Hawthorne Ridge. We swamped the place. I loved its hill-top situation, catching the best of the light and the breeze. It all felt so miniature, so intimate, so appropriate. Each grave is beautifully kept. There are splashes of red and yellow roses against the white-granite tombstones, the lawn trimmed like a bowling green. I kinda felt I would have loved to stay there by myself for a while.

We all watched as the Tipperary student in her blue and gold Gaelic top spread a little earth from the soldier's home parish on his grave. It was a lovely emotional moment for her and she shed an unembarrassed tear or two.

Now, in this monochrome German cemetery, our brightly coloured gear seems to jar with the grey dilapidation of our surroundings. I glance at Lena across the circle. She's wearing her purple 'Find The Fallen' shirt above cream-coloured slit-knee jeans, her skin showing through like chocolate in a torn Galaxy wrapper. Her head is down. There is a sadness about her, but I am not sure whether it is to do with this depressing place or if this is just her default emotional state. I have noticed that she does not seem to be hanging around much with anyone from her school. She is not part of any clique, as I had feared she would be; in fact she seems to be a bit of a loner, which I find hard to get my head around. A girl as pretty as her would have guys buzzing around her like wasps at a honey-pot if she was at my school. I've only seen her chatting once to one other friend, a girl of African background, I am guessing. It's all a bit of a puzzle to me.

When we have done our minute of silence and are allowed to wander around again I make sure my wandering brings me across Lena's path. We meet beside a different kind of grave. Whereas most of the graves are marked by a dark cross this one has a proper tombstone. Small stones have been placed on top and, as I go around to read the inscription, I suddenly realise in surprise that it is the grave of a Jewish soldier.

"Jeez, this is random," I say.

"What is this?" Lena asks.

"'Albert Wolff, Kanonier'," I read. "I think that this is a Jewish guy. He has a Star of David on his grave, not a cross."

"Kanonier. He was a gunner. But I thought that the Jews were being...how do you say? The Holocaust? All Jews were being killed by...?"

I can understand her confusion.

"Ah, that was later, in Nazi times," I tell her. "Hitler and all that. The Second World War."

"Ah yes, of-course. Sorry. I am being stupid," she says, slightly embarrassed.

"No, you're not," I say. "I had the same thought myself. But there is something very haunting about seeing a Jewish German soldier's grave. And there seem to be several of them here."

She looks around and starts to wander away towards another similar grave. Slowly I follow her, trying my best not to be distracted in the poignancy of this moment by my rear-end view of her sinuous form as she meanders slowly through this forest of low crosses. I

am so tempted to take out my phone and video this bizarre image... these columns of stark tomb-markers, rigid and spikey, as a canvas for the loveliness of this languidly feminine walk. Life and beauty strolling through these silent monuments to tragically cold death.
"How do you feel about all this Lena?" I ask as I catch up.
No answer; she just stares at the tombstone of Nathan Frank. I think she hasn't heard me. Then...
"I do not know what to feel. It is all so sad. So many lives wasted."
"Do you think it feels different for a German?"
"I don't know," she says as she starts to wander on again. "You should ask one."
Wow, that is not the answer I am expecting; I don't know what to make of it and it throws me completely. I want to ask her what she means by it...like it's a denial of her nationality, is it not, but I can't quite bring myself to ask. When we reach the coaches she turns back to me.
"You ask me what I feel about this," she says. "I ask you what do you feel about the war in Syria? The war in Iraq? Terrorism in Turkey?"
Again I am taken aback. This is very out of the blue and my face must show my shock and confusion. This would not be a good time to be telling her that my own father fought in Iraq. I hope she cannot read my mind.
"These soldiers are dead for a hundred years, you know? Today many ordinary people will die in Syria, many children who are not having guns, knowing nothing about war. That is why I am saying this," she says.
"Yeah, I take your point. We should talk more about this," I say as she leaves me to climb into her coach without a backward glance.
Yeah, we absolutely do need to talk more, about this for sure but about a whole bunch of stuff, like about who she is, what's her story, what's her connection to Syria or wherever? I need some space to process all this but I am not to have any just yet.
Teacher James taps my shoulder and says, "So Patrick, tomorrow, when we have our ceremony at Thiepval Tower, would you be prepared to sing for us?"
"Sure," I say. "What would you like me to sing?"
"One of your own songs perhaps? Do you have anything suitable?"
My only song that is relevant is the one about my ancestors; I wouldn't mind doing it but I sort of think it is a bit rough for this

particular context. I'd have to change some of the lingo in it. The Germans might find it offensive.

"I'll think about it," I tell him. "Maybe something like 'The Green Fields of France'? Most people know it; they could join in."

"Good idea," he says, "but keep that song you sent in for our wee concert on the final night; it's too good to miss."

Thanks man!

That conversation I had earlier with Lena has left me a bit unsettled. Did I say something to annoy her? Did I step on some cross-cultural land mine without realising or was it just her idiosyncratic mood-swing thing? I'd love to be able to figure out why she seemed to turn so bitter in her attitude. The thing is that even if I got the chance to ask her maybe it would make things worse. I should just let things be; it might only complicate the situation to try to tease it out. Like, I can't just walk up to her and ask, "Did I say something that bugged you back in the German cemetery?" When would I even get the chance to chat to her on her own anyhow?

As it happens I do get a chance, a brilliant chance. I am heading out the door with some of the Irish lads for a wander around the hotel area in the evening when, out of the corner of my eye, I see her sitting alone in the dining room. I excuse myself from the gang, saying that I am going to the loo and will catch up later. Then, as I stand outside the door of the diner, I have second thoughts. This is outside my comfort zone; it's not like I have had a bunch of experience of this kind of thing. I think I am being a bit naive and suddenly start to feel very awkward. Am I making a fool of myself here, forcing things too much with this strange girl? And yet, as I study her from behind this frosted glass and notice the slouch of her shoulders as she bends over the table, focusing intently on something, I think, 'No, it's not just me who is the needy one here. Lena is far more confused than I am.'

I push open the door and go to her, coming over all confident as I try to cover my nervous tension.

As I approach I see her look up from whatever she is writing. Quickly she closes her folder, leans over it like she's trying to hide it under her arms, as if she is embarrassed to be caught at something. She doesn't meet my eye as I sit down opposite her at the table.

"Hi," I say.

No reply; she just looks away.

"So you do some writing then?"
She obviously does not want to talk to me but her manners are good enough to guarantee a brief reply at least.
"Yes, some writing," she admits, still that closed look to the side.
'Come on, girl...loosen up,' I think. 'Talk to me.'
"What sort of stuff do you write?" I say.
"It is nothing."
"It can't be nothing," I argue with a smile that is meant to say, 'Don't feel any threat here Lena; I just want to talk, about anything.'
Still she says nothing, just looks away, slightly bored.
"Do you keep a journal or what?" I ask.
"It is a bit like that. It is not important. Please don't ask me about it."
"I am sorry," I say. "I am just curious, that's all, cos I like to write as well, you see. So when I see someone else writing I get curious."
Silence from the other side of the table. This is some craic.
"Ok," I say, getting up. "I'm sorry I disturbed you."
"It is alright," she says with a small shy glance up at me. "I am not in a mood to talk at this minute please; is that ok?"
"Of-course Lena. I just wanted...look, if I said something at your cemetery today that hurt you I am sorry, that's all."
"You did not say anything wrong," she says. "It is me only, my own thoughts and problems. Please forget about it."
"That's good," I say. "Right, chat to you later."
And I leave her hugging the folder to her chest, her chin resting on it like it's a prayer book.

Chapter 14

Bernie Doherty is at **Home** alone feeling frustrated
Sunday 26th June 2016

U ok Patrick? I tried foning; what r u playing at? U promised 2 call me. I'm worried now. Been 2 days. This is Bernie, ur mum, remember me? XXX

The skitter!
Not a single phone call from him since he left. He was to phone when he arrived safe in France; that would have been on Friday night. It's now Sunday evening and not a word. He wouldn't even answer his phone when I tried, several times. OK, he did answer my text yesterday, just about.
Such a comfort to me that boy. So considerate.
Well, if he answers his phone now he'll get an earful.
It's ringing....still ringing...he won't answer....ringing....he's likely wrapped around his Fräulein....
"Hi mum."
"Patrick, you ok?"
"Yeah, everything's fine."
"You were meant to phone me, to tell me how..."
"Yeah, I forgot sort of. Sorry."
"You forgot, you ungrateful wee...! You have to realise that when you make a promise you must stick to it. I was worried..."
"Hey, I said I'm sorry. If you are going to go on a rant about it I'm hanging up."
"Ok ok, don't hang up. So...what have you been up to? How's it going?"
"Going dead on."
"And...g'on an tell us about your wee blonde?"
"My wee blonde? What are you on about?"
"The girl you have fallen for?"
"Mum, I'm hanging up here..."
"No don't Patrick. I'm sorry I'm just kidding. What's it been like so far?"
"So far pretty good. I did a song this afternoon at Thiepval Tower. You should Google it! It's huge. We had a sort of remembrance ceremony there. Laid flowers and all."
"What did you sing?"
"You know the song about Willie McBride? 'Green Fields of France'? Sang that. Went ok. The girl from Clare played a slow air lament sort of thing; she's brilliant on the flute. I'll probably get to play with her at the final concert tomorrow night."
"And what about your soldier...Hugh whoever? Did you find his grave?"
"No, sure his body was never found. His name is up on the tower. I saw it. Laid a flower for him."
"Good for you. Did it feel weird?"
"Yeah, it was. Like, I was thinking that this poor bloke from Scot's Hill was just an ordinary guy, and there is his name stuck up there on that monster of a tower

along with 72,000 others. I wondered if I was the first person from his home-place to even come looking for it. It did feel sort of tragic that nobody actually knows where he died, where his body is; it's all so anonymous, so random."

"I can imagine. And the Germans? Are you getting on alright with them? How do they react to all those cemeteries and stuff?"

"Aye, they seem nice enough; haven't had all that much chat with them, to be honest."

"Really? But sure you spent ages getting to know the one you were teamed up with on FaceTime, did you not? Is she ignoring you or what?"

Oh boy, my motherly instinct has struck a chord there, I think, for suddenly he has nothing to say. Silence; then...

"How do you know she is a 'she'?" he says. "Could be a 'he'."

"I doubt that very much son, not unless your orientation has taken a dramatic turn to the left. I'm your mother, remember. I think I know when you've fallen for somebody."

"I haven't fallen...would you give over mum. She's just a girl."

"Oh yeah? What's she like then?"

"She's ok; just a normal girl."

"Yeah but do you get on well with her like? Is she nice to chat to?"

Weary sigh, I think by the sound of it. Nothing else coming from him.

"What's wrong?"

"I don't know; nothing's wrong. She's just...just very different."

"Germans can be like that; not the warmest people on the planet..."

"Mum! You're talking nonsense again. For a start these ones are from Bavaria and they hardly even think of themselves as German. They're all fine, so they are."

"Except for your woman?"

"Well, I have to admit...she is different; she's very quiet but when she chats she is really nice to talk to. But...she is just a bit hard to fathom. Like I'm never sure where I stand with her."

Ok, Ok, this is good; he is talking to me about this girl, great. Just don't push it, Bernie.

"Is she pretty? Have you taken any pictures yet?"

"I haven't, to be honest; sort of forgot. Too busy wondering what she's thinking."

"Is she on Facebook?"

"Don't think so."

"Well be sure to take a few good photos...and send me one."

"Send you one? So you can stick it on Instagram and embarrass the life out of me? 'Patrick's babe from Arabia'! Sure I'll be home on Tuesday, for God's sake. That's only two days away."
"So it is. What do you mean Arabia? Is she not German like?"
Another sigh.
"I don't know where she's from. Middle East somewhere I'm guessing. I'd love to ask but I think she's too sensitive about her background, so I don't raise anything to do with it. Anyway, as I say, there's only a couple more days left to..."
"Yeah, you'd better go and work on her; you wouldn't want to be coming home wondering, would you?"
"Give over mum; you and your fertile imagination."
"I don't think it's my imagination is the problem here, do you? Anyway, Josie is still here, if you are interested in your sister."
"Ok."
"Are you eating ok? Is the food good?"
"Yeah, it's grand."
"Do you want to speak to Josie?"
"Naw, it's ok; I have to go here."
"Right, ok, take care of yourself."
"Ok, see you Tuesday."
"Yeah. Bye, bye bye!"
I hang up and turn to Josie.
"Why will he not talk to me any more?" she says.
"Probably because you normally won't talk to him. Every time he sees you your head is either stuck in your computer or some magazine. You need to give him some time, for himself like. He needs you."
"He needs to grow up and stop treating you like an afterthought; selfish wee bugger. He's getting more like his father every time I see him. You need to put your foot down."
She doesn't stop to listen to my protest about this last comment, just storms away upstairs to her job search.

Chapter 15

(Patrick McAleese)

We are all gathered in the foyer for our last night together in Albert. The Germans will leave straight after breakfast; we will fly home later. This is meant to be a chance for us all to feedback about the whole experience. Later we are to have a mini-concert; there's a small PA system and a mic; someone has set up a keyboard; a couple of guitars lean their heads together in the corner, mine being one of them. At least it has done better than I have at getting close to its German counterpart.

But for now we are in groups, bigger groups than the last time but, as before, I am in the wrong one. The chat is very revealing though and I have to admit that I find all the attitudes and points being shared to be really interesting, especially from a few of the German students.

We talk about the trip of-course but at times our discussion ranges much further, especially into WW2 and Nazi-related issues. One girl in particular shares an experience which, from the nodding heads, seems to be a common attitude that many German kids have encountered. Someone had told her, "Sure you Germans owe it to the world to take in all the refugees you can, after what you did to the Jews back in the day!" She found this very hurtful, from someone she had thought of as an English friend. It wasn't the only example of this feeling, this idea that the current German people need to be continually reminded of the two World Wars and so be punished for the mistakes that Germany made...a 'rubbing their noses in it' type of attitude that should have passed out of public consciousness years ago.

One guy expresses it brilliantly. "The trouble which comes from a visit like this is that we can get the feeling that we as young Germans are somehow still to blame for all the soldiers who lie in cemeteries here in France. We are expected to carry some guilt, all these years later. Do English children experience this? Should they feel responsible for what the British Empire did to its colonies? Should Americans feel guilty about stealing the land of native tribes? Should Irish young people feel guilty about the violence in a part of Ireland? I don't think so. So please...we are not to blame."

He gets a round of applause for this. I find myself thinking of a possible line for a song.

"Let them off the hook of history."

James intervenes to say, "I hope that none of you have felt such a vibe from us during this trip? If so, I can only apologise..."

It is a slightly awkward moment and Oskar is quick to assure him that this is not the case. His students nod in agreement.

Later we all have to say what has been our highlight of the trip. The majority of responses have something to do with the whole experience of meeting and getting to know 'the others'. Only one or two mention the graveyard bit. This is very warming for the leaders. When it comes round to my turn I find myself glancing across the room to Lena; she is looking at her feet though. I cannot be completely honest in my answer but secretly I am hoping that she can interpret my response in a personal way.

I say, "Yeah, basically for me...it's been really nice to get talking to you guys from Bavaria."

How bland, I am thinking. It would have been more honest to say something like, "My main disappointment is that I have not been able to get the chance to talk properly to one in particular and, with the event being nearly over, I am kicking myself that I have been so shy about this, and so internally preoccupied by it all."

One or two mention today's tour at the Ulster Tower and the Newfoundland Memorial. "Amazing to be in the actual trenches."

When it gets to Lena, though, I am in for a lovely surprise.

"My highlight is the music of Caoimhe and Patrick at the Thiepval yesterday," she says quietly.

Wow, I'm well chuffed. I do my usual bit of instant neck-colouring; she said that in such a natural way, not a hint of cringe or insincerity. I get one or two curious looks and cunning smiles from people like Katie and Aisling.

I watch Lena for a while but she does not even come close to looking in my direction.

'Please girl, just one smile. You are such a torture,' I am thinking. 'And there's only a few hours to go until you disappear forever, back into your hiding place!'

I go out to the loo but it's just an excuse. I write a text.

> Thanks for that Lena. Do you fancy going for a walk after this? Patrick x

Do I press send though? Delete the 'x'? Delete the walk idea? Do I say that I want to talk to her, or need to talk to her? Do I just forget it?

I stare at the screen for a while.

I remember someone saying that generally in life your regrets are the things you don't do, instinctive, spontaneous things that you miss out on because you are too cautious. It stuck in my mind as smart advice; I sure hope so. As I am about to re-enter the foyer I press send and see the text disappear to determine my fate.

I go back to my seat and watch her as she feels her phone vibrate in her pocket, takes it out and reads the text. Instantly she looks across at me, blankly at first, then a typical little underplayed smile behind the half curtain of her hair and a faint nod of her head.

'Bingo!' I think and the adrenaline kicks into my system in immediate anticipation. Wow, I just did that. I try to retune into the discussion but my mind meanders and I'm lost in my wonderings about how strange this feeling is, this bizarre intersection of two insignificant little lives which somehow have found their way out of their normal orbit and are now smiling across a room full of randomers at each other in an Ibis Hotel in Albert.

Then my phone pings and I see a reply.

> I am hoping you might ask this. X Lena

I can't bring myself to look across at her; I'm just way too excited. This concert thing cannot be over quickly enough. 'Thank you God,' I think, which is kinda inconsistent, 'cos I don't really think there is a god in the first place, never mind one who organises my love life.

The concert arrives and I go through the motions of engagement with the various performers. Once again I have to admire Caoimhe's smooth flute playing. She plays a set of quick tunes, I strum along on guitar and three of our Irish girls skip their way through some lively jigs, to great applause. We hear a few German songs and a brass duet; they seem to like such music in Bavaria. Then it's my turn.

I have two songs to do.

I give them a short introduction to "My Warring Family" as I'm getting my guitar tuned up; I always think that doing these two things simultaneously looks very professional. Then it's into the harmonic intro, then A major and the song itself.

> *Daddy was a soldier man*
> *Bedtime stories, gun in hand*

At the end it seems to have gone down very well; there are a few whoops in the wave of applause.
Then I say, "You probably have all heard this next song and if you know it you can join in. It's a U2 classic and it's called 'One'."
Great reaction to that. I get wired into the song. It is a song that never fails to bring out the best in me and I sing it often back home. It's only when I get further into the song that I notice the relevance of the lyrics to this particular situation with Lena.

> *"Did I disappoint you*
> *Or leave a bad taste in your mouth*
> *You act like you never had love*
> *And you want me to go without*
> *Well it's too late tonight*
> *To drag the past out into the light*
> *We're one but we're not the same*
> *We get to carry each other, carry each other."*

As I'm singing this I cannot help but look at her. She meets my eye and is drinking in every word, every meaning. This is just the most fantastic experience I've ever had doing a song on stage. It's like it really means something, it's a very special connection, a very special moment...and I almost have a catch in my throat as I scream out in my best Bono imitation.

> *"I can't be holding on to what you got*
> *When all you got is hurt*
> *One love, One blood, One life*
> *You gotta do what you should*
> *One life with each other*
> *Sisters, Brothers, One Life*
> *Carry each other, Carry each other!"*

At the end they are all standing up, arms raised, singing along at the top of their voices. I close my eyes and it's easy to imagine that I'm on main stage in Croke Park. My guitar is taking such a hammering that I break the E string but it doesn't bother me. I finish the song to massive yelling and applause, on a total high. I look across at Lena and she is smiling, hands above her head, the happiest I've seen her look since we got here. That smile alone is worth it.

I had imagined that my song was to have been the final one...like it would be difficult to top. Nothing if not arrogant.

How wrong I am!

Herr Fischer comes to the piano and sits down. Oh-ho, I think, we are going to have some Beethoven, some classical German piece to settle us back down, or maybe he's a blues specialist or a frustrated Elton John wanna-be-rocker. The German kids are all whooping again and whistling, all very enthusiastic about this, whatever it is going to be...the man has 'previous' with them and they are up for whatever he's going to do. They start chanting 'Oskar! Oskar!' I can't quite imagine folk in The Academy back at home ever being in a situation where they chant a teacher's name in this way. 'Deccie! Deccie!'? Not likely, not even 'Mrs Kelly! Mrs Kelly!'

He holds up his hands for quiet and they settle. He says something in German and they all laugh knowingly.

"No, no," he tells us, "I am not going to play but I am going to accompany. I have been...how do you say in English? Collaborating? Yes? I have been collaborating with one of my students to prepare a special arrangement for you all this evening. I did not ever realise that this student of ours was a singer, I was 'in the dark', as you say; she has been hiding her light under...under whatever you hide your light below. I only found out because one evening I was passing a church back home in Fremdenheim and I heard a beautiful sound, a song being performed by a wonderful voice. I was so drawn by this voice that I found myself going inside the back door to listen and when it was finished I looked to the front to see who the singer was and I recognised her. She was one of my own students. Surprising for me...I had not known. So we have worked together and tonight she shall sing another wonderful song, from years ago, one you may have heard of as well."

He pauses and I can see everybody looking around to try to figure out which of his students he is referring to. I'm doing the same myself. Everybody is looking at each other; nobody is owning up or moving forward. Dramatic pause over, he speaks again.

"So, to sing John Lennon's wonderful song, 'Imagine', please welcome....Lena Rosenthal!"

Jeez, you could knock me over if you breathed on me. Never! She is a singer? Why do I not know this?

Everyone is cheering but I watch her as she climbs over some people on the floor to get to the mic, and I see that she is looking very strained and nervous; she is not finding this easy. I give her the thumbs up as she glances my direction while Oskar plays the familiar introduction. Straight away I recognise that he has great touch in his phrasing. Lena gentles her way into the song. I notice that she has started at the second verse, which puzzles me, but not for long. As she gains confidence and momentum I am spellbound.

> *Imagine there's no countries, It isn't hard to do*
> *Nothing to kill or die for, And no religion too*
> *Imagine all the people, Living life in peace*
> *You may say I'm a dreamer, But I'm not the only one*
> *I hope some day you'll join us, And the world will be as one*

Yeah, absolutely spellbound. She is pure class. What a voice! Perfect for this song in that it is a simple voice, no great power, no forced vibrato...it's an untrained voice with a gorgeously folky texture, a voice that has not had the beauty disciplined out of it. The more I listen to it the more intrigued I am; that silky, natural tremolo that no amount of expert coaching could ever produce. Hundreds of top singers would kill to be able to achieve this sound.

Out of the corner of my eye I see that some of the others have their phones up. Dah, how dumb of me...I should be filming this. I get the phone out and start recording. This is one I am going to wear out in the future, I am thinking!

She sings the last verse and then goes back to reprise the 'Imagine there's no countries' bit, this time with more soul and freedom. God, she has me trying to hide my emotions here, and I have a feeling that I'm not alone, as she ranges up into the higher octave for 'And no religion too'. Eyes up to the ceiling now as she belts out 'Imagine all the people living life in peace'. Wonderful...and we are all joining in with her in the final chorus as her arms rise high and wide in a sort of cosmic embrace which every single person in the room copies. It's kind of like the closest thing to a worship moment that I have ever been in and I know, as I look around at the faces, that I am not alone in being really moved by this synergy. It's like some form of electricity has produced a bonding fusion between us,

Germans and Irish alike, students and adults...and it all came from Lena's performance.
So moving, and when she finishes none of us quite knows how to react, then there is a wave of clapping and cheering and it feels like a fantastically perfect finale to our experience. Not quite my finale though, and I go to Lena, having waited my turn as she receives the congratulations of her friends. Eventually she is free and I stand in front of her.
"That was brilliant," I say. "Lena, the legend! You never told me you could sing."
"You did not ask me."
"Your voice is absolutely class, Lena. That was fantastic," I tell her.
"No, I think your songs are much better," she says. "You do it with so much...I don't know how to say..."
"Bluff?" I say.
"Bluff? What is that?"
"It's kinda the opposite of 'sincerity'," I tell her.
"No, not like that. You were sincere and you are so confident when you sing," she tells me.
I think we have debated this long enough. I want to get this walk on to the agenda; there are only a few hours of possibility left.
"So...you want to come for a walk then?" I say.
"No, I think it was your idea," she says with that hint of a smile, "but I will come if you still want me to."
"Of-course I want you to come. Should we take some supper here first or do you want to go now?"
In answer she just takes off towards the door and I follow. It's eleven o'clock and we have only an hour before our curfew is supposed to have us inside. I'm not too bothered about that, though. I've been waiting for this moment for ages.
She waits for me outside the door and we set off towards the town centre. Suddenly it's all very awkward. I can't think of how to start all that I want to say to her. Above all I just want to listen to her, but how do I give her the chance to talk, to open up, especially if she doesn't want to?
"So, how have you enjoyed the visit?" I begin. I sound more like her form tutor or something but it's a start.
"I have enjoyed it very much."
"What especially?"
"Especially? Ah yes, the best bit. You know that already," she says.
I'm puzzled. "Meaning what?"

"I was saying the truth when we were telling about our highlights," she says. "I enjoyed best your music with the flute girl."
"Really?"
"Well, it was my best moment until this evening. Now my best memory will be the songs tonight."
"Mine too," I say. "Your performance was just fantastic. And a brilliant song to do..."
"I was talking about your songs actually," she says.
"You're too kind," I counter but I am delighted she would say that.
"So you didn't really enjoy all the cemetery visits?" I ask.
"How can someone enjoy these places?" she says. "They were so sad. So many. My mind could not make any connection to it. I did not understand....all the Irish students, putting flowers on graves of men they do not know, strangers. What was I supposed to feel?"
"But, because we have found out all about these soldiers some of us feel that we have gotten to know them. Like I have met a close relative of my soldier. Some of us have gone to their homes. Do you understand?"
"I know about that but it is very difficult for me. For me, I do not understand. We are reading all their names and walking over their bones but these men, they are not there. They are in heaven or....wherever they are gone. Putting flowers or soil on their graves does not mean anything to them. They are with God."
She has a point alright.
"Yeah, you are right. Maybe it's more that the ceremonies, the remembering and all, is actually more for us?"
"I think so, but not for me, I think."
It suddenly strikes me that now I get why she had left out John Lennon's first verse when she sang earlier.
"I was wondering why you did not sing the first part of 'Imagine'," I say. "You believe in all that religious stuff, God and all that, so you did not want to be singing 'Imagine there's no heaven'."
"Is that wrong from me?"
"No, it's not wrong; just interesting. I like that you are so individual and you have the courage of your convictions not to sing something you don't want to just because it is in the song. And by the way, I like it that you write as well."
I notice that she looks away from me again. What is it about this girl and compliments? She doesn't seem to like to hear anything good about herself.
"So what sort of things do you write about?" I try again.

No answer for a bit. Then, "Private things."
"Ah ok," I say. "Sorry."
But I won't let this go.
"Me too. Stuff that I would struggle to tell anyone in a normal conversation, but stuff that really matters to me."
She looks up sideways at me as we cross a street. "And these things you always write into songs?" she asks.
"Yeah, I suppose. Mostly that anyhow. How about yourself?"
She looks puzzled. "Sorry again; I am not understanding."
"I mean what sort of format do you write in....like when you were writing earlier?" I prompt. "A diary or a blog or what?"
"Ah I see," she says. "Sometimes those things but the main one is poetry. Not good poetry but just for me."
I'm impressed. "Brilliant, that sounds great. So you were sitting in the dining room alone writing a poem and that's why you didn't want me to disturb you?"
"No, I did not mind you....well, yes actually, because I was at the most...how do you say in English...perhaps 'sensitive' is the word?"
"Yeah, the climax of the poem, the most intimate part?"
"I think so, yes," she says.
"And how about if you let me read it?" I try again with my most gentle, most beguiling smile. "Please?"
She reacts well to the smile with one of her own and doesn't answer straight away. Then, "There are things which are too personal. I could not show anyone some of these things, but some lines are OK for you," she tells me.
"Ok, that's good," I say, "but who gets to read the other lines? Like....what are they for if they never get to be read by anyone but yourself?"
She thinks about this.
"They are only for me," she says firmly. "Me and God."
"You and God?" I say. I can't help the tiny hint of cynicism in my voice and it draws another little glance from those ebony eyes.
"There is nothing a problem with me writing from inside my heart for God to read," she tells me with that lovely innocence she has about her. "It is a poem but it is also a prayer or a...what is the word?....A confession, you know what I mean?"
"Yeah, I get that," I say. "It's kinda like cathartic, to write down your emotions and stuff, yeah?"
"This word I do not know," she says, "but, for you, your songs are for other people to listen to; for me, I write for God to hear me."

Now I am all the more curious; curious and determined to get inside this duet of her and her God and make it into a trio. That's the only way I am ever going to get inside her pretty head.
"Ok," I say. "Right, here's a thought for you. How about if you ask God if it's ok to let me read some of your poems as well?"
Suddenly she laughs right up into my face.
"I think he is happy for you to read my poems but you will not understand them," she says. "You see, God understands my German!"
"'Course he does," I laugh back. "I will just have to use Google Translate, won't I?"
"I don't think this will work for poetry though," she says.
"Maybe, but let me try, please?"
She just smiles but I sense that I have taken a step forward into her mental sanctuary. It's a good feeling and the night is not done yet.
We walk on for a bit until we are outside a late night cafe.
"You want a coffee?"
"Yes please, maybe just a cool drink."
So we are sitting across from each other at a small stainless steel table in the darkest corner of the cafe. Only one other couple is in the place, heads together across their table. Sounds like some slightly depressed French pop artist playing on the in-house stereo. 'Samedi soir sur la terre', he croons over his melancholic guitar. Well, this is Monday night in northern France and I am the polar opposite of depressed.
I have to somehow get the courage to try to tell this girl what I am feeling, but I am so hesitant; I do not want to scare her off or annoy her on this our last night. I make a tentative start.
"Lena, can I tell you...look, I have really enjoyed meeting you here."
"Me too," she says, looking down into her orange juice.
"But...it's been so busy, so much going on and so many people that I sort of feel it's all over and I haven't had enough time to chat to you, do you know what I mean."
"It has been...difficult, ja."
"There's so much about you that I don't know."
"Like what?"
Now that's a question; where to start?
"Just...like...well, I know now that you are a class singer and that you like to write poetry but that's near enough all I know about you."
A pause, then a whisper. I struggle to hear her above the sound of the song.

"Why do you want to know?"
"I think you should be able to guess that."
"No, I cannot guess what is in your head."
"Oh come on, don't play the innocent."
"I do not understand that, 'play the innocent'"?
"Ok...look...you must have noticed that I find you..." I run out of words, then try again. "I think you are just about the most mesmerising girl I have ever met."
She stares at me in a sort of blank puppy-dog way.
"I am sorry. My English. I do not know this 'mes...' whatever you said."
"Mesmerising," I repeat.
"Ok, wait," she says. Out comes her phone and her thumbs go quickly to work. "I am curious, so I will check my dictionary."
I spell it out for her.
A few seconds later she seems to be a bit startled by what her translator app tells her.
"'*Hypnotisieren*'! You think that I am hypnotising you?"
Oops, we are about to be lost in translation here.
"No, no! At least not in a bad way. It means...like fascinating. Like I am so curious about you..."
"You should not be curious about me," she says with just a hint of annoyance. "I am nothing to be curious about. I am just me, simple."
"No you are not simple; you are very complicated; in a really nice way, don't get me wrong. That's what gets me. You are so intriguing."
"I do not know intriguing also," she says. "This language is such a..."
"Yeah, I would love to learn German...or whatever language you are best in."
She looks at me sharply, suspiciously almost.
"Why are you saying this? I only speak German; of-course I only speak German."
"And Bavarian, and English," I say, covering my clumsy suspicion, "and you are very good in English."
"Thank you but I do not think so."
We sit quiet for a short while. Then I sit forward, trying to engage her eyes more directly.
"How do you feel about this, Lena?"
"What do you mean, 'about this'?"

I rub my hand over my mouth, thinking; how do I get inside her shell? How do I tell her what I am feeling without annoying her again?

"Ok...look, if I tell you what I feel you won't be angry with me, will you? You don't have to agree but...just hear me out."

"I don't understand 'hear me out'," she says, "but I will listen. Tell me. I promise I will not be angry."

"Good. Thanks. So, does this sound weird? I feel like, like somehow this was meant to be, that we were supposed to meet. Does that make any sense?"

"A little," she says. "You mean that God planned it for you and I to meet, to know each other?"

"I don't know about God doing it," I tell her. "I don't really do the God thing, but I feel like this is not just accidental. If it is just an accident then it is one of the nicest accidents that has ever happened to me."

She gives me a very tender smile, self-conscious but warm.

"I do not think you can mean that."

"I do. I totally mean it."

"That is so nice...but I do not understand why you would say this."

"I mean it, that's why."

"But you say you do not do God? Who else does this...this accident, if not God? Are you not Christian?"

"I was baptised but I don't understand how I am supposed to believe in God when there is so much wrong in the world. And anyway, our meeting is just a chance, right? Fate. You don't believe anything else surely? All the religious stuff? Like, I know you go to church, and I'm glad about it because if you didn't then Herr Fischer would never have heard you sing and you wouldn't have been singing tonight and I would never have known how talented you are...so, thank God for church like."

"You need to slow down so I can understand all this," she says.

"Anyway, I don't want to waste time talking about God any longer when I should be listening to you."

"And what do you want me to say?" she says.

"Ok, for one thing...I want you to tell me if you want to keep in touch with me when you go back to Germany and I am in Ireland?"

Ah-ha, she is pretending to give this deep consideration, finger up to her beautiful pursed lips. She looks so lovely with the low light of the cafe doing a sort of highlighter thing with her dark hair.

"Why would I want to do that?"

"You are such a tease," I say. "Well, do you want me to FaceTime you again or what?"

"But you would have to look at me on the screen," she says. "You could email me instead, or a small text every month."

"Is that what you want, just an odd text?"

"No, of-course it is not," she says, sadly, I think....and then, after a long thoughtful pause, "But what I want I cannot have, can I?"

"Why? What do you want that you cannot have?"

Oh my God. She puts her head down in her hands and after a bit I think she is crying, very softly crying behind the veil of her hair.

"Lena, please...what is wrong? What have I said? Why are you so sad?"

I am right; she is tearful and it takes her a while to adjust herself and come back to me. She grabs a serviette from the centrepiece on the table and puts it to her eyes.

"I am sorry," she says. "I am so stupid."

"No you're not," I say, reaching out to take her hand across the table. She only lets me touch her for a moment, then she pulls away. "What is it? Please tell me."

"I'm sorry," she repeats. "You ask me what I want but I cannot tell you...or anyone. I want...I want you to know that it is not your fault. I want you to think of me, of-course I do, but you will be very far away and I cannot let myself have the thought that...that this will continue. I cannot allow myself to feel...to feel what I want to feel, because there is no point. Do you understand? You will go away of-course, and of-course in a while you will forget me and for me you will be just another memory. This is life. We should not become...connected too much, yes?"

"Ok," I say. "Now I understand, but you are forgetting one thing."

"What is that?"

"You say that it must have been God that brings two people like us together, yes?"

"I think so, yes."

"Well, if that is true, then why would he do that just to make you feel good for a bit and then feel disappointment and loss, know what I mean?"

She thinks about this.

"That is not fair," she says. "You are the one who does not think this. You imagine that above us there is only sky...not God, so why are you using this God argument against me?"

"I'm not using it against you. I'm only trying to say that you might be right. Maybe there is some greater being engineering these circles of our lives. Some wonderful love-God in the sky, sort of a cyber-Cupid with shares in FaceTime and dating apps."

"You are mocking me, I think."

"No way. Look, let's keep it simple. A simple question, ok? Do you want to stay in touch?"

"If you would like me to, I would like to as well."

"Brilliant," I say. "Now that was easy, wasn't it?"

She picks up her phone and opens the screen.

"Do you have 'Find My Friends' on your phone? The app?"

"I don't but I can get it easy enough. Why?" I ask.

"Then I can know where you are in the world. This is something I like to know of, when I am alone and thinking, back at my home, you know," she tells me.

I'm not sure I understand this but I am well happy that it is a sign of her wanting me in her life, wanting to stay in touch, hopeless and all as it may seem.

"Cool," I say, "and is it ok if I send you songs, and you send me your poems? And recordings of you singing too?"

"How will this be possible?"

"I record on GarageBand and then I can email them or you can listen on Soundcloud; you can record the same way."

From behind the counter we hear the voice of the café man. "Cinq minutes, s'il vous plaît. I close."

We have finished our drinks and it must be close to midnight so we get up and leave. We walk back with very few words between us, strangely so, when there's so much more I want to say, and to hear. When we reach the hotel I don't want to go in just yet. At the door I stop and reach for her hand. She takes mine and doesn't resist as I pull her round to face me. She comes into my arms but keeps her face firmly from mine, her head on my shoulder. It's all very sister-brotherly. A slightly stiff hug is all she seems to be comfortable with. Ok, I'm good with that but I squeeze her tightly to me. She's got to know.

The scent of her hair is in my nose, a very natural human aroma, wood-smokey if anything, and I plant a long kiss there on top of her head.

"Lena, don't be so hard on yourself. You are very special. I don't know you very well yet but already I love just about everything about you."

"Thank you," she says, "but, remember, you do not know everything about me."
"True, but we can work on that, can't we?"
"Perhaps," she says and we stay together like that for ages until James taps the window and waves us to come inside.
'Tonight is a night I will never forget,' I think as I try to go to sleep.

Chapter 16

Bernie Doherty

He's home, pretty much unscathed, from what I can gather.
I was working yesterday so I persuaded Josie to drive down to Dublin to get him. It worked out well for she had stuff to leave in Belfast. She didn't object too much. I had half-hoped that travelling together might give the two of them space and time to talk but it may have been a vain hope. Certainly she was giving nothing away when they arrived back. He went to bed more or less straight away. I couldn't get any more than a grunt out of him.
It is strange how the two of them have pulled apart in the last few years, especially since she went across the water. And the thing is, I don't seem to be able to talk properly to Patrick when Josie is here. If she is in the room or in the conversation he just goes into a dour grump, incommunicado. Monosyllabic answers, if he answers at all.
So when I was working today I was hoping to God she would be out when I get home...and hoping he'd be at the house so I have him all to myself, ask him a few questions.
Both hopes answered.
"Where's your sister?" *I ask as I come in the door.*
"Search me. She hasn't been here since lunch time. Somebody picked her up I think."
"You think? Somebody? Who? How do you know?"
"Sor-ry! I hadn't realised she was in lock-up. Was I meant to warn the public?"
I start to set the table.
"Well, to be honest, I'm sort of glad. Means I can hear all you got up to when you were away, just private like; straight from the horse's mouth."

He says nothing, folds up his lap-top and heads upstairs. Great company; such a blessing having a son and daughter like this as you get older.

As I'm sticking the pie in the microwave I see his phone sitting on top of it. Not often he leaves it so invitingly. Instinctively I pick it up and press the home button. I won't know his passcode so there's no harm in looking at his screen-saver, is there? Or is there?

The wallpaper photograph is brand new.

It's a selfie, but 'him-self' is not the only person in the picture. He has his arm firmly wrapped around a girl, pulling her close like she might evaporate if he doesn't, like he doesn't quite believe she is for real. My fingers go to the screen to try to enlarge her face. Agh, that won't work of-course, not without the screen being live.

Both faces look a bit surprised, happy and surprised at the same time in that way that only a selfie can look. She is a fair bit shorter than Patrick, long dark hair and quite a pretty wee face peeking out from under it. There's a coach in the background. It's not a great photograph but, from a first look, I would say this girl is more 'striking' than she is 'beautiful'. Is she brown-skinned or is it just that the shot is taken at night or in very dull light? I'm not sure. At first glance she looks a bit Mediterranean I think. For some reason, no idea why, that Egyptian doll springs into my mind…what's her name? Cleopatra, of-course. She has what I would call 'Cleopatra-features'. Even in the hazy light of the photo I can tell she has the high cheekbones and the dark eyes.

Well, well…my Patrick!

When we begin the dinner I can't wait any longer.

"*So, how was the trip? You haven't told me a thing about it.*"

"*Not much to tell,*" *he lies.* "*It was good.*"

"*'It was good', that's all? Good? What was good about it?*"

"*Pretty much everything,*" *he answers.*

"*Come on Patrick; you can do better than that.*"

He munches away at his salad without answering.

"*Did you talk to Josie about it on the way back?*"

"*Not really,*" *he says.* "*She wouldn't be much in a bother about it.*"

"*Did you tell her about your FaceTime contact?*"

"*No, why should I?*"

"*But you'll tell me, won't you?*"

"*Mum, give over.*"

I bring his phone from the worktop, click it on and give it to him so he knows I've seen the wallpaper picture.

"Jeez mum, why can't you mind your own business?" he says.
"Because I'm a mum; it's part of the job description," I explain to him. After I've given him a few moments for this truth to sink in I begin the interrogation....in the gentlest possible manner.
"She's very nice."
Nothing.
"Are you allowed to tell me her name?"
I watch as he does that facial grimace thing again, and then I beg.
"Please?"
Eventually he leaves down his knife and fork....now there's a thing...and speaks.
"She's called Lena."
"Lena? And she's the German girl you have been talking to online?"
"Yip."
"And she's...she is German, yeah?"
"Agh mother, would you come out of the ark and catch up. Of-course she's German."
"Just thought to look at that picture she might be middle-eastern or something. I'm just saying."
"Never thought you'd be prejudiced against somebody just because they're not pure Derry white-man."
"I'm not prejudiced; I'm just curious, that's all. And you get on well with her?"
"Naw....can't stand her."
"She seems lovely." Then after a pause, "So, you two hit it off? That's nice. No, seriously, I'm pleased for you."
"She's just a friend mum."
"Yeah, ok. But you're....like very good friends, yeah? Going-out-sort-of-friends, yeah?"
"Yeah, yeah," he says with fake enthusiasm. "We're going out, sure. I'm taking her to see a movie this weekend; the Berlin Odeon, I think."
That bit of sarcasm did shut me up for a while. Then I changed tack.
"So you found your man's name, your soldier? How did that feel?"
"It was ok; it was a bit weird. There were stacks of other people around and it was a bit of a crush in the tower itself, until we got away to a separate memorial just by ourselves. That's where I did the song and all."
"Yeah," I said, "I suppose the crowds are starting to gather up for all the big centenary events next week. It's been on the news. And what about your singing? All go down well?"
"It was ok. Lena turned out to be a singer as well actually."

Now this is nice, and pretty significant too. He is introducing her back into the conversation. I can't ignore this opportunity but I take it gently.
"Is she? That's a neat coincidence. Any good? Who does she sound like?"
"Sounds like....herself really. Maybe a bit like Nora Jones meets Regina Spektor. She's very good," he says.
"What did she sing?"
"'Imagine'."
"Imagine that," I say stupidly, regretting my attempt at humour straight away.
"Yeah, imagine," he said dryly.
"And imagine my wee son falling for a girl from Germany."
"Wise up ma. She is just someone I met."
"Yeah but it's fascinating like, that she's a singer and she's the one you got paired up with... and there you are in the picture, obviously very close to her."
He shakes his head in mild denial.
"Come on. I didn't come up the Foyle in a bubble son."
"Well, sure if it fascinates you then I'm delighted for you," *he says with pleasant sarcasm as he gets up from the table.*
"Are you not gonna show us some of your photos?"
That pained look again as he hesitates. "Slide on, ma."
"Please?"
"Why?"
"Just; need something to cheer me up."
"This cheers you up, does it?" *he says, fiddling doubtfully with his phone. Good; at least he's thinking about it.*
"It does. Please?"
"I didn't take very many," *he says, parking himself beside me, phone in hand.*
He thumbs quickly through some shots. Mainly I see groups of young wans posing in very neat-looking cemeteries. Even though it is a very hasty flick-through, it wouldn't take a detective to notice one particular face in the vast majority of the pictures.
The final photo is the one that he now has as his wallpaper. Him and her. He didn't dwell on it, not in my presence anyhow.
"Let me see that video that you skipped past so quick, the one before that last selfie," *I ask him.*
He makes a show of reluctance but I know my Patrick; it is only a show; he plays the clip. And he is right...this Lena is some singer. It is funny sitting beside him watching it and the mother-thing in me sensing my son's pride in this girl, the soul-joy in his connection with her. I have a strange stirring of happiness and

trepidation for him. How is this all going to pan out for him? How will he be whenever things move on and the two of them start to forget about each other, when the cold winds of reality blow away these feathery infatuations? I just hope he doesn't get himself hurt.

"She's very talented, isn't she Patrick?"

"I think so."

"And very pretty. Is she nice to talk to?"

He gets up and stretches.

"Naw, she's cat altogether ma. Couldn't stick her."

He heads to the door.

"Hey listen...thanks for showing her to me," I say.

"No worries."

"And you'll keep in touch with her, will you?"

"If it keeps you happy I'll keep in touch with her. Is that ok? Maybe bring her home for tea some evening, Meet the Fockers, like...and you can make sauerkraut and frankfurters for her. Make her feel at home."

He disappears upstairs to his iPad. Can't he be the wile sarcastic wee skitter when he wants? It seems to be all in good fun though. He knows I am pleased for him. I am pleased for me too. It might help him move on from that man-eating Madison doll who was only a fantasy for him, and not himself alone either from what I hear. This Lena girl might help him mature a bit now that he's about to leave school and move on with his life. And let's face it, it is not as if it is going to go anywhere, is it, with her being in Germany, at school or whatever she is doing, and him being in Magee...that's if he gets in. There is little or no chance that they will ever see each other again, except on FaceTime of-course. I have the unpleasant thought that isn't it just as well that the two of them can only see each other and talk on screen, and that so far nobody has been able to come up with an app that would enable them to 'get physical' in any shape or form....at least I hope that is the case! You never can tell with these young wans nowadays though, can you? For all I know some perverse wee brain-box is sitting at his screen, (or her screen of-course,) at this very minute and is just about to introduce some more intimate version of FaceTime. The mind boggles! What will they decide to call it? No, don't go there! Heaven preserve us!

I sit back down at the table and run my fingers up in under my blouse and below my bra at the side, gently stroking an area which has been irritating me recently. Yeah, I should go and get it checked sometime soon.

Chapter 17

(Patrick McAleese)

This is not getting any easier.
I watch my customers queue for ice-cream, their eyes glistening like sorbet, little dribbles of saliva virtually starting to drool from their lips. Fellows and their girls in the port for a Sunday afternoon walk on the prom, holding hands under their tables as they gorge themselves on Banoffee Sundae and Vanilla Waffle. Older couples reliving their courtship days but staring away from each other out the window at the north Atlantic with its fifty shades of grey; Knickerbocker Glories haven't done it for them this time either.
In the three weeks I have worked here in Moran's since coming back from France I have clocked up exactly 140 hours and earned something over £900. Another three weeks and I'll be up around the two grand mark and close to where I need to be to buy and insure this bike. Then a couple more weeks to build up some cash for uni, all being well. But after the highs of the trip to France it is all a bit of a come-down emotionally.
I've talked to Lena every couple of days since but it is so annoying; it is actually getting more awkward and frustrating as time goes on. All I want to do is continue where we left off but the distance between us, both physical and psychological, really bugs me and I am not sure how long I can put myself through this agony. I don't want to stop chatting online with her, no way, but I kind of run out of things to say. Maybe we have been trying too hard, chatting too frequently.
There's only so many times I can tell her about work, about nights singing in Sailors, about those few-and-far-between bits of craic with my circle of mates which bring some relief from my confined, boring existence here. At the same time, there are so many things I want to ask her about her life, not about the mundane day-to-day stuff...more about what she thinks about, what makes her tick, who she is and why she is....why she is just that bit different, I suppose. Like, why she does not seem to have any real friends in that group of pupils from her school? Naturally I'm not about to ask about this but I do find that all a bit rare; to my mind she is one stunning-looking girl... so why did she always seem to be on her own on our trip? Everyone ignoring her, especially the guys...like are they blind

or what? She's a babe. I don't recall any of them chatting to her, at least not up until she sang that last night. Does she have other friends in school who just didn't happen to be on the visit or is she generally just unpopular?

But of-course I can't go there, not on the impersonal medium of FaceTime. I dare not risk questions that might upset her or switch her off, and I seem to know instinctively that there are pages in her story that I cannot turn over, whole chapters even that, for the minute anyhow, I cannot read.

So the relationship struggles on without any natural momentum. I feel like those surfers I watch in the bay, paddling around in circles on a calm day, hoping for a decent wave to make all the expended energy worthwhile. The surf is not happening.

Then I get an email this evening, exactly the boost my sagging spirits need.

Hello Patrick.

I hope it is ok if I write to you? When we are talking on FaceTime I am getting confused sometimes and so I do not think what to tell to you. So it is better if I put my thoughts together by writing these thoughts. But I am not meaning that you must stop Face-Time please because of this. I always like to see you, of-course.

When we were in France you were very nice to me, very kind. I want to thank you for that. You are good at listening to me, even the times when I am not talking. You are able to know what is inside my head and you do not make me feel bad for being a person who is shy, not confident.

When I am with you I want to be able to be myself but it is difficult. This is a little because of language but it is also because of me.

I know that you are 'inquisitive' of me.

(Is that the correct word? I am using Google and my dictionary to English but it is not very easy to give the proper meanings.) There are many things to know but many things I also do not know. Also there are many things I am not happy to tell you. And so it is difficult to explain.

My life is complicated. I am not able to tell much to you. I hope you forgive that I am like this and like me as I am. That is why I was crying a little when you hugged me at the hotel. I felt that you were liking me as I am and that you were understanding me. They were happy tears but also sad tears because you were going away and we might never see each other again. I am sorry if this is stupid emotion girl talking.

Also I am curious about you. You are very talented as a singer and a writer of songs. How did you become like this? I could not write these songs. The song about your fathers was very good. I want to hear other songs which you have written if that is ok.

I like to sing but only the songs of somebody else. And so far I only have been singing in church. Once at a wedding. It was very difficult for me to sing to all my friends and all the students from Ireland, especially you. I was worried that you would laugh at me and perhaps you would not want to go to walk with me after my singing. I will not forget that night in Albert. Thank you.

When you have the new motor cycle which you tell me you must be careful. I had fallen off my bike last year pushed by a car. It was a miracle that I was not injured because I fell on to a small grass hill beside the pavement.

My birthday is Thursday 21, I am 17. Later I will be having my results of examination. If they are ok I will move from Realschule Fremdenheim to a bigger college where I will hope to study Health.

When I came home from France my mother told me that her grandfather was fighting in that war, also on that western front. He wrote his memories of how he was almost killed by a shell and the story of how he survived. I had not known of this story before. She is very proud of her grandfather.

Now I come to the end but I do not know what to say. I feel that I might not send this stupid email to you because you might laugh at me. My English is so bad. It is a pity you do not speak German.

But you can google, yes?

Remember the evening you try to talk to me in the eating area in our hotel? I was rude to you because I did not want to talk then. I say sorry for that now. I was writing a poem (not a good one) about my feelings in the cemetery of Germans that day. I will let you see it now (even if you cannot understand the German).

These were some of my small thoughts on that day.

Schatten und Geister.

Menschen streifen diesen Ort,
wie als wäre er ein Schatten,
Dunkelheit, aus einer andern Welt.
Geister einer andern Zeit.

Hier regiert die Einsamkeit,
fern von unserm Alltag.
Alles verfallen.
Staub liegt auf den Grabsteinen
Ignorierte Zeugen des Todes,
eine Zeit, die wir lieber vergessen würden.

Kreuze für tote Christen.
Davidsterne für tote Juden.
Sie liegen in tausenden zusammen,
im Schatten der schützenden Bäume

Ich kann nicht trauern.
Ich kannte diesen Soldaten nicht, Albert.
Eine Verbindung gibt es nicht wirklich.
Er ist ein Fremder, verloren in der Zeit,- im All.

Ich gedenke ihm, doch rührt sich nichts in mir.
Das Vergangene ist nicht mehr zugänglich.
Ist mir leider nicht gerade fremd...
Und die Kälte steigt in mir auf, -wie ein loderndes Feuer

I hope that you can translate these words and understand, especially these feelings.
Ich vermisse dich.
Bye now Magdalena xxx

I don't remember feeling this good about any letter I have ever gotten before. I read it again, a couple of times actually, the English part, and I catch myself smiling inwardly. I'm curious about this last expression and of-course about her poem so I go to a German-English app and start working it out.
'*Ich vermisse dich*'; ah lovely...'I miss you'!
Then to the poem.

Shadows and Ghosts
People roam this place,
As if it were a shadow,
Darkness from another world,
Spirits of another time
Here reigns the solitude
Away from our everyday life
All is decayed
Dust lies on these tombstones
Ignored witnesses of death
A time we would rather forget
Crosses for dead Christians
Stars of David for dead Jews
They are found in thousands
In the shade of the protective tree
I cannot mourn
I did not know this soldier, Albert
There is no connection really
He is a soldier lost in time and space
I remember him, but nothing moves in me.
The past is no longer accessible
It is unfortunately not just foreign to me
And the cold rises in me like a blazing fire

Fantastic thoughts; I have no idea how good or bad the poetry is in German but some of it translates beautifully into English. Now I start to feel I have some kind of a window into this girl's mind and I so appreciate the chance to look. It was obvious that she had been moved in some complicated way that day when we stood in the German cemetery and it seems this poem is the result. I feel very honoured that, for all her seemingly introverted persona, she has trusted me enough to want to share this with me.
I need to send her a wee text.

> Hi Lena. Danke so much 4 the email; loved it, and especially your poem; very cool. U have a brilliant way with words. Chat 2moro. IVD too. xPatrick

And so to bed, to lie and listen to her sing 'Imagine' yet again.
I waken just before six and a song that began its life in the Hotel in Albert is trying to break out of its chrysalis in my head; that's what it feels like, a struggle to be born. The only thing to do is to get up and write it down before it sprouts butterfly wings and flies off and leaves me, as it certainly would if I go back to sleep. This has happened before, so many great ideas never actually seeing the light of day, literally. I get the guitar and an old notebook and start to work on it.
Sometimes my best song-writing just happens like that; it's like it has already been written somewhere else, in some different reality, and all I am is a kinda lightning conductor to transport the thing into existence in the here and now.
The lyrics are based on what I wrote back in June and are about those moments when I first saw her, what I wanted to say to her and then the last few moments, near the end of the trip.

1.
I catch your glance across the crowded room
Your eyes wide open like a harvest moon
I think I see below your thin disguise
A special something that I recognise
You give me feelings that I can't explain
I'm like a moth drawn to the flame
2.
Hey, do you know how beautiful you are?
Hey will you walk with me below the stars?
Excuse me but I think I know your face
Remember when I met you first in cyberspace
You have me tongue-tied so I can't explain
I think you probably feel the same
3.
That night I held you by the hotel door
I wondered what the future had in store
I kissed your hair and when you raised your head
Your chocolate eyes melt into mine instead
You did not speak, you did not move away
Your smile said all that I am trying to say.

Not quite sure what to call it as a song, maybe something like "Tongue-tied", because that sums up how we both were at the start. Feels so good to have written it and without really consciously trying. And as I sit in my bedroom watching the light through my curtains playing haphazard patterns on my postered wall I suddenly have an even better idea!

Why don't I record the song for her and send it for her birthday?

I don't have to think twice. GarageBand makes it all so easy. I have it set up in no time. I record my acoustic guitar first, stick on a few effects, then lay down a simple bass line and a very sparse keyboard track. All sounds pretty decent.

By 8.30 the backing tracks are finished. The front door bangs behind my mother as she leaves for work. I take a wee break and skip down for some cereal in nothing but my boxers.

Totally forgot about Josie being in the house. She takes one look at me and pretends to be sick.

"Jeez Patrick, would you ever put some clothes on. People from the food bank will start donating to us if anybody sees you like that!"

"Jealousy will get you nowhere sis," I say. "You don't look too hot yourself without the old paint-job!"

"At least I can see myself when I stand sideways to the mirror."

"And that must be a horrible shock for you," I shout back as I scramble back up the stairs, Wheatos and yoghurt in hand. I do some vocal exercises to clear the tubes of morning gunge and lay down the vocal track. Three takes, a bit of editing and effects application and I am happy that the thing sounds listenable to.

As I hear it back I wonder will I ever have the courage to sing the song in public, like in 'Sailors'. At the same time, inside myself I recognise that that isn't really a priority for me any longer; as long as it goes down well in a certain bedroom in Bavaria I will be happy.

Chapter 18

(Patrick McAleese)

Bought bike today. Suzuki GZ125, blue, sharp looking for a 2010 model. Had to give Barry's dad £1550 but I think it's a good buy; he's always been very decent to me, on account of Barry and maybe a bit on account of my dad having disappeared, so I trust his judgement. Even delivered it to me in his trailer.

Now for lessons and the oul test!

Was excited to be FaceTiming Lena, this being her birthday. Earlier I sent her my song by email and texted to tell her; wanted to see her reaction when she opened it and listened first time. Tried FaceTime three times before she answered. Frustrating but worth the wait.

The conversation went something like this.

Me	Hiya.
Lena	Hello.
Me	Happy birthday!
Lena	Thank you.
Me	I tried for ages.
Lena	Yeah...I am sorry. Too much going.

She looks down at her T-shirt and shifts the camera angle slightly

Lena	Do you like my top?
Me	Of-course I like your top. Ever since I saw you in...
Lena	Patrick! No, I am meaning my shirt. I got it for €5 in a shop...how do you say, for clothes that people want to give away?
Me	Ah, a charity shop.

The T-shirt, by the way, is green with a shamrock motif and the words 'Gaelic Girl' emblazoned across the chest. It's like something you'd see at the Lammas fair!

Me	Very nice. Suits you. Wish I could be there to give it a warm welcome.
Lena	I am glad you like it.
Me	Just gotta be careful where you wear it if you ever get to come to Norn Ireland.
Lena	I do not understand....I thought it would be ok?
Me	It is ok. I love it. It's just that some people where I live might have a different take on it. Don't worry about it....it's too complicated; I'll try to explain it to you sometime. Hey, I really loved your poem about the cemetery.
Lena	Did you? It was just some silly words. I think it is not very good.

Me   No way Lena; it's brilliant. I love the last line...'Coldness rises in me like a blazing fire'....something like that anyway.
Lena   (thinking about this translation) Yes, I think it means this. Do you think it is ok?
Me   Absolutely. Two opposites together; it's great. You must keep writing.

She says nothing to this, just looks away off-camera for a bit. I decide to switch the conversation.

        So...how's the birthday? Did you get my song?
Lena   Your song? What song?
Me   Ah no, you didn't get it? I emailed it to you a while ago.
Lena   I am sorry; I have been at Murnau with my family. We have only now returned. I did not see emails. What song is this? You are writing it yourself again?
Me   Yeah, it's my own song. It's kinda about you; that's why I wanted to know if you liked it.
Lena   Oh, this is bad. I am sorry. Should I go now to my emails?
Me   Can you do that, maybe on another computer?
Lena   Perhaps.

I see her get up, phone in hand, and leave her room. As she wanders through her house she is still talking to me, her image bobbing about, sometimes on screen, sometimes not.

Lena   I will ask if I can use the computer in the library.
Me   You have a library?
Lena   My father's study; he is a...what word is it? A minister.
Me   Yeah, I wondered about that. I saw he had a white collar that last time. But how come...?

She has entered some other room where her folks are, I am guessing. She must be holding the phone to her body as I can see nothing but greenish shadows for a bit. I hear her speak in German, presumably asking to use this computer. She is being careful not to let her folks see who she is talking to, or maybe not wanting me to be seeing them, I don't know. A few seconds later she seems to be in the 'study', judging by the bookshelves as she props the phone on a desk.

Lena	Give me a few minutes as I will get this computer working.
Me	So what have you been doing today?
Lena	Ah...in town today for buying presents, new clothes; and we ate my favourite food in my favourite restaurant.
Me	And you are seventeen now?
Lena	Ja. Do you think that is very young? I was just sixteen when we met. You are so much more...how do you say?
Me	Mature? Wise? Intelligent?
Lena	Ha ha, whatever you want to say.
Me	And will you go out anywhere tonight to celebrate?
Lena	I think we will walk in the mountains, my friend Gaby and myself. Watch the sun setting, then have some ice-cream in the village, perhaps hear some music.

I am interested and delighted that she has mentioned a friend, this Gaby, the first time she has referred to anybody other than her immediate family in our chats. I am presuming that Gaby was not one of the girls from her school who was on the trip; certainly I cannot recall Lena ever showing much connection with any of her fellow class-members in Albert.

Now she seems to have gotten into her emails.

Lena	Ah good, I have your email, let me open the attachment. What shall I play it with, what programme?
Me	What programmes do you have? I made it in GarageBand.
Lena	I do not have this programme. Perhaps I may open it with iTunes?
Me	Yeah, try that.

I see her work at the computer; this couldn't have worked out any better. I get to see her immediate reaction. She won't have time to analyse anything; she won't have time to come up with any defence against the honesty of the lyrics, that is providing she actually understands them all first time around, maybe too big an ask.

What if she reacts badly? Maybe it will all be too much for her. Have I been misunderstanding her, reading too much into her email. I just hope this doesn't totally embarrass her or drive her off in a panic.

Frantically I revisit the lyrics in my head. Is there anything too intimate, too extreme in there? What will I say if she asks me to explain anything? I can't be too overt about my feelings, particularly as I haven't been capable myself of analysing my own thoughts. Pity I didn't send the lyrics first.

She seems to have deliberately turned away from the camera as she listens, so that I cannot see her reactions, so I am in a state of limbo as I wait. The first time she turns back to me, however, is when I sing the line, "Hey, do you know how beautiful you are?"

She stares almost sadly at me from the screen, a slight shake of her head as if in denial of what I am telling her, like I am trying to humour her and she is having none of it. The sadness morphs into the tiniest of smiles, though, as she understands the next line; "Hey will you walk with me below the stars?" Then she turns away again, head down as if to concentrate. We almost reach the end of the song before I see her face again, an ironic smile as she understands "Your chocolate eyes melt into mine instead."

I wait; she is slow to speak. Eventually...

Me	Well?
Lena	I do not know what to say.
Me	Try something. Is it Ok?
Lena	It is so beautiful Patrick, but I do not deserve all the things you say.
Me	Of-course you do.
Lena	No. You can not write all those things of me Patrick, you must not. They are not true things.
Me	What part isn't true?
Lena	I am not understanding all the words, it is too quick...but you ask me about if I know how I am beautiful. This is not so. You are in your imagination and this thing is not real.
Me	Look, I don't want to argue with you on your birthday but I was writing a song about how we met and about what I think of you. So I am telling the truth, my truth. If you have another version of the truth, then it is something in your head and you have to deal with it. I was writing what I believe.
Lena	It is embarrassing to me that you think of me like this.
Me	I don't understand that. Why can you not just believe me that this is how I think of you? I am not trying to exaggerate what it was like to meet you, I'm not trying to butter you up, honest.
Lena	'Butter me'? What does this mean?
Me	Like... I am not simply trying to make you feel good, or say things to make you like me, you understand?

Lena	I think so...and you do not have to try to make me like you, by the way. I have another question. What is it meaning that you are 'like a moth' in the fire... something like this?
Me	Ah yeah; 'I'm like a moth drawn to the flame'. Do you know what a moth is? Small insect, like a butterfly?
Lena	Ja ja...we say it almost this way. 'Motte'.
Me	And you know how they are attracted to fly close to a light or a flame?
Lena	And sometimes they get burned, their wings?
Me	Yeah, that's the idea.

She frowns for a second and turns away.

Me	Lena, what the heck?
Lena	You think I am dangerous to you, this is the meaning, yes? You are afraid that you will be burned because you are coming too close to me and so...
Me	No, never! That is not the meaning, not at all. For God's sake girl, can't you see when something is simply a compliment and accept it as such?
Lena	You are getting angry with me.
Me	No, I'm not angry, just frustrated by the...I suppose by the language thing. I did not mean that you are dangerous, no way. What I meant was simply that you attract me...kind of like how a moth can't resist being attracted to a flame.

She doesn't seem convinced. I try again.

Me	It's like...you know how a magnet works? Like that, except that the 'magnet' idea is way too cold. It's more like a bee can't resist the scent and the colour of a flower. That's how I feel about you.

I notice that while I have been saying this, she has turned back to look at me, and a coy smile has spread from her eyes to her mouth so that now she is almost laughing at me, in the nicest of ways.

Me	What's so funny?
Lena	So I am a flower and you...most probably you do not know what my name means?
Me	Lena? Or Magdalena?

Lena	No, Rosenthal. This name means 'a valley of roses'. That is why I am laughing. It just sounded so nice to hear you say it like this, that is all.
Me	Brilliant! What a name! Legend!
Lena	But I am also a rose with chocolate eyes? Why do I have chocolate eyes please?
Me	Yeah, that bit doesn't quite work now, does it?

At this point in the conversation she is disturbed by someone coming into the room; I see her look up and hear her father's voice off screen. Maybe he needs on his computer, or maybe her meal is ready, or maybe he has figured out that she is chatting to some random Irish guy who is a thousand miles away but who cannot take his eyes off the "Gaelic Girl" logo on her T-shirt. Either way it seems to me that this conversation is over. She turns back to me on screen.

Lena	I am now to go for my birthday dinner Patrick. I am sorry. I would rather be staying here to talk some more to you.
Me	No worries. Enjoy. We'll chat again soon.
Lena	Thanks for the song. I love it. You are so talented.
Me	No way, I'm just well inspired at the minute....all your fault.
Lena	Ja, always my fault. I must go now. Bye Patrick.

She blows a little kiss at the screen and I return the favour. The screen freezes and my heart gives a strange wee lurch.

About a week later I am watching Alec Baldwin do an incredibly funny take-off of Donald Trump on Facebook when I notice an email arrive on my screen. An email from Lena, unexpectedly. I leave 'The Donald' to his own ego and open it immediately. I discover it contains a sound attachment.

Hi Patrick,
I could not resist this idea, to sing with your beautiful song. I was always singing it inside my head; the only times it was not in my mind was if I was asleep. Sometimes I would even dream the song. Is that strange? So I had the idea to buy the app you told me. I copied your track to the app and so I can put my

voice into it also with some harmony. I hope you are ok about that. It is a song of you but also of me, so I want to be in the song, if that is alright? Please listen to it and tell me it is ok to do this. I feel good about being in the same song, along with your lovely singing as well.
I hope you enjoy. If you do not, I ask you to forgive and delete the song. But it is nice to me to feel that I am with you a little.
Love, Lena

Fantastic! I open the track and there she is, singing a wonderful harmony to my melody. Her voice as magical as ever. Wow! I am dying to let somebody else hear it, to put it on Facebook; it is too good to be kept to myself, to ourselves.
But I can't, can I? It is too personal. Frustrating and all as it is, (because in my opinion music is always meant to be shared, it is a social thing at its very root), nevertheless, this has to stay with just the two of us at the minute. Maybe sometime will come when this song can be a public statement, a declaration in duet. For now, though, it feels like it has to be time-capsuled as the best thing I've ever written and the sweetest collaboration I may ever experience.

Chapter 19

Bernie Doherty---18th Aug 2016

So nervous for him this morning.
I am off work for an hour or so, (kindly permitted to me by my infinitely understanding boss, Mr Johnstone, who, as he constantly reminds me, has not got a misogynistic bone in his body), so that I can take Patrick up to The Academy and be with him when he opens his envelope and reads his A Level results.
"I do understand your unique circumstances, with there being no man on the scene, and sure can't you make up the time maybe later in the week when it suits you," he droned at me when I asked if I could be late in. Then..."What about your daughter? Will she not be there to take him?"
I didn't like to say but the idea of Josie being of any use to Patrick if his results are poor is as unlikely as Mr Johnstone voting 'yes' in a gay marriage referendum. Apart from anything else the girl is so preoccupied with her own lack of a job that

she hasn't a thought in her head about anybody else, which is why I haven't even told her about my own worries. She has enough on her plate.

It was a nightmare to get Patrick out of his pit and ready at a decent hour this morning but now here I am, sitting outside the main office waiting for him to reappear with the dreaded envelope.

After he'd left me he wasn't long getting lost in the crowd of sixth formers milling around the entrance as they waited for the school to open its doors. For a while I could see him chatting to Barry and a couple of other fellows. Madison long-legs was there in the centre of a circle of devotees but Patrick never looked the road she was on, bless him. Then one or two teachers arrived and ploughed in through the melée to get to the door. One of them turned and I could see him talking to Patrick in what, from my distance, seemed to be a very friendly manner. I wondered if that is the History teacher, Donaldson or something, if I remember rightly. It was a long conversation anyhow and was only ended when the main doors opened and the students surged inside.

So I am still waiting. No sign of him re-emerging. I look at my watch. Twenty past ten. He has been in there near enough twenty minutes. It's going to be eleven before I get to work if he doesn't hurry up. I hope nothing is wrong. What could be keeping him? I told him to be quick; what could be the matter? Maybe his results are a disaster and he is having to get advice from the Careers staff about the Clearing System? Might he finish up in Wales or some other God-forsaken place studying Media or something? I hope to God not; he will be so disappointed if he doesn't get into Magee to do his beloved music course. University of Ulster at Magee is only a mile or so away from where I was reared but, having said that, I think I was only ever in the sober old building once in my life, strangely enough for a play about Bloody Sunday, maybe a Friel play...can't mind now.

Ok, here he comes across the car park now, his mucker Barry on one side of him and a teacher on the other, nice looking girl, Miss Kelly, his music teacher I think. They all seem pretty happy; Patrick looks like he's buzzing, unusual for him. I get out of the car.

"How are you, Miss Kelly?" I say sticking out my hand.

"Mrs! Mrs Kelly!" says Patrick.

"It's alright," says the teacher, "I'm good Mrs McAleese. And yourself?"

I resist the temptation to tell her that I am Ms Doherty and I can sense that Patrick approves of my tact.

"Grand, just a bit nervous sitting out here waiting. How did you get on? Are you pleased?" I say turning to Patrick.

He grins his sloppy, half-sided grin but Mrs Kelly answers for him.

"I should say he is pleased," she says. "Top grade in music, an A*. Brilliant, one of only two in the class."

"Congratulations," I say. "What about the others?"

"They're alright," he says. "B in History and a C in English Lit. I'm happy enough."

"So you'll get into Magee?"

"Aye, no bother. Thought I mighta got a B in Lit but…"

I turn to Barry.

"How'd you get on Barry?"

"An A and two Bs. I needed an A in I.T. And that's what I got so…happy days. Should get into Liverpool Hope with that."

"Isn't it amazing to see them all at this stage, A Levels under their belts and heading off to Universities all over the shop," says Mrs Kelly. She is so enthusiastic, so full of genuine happiness for them that I am quite moved; no wonder Patrick put so much into his music studies; this girl would inspire a tone-deaf chapel wall. Didn't have teachers like this in St Bernadette's back in the day when I was in school. All too busy with the twelve inch ruler, measuring how far your hem was above your knees. We were an all-girls school, for God's sake. Who was going to be tempted? The caretaker was the only man about the place and he was half-blind from some RUC man's baton in the Battle of the Bogside!

"Look," I say, turning to the car, "I have to be going to work, I'm late already but I just want to say a big thank-you for how much you put into Patrick's time here in The Academy. He has loved his music; he's got so much out of it and that is down to you entirely, so thank you very much."

"Not at all," Mrs Kelly says and beams at my son. "He has so much music inside him naturally that he was never going to do anything but succeed in it. You should be so proud of him, especially now that he is recording his own songs with his German friend. You never know where they'll end up, the pair of them."

"His German friend?"

"Yes. Isn't he the right dark horse! Another Glen Hansard in the making. And he tells me he has never even seen 'Once'."

"Once?" I ask, a bit bamboozled by all this effusive praise and cultural in-references.

"Yeah, the movie? Fantastic soundtrack. Maybe you haven't seen it either. You should, both of you, together like; now there's a real mother-son treat in store for you. It should be on Amazon; check it out. 'Once'. Irish singer-songwriter meets a Czech singer on the streets of Dublin; the rest is history. I won't spoil it for you."

Ok, enough, Mrs Barry Norman! I look at Patrick. His face is somewhere between rosé and Pinot Noir but, in his embarrassment, he hasn't lost any of his satisfied glow. As I watch, Mrs Kelly steps forward and gives him the warmest of hugs and his facial tone moves further along the colour spectrum towards a full-bodied Port shade. But fair play to my boy, his return hug is every bit as enthusiastic and I am every bit as proud of him as his inspirational teacher is, only more so.

We give Barry a lift back to Coleraine and I listen to the two of them chatting happily. Patrick has never been one to form intense friendships but there's no question that Barry has been his best mate throughout their time at The Academy. I wonder will they keep contact or will there be a parting of the ways. My own situation, particularly because of my relationship with Robbie, meant that I had little or no contact with any of the girls I had been friendly with when I was at St Bernadette's. Facebook and all that other social media stuff is good nowadays in helping young ones to maintain friendships, even at a superficial level, but I have very few friends from my Derry past; it is just how life has panned out for me. And that has affected Josie and Patrick too. I have no doubt that the particular 'cutting-off' from...I suppose from family, on Robbie's side and, on my side, from family and friends and the wider community which nurtured me as a child, those realities of our personal histories have narrowed down the range of social exchange for our children. How it has affected them I am not entirely sure. I would need to have some psychologist come and analyse us. Psychologist or psychiatrist...take your pick!

When Barry gets out of the car I light on my secretive son straight away.

"So, you tell your teacher about your recording projects with your German girlfriend but you don't tell your mother?"

He looks out the window as if the passing sports field is suddenly of great interest to him.

"Come on! How do you think that made me feel, not having a clue about the fact that you have been recording songs with her?"

"You are just jealous ma."

"No I am not! Well, actually, yes! Yes, I am bloody-well jealous Patrick. I'm jealous of you and Lena. I'm jealous of you and Mrs Kelly. I am sorry for that. But, before we go any further about my problem with jealousy, let me tell you another home truth, alright?"

"Here we go," he says resigned. "Another of the famous 'Home Truths'."

"This one is easy to hear though. Here it is. I am SOOO proud of you Patrick. I am so delighted for you. You haven't had it easy in the last few years but, to your

great credit, you got your head down and you worked really hard and look what you have achieved. Brilliant. You didn't let your father distract you..."
"Chance would be a fine thing," he interjects.
"Yeah, sure. You didn't let your trip away distract you. You didn't let your music distract you. You have done..."
"My music distract me? That's the point ma. It was my music that saved me. That is the one thing that gives me a buzz; that is what I am all about, don't you see? Without music I would have given up on school. Even Mrs Kelly...at times she had to talk to me, just to keep me focussed on the other stuff. She's been a total legend. You should be thanking her, not seeing music as some sort of distraction."
"And I did thank her, or were you not listening back there? I thanked her."
"Yeah, ok, you thanked her."
"I didn't mean all that the way it came out. Sorry, ok? I'm trying to say you did brilliantly and I am very proud of my son, alright?"
"Thanks."
"And I am dying to hear these recordings."
"Mum!"
"Why not? Why shouldn't you play them for me? I'm not going to be critical or anything. How does it work anyhow, her there and you here?"
He scratches his head and half-smiles.
"I write a song and record it, then I send it to her and she records some on it as well. It seems to work. Sounds cool, even if I say it myself."
"Lovely. And have you not let anybody else hear these songs?"
"Not yet, but I will."
"Who?"
"Mrs Kelly wants me to send her a copy."
"Ah right, Mrs Kelly. And what about Ms Doherty? Will you send her a copy?"
Silence. After a bit though, as we reach the house, he replies.
"Ok, I'll play a song for you. Why not? But you keep it to yourself, right? Don't tell Josie or anybody."
"Alright, deal."
It is a moment of unusual closeness. My boy is becoming a man. He can talk to me like he might even be a potential adult and I am someone over and above being his mum. For a split second I almost tell him that I have an appointment with a consultant...but I don't. I haven't told Josie either. Poor Josie; nobody is telling her anything.

Chapter 20

(Patrick McAleese)

I had been sitting in the refectory in Magee, chilling after a fairly intense morning spent in lectures, looking forward to getting on the bike and heading home early, when my phone vibrated in my pocket. I looked at the number, didn't recognise it and opened the text, curious.

> Hi Paddy, ur dad here. I'm home for a few wks. Want to meet up with you & Jos. No need to tell Bernie. Could yous be in the Causeway Coast for lunch on Sun next. 1300 hrs. Dad

My good lord!
I felt a strange churning in my stomach; so long since I'd felt that sensation. Never quite been able to analyse this feeling. The best I can do is compare it to the feeling, as a child, of opening a Christmas present that I had been promised and was really looking forward to and discovering it was only a tacky, plastic copy of the real thing, some mass-produced Chinese alternative bought off the back of a lorry in a seedy car-boot sale. Queasy disappointment.
What is he after now? I haven't seen him in ages; thought about him even less, if that is possible. He is someone I have deliberately cut out of my consciousness.
I found it near enough impossible to tell mum. When I did she did the predictable reaction; initial silence followed by a ten minute rant of stale hurt and resentment. I know those lines pretty well; it's just a case of waiting it out until she chills and then reassuring her of my understanding and my undying loyalty. Oh mum, still so vulnerable, despite the bullet-proof vest of stoic denial.
After a few changes of mind and chat with my sister, we keep the appointment, Josie and I. Her first time as my pillion passenger. Her last too, if she is to be believed. My sides still hurt from her iron grip.
Dad is waiting for us in the bar, black pint in hand like a badge of belonging. A shaking of my hand, a limp, slightly guilty-looking hug

for his daughter who has kept her helmet on for the 'reunion', maybe for extra defence.

"So you got a bike then?" he begins.

"Yeah."

"What is it?"

"Suzuki 125."

"Great. Take it easy though. Don't wanna come off it."

"Wasn't planning to."

"What yas drinking?"

"Nothing for me thanks". I get a coke anyway. Josie has a white wine spritzer.

The waitress takes us to sit at a window table which is good 'cause I can look past him at the horizon where northern Atlantic meets sky; all so blue, so unchanging, a constant since my babyhood.

He has lots of questions as we pretend to be studying the menu.

"What's the score with yous now? What are you doing with yourself Josie?"

"Not much; still looking for the right job."

"No job yet? After four years in your bloody university? And in the meantime....what are you doing? You're not just sitting around under your mum's feet waiting for something to land on your lap, are you? See when I was your age..."

Josie interrupts sharply. "No, of-course I am not sitting around. I do a few shifts on the street in the Port after the bars close! Lots of nice men around."

Jeez, what a sarky bitch my sister can be when she wants! Sharp as a pin! Robbie does a bit of a head-jerk, stares at her, then picks up on her irony.

"Bloody hell girl! That was cheeky; you didn't lick that off the wall, did you? There was no need for it. I was only asking..."

"I work part-time in Lidl. It keeps me in drink and fags," she says, not letting up on the attitude.

"I don't know what to make of you, Josie," he says after another hurt look at her. "You have so much potential and you end up working in bloody Lidl."

"Who said anything about 'ending up'? I told you, I am still looking for a job. I have an interview with the Belfast Trust in a couple of weeks. Jobs are scarce at the minute, with the cut backs and all in the Health Service. It's not like you have any right to be lecturing me anyway, is it?"

The waitress stands awkwardly by our table. We order. He has a steak, I can't rise above an Atlantic burger, whatever that is and Josie settles on a Caesar salad.
"What about you, Patrick? You still studying?"
What sort of a question is that?
"Yip."
"What stage are you at now? 'A' levels?"
Last time it was G.C.S.E.s. At least he's got the order right.
"No, I got those past me. I'm at uni."
"Ah right, so you are. Shoulda remembered that. Queen's, is it?"
"No, not Queen's. I'm at Magee."
"Magee? Good God! What took you there?"
"I'm doing music."
"Thought you were academic, like history or geography or something? Music?"
He says 'Music' like I had told him I had taken up child abuse.
"Aye, music. It's a good course. I'm loving it," I tell him.
"Alright, but what are you going to do with it? Teach, I suppose?"
"Maybe. Haven't thought that far ahead yet."
"That's the thing, you see. You guys, your generation, yous don't think ahead. No planning, then you finish up in some dead end job, no prospects, no decent money coming in."
"Yeah, you're right," I hear myself saying. "But chances are I won't finish up getting shot if someone doesn't like one of my songs. Like, being a soldier, in some war zone; now that is a 'dead end' job."
"Very droll son," he says, but he knows I have trumped him in that exchange. The young bull scores a painful dig into the old bull's ribs.
"And where do you stay over in Londonderry? You in halls or what?"
"No, sure I have the bike. I ride over most days. If I have to stay over I go to aunt Majella's. She kinda likes me staying. Gives her a bit of company, now uncle Seamus is dead. She's nice, Majella."
He shakes his head, almost in disgust I think.
"So you are hanging around Shanty Town in your free time? You be very careful, Patrick. Don't be getting mixed up with anything. That place was the hood capital of Northern Ireland when I was serving there, probably still is."
I nearly choke on a bite of burger.
"This is 2016, for God's sake! That was the eighties. There's been a bit of a change. The peace process? Or haven't you heard of it?"
He shakes his head doubtfully.

"That's as maybe; in my opinion it's all a bit of a con. Anyway, I'm still not happy about you spending your evenings in places like Shantallow."

"But Dad," I say, forcing the sour word into my mouth and back out again like it's a rancid grape or something, "it doesn't matter whether you are happy or not. I am coming twenty, I am my own person. You are away in war-land or wherever. You don't have a say, remember?"

"Yeah, right," he groans after a sullen glare.

We eat in silence for a while. Then after a bit he picks up on my 'war-land' comment and starts into a passionate description of some of the places he's been recently, some of the action he's seen, some of the frustrations of not being allowed to 'clean-out a situation' like he's been trained to do. What is he like? As if either Josie or me give a damn about any of this! I stare out at the flat, blue sea and think my own thoughts, not even bothering to pretend that I am interested. Josie is finished eating and excuses herself to go to the loo. He catches on to our disinterest eventually.

"So wee lad, tell me about yourself."

'Wee lad'! Jeez!

"Tell you what?"

"Whatever. How's it going at home? Oh aye, tell me about the trip to the Somme. I was proud of you for getting selected for that, really delighted for you. How was it all?"

Now this I could talk about but what I might tell him would not be the kind of vibe he would be wanting to feed on, so I hold back in a cool misty blandness.

"Yeah, it was good. A great experience. Some lovely people with us, from all over Ireland."

"What was the highlight?" he asks as Josie arrives back at the table.

"The highlight?" No way am I being honest about that question, so I go with the expected. "I suppose it was finding my soldier's name on Thiepval Tower and then getting to sing there."

Josie cuts in with the counter.

"His highlight was scoring with some wee German doll, I hear."

He looks at me, a slow lech of a smile coming over his face.

"Oh ho," he says. "Good lad, Patrick. The apple hasn't fallen far from the tree after all. So you pulled, eh? What was she like? Tall and blonde with legs up to her oxters?"

"I don't want to hear this," says Josie. "You're a pair of sleaze-balls."

"You're the one that brought it up," I say, "so why can't you just mind your own business? It's not like I see a crowd of fellas lining up at our house to take you out."
"Bastard," she says.
Robbie jumps in, peace-keeper that he is.
"Here, come on you two. That's enough of that. Right, let's change the subject. How's you mother nowadays?"
Josie and I look at each other.
"She's OK, far as I know," I reply.
"No company on the go?"
"That wouldn't be any of your business," Josie barks.
"No, you're right, it wouldn't," he says, just a shade of regret in his tone. "Agh, I'm sorry. It was just a daft idea from the beginning, her and me; nicest looking girl in the country but her and me was like oil and water."
"Yeah, and the oil and water mixed and produced Patrick and me," says Josie. "How do you think that makes us feel? Like we are some kind of disastrous accidental consequence? Jesus, you people!"
"Sorry girl, I didn't mean it like that. It came out wrong. I'm sorry."
Not often he is given to apologies so we accept it and sit quiet for a bit. He drains the last of his pint.
"What about puddin'?"
"No, nothing for me," we say together.
"Another drink for yous then?" he says.
"No thanks," I say. Josie shakes her head.
"I'd better not have any more either," he says. "Driving back to the city now. Changed place these days, Belfast. All very modern getting, very cosmopolitan. You can't go into a restaurant but you're having to deal with somebody from Italy or Poland or somewhere. I'm dying just to hear a Belfast accent at times. Hopefully this Brexit will sort it out. Send a lot of them back to where they came from."
Josie and I look blankly at each other again. I want to take him on but I see her compress her lips and shake her head very slightly.
"Well, if it sends them back," I say, "all the restaurants will just have to go self-service for there will be nobody left to work in the places."
"You think?" he says. "Maybe you'll have a better chance of getting a job with your music degree when they go, serving in MacDonald's or some place."
Cheeky bugger.
I've had just about enough of this.

"I'm sure you wish you were in the U.S.," I retaliate. "You could get a job on Trump's Great Wall of America, keeping out the Mexicans and the Muslims and all them terrorists."

"Look son," he says, "you may laugh but the world is changing. People have every right to demand more protection from their governments. Look at what is happening on the continent. Where would you be safe these days? We have to get control of our borders again. That's all Trump is trying to do and fair play to him for it, though I don't think he has any chance of getting elected now, after that pussy-grabbing remark. The religious people won't vote for him any more. I just hope Theresa May will have the same attitude. Secure our borders. Get the place back to what it used to be like."

"Yeah, maybe re-invade India too; like they must be such a mess since the Brits stopped ruling them," I say and stand up. There's only so much garbage you can listen to in an afternoon. "Right, need to go here. I have work to be doing for tomorrow."

He stands up as well, reaches in his jacket pocket and brings out two brown envelopes. He thrusts one at Josie. She hesitates, then takes it with a tiny 'thank-you'. I do the same.

"There you go," he says. "Just a wee something for oul times sake."

Again I echo Josie's thanks and grab my helmet.

He sticks out his hand and I shake it, that old tight feeling in my gut again. I turn away as Josie gets a sort of awkward hug.

I sense him watching us from the hotel window as we cross the car park to the bike; neither of us looks back.

We hit the road in mutual silence.

Chapter 21

Bernie Doherty

They arrive back home in a strange mood, as I sort of expected they would. There isn't a lot of craic from them, that's for sure. I can barely get a word out of either of them.

"So how was it?"

Nothing, not a word. Just a dull shadow of disillusionment flitting across their eyes before they look away. Predictable.

Why does he do this? Why not just fade totally out of the picture and leave us be? He has no right to be re-entering our world every so often, rubbing and tearing at old wounds which have been healing over as best they can. His kids do not need him, absolutely not. But I need them. I need them to sit down and listen to me for a while. They are all I've got.

I notice Josie at the fireplace fiddling with an envelope, ripping it open, throwing it into the hearth and sticking something in her pocket. I can't resist.

"What's that Josie? Did he give you something?"

"Yeah, he did," she says in her bored monotone. "Just some hush money."

I see Patrick fish a similar one from his jacket.

"Yeah, he gave us these," he says, opening his and counting a wad of notes.

"Two hundred and fifty. That was nice of him. Must have won big on a horse or something. How much did you get?"

Josie gives him a dark look. "Didn't count," she says. "Likely the same as you. Don't know if it was worth it though, having to listen to him. You are well rid of him mum."

She starts to head for the stairs but I call her back.

"Would you sit down a minute," I say. "I have something to tell you."

Josie hesitates, then comes slowly to the couch.

"Tell me? Tell me what?"

"You too, Patrick," I say as he makes a dive for the kitchen.

"Alright, give me a minute. Anybody want a cuppa?"

I wait while he boils the kettle and gets tea for the three of us.

Josie can't help quizzing me.

"What is this? You'd better not be about to tell us you've met someone?"

"No, no," I say. "Chance would be a fine thing. Nothing like that."

"What then?"

"Wait for him," I say.

This has been building up in me for a good while, this need to tell them. It is their right to know but I am a stubborn lady by nature, stubborn and deep-down scared shit-less, I suppose, by what may be up ahead for me. The thing is that until I'm sure of where I stand, is there any point in worrying them too? That is the real reason I have stayed silent, or at least that is what I tell myself. Now that I have stepped out over the threshold of my bunker, I know that I am terrified of how they will react. Even now I want to chicken out. Can I quickly think of some alternative story to distract them with? What about...but it is too late. My mind goes blank as Patrick comes back from the kitchen.

"Right," I say. "This is difficult but I suppose I just have to come out and say it. I have been to the doctor, for tests."

"What?" Josie's reaction is typically dramatic. Patrick just sits and stares at me. "Tests for what? What's wrong with you?"

"A while back I started noticing a lump, in my breast like. I thought it might go away of its own accord and I waited, but it didn't. So I went to Dr Forbes and he sent me to the clinic, the breast place. They took a wee sample and sent it off for analysis."

"Oh mum! Why did you keep this from us?" Josie jumps towards me.

"And did they give you any results? Do they know what it is?" Patrick is sounding high-pitched like he always does in this kind of unusual circumstance.

"No results so far. I have to go and see them on Tuesday. The clinic doctor is not sure if it's a cancer thing. He did a mammogram and an ultrasound but he wasn't sure. It might be, but it might not be. That's why he did the needle biopsy. If that shows up any cancer cells they will take the whole thing away, just to be sure."

"Oh God mum, that's terrible," Josie says getting up and coming to hug me. Patrick sits in shock, not sure how to react to this. To be fair to him though, I see that he is affected by my bombshell. He looks kinda dumb-struck. I can see his fertile imagination is already running away with him. I have to try to get him to see this thing in balance.

"It's not terrible Josie, not yet. There's lots of folk in far worse positions. It may only be a wee lump, something benign. They told me that not all of these things turn out to be cancer. In fact something like four out of five of them aren't dangerous, aren't malignant. So the chances are I am ok. Don't be worrying yourselves about it, alright. Patrick? Alright?"

He sits head down. No reply.

"Why did you not tell us earlier?"

"Agh Josie....it wasn't easy. This is why...now...seeing yous react like this."

"Then why did you tell us now?" Patrick sounds angry. "You could have kept it to yourself until you were sure one way or the other."

"Well, I could, but I'll have the results on Tuesday. If I'd kept it from you till then you would have been mad at me, wouldn't you?"

Josie defends me.

"You are one selfish boy," she tells him. "You would rather she had to suffer all the worry herself rather than bother you with it. It must have been hell for her to keep this all inside for the last while."

"I suppose," he says. "But it's just hard to know what to do with it. Like...what am I supposed to think now? The way my mind works, my imagination jumps straight away up ahead to the worst possible scenario. I can't help that. It's just the way I am. So I'm thinking the worst, while you two are wondering what to make for tea or whatever."

Yeah, that's my Patrick alright; that's why I kept my secret until now.

"You don't have to be like that," I tell him. "You should be positive, think for the best, not the worst. It won't make it any better to be negative, will it?"

"It won't make it all go away just by being positive either," he says. "There's lots of people in the graveyard who died clutching their rosary beads, all full of faith and positive attitude!"

Josie rounds on him.

"You should just shut the hell up, Patrick. Who needs that rubbish at the minute? Think what you are saying here. Mum has just told us she may have cancer. Can you not see she needs us to support her. We are all she has got, you self-centred moron. Get a life, for God's sake!"

That was pretty harsh Josie, but she does have a point. I do need them, I really need them, both...maybe for the first time ever, or at least for the first time since the bother with their father. I lift my head to look across at Patrick and as I watch him, crouched forward in his chair, hands over his face, I see the first wee ripple of emotion in him. I want to hug him but it's awkward as Josie is draped around me on the couch.

"Come over here son," I say, making room beside me. He does, slowly, and sits down beside me. I put my arm around him and feel a gentle shudder of emotion working its way up to the surface of him, no noise, no words, no tears. We sit like that, the three of us, for a good five minutes. No more language, just the primitive bonding of family, such as we are. David Attenborough would have the precise prose to describe this picture but for us, we are just living it.

"I do need yous," I say. "I need you to understand me and be patient with me. And make a bit of an effort to get on with each other instead of squabbling all the time. This is going to be ok, right? We will see it through together, if we are strong together and stay together. Alright?"

Josie does a lovely thing. She reaches across and takes Patrick's hand for a bit, then she releases it, gets up and hurries away upstairs.

Patrick sits where he is.

"I'm sorry mum," he says. "Do you want me to stay at home on Tuesday and come with you for the results?"

"No, I do not!" I tell him. "Sure Josie is here. She can come with me. You go on to Derry as normal."
"As normal?" he says. "What does 'as normal' mean now?"

Chapter 22

Patrick McAleese is at **72 Bannview Close, Coleraine** feeling 'empty'.
Friday 16th Dec 2016

Finished uni today for the holiday break and should be happy about that but...
What happened with my mum in October has knocked me back on my heels...I mean my mother's health scare.
You can be sailing along all cool like, enjoying the scenery of life, living 'the mad dream' as a first year uni student, and then something like this happens and everything gets all shook up. The things you take for granted are suddenly not half as certain as they had been. You feel under threat and the thing is that you are pretty much powerless to do anything about it. It's like chance has conspired against you to say, "Hang on buddy, how do you like this one?" And from out of left field...Bam! You did not see it coming; you didn't even know there was a left field.
I have found it hard to concentrate since that Sunday when she told us, sometimes worse than others but always the nagging feeling that nothing really matters. What I am studying is meaningless, irrelevant. Even the composition classes that I loved those first few weeks are heavy going now. So are the possibilities of joining a couple of other musicians from the course as singer-guitarist in a band doing original songs around the pub scene in Derry. My bike journeys over there that were sort of enjoyable at the start have become endless ruts of darkly depressing thoughts. My song-writing has dried up. My guitar stands forlorn in the corner, out of tune and staring at me accusingly.
Even my feelings about the whole thing with Lena have been affected. As a relationship, it all seems so distant, so impossible, so pointless, and yet I cannot bring myself to move on from it, which would be the logical thing to do, or at least to try to do.

I haven't really made any decent friends in Magee, possibly because I am not around there much for the student night life. I did enjoy the Fresher's dance back in September, hooked up briefly with 'Juanita' from Omagh, a trainee nurse who seemed to be 'only interested in me for my body', (as I told Barry later). I just couldn't have any enthusiasm for the whole thing; the thought of Lena had me well inoculated, I think. Since then I haven't really hung around there to socialise, apart from a few drinks with that couple of guys, (the ones who want to form a band), when I was staying over on a Monday night. At the same time I am really glad that I made the call to be at home. I am there for my mother, all the more important now that Josie has moved out.

Big sister finally got her job in Belfast and is staying in the city, though, to be fair to her, she comes home at every opportunity. Mum is pretty positive, despite her hair starting to fall out. She's had it cut short and she actually looks younger I think, younger and thinner. Maybe it's the new make-up. After the lump was removed the oncologist people told her that they were very confident that they had gotten everything but that she should have the chemo for six months and then a few weeks of radio therapy, just to be sure. So she goes to the City Hospital every fortnight for that. The train is really handy for her and she can be there in an hour and a half. If she's not feeling too well after it she can go to Josie's flat up the Lisburn Road for a while.

It has been a crazy year, this 2016. Crazy and disturbing, both personally and in a wider sense. Brexit was the first major shock, but it was only a mildly jarring event compared to what has happened in America. Seems to me that the whole idea of democracy is hugely over-rated when you have the world's leading example of the system electing a bullying, sexist, racist, serial-bankrupt like Trump. Ok, they didn't exactly have a great alternative in Hilary but I just cannot get my head around it. And this 'wee country' of ours isn't much better, with its 'burning issue', the scandal around the scheme known as the Renewable Heat Incentive. I watched last night's Nolan show when I was round at Barry's house; his dad was hopping mad at the TV as that smoothie politician had some minister praying over him before the interview, asking God to give him the strength to tell the whole truth.

"What sort of an idiot goes on TV and does a charade like that?" he said. "What sort of a man in his position has to have prayers to help him be honest?"

"A politician maybe?" I suggested.

"This country is a feckin' joke! What did we do to deserve politicians like that?"

I could have answered that but I'm not sure he would have wanted to hear it.

I have been hoping to hear from Lena but she hasn't contacted me for a while. Back a few months ago I had had such a good plan for this Christmas break. Before I knew about mum's problem I had a whole scheme planned in my head to fly to Germany for a week, just to spend a bit of time with Lena. I had checked prices of flights from Dublin to Munich and Memmingen, how I would get to Fremdenheim, possible places where I could maybe stay when I was there...mad. It was meant to be a surprise for her but of-course I would have told her about it sometime before, just in case she and her family were going elsewhere. Thankfully the idea had just stayed as an idea because now there is no way I would be leaving mum, especially around christmas.

It is at least three weeks since I have FaceTimed Lena, maybe more. I do feel guilty about that but it has been busy, plus this gloomy cloud hanging over me lately has put me off trying to be all sociable and happy and positive with Lena. I need to contact her, yeah, but it is not as easy as it had been.

I can't really get a handle on my feelings about her at the minute. I would love to have her near me right now; I could really use her wee smile, her hugs, her support. But cyber-contact is a very poor alternative. I felt this when I first told her about mum. It's not that I was emotional or anything...I wasn't; it all just seemed so strangely distant. I wasn't sure that she even understood. She certainly did not seem to know how to react. Yeah, she said she was sorry, but it was a strangely cold moment for me, cold and awkward to the point that I was nearly sorry I had told her. It was like she couldn't quite think how to empathise with how I was feeling.

Actually, when I think about it, that was possibly the last time I was speaking to her online...and it may be one of the reasons I've not been rushing back to talk. There have been a few brief texts but not the face to face chat that had been my oxygen after the summer. Still, I know I should call her. If only I could make up my mind on how I feel about the relationship.

'The relationship'? What relationship? It is not as if I am going out with her or something. Yeah, she is some girl, beautiful, cool. I like her a lot. I like her better than any girl I ever met, and I know she

likes me too but it is not as if I have ever told her how I really feel about her. Nor her me, for that matter. Yeah, the connection with her is massively strong; how we met seemed to be such a meant-to-be thing; how we were with each other that last night in Albert, one of the best feelings of my entire life. Her emails have been lovely and when we have shared songs and ideas on FaceTime... yeah, it has been very special.
But!
But it is all so frustrating, being this far apart, missing the actual contact, the look she has in those smokey eyes, the evocative scent of her hair, the touch of her body against me. If I had a fiver for every time I have lain in bed and stared at her image on my phone I could have paid for a flight to Bavaria twice over.
I need to know how she feels about all this.
I need to know does she feel it is time to move on. Maybe, for all I know, she is seeing somebody else and would love to be honest enough with me to tell me...but she doesn't want to bring it up, doesn't want to hurt me. Would I be doing her a favour to say some sort of goodbye, even for a time-out?
I don't know. I need to make contact again. Right, I will call her and play it by ear.

Her face appears on screen; she seems to be walking.
Pretty as ever, a low sun catching the side of her head and making her hair shine like washed coal as it bounces to her rhythm.
"What's up?" I say.
"Nothing is up, just coming to my home from school. How are you?"
"Good," I lie. "Sorry I haven't been in touch for a while. Been shocking busy at uni and stuff."
Her head bobs about above her multi-coloured woollen scarf and her eyes only flick down to her screen occasionally. I see her look off to the side and say something. She is obviously walking with a friend.
"Sorry," I say, "do you want me to call you back when you get home?"
"No, no," she answers quickly. "I am almost at my home just now. You want to see how it is looking, our house?"
The camera moves around from her face to show me her home and, as it does, the image of a guy suddenly flickers across the screen; it

is the briefest of looks but even in that millisecond I notice his broad smile and his blonde hair and my heart gives a tiny lurch of jealousy. I see what must be her house, large, two-storied, wooden, quite alpine looking for a house in a town. Then I see the street ahead, a fairly typical village street with traffic lights not far ahead. From what I can see it seems to be a wintery scene. I hear Lena say something in German to her friend and the image of his back walking on along the snow-covered pavement is briefly on screen. Seems to be a pretty tall, athletic-looking type. He shouts back over his shoulder.
Back to Lena's face. She seems fairly happy for once. I so want to ask about the guy but obviously I am not going to. Let's see if she mentions him as we chat.
"I sort of forgot you might be still at school," I say. "No holidays yet?"
"No, not yet. We have three days next week. You see we have snow here now," she says and I see her image darkening a little as she enters her house. I hear her bag clattering to the floor. She seems to be taking off her shoes. She calls something to whoever is in the house, presumably something like, "I'm home, mum," and then I sense her run up the stairs. I wait.
"I must go to the bathroom first," she says.
"Sure, go ahead," I say and I wait a bit longer, looking at the still image of her ceiling on screen.
She comes back eventually.
"I am sorry," she says. "That could not wait. You know about this thing..."
I am not sure at all what she means but I let it pass. I just watch her as she seems to be placing the phone again.
"So, what's the craic?"
She should know this expression from previous calls but I see her struggle briefly to remember it.
"The craic? The craic is all ok," she says. "How are you?"
That's two or three times she has asked me that already. It all feels a bit stale, even though I am enjoying looking at her on screen.
"Good. A bit bored though," I say.
"And your mother? How is she?"
"Mum's handling it all pretty well. She has times of sickness and she has lost a fair bit of hair but she is very brave."
"It must be very hard for her."
"Yeah, it's not easy."
"And for you too...it is difficult, yes?"
"I am ok,"

"You do not seem to be as you were before; you seem to be in...how do you say? You seem to be in a bad atmosphere, a bad mood. Are you sad?"

This is all a bit direct and, despite liking a frank conversation with her as much as I do, I cannot bring myself to answer it honestly.

"I am alright."

"I do not think you are, Patrick. I wish I could be with you at this minute. I really wish I could."

I find this just so genuine, so lovely, that it breaks through my defence mechanism. It affects me and she knows it. I can't respond for a second.

"I miss you, Patrick."

"Ah, that's lovely Lena. Do you know something? I haven't told you this before but I'll tell you now. Before mum took sick I had a secret plan to fly over to you during the christmas holiday. I honestly did."

"You were going to do that," she stutters, "Fly over here for christmas?"

"No, not quite that; just fly to Germany and get to your house somehow, see you, maybe stay nearby for a day or two....not all of christmas, that would have been too much like an invasion."

"Wow," she says. "That is so romantic. You were actually making a plan to do this?"

"Yeah, well...I looked up flights; I even looked at the best way to get to your town. But just when I was about to tell you my plan mum got news of her illness, so I had to forget about the idea."

"I am so impressed," she says. "That would have been a great christmas present, for me anyhow. I am sorry two times now that your mother has been sick. Would you really have done this?"

"Yeah, why not? Would you have been OK with me gate-crashing you at a special time like this?"

"What is gate-crashing? I have not heard this word before."

"Means sort of arriving unexpectedly, uninvited, maybe unwelcome. Coming to see you and it being awkward."

"You would not have been unwelcome," she says. "You know that."

"What about your parents....and your friends?"

"My parents? No problem, I think. They are quite old in their customs and they are much in protection of me, but they would like you, I know they would."

"And your friends?"

"No problem. Ah that is a pity. I would be looking forward so much more to christmas if you were here. Now it is only singing and eating and presents and all that stuff."

"You are going to be singing? Tell me about that. Where are you performing?"

"In church. As usual in church, the singing of carols. We will have a small orchestra and some singers who are guests as well."

"Ah ok."

"Yeah, not too much exciting, is it? Are you singing anywhere? What about new songs? Are you writing?"

I wish.

"I haven't written anything for a while," I tell her. "The muse seems to have dried up."

"The muse?"

"Yeah, you know...ideas. Haven't felt inspired to write anything. Maybe it's to do with my ma and stuff. Just all seems so pointless and it doesn't fit well into a song."

"You know Patrick, that is exactly what you should write about. How you are feeling about this. Some good songs come from pain and worry, is this not so?"

"It may be," I say, "but I am struggling for words. Even to write about life and love and happy times; the words won't come. I just feel bored by everything. It's so pointless, even this."

"How do you mean? Even this?"

"Talking to you and not being able to be close to you. Do you not feel that?" I say.

I have to wait for a long time before she answers me. Her head goes down and her hair seems to make its way across the front of her face like the protective curtain it was the first time I saw her. I sense a deflation in her as she looks back up at the screen.

"I do feel this too, only sometimes. Other times no," she says simply. The silence that comes between us now is deafening.

We have both been honest. We are both realising the stupidity of this, this pretence that we can be any more than two needy teenagers who found a flash of fascination and comfort in each other in the weirdest of circumstances at a particular point in our little lives.

"Life feels a bit cruel to me at the minute," I say. "I know that I shouldn't be thinking this but...I was so happy to have met you; it all felt so right. Plus I did well in my exams and stuff, and I got into the course I wanted to do in uni. Then my mother gets sick...and the distance between you and me seems to get wider every day. It just bugs me so much that I can't..."

I fade out. What I am feeling is so irrational, so selfish.

"I have these feelings very much too," Lena says after a pause. "For me these feelings are very often, very usual, but I did not think you would be in depression like this. You are always so confident, so much.... in good feeling. You always make me feel better."

"That's nice of you to say," I tell her. "It must be a phase I'm in at the minute."

She stares silently at her screen for a bit. I look at the line of her face around her jaw and cheek-bones and eyes and the shape of her mouth and I see again a hint of sadness, even some kind of pain I would say, somewhere on the other side of those intense eyes. Eventually she speaks again.

"It will be ok, after some time it will be ok," she says. "You will feel better."

"I know," I say. "You are probably right. I am not brilliant company for anybody at the minute. Least of all you."

"No, it is the other way around. I make you feel bad...because you have been so lovely to me and yet I am so far away. You need someone to love who can be with you but I am in Germany and I cannot be what you need. This is the true fact about us Patrick."

I want to counter this argument; everything in me wants to tell her that this is nonsense, that I need her even at a distance, that she means so much more to me than anyone bar my family. But I find it hard to argue back to her.

I say, "You don't make me feel bad, no way. But I am doing that to you. I call you up and load all my stupid shit on to you. You don't need that. You don't need the hassle of a boyfriend a thousand miles away from you in Ireland who gets all screwed up because he cannot have what he wants....Like, I see you with your other friend today and I imagine you in your school with stacks of fellows chatting to you and wanting to be with you."

"This is not so."

"It is Lena. So I need to say to you...that...I do not want to hold you back from being with anyone else, ok? I don't want you to think of me as someone you have to be loyal to, as if I owned you or something, do you understand?"

She sits head down for a while, processing this.

"I understand some of your words," she says, "but nobody is asking to be with me. I do not have any other boy with me, honestly. What kind of person do you think I am?"

"Ok," I say, wanting again to ask about her obvious happiness with the blonde guy on the pavement but not able to. "I am just saying that you should be free to be with whoever you want, that is all."

She waits for a while, staring off at an angle, chin on her hand.

Then..."And you? Do you have a new girl?"

That was very brave of her to ask me like that.

"No way," I say. "It's not that."

"But you would like to have? You have seen someone else in your college perhaps?"

"No, I haven't. Listen Lena...I could see a hundred girls and not see anyone I would rather be with. You must know that?"

"I know that you are changing," she says, "and I understand this, that people change, that things change. It has happened to me too, before. I have had some big troubles in the past but you have helped me. I believe more in myself now. I am glad of all that."

"Me too," I say. That is one of the best things she could have said to me. "It is just this frustration of not knowing if I will ever see you again."

"Do you want to stop this?" she says. "You would like to tell me to leave you alone? To go away because we may not ever see each other again? To stop writing to you or stop talking together like this?"

"I don't want to tell you this," I say lamely. "I will always have you in my heart...and I will always live in hope that I will see you again and maybe be with you. But I just don't want that to be like a prison for you. You must be free to be your own person and be with whoever you want to be with and live your life to the full...just in case it doesn't work out that I can ever be...you know?"

"I think so," she says slowly. "And you too. You must be free as well. And thank you for being honest with me."

"Thank you for understanding."

"So...do you want me to stop writing to you or texting or FaceTiming?"

"No, of-course not," I say emphatically. "I want to know how your life is...all that stuff. Please stay in touch; promise me you will?"

"I promise."

"Good, thanks."

"And you must tell me too. You will tell me about your mother and all?" she says.

"Yeah, I will," I say. "And Lena..."
I stop there.
"Ja?"
I have to tell her, even now at what might be the end. She has to know, she deserves to know.
"I haven't said this before, but I guess you know anyhow."
"I know what?"
"Ah, now it is awkward, just as I'm about to hang up on you, but...here goes. Thank you for being so...special. You are lovely beyond any words I have and...I love you. There I said it."
She reacts quite emotionally to this. I am really pretty shocked as I watch her trying to get herself together. When she does turn back to the camera I see her hand come forward quickly to the screen.
"And I love you too Patrick. Goodbye."
I start to speak. "Goodbye but only for now..."
But by the time I have gotten halfway through she has already disconnected and I am left staring at her image, unhappy, slightly distorted and frozen on the screen.
My instinct is to call her back straight away and take back everything I have said except the last few sentences. I know she will be suffering, crying more than likely.
But I know I should not do that. This is for the best, tough and all as it is.
Time to try to move on.

Chapter 23

Bernie Doherty is at **Cancer Centre, Belfast City Hospital,** feeling hopeful.
Thurs 23rd March 2017

Final chemo today, thanks be to God. Patrick has taken the day off to be with me when I meet the oncology team and hear about the next step. Apparently there isn't much happening in Magee on a Thursday.
"Why should Thursday be different?" I asked him.
I appreciate him being here with me. I noticed straight away that he did not find it easy coming in here. He looked very strained, his eyes darting around at the faces of the people, meeting other eyes and bouncing away to the posters on the walls. I

well remember this feeling the first time I came into this ward myself, sort of like as if you are entering a correction facility. You'd done something terrible and you were here for the lethal jag. The actual injection, which lasted for over an hour, may not have been lethal but nearly made me wish it had been, for I was so unbelievably nauseous afterwards, boaking up in the toilets for twenty minutes.
"Not everybody has the same reaction," I was told but looking at those poor faces it wasn't hard to suss out which ones had been through it all before; the resignation swilling around in their sad, downcast eyes; the short cropped hair and the wigs. Sometimes over the months I have seen a middle-aged couple come in looking like rabbits caught in the headlights, staring around for an escape route. I'd try to work out which one was the healthy one and which had the dreaded 'big C' lurking somewhere in their unlucky body. It was usually impossible. Both looked equally terrified. Some smart wee nurse would come with her prearranged smile and lead them off to an interview room but seriously, they could not have looked any more scared had they been heading down a corridor to a gas chamber, God love them.
I'd probably been the same myself. And the thing was that in those early days of treatment not a soul spoke to you, the other patients I mean. Everybody seemed to be locked into their own wee world of trepidation. Eyes did not engage. Queries remained unasked, except for the very odd exception. The Friends of the Cancer Centre volunteers were a big help early on, getting me coffee and a biscuit. No vodka though, but I did keep asking in hope.
It is nice having Patrick here with me today. I have sensed a bit of a change in him lately. He has seemed at a loose end at times, lonely even. With Barry away and with the whole German connection seeming to cool down he has definitely become more introverted. He has even asked me for a loan of money, which isn't like him. There doesn't seem to be as much work in that pub he sings in, less punters around in the winter of-course. That applies to the ice cream business too.
It is especially good for him to be here today and meet the staff who have been looking after me. They are the best of people. You'd think that seeing all these poor condemned patients day after day they'd get a bit blasé, immune to the sad hopelessness of so many of the cases. No way! I have seen nothing but sheer human goodness and the best of care and professionalism from every single one of these cancer staff, from admin people to nurses to doctors.
We go down a corridor to a side office. They seem cramped for space in this place all the time. A nurse takes us in to meet the main oncologist who's been looking after my case. She and her side kick, a young doctor from Eastern Europe, I am guessing, are very welcoming, very smiley as they shake hands with Patrick. I have the sense that this is a sign of good news; they could not possibly be about to tell

us that my cancer has come back or has spread, not after smiling their way through the introductions like Mormon missionaries.

"Well Bernie, you will be keen to know the results of your blood tests and the last scan."

Just what you would know!

Short pause. Patrick sits forward in his chair, nervous as a kitten.

"The scan shows no further sign of cancer. No spread to other organs. We think that at this stage you are pretty much clear."

"That's brilliant," I say. "Thank you very much....that's a great relief, isn't it Patrick?"

"Too right," he says.

"No more treatment then?"

"Well, you need to complete the final chemo today, and...", they look at each other...."we would be recommending that you take the short course of radio therapy as well just to be absolutely sure. How do you feel about that?"

"No bother," I say. "Yous know best and yous have been great already."

So it is that an hour later I am lying on a reclining chair in a side cubicle, all connected up to the drip, feeling more than satisfied with myself. Patrick is watching Countdown or some other pointless programme on the wee TV above the bed.

I hate the feeling of this poison dripping slowly into my blood stream, especially now that I have the good news that I am clear. I'd rather be heading to the Crown Bar for a celebratory drink before catching the train back up north. It will be a few days before I can allow myself that pleasure.

Patrick's phone bleeps the arrival of an email and I watch him take it out to read. Suddenly he sits up straight in his chair; I sense excitement in him and a smile spreads over his features. I can't wait to ask what the big deal is that is so cheering him up.

"Well?" I say.

"Well what?" he says still reading.

"What's the bars? You're getting all worked up? A record contract or something?"

"Naw, nothing like that. It's Lena."

"Oh right. Remind me who Lena is," I ask, but I know right well.

"Lena from Germany. She is coming to Ireland," he says and I swear he is on the edge of some kind of jig of joy, at the same time trying to hide the grin in his eyes.

"My word, and what is bringing her here? Is she coming to see you...like is she coming to Coleraine?"

"No, no. Sure we've been split up for three months."

"Have you not heard from her in three months?" I am curious.
"Well, not exactly; just a couple of texts."
"So why is she coming to Ireland?"
"She's coming to the south; some sort of cycle-ride thing."
"And when is this?"
"Easter time, like three weeks away."
"That's lovely for her," I say. "So she doesn't want to see you?"
That sort of takes the wind out of his sails for a second.
"Here, read it," he says.
"No way. I don't want to read your private emails. I'm not that kind of mother," I say.
"Oh right? Well, listen then," he says and he proceeds to read the whole thing to me. Very open of him, this new son of mine.
'Hi Patrick; I hope you are well and your mother is making a good recovery. I say a prayer for her every night. I have some good news for you. Myself and my friend Gaby are coming to Ireland to cycle around the Ring of Kerry. We are coming at Easter, from April 16 to 23. We fly to Dublin and take a coach to the south. We have hired our cycles already in a place called Killarney. Also we want to see The Skelligs, (but it may not always be possible with weather.) 'Star Wars' was filmed there but of-course you know this; we are both big fans of 'Star Wars'...do you like it? Also if we have time we will visit the town Dingle. We will stay in Youth Hostels every night. Gaby's father did this route when he was a youth in 1979 and wants Gaby to have the same experience. I would prefer to cycle in the northern division of Ireland nearby to you so that I could see you but I have to follow my friend's idea this time. It is exciting for me to be on your island but I do not expect that you will be anywhere near where we are riding, so I will just appreciate the scenery instead. Pity! I must go back to my study now; I have some exams just after I return from Ireland. Say hi to your family. Love, Lena.'
"There you go," he says quietly.
"That is nice for her."
I watch him closely. I have nothing else to be doing. I can almost hear the gears of his mind clunking over. In spite of himself he is missing this lassie, that is for sure, and, what's more, she is missing him...why wouldn't she? And that 'missing' feeling is driving his imagination yet again; he is scheming, I know it. How is he going to solve this quandary of being on the same patch of land as her and yet three hundred plus miles away and not being able to see her?
No doubt the same boy will come up with something. I wonder will he tell me what.

It is really strange watching him growing up to this stage where he is right on the threshold of being his own person and seeing the different quirks of his personality become more fixed. I can see traits that he inherits from me and traits where it is obvious that some of his father has made its way into his character. Then there are the bits that are just pure Patrick. They don't seem to have any relationship to either side of his genetic background. The singing.... and this creative instinct in him, for example...no idea where it comes from. His father could only sing when well drunk and then only party songs and ballads, like his perennial party piece, 'Brothers in Arms'. Myself? I was nearly expelled from Derry for being the living contradiction of the Phil Coulter line, 'There was music there in the Derry air'. There may have been but it blew past me without consequence.

Then there is this 'secretive-planner' thing that Patrick has; again, that has nothing to do with either of his parents. Robbie could plan, yes, but the world and his aunt would know all about it. I can plan the dinner but not much further ahead than that. That's always been my problem. 'One day at a time, sweet Jesus' has gotten me nowhere over the years. So, to watch him now as he starts imagining how this is all going to work that he will get to see his woman, and to realise that he will most probably make it happen and that I will know next to nothing about it. It is all an exercise in trust, in faith. Yes, blind faith...but then blind faith hasn't exactly let me down in the beating of this cancer, has it?

Chapter 24

(Patrick McAleese)

There is no way that Magdalena Rosenthal is going to be on the same island as me for one whole week and me not get to see her...no way!

I check my phone diary. 16th to 23rd April she says she is here. I am down to be working every single day in the Port. I need to be working for I am pretty much skint at the minute. How am I going to manage this?

I have to see her. I have to get time off, even one day, to travel down to Kerry. I'll ride down. Actually...two days then...one to ride down, stay the night, one to ride back. I'm sure six hours should do it, so I could maybe take one day off, get up early and ride back to do an evening shift. It will cost me a few pound but I don't care.

I call in Moran's to chat to my boss.

"Gina, you know the way I said I wanted to work every day of my holiday from uni?"

"Yes Patrick. You have changed your mind? It's a long stretch."

"No, not exactly changed my mind, but you see that second week...is there any chance I could maybe take one day off?"

I notice that my hands have developed a mind of their own here and have come together into a sort of praying mode, buddha-like.

Gina loses her vanilla smile as she thinks about this.

"Well, it was your idea in the first place. What changed your mind?"

"Ah...there's this friend I have to see. She's going to be in Kerry for a day or two and I want to go down..."

"A girl called Kerry did you say?" Gina asks, already distracted and moving back to her screen to solve another problem.

"No, no. She's Lena; she's from Bavaria. She's just going to be in Kerry doing a bike ride."

"Ah right. Well it's your call. She must be some girl if you are giving up a day's work for her. Mind you, why anyone would want to come to ride a bike round Derry I have no idea. But take whatever time you need. I won't ever stand in the way of romance. Bring her in sure and we'll see if we can rise to a free ice cream for her."

"It's County Kerry, not Derry," I begin but Gina is already leaving me. How did anyone ever get exactly what they ordered back in the day when she was front of shop?

Now to tell Lena.

Email of-course. We kinda backed off from FaceTiming, after that last episode. It just seemed a natural development. Maybe it is because there was so much pent-up frustration in the face-to-face visual thing. Certainly I have found it easier to text, be a wee bit more in control of what I am saying, not having to try to read her body language and judge her moods and reactions to me. I still absolutely love it when she has gotten in touch, this last email being almost like a dream come true.

So I sit down and start an email to her.

Halfway through I stop. I have another idea. A class one.

Why don't I surprise her? I will not tell her that I am coming. I will just ride down and find her. I will be able to use 'Find My Friends' on my phone to track her down. What a great app this is, and how glad I am that she asked me back last summer to connect our iPhones using it! At the time I was sort of reluctant to agree...like why does she want to be able to know where I am all the time? I'm not sure how much she used it, if at all. I used it once or twice but the places meant nothing to me and the novelty soon wore off. Now it is going to be massive in this game of surprise that I am planning.

So my answer to her email does not mention the scheme, not a hint of it. Nice and bland, 'delighted for her to see Ireland,' etc.

"Shame it's County Kerry though," I tell her. "I've never been there myself; I hear it is very beautiful but it is the other end of the country from me and sadly I am working all that week. I am sure you and your friend will have a brilliant time. You must make a point of visiting a few pub sessions, musicians playing Irish music. FaceTime me afterwards and tell me all about it."

I am laughing as I write these lies, imagining her face when she sees me waiting by the side of the road on some Kerry cliff edge. That is the plan anyhow.

I suppose I'd better tell mum though, just so she knows where I am if anything goes wrong. She will not be impressed but I am prepared to risk that. This is too good to pass up on.

The night before I take off I am way too excited. My imagination is running riot. I lie on my bed and Google 'Coleraine to Killarney'. It is only then that the scale of the thing hits me; this journey I am taking on is near enough three hundred and fifty miles! Estimated time six and a half hours....and that's only to Killarney. Lena will be way further on than that, out on the Ring of Kerry somewhere. Last night she was in some place called Cahirsiveen, according to 'Find My Friends'; that is another fifty miles or so; the whole journey could take me eight hours plus, if I stop for food somewhere.

Am I mad or what?

What if I ride down all that way and can't find her? Maybe she will not be in a wifi zone, or out of coverage and her app won't work. I could be searching Kerry for days and miss her. I could just phone her of-course and forget the surprise idea. It is all a bit risky.

And....I still have to tell my mum! No time like now for that. I go back downstairs and break the news to her.

I notice that somehow she does not seem to be shocked by this idea of mine, like she half-expected it. Better still, she does not try to put me off the idea.

"Ok, but promise me you'll not fly on that wee bike of yours. Leave yourself plenty of time, alright? How long is it going to take you?"
"Not sure; maybe seven or eight hours," I say, flippant as you like.
"My God, Patrick! Hopefully she's worth it, this kid. Eight hours on a motor bike? I thought yous had sort of cooled the whole thing off a bit, her being so far away and all?"
"Aye well, maybe we had," I say. "Anyway, she's just a friend."
"Wish I had a friend like that," she says.
She rummages a bit in her purse.
"Here...put that towards your petrol." She hands me two notes.
"Thirty quid, ma! Thanks! You trying to get me married off or what?"
"Aye well, you never know," she says. "You need to stop somewhere and change it into Euros, for the tolls like."
I'd forgotten about that.
"So you'll ride back up...when?"
"Probably the next day. I have to work that evening. And anyway, she goes home on Sunday."
"So you're just going to see her for one night? Where are you going to stay?"
"Haven't really thought about that. I'll find somewhere."
"You're likely hoping you can slide in beside her in some hotel somewhere," she says.
"There's another girl with her so it won't be like that," I tell her.
"You think? We'll see. Just come back safe to me afterwards."
Back up to my room, but not to sleep. I need to leave about nine, just behind the rush-hour traffic to Belfast; that should have me into Kerry well before six in the evening . I lie there estimating all this, thinking about the possible things that can go wrong, like phones not working, then imagining her surprise when she sees me.
It's been a while since any inspiration has stirred me to write but now some lyrics drift into my head, so I start scribbling.

Hard to think of you so close and yet so far away
Out of reach but in my mind every single day
See you standing on a cliff above the loud Atlantic roar
Your long hair streaming in the wind by a wild romantic shore

My Magdalena
Imagine your surprise
My Magdalena
Can't wait to see your dark smiling eyes

It is definitely not my finest but it's a start, and I can see myself stopping the bike several times on the journey south to add bits to it. Every road-trip needs an anthem; maybe this will be it.

Chapter 25

(Patrick McAleese)

I have made good progress on this journey so far. Reached the outskirts of Dublin by lunchtime and stopped in a motorway cafe for a bite to eat. Then headed out the M50 around the sprawl of the city's growing beer-belly and down the M7 towards Limerick. All pretty easy so far; boring if anything, hour after hour of flat motorway across farmland and bog, with not as much traffic as there had been on the Belfast route. Thankfully the weather is dry, little or no breeze so riding is easy. I hope it's like this tomorrow when I am on my way back north to be in work at four o'clock.
I've had a lot of time for thinking but no time for regrets. I'm committed to this now...and I have to admit to some sense of pride in my scheme and in my internal driven-ness to make it happen. I won't forget my first road trip through the guts of Ireland, that's for sure. Fingers crossed it will not be in vain.
By half three I'm approaching Limerick. I pull off into a service area to check 'Find My Friends'. No sign of Lena's phone at the minute; 'location not available'.
No panic though...she is probably just out of cellular coverage, maybe in the mountains or somewhere. Last night she was in a town called Castlemaine, according to the app. Her email mentioned going to Dingle, but then again she may have headed back towards Killarney. Either way my hunch is to head there; should only take me a couple of hours and I will be a lot closer to wherever she and her friend have reached. So that is what I do.
As I ride I get to thinking about her friend, this Gaby. I wonder what she is like? I don't think she was on the trip last summer; Lena didn't seem to have anyone on that visit that she was hanging around with; I can't recall her mentioning Gaby before. Hopefully she will have a bit of tact and get offside while I talk to Lena.
The road to Killarney is quite good but it is not dual carriageway, plus it seems to go right through the middle of a string of villages. I

stop in two of these to check for Lena's whereabouts; no luck; she is still out of coverage, it seems. This all slows me down. I don't know the road well enough to be taking risks passing lines of slow cars. I am getting into Killarney way later than I had thought, just after six. No matter, as long as I can track her down I will be fine.

I do a quick reccie around the famous town, then find a cafe. Maybe I should just call her and find out where she has holed up, but I don't want to spoil the surprise. I check the app again.

Relief! As I tap her name on my phone the blue circle ripples out from her present location. But where is it? My fingers work the screen and I see the name 'Dingle' appearing. Damn! My guess was wrong...she has headed out west along the Dingle Peninsula rather than back towards Killarney. From what I can see as I focus in on her location she is right beside what seems to be a major junction or a roundabout just as the N86 enters the town. She is likely in some place with public wifi. I have a closer look on Google maps; yes there are two likely venues there, a hotel and a B&B/hostel place. If she stays there I can find her; I just have no idea how far away it is.

A quaint old waitress brings me coffee and sandwiches. She reminds me of someone, can't think who. I ask for her help.

"How far is it to Dingle from here?"

"T'would be forty miles I'd say," she sings.

"Jeez, forty? And is it a good road? Like how long will it take me?"

"I suppose it will depend on how fast ye will be at the driving," she smiles. "Is it a car ye are in like?"

I've seen some horse-drawn carriages parked down the street and I am wondering does she imagine I am going to take one of those.

"No, a bike."

"Ah, a bike itself, is it?"

"Yeah, a motor bike like."

"Ah right. It would take ye a lot longer on the pedal thing alright! Well I would be thinking an hour, for there can be slow bits where there be's traffic, d'ya know?"

"I know alright," I say back and I catch myself sort of mimicking her idiom and accent; she should take that as a compliment because this has to be one of the prettiest accents I've heard in a long time, nothing like the thick Ulster-Scots I hear around me in North Antrim.

I scoff the sandwiches, drain the coffee and hit the road again.

There is a bit of a west wind now and I am riding straight into it, which doesn't help my time, nor my patience. I have to wait at road-

work lights on two occasions and I get held up behind a huge tractor and muck spreader on the most bendy part of the road.
Eventually I reach Dingle. Unbelievably it is a quarter to eight. As I hit what I think is the roundabout that I'm looking for I scan the nearby buildings. Yeah, there is the hotel but I am guessing it is way too posh for Lena. Across the road there is a slightly more dingy-looking joint; Harbour House Hostel. That looks the kind of place a couple of German girls would be hiding in. Brilliant. I pull in, park the bike, take off my helmet and make my way in to the foyer.
No one around; I have to knock a door and a dreamy-looking girl appears from the back room, tea towel in hand.
"Hi, I am looking for a couple of friends of mine who might be staying here at the minute," I say.
"Ok, who would that be?" she says looking down at her register.
"It may be under the name Magdalena Rosenthal, or maybe Lena, or Gaby somebody," I say.
I follow her finger down the page until she gives it a triumphant jab.
"Yes, they're booked in. German couple I think. They left their bags and went for something to eat, not half an hour ago."
"Any idea where?" I ask.
"Not a clue, but they were asking for the best place to hear some Irish music after," she tells me. "I told them if it was me I'd go to the Court Bar in the Mall. Always a good bit of craic in there. They might even have gone there to eat as well; they do great bar-food now."
"Great," I say; she tells me where to find it and I'm on my way.
I find the Court Bar no bother and park the bike in a little yard out at the back of the joint. Should be safer here. I notice that my heart is thumping way faster than normal. After nine months of waiting and nine hours of travelling I am about to walk in on Lena and surprise the life out of her. I can't wait to see her face.
Helmet in hand I push open the back door of the place and enter through a narrow porch. I pause at the door into the bar and stare through the beveled glass at the customers in the restaurant; it is a very distorted view but even with the bending of the images I think I can see Lena straight away, her back sort of sideways to me, the shine of her long black hair unmistakeable. Yeah...it's her; she turns her head slightly...it's her! I've finally had some good luck on this hunt, finding her so easily. Fantastic! I think she has a wine glass in her hand as she stares across the table at...at Gaby.
Gaby?
My heart gives a strange lurch.

Across the table from Lena is a guy.
A male!
A fellow!
Gaby is male?
Oh God no!
It had never crossed my mind that Gaby was anything but a girl! Gaby? Gabrielle surely? Why did Lena not tell me this?
Gaby is a bloke, her bloke!
Yes, he is very much male. Tall, broad-shouldered, longish blonde hair, athletic.
Haven't I seen this guy before? Yeah, I think so; the guy who was walking her home from school back a few months ago when I FaceTimed her. I remember a hint of these same feelings back then.
I stand at the door and there are no words to describe the pain I am going through. This can't be happening to me...not after riding three hundred plus miles to see her.
Literally I feel like a hot knife has been stuck into me, somewhere in my chest. No other way to put it. I'm devastated! How will I tell my mum? Suddenly I want to phone home to her. I want to cry. I want to hurt somebody, mainly this Gaby! What right has he...actually, it's not his fault! It's her! Why could she not have been honest and told me? I have been fooled by her. The wee....! Oh Lena, why? Why have you done this to me?
Someone comes pushing in past me at the door and I have to stand back; I move quickly to make sure that I cannot be seen through the open door, if Lena should happen to look around.
I turn and head back to my bike. I stand beside it, thinking.
I can't bring myself to go in there and confront her. I am not that kind of guy. The conversation would be too difficult.
God...all my dreams and schemes! My stupid songs...so naive, so innocent. If I had my guitar right now I would leave it in such a state that no one could ever play it again.
I need air. I need to breathe, to think.
I put my helmet back on, then take it off again to wipe the hurting juice from my eyes; the last thing I'd need now is to crash into something in this strange place because I can't see the road.
In five minutes I am heading back out along the road. My thoughts are blacker than I have ever experienced. My language is not good; the wind whips these angry, shouted curses away from my mouth and dumps them into the Kerry bogs.

First Madison. Now Lena. Lena! God but I have had no idea how much you have come to mean to me, Lena Rosenthal. Why? Why did I fall in love with a frickin' German girl who does not know her own mind and who has played me like a trout on a line?

Over and over in my mind I replay what I have just seen, the raising of her glass to this Gaby character, the smile into his eyes, the happy oblivion that she is in, not knowing that I am watching. I start to wonder will she ever know. Will I tell her? Will I ever speak to her again? Will I FaceTime her when she gets home and tell her that I stood outside and watched her with her German boyfriend, saw her loving his company? Tell her that I turned and walked away, carrying my hurt like a dead pet? Tell her that I didn't even have the courage or the manners to hide my disappointment and go in and have a chat with her? And him, of-course.

I reach a tiny village called Annascaul, maybe fifteen miles along the road home. Through the evening gloom I see a striking-looking pub; it's painted bright blue, the colour of a synthetic energy drink; I had noticed it on the way past, lit up by the setting sun. I could do with a coffee and time to clear my head and make a plan so I pull in by this 'South Pole Inn'. A name to match my feelings as I cannot feel much further south or much icier than I do at the minute.

Inside I can't help but notice that the walls are covered with pictures and newspaper clippings and memorabilia. This would not be unusual in an Irish pub of-course, but there is a distinctive feel to this place. Standing at the bar waiting for service, I read the name 'TOM CREAN' on a brass plaque above the beer taps. I'm curious, despite my self-pity.

The barman comes to me.

"Yes son, what'll it be?"

"Would you be able to do me a coffee please?"

"A coffee it is," he says with an air of slight resignation.

I feel the need to explain.

"I'm on a motor bike and I have an eight hour journey ahead of me."

"Definitely a coffee then," he grins and sticks a kettle on. "Mind, if ye ride for eight hours in Ireland ye will fall off the edge; I'm just warning ye now!"

I like his sense of humour, contrasting with my own darkness.

"Not if you're riding to Coleraine," I say. "It took me nine hours on the way down."

"Coleraine? That's in County Derry, isn't it?"

"It is," I say. "Only just."

"Ye wouldn't have much of a team up there this year. Down to division three now, aren't ye?"

"So I hear," I say.

"Do ye not wish you were from Kerry now?" he says. "We're after beating Dublin at Croker to win division one. I was there myself."

"Ah right," I say, not really wanting to argue Gaelic football with this talkative Kerryman.

"Are ye far from Derry, the city itself?" he says. "My wife went to the university there....Magill or something?"

"Magee," I say. "I go there myself at the minute."

"Now there's a coincidence. She's a Donegal girl. Inishowen, if ye know it. Did nursing at that Magee place and then gave it all up to come to God's County and marry me."

"Good for her," I say. Lena is filling my thoughts so I'm a bit limited in how I am answering this guy. He puts the coffee in front of me and I give him five Euros.

"Not at all,' he says, pushing the note back into my hand. "It would be a sad lookout for Kerry if we couldn't give a poor Derry boy a cup of coffee for his journey."

"Cheers," I say, then pointing to the brass plate, "Who is your man?"

"Who?"

"This Tom Crean?"

"Tom Crean?" he says incredulous. "Are ye Irish at all son? Tom Crean? Ye never heard of him? One of the greatest Irishmen who ever lived? Scott of the Antarctica? No? Tom Crean was on no less than three expeditions to the Antarctic back in the day. Very famous. His picture has been put on a Norwegian aeroplane just last week."

"And what has he to do with here?"

"God but ye are far from home son," he says pitifully. "He was from this village. This was his pub. Look, take yerself over to that table there and sit down and have a read at some of those books and those newspaper things. It will open yer eyes. He was a hero, one of the bravest men ever to come out of Ireland. Go on now!"

I sit at the table, drink my coffee and scan the walls. I read the back cover of a book called 'Ice Man'; this Crean fellow apparently spent four hundred and ninety two days floating on a melting ice pack in the Antarctic Ocean. The more I read of the newspaper sections the more impressive it all sounds. I do feel a bit uneducated that I haven't heard of him before.

'A thirty five mile hike alone in severe blizzards across ice fields to save the life of his dying fellow explorer,' I read.

I must find out more about this guy when I get home.
When I get home.
This coffee is utter dishwater.
Lena...My Magdalena!
Suddenly I realise that I have to go back. I have to talk to her. I will kick myself for all time if I don't. Actually I sort of kick myself for my reaction back there in Dingle. I am annoyed that I couldn't swallow my hurt pride and go in and be normal with her and her boyfriend. What sort of a selfish, spoiled child am I that I took such a reaction to the bursting of my ego-bubble.
I down the last of Bird's Instant...it was free after all, do a quick internal salute to Tom Crean and head for the door.
The barman calls after me.
"Hi Derry! Safe home to the black north!"
I give him a wave of thanks and soon I am racing back on the road to Dingle.

Chapter 26

(Patrick McAleese)

I am back in Dingle in less than twenty minutes.
At the rear door of the Court Bar it suddenly strikes me that now, at a quarter past nine, Lena and Gaby may not be in the place. They may have decided to wander the streets, may have found another bar, may even have gone back to the Harbour House for an early night together. Oh damnation, the very thought of it! This epic journey may be all for nothing.
Doubts rise in me again. Am I wise at all? I should be in behind Gina's counter dishing out safe little honeycomb ice creams.
Anyhow, nothing for it but go in here and have a look around. I take off my helmet and gloves and open my leathers. As I push open the door I see that the room is nearly deserted; there are only one or two couples drinking around the tables of the restaurant. The sound of Irish traditional music is filtering through from the front bar and I make my way in that direction. There's a loo on my left so I visit that first, all the time thinking, "Why am I delaying this? How is this meeting going to be if she is actually in here? Will I be coming back out of here in ten minutes with my tail between my legs?"

I open the door to the crowded lounge. All eyes are pointing in the direction of a low stage which holds three musicians, each giving it all they've got; uilleann pipes, fiddle and guitar, sounding very professional. I study the backs of people's heads but there's no Lena. I move forward to see around the corner of the L-shaped bar and suddenly she is there, at the furthest end of the bar.

And at that very moment I see her raise her head and see me, stare at me through the gaps between the swaying bodies, the punters with their dark pints in hand. I simply stand there and look back at her, trying to judge her reaction. For a second I think she does not recognise me. Then her hand goes to her mouth, like she is not sure if it is me or just a doppelgänger. The expression on her face, even from this distance, is absolutely priceless. Disbelief, sheer shock, maybe even dismay. Is that a reaction to me catching her with this Gaby person? I see her hand come from her mouth and point out through the crowd and I see her lips move as she says, "Patrick?"

Then I am ploughing through the people, spilling Guinness from frothing pints and pushing large tourists out of my way. I only get halfway across when she is suddenly in my arms, holding me so tightly, whimpering like a lost child that has just been found by her daddy.

"Patrick, Patrick, Patrick!" She just keeps saying my name over and over, plus a whole string of German stuff which I haven't a clue about.

I hold her and bury my face in her hair again. I am sure people are watching all this, wondering, smiling at us, but I don't give a damn. She won't let go. She won't stop crying. I want to look at her face but she has tucked herself into my jacket and I can see or hear nothing; at the same time I am just feeling very loved, very appreciated and very confused at the same time.

"Lena," I say eventually. I speak close into her ear to be heard above the music and conversation. "Welcome to Ireland."

"How did you find me?" I more read her lips than hear her actual words.

"It was thanks to your 'Find My Friends' app. Remember?"

"Oh yes," she says. "Patrick, Patrick. I can't believe this, that you are here."

"You are not angry with me?"

"Of-course not. I am so surprised but I am happy too. Why do you think I would be angry? I could not ever be angry to see you."

"But...you are with your friend?"

She is struggling to hear me.
"Can we go to talk somewhere? This is too loud," she says.
"Sure, we can go back to the restaurant where you..." I stop there. I don't want her to know how stupid I was before.
She holds my hand and follows me as I half drag her through to the back room and the sound of the tune dies in our ears. She sits down across a table from me. She is full of questions.
"This is amazing. You are here! How long can you stay with me? I fly home in two days time."
"I have to go back to work tomorrow."
"Tomorrow? And how long is your journey taking you?"
"About eight hours, non-stop, on my bike," I tell her.
"You came on your motor cycle for eight hours today, just to see me?" She is incredulous. She reaches across the table and holds my hand again. 'This girl is changing,' I am thinking. 'Either she is losing her inhibitions or she really is massively glad to see me.'
"Actually, I left my home this morning at nine o'clock," I tell her.
"So how many...that is twelve hours of travelling, is it?"
"Well, I didn't actually ride for twelve hours...I stopped sometimes for food and....for various things, but I am here now, so that's ok, isn't it?"
"It is ok but more than ok! *Ach du meine Güte*, I can't believe it. I hoped you would come. I wanted you to come but I could not ask you...because...."
"Because of what?"
"I don't know...I was not wishing to be...how do you say? I cannot think of the words, Patrick. I did not want to make a big demand of you...because after you had talked to me at Christmas...you know? About being free, and being your own person and all this? I did not know you still wanted to be with me."
"Well, I am here now, am I not?"
"Yes you are. Oh I am so happy!"
She sure looks it too. And she proves it by getting up from the table and giving me another hug, sort of awkwardly because I am still sitting and she is bending over. I solve the thing by pulling her onto my knee and holding her around the waist again. She is so light on my knee, like a fairy girl might be, if you believed in such a thing. It feels so great to have her this close, after such a long time and such an unreal day.
I can't get over the change in her. She seems so much more content, more together as a person. So far I see none of her old

shyness or that strange vulnerability that seemed to be her main emotional characteristic. Maybe the poor girl is a bit bi-polar. Maybe it is this new relationship with...

Suddenly I remember Gaby. She hasn't mentioned him and I didn't see him in the bar, largely because I couldn't take my eyes off her.

"Hey, what about your friend, Gaby?"

"Oh he is alright. He is loving the Irish music. He will not even notice that I am gone to you."

Interesting.

"I have so much to tell you and so little time to say it; this keeps happening to us," I tell her. "It's always last minute, isn't it? Like in Albert."

"Yes, it is like then. How is your mother?"

"She is good. Almost finished her treatment and it seems to have worked. She had good news last time at the hospital."

"Thank God. I am happy for her, and for you."

"So how has your trip been? No problems?"

"Yes, no problems," she says. "Gaby had it all planned perfectly. He is very organised. You country is very beautiful. Everything is so lovely. The people are so friendly."

"Glad you think so. Next time you must come to Northern Ireland," I say. "It is even better, and even nicer people. I so want to show you around my area. You should come in the summer."

"I do not think my parents would allow me to do that. This time it is good. They know Gaby well so they were happy for this visit, but I think they would be not so happy for another trip."

"They know Gaby well then?" I say, fishing.

"Yes, he is living nearby. We are good friends for many years."

I want to ask more but it seems not to be the right time.

"Tell me about your studies, and tell me about your songs," she says, changing the subject, I think.

"Studies are fine, a bit boring at times. I haven't been writing so many songs of late...just one...about you, actually."

"Oh? I want to hear that one, please. Will you tell me?"

"It's not finished yet. I still have to write some more verses."

"I am curious," she says, then, changing the subject, "Hey, you are staying here tonight, yes?"

"I guess I am."

"Where are you going to sleep? Do you have accommodation arranged?"

"No, not yet. I haven't really thought that far ahead yet. Maybe get a room in here."

"No, not in here. You must come and stay with us. We have a booking, in a hostel nearby this place. You can sleep in our room."

Our room? They have a room together? Of-course they have. My heart sinks again and, at the same time my brain is trying to reconcile how lovely she has been to me in the last few minutes with the fact that she is sleeping with this Gaby guy.

"Thanks...ah...I don't know. That would feel too weird...like..."

At this point the door from the bar opens and Gaby puts his head in, looking around, his face showing concern. He speaks in German to her and Lena answers him easily, getting up from my knee. Then some introductions.

"Come and say hello to my friend Patrick, you know, the boy I have told you about so many times. Patrick, this is Gaby."

I stand up and shake his hand. He seems friendly enough in his greeting, no problem there; a handsome guy alright, taller and better built than me. I can see why Lena would fall for him but I am still confused about all this. She has returned my affection and with interest tonight. I could not have asked for anything more encouraging. But here is her new lover, impatient to have her back to himself.

Gaby speaks briefly to Lena in German, then to both of us in English. "It is very good, this music; very Irish, I think. I love your Irish music."

"Thanks," I say, as if taking some personal credit for it. "Glad you like it."

"Hey Gaby, Patrick has nowhere to stay tonight. I have told him he can sleep in our room. That is ok, isn't it?"

"Sure," he says. "Of-course."

Then he speaks to Lena in German again, asking a question, I'm guessing. She laughs and replies and my poor twisted mind is reading all kinds of suspicious stuff into that snippet of conversation. 'What is the German for three-some'? I wonder. It is fairly obvious that Lena's laugh is at my expense. This is just a pure bizarre situation and I am feeling well on the 'wic' side of uncomfortable.

Then Lena comes to my rescue...or at least she thinks that is what she is doing.

"Gaby is asking if we want him to sleep somewhere else," she says, "but I am telling him it is ok, yes?"

My confusion level is rising with every sentence here.

"Sure," I say, "but look, I don't want to come between you two. I can get somewhere else to sleep and see you in the morning."

Lena and Gaby give each other a slightly confused look. He says something to her, short, clipped, and her face immediately shows a moment of terror. She jumps into my arms, nearly knocking me over, hugging me like there is no tomorrow. I am totally knocked out by this, completely confused.

"No Patrick, no! You are mistaken. You cannot come between us. Gaby and I...we are not together."

"But...I thought...I'm sorry."

"No, I am sorry. I know now how this must look to you. I am so silly," she says. "We are just good friends and also...."

She stops there and looks at Gaby.

"And also," Gaby continues, "I am gay, you see. So your Lena has been very safe with me."

Oh my God; they're not... he is gay! This is a lot to take in all at the one swallow. As the whole muddy water clears in my head I find myself releasing Lena, turning to Gaby and giving him a hug. I'm not quite sure why, probably relief. He is laughing now, so is Lena.

"Gaby," I tell him, "I have never been so glad to hear that someone is gay as I am right now. I was so confused."

"I can see that," he says.

"And hey, thanks for looking after Lena."

"No problem, my pleasure," he says.

"You should be thanking him for bringing me here to you also," Lena says. "It was his idea and I could not resist when he asked me to be with him."

"Yeah, thanks for that. You did good."

"Are you sure you two do not want me to disappear to some other place tonight?" Gaby says. "I do not mind; it will give you some privacy."

I kinda like his suggestion but it's not up to me to say.

"No, do not feel like that. We will be talking and you will be asleep," Lena tells him. "It is ok, isn't it Patrick?"

"Sure," I say. "We will probably bore you to sleep anyhow."

"Fine by me," he says. "Listen, we are missing all the brilliant music. Please come back to the bar with me because there is a big Irish farmer who seems to want to get to know me better and I am not liking how he looks or how he smells. I need your company, please."

We go back to the bar.

As I buy them both beers a girl gets up from the audience and goes to the stage. She chats with the musicians and soon they are accompanying her as she sings some famous Kerry song. She is good too; big applause when she finishes.
"Anyone else now? Open mic time," says the guitarist, "after we play this next set of jigs."
Lena looks at me. I can tell straight away what is going on in her pretty head.
"No way," I say.
"Please Patrick; one song? It will make tonight even more special."
This girl can charm me to do anything she wants.
"Ok, but only if you will sing with me?"
"I will make a mess of your song," she says.
"No you won't. Sing with me. Sure nobody here knows us."
"What song?"
"The one we did on GarageBand ages ago, what's-it's-name? 'Tongue-tied', right?" I tell her.
"But...the words. I do not remember them all."
"Got them on my phone. Look! Here you go, no excuse now."
So it is that we are performing live together, for the first time on planet earth, in some Dingle pub, with not a second of rehearsal. I borrow the guy's well-battered guitar and retune. It's a lovely bight sounding Taylor. Lena drops in the harmony accompaniment at exactly the right times, her voice like honey. It works beautifully and the whole bar comes to a silent stand-still until we finish, mobile phones all over the place filming.

> *I kissed your hair and when you raised your head*
> *Your chocolate eyes melt into mine instead*
> *You did not speak, you did not move away*
> *Your smile said all that I am trying to say.*

Then it's bedlam; I've never had such a response to a song and there is nobody knows better than me that it is all down to the gorgeous voice of this beautiful eastern babe beside me, a bit to the obvious chemistry between us as well.
As I give the guitar back to its owner he sticks out his hand.
"I'm Eoghan," he says grinning, "who the hell are ye?"
I introduce myself briefly, a bit embarrassed by the applause and back-slapping.
"Ye bin singing a good while together?" he asks.

"Naw, this was a first, actually," I say.
"Ye serious?"
"Yip, a virgin run; never sung together before tonight."
"Yer having me on?"
I just smile and shake my head.
"Well, I don't know where ye found her," he says, "but whatever ye do, don't lose her. Star-quality like; she's amazing. Ye are as good a duo as I've heard in a long time."
"Cheers; lovely audience," I say.
"Where are ye from with an accent like that?"
"Coleraine in the north; she is from Germany."
"Feck sake! A long-distance act, are ye? Well, one of ye is going to have to move," he says. "I'm serious! Ye have something special there. Good luck now."
And he leaves me to go back on stage with his trad mates.

Later I am cuddled up in bed with Lena. We're both fully clothed. Gaby is asleep in the bed opposite, as far as I can tell. We chat half the night away; yeah, we kiss and stuff but it is all just so lovely and so innocent. It is just the best feeling in the world to be with this girl, to feel so loved by her. God, am I ever glad I made the journey; even more glad that I had the sense to turn around in that pub and come back here. What a mistake I nearly made.
I don't confess to her that I had initially chickened out after seeing her with a male Gaby and headed away before turning. She does talk about him though; it is all so unreal; we are lying there totally entwined around each other like we are Siamese Twins who are resisting separation and meanwhile she is chatting so warmly about this other guy in her life.
"He is the best person to be my friend," she tells me. "Always he is the first person to listen and to talk to me, when I am needing this."
This bit of the dialogue does not make me feel very good about myself, considering that I have sort of abandoned her in the last few months, but I say nothing. I let her talk; she seems to need to say so much to me and we only have tonight.
"When I was in a difficult sad time in my life Gaby was the only one of my friends who stayed with me. He was not being embarrassed to be seen with me in school or in my town. I will always thank him a lot," she says.

"So do I then, both for that and for him bringing you here to me."
She laughs softly at this and whispers in my ear.
"I did tell him all about you. It was him who was making me write the email to you, about coming to Ireland. I was too afraid to do this."
"Why would you be afraid to tell me? Imagine how I would have felt if I had found out after!"
"Yes, I know now, but before...I thought you might be annoyed, as if I am following you...how do you say? Like a stalker?"
"Oh yeah? Well, you see how annoyed I am. I am the one who came to stalk you, if you think about it."
"And I am so happy you did this," she says and we kiss again.
After, I decide to ask about what she said earlier.
"So what was this difficult time you were talking about?"
I wasn't ready for her reaction. She turned away from me in the bed, still with my arms around her but I was aware of her body becoming hard, like taut and quivering a little at the same time.
"Sorry Lena...I shouldn't have asked. I wouldn't have mentioned it except that you did...hey girl, I'm sorry; come back to me."
She did, slowly, and I stroked her hair and her face in the darkness until I felt the rigidity melt and her feminine softness return.
"Please don't ask me Patrick. Not now. I am so happy now. I do not want to spoil this moment. I want you to keep liking me and so I cannot speak..."
"Listen, nothing you can tell me will change me liking you," I say.
"Ok, and sometime it will be right for me to tell you, but not tonight."
"No problem, babe. I just want to know everything about you."
"And I want to know all about you too. Like, why you play guitar so well, and how you can write these amazing songs? How have you become this person?"
I think about this, half-smothered by her hair stranded across my face, drowning in the wonderfully natural scents of her body.
"I don't know," I say. "Just something inside me feels I have to do it; I have to let these words out of their cage, get these tunes out through my fingers. If I didn't, they would sort of stagnate inside and poison me, does that make sense?"
"Then you must keep doing it. After this night I cannot think of you being poisoned. I cannot be losing you again."
We are still going well after four in the morning. When I mention her family though, she tells me she is getting too tired to talk and that I will just have to meet them myself, which is near enough an invitation, I think. Just before she falls asleep in my arms, spooned

tightly into each other, she half-turns and says, "You have to come to me, you know this, don't you? You have to be with me in my place."

"Yeah, I do sort of know this Lena, and I will come, I promise you. I just don't know how or when. I need to get some money together first. That may take a while."

"No, it cannot be a while. I cannot think that it will be so long again. Please? This summer? Please Patrick, promise me? I need you to be with me."

She bends her arm up so her hand can grab my ear, gently but firmly.

"I will try."

"This summer, promise me?"

"OK, I promise."

This obviously deserves another episode of intimacy and she spins back around to me. Then half way through a long kiss she seems to doze off. No shame for her, after cycling all day and chatting to this time, so I don't take it too personally.

'What have I just promised?' I think, as I drift off, three hours before my phone alarm is set to go off.

🎼

It is 8.15am. I am riding back through Annascaul, past the gaudy front of 'South Pole Inn'. I do a kind of internal salute of appreciation to the place, to the determined spirit of old Tom Crean or whatever it was that persuaded me to turn back last night. Life changing. To think that I nearly missed it too. Incredible! Thank you God....or whoever looks after these things. Actually, just wipe the 'God' bit. It can't be anything to do with someone who doesn't exist, can it? Chance? Maybe...just sounds way too haphazard.

I am experiencing something I have never felt in my entire life, a rush of feeling I have never had before and one I half-hope will never leave me. I say 'half-hope', because there is a downside to this feeling; a physical pain which seems to rise and fall somewhere deep in my chest, kind of like the swell of the sea beside me as I fly along this pretty much deserted road. Every time I let my mind go back to Lena's goodbye kiss this hurt throbs up in me. I had no idea that falling in love and knowing I am loved back in the same way, to the same degree, would have this intense physicality about it. It hurts, yeah, it really hurts...but in the most life-affirming way. I am

smiling ear to ear inside the shell of my black helmet, sometimes even laughing out loud to myself, like I can't quite believe what just happened.
So this is it? This is how it feels to have fallen in love? Wow, just pure bloody WOW!
I want to stop at a viewpoint overlooking a long strand down to my right, not so much to look at the scenery, more to attempt some lyrics to try to put a cordon of words around the essence of this feeling, so as not to lose it sort of, but I know I don't have time if I am to make it back north for the evening shift.
I ride on. I am absolutely flying, both in terms of the bike and in my thoughts. I feel I could easily do the ton along here; everything is so extreme, so vibrant, so real. But I catch myself on and slow down a bit; no point in killing myself right now, now that I am on the emotional high of real love for the first time. Yeah, the first time; every other time was just me trying, experimenting, lusting, fancying somebody, nothing much returned. With Lena this is so different; it is the fact that she feels the same way, that she loves me, that she needs me so much. Last night was the best night of my life...and we didn't even make love; but I know we will, sometime soon, I just know we will, and it will be perfect because it is love and it will be in the knowing that we somehow strangely belong to each other, that this is all meant to be and has been, right from the start, from that first second I saw her on my iPad. Lena Rosenthal, my God, Lena Rosenthal...you are the most fabulous girl on the planet....and you are mine!
The feeling does not leave me as I roar into Tralee.
I start to fantasise about being with Lena in her country, walking an alpine track beside a rushing river in some idyllic valley, alone together, high in the mountains, away from the world, just the two of us. Can I make it happen? Can I somehow manage to come up with a way of getting to Germany this summer? What on earth will my mother say about it? Actually, you know what, she might be perfectly ok with it; she has been very understanding of all this recently, very supportive. I should give her a ring to say I'm alright and I will be home by about four or five this afternoon.
So I pull into a service station beyond Tralee and phone her. She seems to be delighted that I do, full of questions, especially about Lena. I have to cut her off.
"Mum, this call is costing me a fortune. Sure I'll see you tomorrow."
She hangs up reluctantly.

God love her, I think she is getting some vicarious pleasure from me and Lena, in the absence of any real love in her own life. Now there's a thought I never had before. How would I feel if she found somebody else? Well, if it would make her as happy as this has made me, let it roll.
Lena, Lena.
A lyric is kicking off in my head, like it or not.

> *I will come to you, Lena*
> *We will walk in the mountains*
> *I will come to taste your honey*
> *Lie with you in a valley of flowers.*

Chapter 27

Bernie Doherty

It's driving me mad, this need to know what he got up to when he was in Kerry. But all he wants to talk about is this daft notion that he could go to Germany this summer. He's been on about it till he has my head deeved.

"How's your money situation? You'd have more need to be working here all summer, would you not?"

"Sure am I not doing every hour I can get at the minute and I'll keep on doing that until the end of June. Then I'll go.

"You haven't a clue, son. How do you think you will you survive money-wise when you are there? It's not like you can learn German and get a job."

No response, just that wee half shake of the head.

"That was a question Patrick. Seriously, you can't expect me to be bailing you out at your age. How will you get money?"

"Busking."

My face turns into a question mark. "Busking", *he says, like he has all this thought out, costed, business-planned, risk-assessed and all.*

"Busking?" *I say.*

"Yeah, busking; me and Lena are good together Mum," *he tells me.* "Honestly. You should hear us. We could make enough to get by on."

"Busking where?"

"In the cities. Tourist places, stations, things like that. Try and get some gigs in cafes and clubs."

"Do you even know if it is legal? They might have rules against street singers over there, d'you ever think of that?"

"Lena is going to find out. It may be we have to get a licence or something. She's checking it all out. She's mad keen to do it."

"I'll bet she's mad keen to do it," I say. "She's just mad keen altogether."

He looks a me a bit accusingly, disappointed. Did he seriously expect me to be jumping up and down with delight at the idea of him disappearing for the whole summer to play music in Middle-Europe? He hasn't got a baldy.

"Did you get to do it together down in Kerry," I ask, no sarcasm, no innuendo intended…well, not much anyway.

He turns away but I catch the ghost of a half-smile at the side of his mouth as he does. 'So he did,' I think.

"Yeah, we sang a song together in the pub in Dingle," he covers. "Mum, you have no idea how well it went down. She brought the place to a standstill. It was a noisy bar, full of tourists, all chattering away but when we were halfway into the first verse of the song it all went quiet, totally quiet….until the end. Even the bar staff were listening. You should have seen it. This man afterwards, one of the musicians, he was raving on about it. He said we could go anywhere."

"Anywhere? So you think Germany? He probably meant like Tralee, or Derry or somewhere. You pick Germany?"

"Yip, cos that's where Lena is."

"Aye and if she was on Mars you'd be phoning Elon Musk to book a flight by the sounds of it."

He just laughs at me.

"You might actually be right there," he says and I realise that I know all I need to know now. This is serious. I've lost him to this lassie, possibly for good. Auf Wiedersehen pet!

"Last heard of busking in Bavaria," I say as I struggle up and go to make the dinner. "Well, it has a ring to it, that's for sure."

He follows me to the kitchen. Unheard of. What's coming now?

"Mum," he says.

"That's me."

"She is…she is…brilliant."

"Good," I say, "brilliant at what? Singing like?"

"I just mean that you will love her; she is the nicest person I've ever met."

I make a conscious decision to switch from my default Derry sarcasm and give the chap a chance. At least he is talking openly about her for the first time in the month since he saw her in Kerry.

"That's nice, Patrick," I say as I stick the pizza in the oven. "I'm glad for you, really I am. It's lovely to see you smiling. And well done for going all the way down there to see her. It was mad like, but I'm sure she was very chuffed."

"She was. Very surprised at first but it was cool to see her looking really happy for a change."

"Why, does she not normally look happy?"

Ah, nice...he's actually setting the table.

"Not really; she generally had a whole sort of sadness going on when I met her, even right through last year. I was thinking about that on the way home from uni yesterday, just the change in her. She is like a new version of herself."

"Maybe it was just seeing you again?" I suggest.

"It wasn't that; even when I watched her at first, that night in the pub in Dingle, before I surprised her like...she seemed more...more happy, less tense. You could see it in her eyes. They seemed to...like, have a light in them all the time. That was different."

"Well, I'm glad you are both happy. And I am looking forward to meeting her sometime."

"Really? But you don't want me going to her in the summer?"

"It's not that I don't want you to see her. It's just that... Germany seems a long way away. And with all this terrorism stuff going on. Europe is a dangerous place nowadays. I'll be worried sick about you until you are back home and safe."

"But wherever you go now there's always that sort of threat. Sure look at Manchester and London. You would think you would be safe going to a pop gig for wee girls or going out for a walk on a London bridge but look what happened there, and that's in the UK. Germany seems pretty quiet recently. Anyway, I can look out for myself, and she knows the place, we'll be grand."

"Just because it's been quiet means nothing. You young ones! Yous have no idea what it was like to live through the troubles and the police and the army and checkpoints and constant searches. Your generation has never had to go through all that. When I was your age, you'd be walking through Derry and there'd be a car sitting on its own along the street and automatically you'd think, "That could be a car bomb!" So you'd cross over the road and hurry past it just in case."

"Agh ma, that's ancient history," he says. "The world has moved on."

"No way son. We may have moved on a bit in this country but with all this ISIS stuff kicking off... And it's places like Germany that's the target for them. That and France, and England, pretty much everywhere."
"So the logic of that is to go to some wee island off the coast of Donegal and keep goats and catch fish."
"Not a bad idea. Apparently the Germans all seem to love it over there so your girl will be happy."
"No way ma; you can't let the buggers get you down. Life has to go on. Anyway, do you not think I am better to be going now before Theresa gets us a Brexit that will have us all boxed in behind some sort of permanent electric fence?"
He has the table ready and is standing with his back to me, looking into the larder. I haven't quite given up yet though.
"And have you thought where you are going to stay?"
He is quiet for a moment, shifting stuff about on the shelves.
"Is there no tomato ketchup?"
"Sorry, forgot to get it. Do without it for once."
"You can't eat pizza without ketchup. I'll go over to the shop. Where's your purse?"
"It's through there..."
He's gone.
This conversation has me in swithers. I am delighted that he is talking to me about his girl and, if I am honest I am well proud of him and happy that he has found love, finally. He's had plenty of disappointments. I was worried he was a bit of a slow learner on that score. So, yeah, I am really pleased and relieved for him. On the other hand I can't help dwelling on all the negatives. He is only nineteen after all; he hasn't much of a clue about so many things...and she is even younger if I mind right. It is very young to be falling so totally in love. I had always thought it would blow over, like most of those 'holiday romances' generally do. I had been fairly confident that the cyber connections between them that had been cooling over the winter would stop altogether. Another couple of months and their contact would have totally fizzled out. It would have died a natural death in the face of all the obstacles between them. Then the boul lassie makes a move that neither him nor me could have seen coming; she arrives in Ireland. And the rest is history. Or maybe it is less 'history' and more 'the shape of things to come'. You can't really predict these things. I, of all people, should know that.
The front door bangs behind him.
"I shoulda told you to bring milk."
"Too late. I'm famished. Get it after."

We sit opposite each other across the tablecloth and get stuck into Tesco's Stonebaked Margherita with a quick mixed salad.
I still have things to ask him, now that he is in the mood to talk.
"So, going back to my question..."
"What question?"
"Where are you going to stay in Germany?"
"Don't know yet. Lena is going to ask her folks. At the start I might be able to stay with them, just while I find a flat or a hostel somewhere. I'll be grand."
"And getting there? Where do you fly to? Munich or somewhere? Is that near her?"
"Yeah, it's not far away, but I am sort of thinking that if I had my bike there it would save a lot on travel. And we could ride around the place and explore."
"And how would you get your bike over there?"
"It's not great pizza this."
"How would you get your bike over there?" I try again.
"Ride it over."
I look at him. 'Aghast' I think is the word they would write in the old novels.
"You are not serious? Do you know how far it is? Have you any idea what the traffic is like? And the rules of the road over there?"
"Well, like I said, I'm only thinking about it. Don't you be worrying yourself."
"But that's my job, son. Worrying. It's all I have left to do. Worry about you and your sister. What else would I think about?"
After a couple of seconds he gets up and comes around the table to me and, suddenly and unexpectedly, gives me a hug from behind.
"I'm sorry mum," he says. "You shouldn't be worrying. You're already beating the cancer thing. You should be happy. You owe it to yourself now to be happy. You only have one life and you're surely not meant to go through it worrying."
"Yeah, Confucius he say..."
He laughs and goes back to his seat.
"Look, since I found Lena, since I know we are meant for each other...it has changed my head on a lot of things. It's what life is all about, do you not think? Love! That's what I started to realise that day on the way home. It kinda hit me when I was riding past Ballinasloe."
"Ballinasloe? You saw the light riding past Ballinasloe, did you? Not a lot of people would admit to that, I'm betting."
"Likely not. And then I thought about you."
"How'd you mean?"

"Well, you haven't had these kind of feelings for years, not since Dad and you. So it just hit me how hard that is for you. How hard it must have been for you, on your own, no love in your life, just us two to be looking after and worrying about. You must have been so lonely."

I am quiet. This is lovely of him. I feel a lump rise in my throat. I put my elbows on the table and my head in my hands. I can't think of anything to say. It is a special moment, realising that Patrick has this kind of depth to him, this empathy, and in some way it is down to him finding this new love in his own life.

"So, I want to say this, mum," he goes on. "You have done brilliantly through this cancer thing. You are really strong..."

"You think?" I say into my hands. "Don't feel that strong. Just sick mainly. I'm tired all the time and I can't help wondering if I will ever have the energy to go back to work."

"You will, of-course you will. How many more weeks have you of the radio stuff?"

"Finish next week, so just three more days on that blasted train to Belfast. I can't wait to see the back of it."

"We'll have a night out somewhere when it's all over and you start getting back to your normal self, alright? Eat out somewhere...on me? Maybe Josie will come down," he tells me.

I look up and smile at my new Patrick.

"Nice idea son, but are you not saving up for some trip away or something?"

"Yeah. 'Course, but that doesn't matter. We'll go to that new Italian place."

"For a real pizza like?"

He laughs. Then he goes into that serious mode again. After a while he asks me the strangest question.

"Do you think you'll ever be with anyone else?"

My God, what a thing to hear...from my son!

"Jesus, Patrick! What sort of a question is that?" I say, a bit gob-smacked.

"Just wondering. Like...how do you see the future? It's ok by me if you do, by the way."

"That is nice of you to tell me that, but the chance would be a fine thing, as the man says. You can maybe be keeping your eyes open for me in Germany, eh? Now that would fairly get under your father's skin, wouldn't it?"

"Yeah, and you'd love that, wouldn't you?"

"Naw, I'm past all that. Time was I'd have jumped at the chance, just to sicken him; it just never happened, that's all."

He watches me as I clear the table.

"Do you ever wonder how your life would have turned out if you'd married somebody else, like some fella from the Creggan or somewhere?"

"Wonder about it all the time. You wouldn't be here for one thing."

"Or maybe I'd be selling programmes at the Brandywell and spying for the dissidents outside the police station on Strand Road, like my cousins."

"Don't say that Patrick. And Phelim isn't your cousin."

"Ok, second cousin then," he says, standing up from the table. "What a tube. Caught taking pictures of policemen's cars! I have a right collection of relatives, when you think about it, don't I? It's like the world's weirdest human zoo."

He starts a mock tour-guide. "'In this pen, folks, we have the lesser-spotted British Army Corporal, and next door, his close cousin, the Orange-sashed UDA volunteer, not to be confused with the Red-handed UVF Hero in a cage further along. Now over here on the other side of the path, behind the barbed wire, we have the Real-IRA Dissident, off-spawn of a Provo father and a Cumann na mBan mother!'"

"Goodness, you have a way with words when you take the notion," I tell him as he disappears from the kitchen to his FaceTime friend.

He isn't far wrong in his thinking about this disaster of an extended family he finds himself part of.

And his query about how my life might have been different if I hadn't fallen for his father; that thought lived in my head for years. It nearly drove me to Gransha, so much so that I had counselling for it, it and other worries. The 'What ifs?' of life had me tied in knots, the regrets about my choices, the fact that I had been so cut off from my family. All the more isolating because we had been such a close crowd. You couldn't have put a sheet of paper between any of us when I was growing up. And then I kinda drove an armoured car through the middle of us. That was the expression my mother used at the time. I'll never forget it.

Yeah, I made the wrong choice, I know that, and my life narrowed away down to a straight-jacket because of it, especially after Robbie left. But for years I didn't see it. I was loyal to him. I even tried to see the whole Irish thing from his point of view, the pride in his 'wee province', the loyal British subject, Queen and country. It was only very seldom we would argue about it all, mainly because he would get so mad, so unreasonable.

I was thinking about this the other day when those wives or women of the dead London terrorists were rounded up by the police. Do they all believe the Islamic propaganda? Are they big supporters, ready to die themselves in the cause? Or are they just caught up in the situation, kind of the way I was? Trapped by the dominant male? Trapped by misguided love and loyalty?

It was good to see the mother of one of the killers talk about her sorrow for the victim's families and offer her apologies. I wonder will she suffer in her own community as a result? It was certainly very hard back in the day for any of the Derry mothers to come out and condemn the terrible things that the IRA did, like the time they made Patsy Gillespie drive the bomb in his van to the border and blew him to pieces. I mind arguing about that in school. I was seventeen at the time and it just seemed like we were stooping to non-human methods to fight the British. Most women and girls I knew were horrified by it but could anybody speak out? You had to be brave to do that.

Then I go and fall in love with a soldier!

I was lucky. I managed to get away from Derry before I was tarred and feathered like so many girls I had heard of. What was it about fancying a soldier anyway? Was it the uniform? Was it the sense of danger, the subtle musk of khaki and testosterone? It certainly wasn't about his politics or his religion or his values, nor the fact that he carried a gun and may have shot people, for all I knew. No, it was just an irrational, 'crazy little thing called love', as Queen used to sing.

So what I am thinking is this. If it happened to his mother maybe it is somehow in the blood, Patrick falling in love across the fence, I mean. In his case it is a lot easier in some ways. I had the weight of Irish history lying against me. He only has to contend with geography, the distance between him and her, and of-course language, and nationality....though I gather she isn't all that sure herself where she is from or who she belongs to. Maybe neither is Patrick, come to think of it. Maybe that is why they are so drawn to each other. Maybe they'll be really good for each other. That's all I can hope and pray for anyhow.

Chapter 28

Patrick McAleese is with **Barry Kennedy** at **72 Bannview Close, Coleraine**
Sat 11th June 2017

Barry has been round with me since early this morning; far too early, but he wanted to see the Lions match and he doesn't have Sky. I probably wouldn't have bothered watching it; (like hel-looo, it's half eight on a Saturday morning), but I couldn't really turn him down. It wasn't much of a game either, though the Lions won at least. It probably didn't help his appreciation of it that I kept interrupting to chat about the result of Thursday's General Election.

"Shut the frick up about the election, for frick's sake," he ranted. That's how into rugby he gets. 'Frick' is his current go-to expletive, btw...Jeez! As if me asking his opinion about the DUP going into government with the Tories was going to put Owen Farrell off his kick!

"I don't think he can hear me," I whispered.

Anyhow, at the end of the game my ma backs her way through the door from the kitchen, two big plates in her hands. The smell hits us even before she speaks.

"Anybody up for a fry?" she says.

Barry sits forward, eyes lit up. "Happy days! Can't beat an Ulster fry."

"Barry's vegetarian," I tell her.

"No way man. That's great. Thanks Bernie," and we tuck in.

I go back to the election.

"But don't you think it's great like, being able to have a general election without any Russian interference?"

Barry thinks about this.

"Maybe there was though? Maybe it just hasn't had any press covfefe yet!"

Haha Barry, very droll. We are still laughing at that one when my phone twangs, a FaceTime call coming in.

Lena! Brill, but at this time of the day? It's not even eleven in the morning. Usually we chat at night. I hope nothing is wrong.

As Lena and I start chatting Barry looks a bit uncomfortable and seems to start to cram his fry in, as if to get out of my space. I signal to him that it's ok, I'm not in a bother. In fact I kind of like it that he will get to meet Lena. So I tell him to chill.

"Lena, I have my friend Barry here. You wanna say 'Hello' to Barry?"

"Ja, sure," she says, as I turn the screen around so they can see each other.

Big mistake!

"Hi," Barry says, his gub full of bacon and beans.

"Hi, I am Lena. It is nice to meet you."

Good for her; not too put out by this interference of a stranger in our conversation.

Not so good from Barry though.

"Ah, right...but hang on," he says, looking at me with a daft grin on his face just above a dribble of bean-juice. "You're a different Lena to the last one he introduced me to."
Jeez Barry, give me that phone; that isn't funny. Cross-cultural humour like that could bring a crisis in international relations here. I am fighting with him for the phone which he is holding up out of my reach, giggling away like a twelve-year old.
"Let me speak to her Maca," he insists. "I never even got a good look at her."
"Give me the phone, you muppet!"
What on earth must Lena be making of this, the images flying across the screen, the shouting. She's probably disconnected by now. I can't grab the phone off him. I decide to cool it and let him have his moment of twisted fun. He holds the phone at arm's length so I can't get it but also so Lena can see us both. He's grinning away like a fool.
"Sorry Lena; that wasn't fair," he says. "I was just taking the mick. It's nice to meet you too."
Lena looks quietly dour, understandably bewildered.
"Patrick?" she says.
"Don't mind him. He's just an idiot."
Barry still has the phone though.
"Maca never shuts up about you Lena, so it is nice to see that you are actually real."
"Real? How are you meaning?"
"Like, he didn't just make you up. You know? His imaginary girlfriend from Germany that nobody has ever seen. 'Cause he's full of it you know; all the stories, all the conquests."
"Conquests? I do not understand you."
"He's just trying to be funny," I tell her. "Don't listen to him."
"When are you coming to Northern Ireland Lena, so we can get to meet you in person?"
That's a bit better Barry.
"Maybe some day," she tells him, "but Patrick is coming to me here in Bavaria...soon. If you allow him..."
Good for her, a bit of comeback.
"Yeah, so he tells me. But how do you feel about me coming as well?" He gives me a sideways look, faking worry. "Oh, sorry. Maybe he hasn't told you about that yet...he has asked me to come too?"
She absorbs this for a second. I wonder is she believing him.
"Ja, you must come as well," she says laughing.

I take the phone. "Time to say your goodbyes and let me talk to my lady in peace."
He gathers up his plate and heads to the kitchen door.
"See you Lena. I am dismissed. Good to meet you," he tells her.
"He is a strange boy," Lena says.
"He's a head-case."
"Why does he call you this strange name... Maca or something?"
"That's just my nickname around here. Actually, it's my stage name as well, when I perform."
"And he is your friend?"
"Yeah, for ages. He's hard work sometimes. Good lad though."
"But not a good way of being funny I think. He makes me worried by his jokes."
"Yeah, but you do know he was just trying to be the clown, don't you?"
"I think so. Are you ok?"
"Yeah, all good. What's the craic with you then? Everything alright? This is early for you."
"Yes, everything is good. I am away from home at one o'clock today for a while, so I cannot be talking to you tonight. So... now?"
"Ok, that's good for me," I tell her.
"I have been finding out about busking. And I have a place where you could stay, for some time perhaps. And I have to ask you if have you booked your flights yet?"
"Flights? No, I have a different plan now."
"What is this?"
"Well, I was thinking...how are we going to get around when I am there? Like travelling to different places, seeing around, going to perform? You don't have a driving licence yet, and we can't expect your folks to take us around. Buses and trains? Maybe but the cost would be high and times wouldn't always suit."
"So what?"
"I am going to bring my Suzuki, my bike. Take the ferry to Scotland, travel down England, through the Eurotunnel and ride to Munich. What do you think?"
She seems a bit bemused by this as she thinks it over.
"At least we will have a way of getting around together, you behind on the back of the bike, hanging on to my guitar."
"Yes that is good. I have been riding behind on a bike before. It is good; but your journey? Is it expensive? More than flying to Munich?" she asks.

"It's dearer than flying alright, but it gives us freedom to have our own transport, don't you think? We'll not be depending on anyone. We can go where we want."
"It sounds good. We can do whatever we like, when we want to."
She is smiling in her eyes; I can see it, that awesome smile.
"But you must be careful when you are riding. It is a very long journey. I will pray for you every second when you are coming."
I laugh but I do like the thought of that. I so love talking to this girl.
"Right. And busking? Did you find out anything? Munich?"
"Munich is difficult. The municipal people give out permits for certain players, at certain times...and I am not sure how to get these. We could go to the main office in the city and ask."
"Maybe perform for them, live like?"
"Better if we give a CD, or send them a song online perhaps?"
"A CD? Now there's an idea!" I say, thoughtful. She picks up on this.
"What are you thinking?"
"I'm thinking, why don't we record a couple of songs and have them on disc to sell to people?"
"Sell? Which people?"
"Punters, tourists, people who listen to us, folk in pubs or cafes if we can play there, anybody who's interested, you know?"
"Do you think this will be possible? How will we..."
"That's not a problem," I tell her, enthusiasm growing by the second.
"Sure didn't you sing a harmony on to my song, remember?"
"Ja, but the quality is not enough I think?"
"True, but I have a way around that this year," I tell her.
"What is this way around?"
"I will go to my university. They have brilliant studios there for recording."
"They will allow this, you think?"
"Of-course. It can be part of my coursework. They'll love it, Gerry especially; he's the main engineer; he's dead on; we get on well."
"So how would it happen?"
"Just like the last time. I'll put down some basic music, you listen to it on your phones, sing along and record your voice on a separate device. Then send it back and I can work on it. What do you think?"
"I think you have brilliant ideas," she laughs. "Sure, we can try this."
"Cool," I say. "What song would you like to sing? Can't really be covers if we are putting them on CD or online."
She looks puzzled.

"No, your songs of-course. I do not write songs. Not yet. Just some stupid poems."

"We need to work on that, your songs," I tell her. "We can do that over the summer."

"And you must also send me some songs you want me to sing with you. Perhaps I do not know them and I must practice," she says.

"Yeah sure, but you'll know some. 'Nothing Compares To You'? You know it?"

"I do not think so, but I can learn it. Do you like 'City of Stars'?"

"'City of Stars' from 'La La Land'?" I say, a bit surprised. "Never thought of that. You like it, the film?"

"I really love it," she says. "It is a great duo song. It is piano, but I think you can play it on guitar? We could do it so well, do you think?"

"Sure," I hear myself saying. "Just as long as you don't ask me to dance with you at the same time."

She grins. "If you like it I can teach you some Bavarian dances."

"Ok but I draw the line at wearing that weird national costume your men wear, remember that."

"Ah, our *Lederhosen*; I am disappointed," she laughs.

"How about places to play?"

"Ja, I will make some phone calls. We have some beautiful towns nearby. I can try some cafes and bars."

"Great. We need plenty of chances to earn money."

"Yes but we will live with not much spending as well, you think so?"

"Of-course. What did you say about where I should stay? Your folks aren't up for me staying at your house?"

She looks a bit resigned as she answers this.

"I have tried to speak to them about this. It is not easy to explain. They are...how do you say? There is a word but I cannot remember it. Old in their opinions? The church reasons? That you should not be sleeping in the house of your girlfriend. My father will explain to you, if you like."

"No, no. It's alright," I say. "I don't have a problem with that. As long as he is happy enough for you to be with me and doesn't mind having me around."

"That part is ok, I think. So he has asked the parents of Gaby."

"Asked them what?"

"That you stay there."

"You serious? Me stay with Gaby? I don't have a problem with that, he's a really nice guy like but..." I tail off, wondering how all this is going to look, actually wondering if she is having me on.
"Gaby will be away in the mountains during the summer; he has work there. His family has a small house beside their home, a guest house or room, do you understand? For visitors to sleep in if they have come a long way, grandparents and people of the family."
"Ah, I see; we call it a 'granny-flat'. Is that what you mean? Sounds great. And it's near you; we can eat there and have our own space?"
"I hope so. They will make a small charge. You think this is ok?"
"Sounds brilliant to me. Well done. My mother will be happy."
"I will also be happy. You will be near me. It is on the same street."
"I can't wait Lena. I will book my ferry crossings for the last two days of June, so I should be with you early in July."
"Awesome," she says.
"What did you just say?"
"Awesome! It is my new American word. You like it?"
"Not really, but then I guess that they have all the best words on the planet right now, best words folks, you know this, right?" I say, going into my Trump persona. "Nobody got any better words! Period!"
She looks a bit puzzled by this.
"I do not understand," she says. "But I have another question. How will you bring your guitar? Not on your bike I think?"
"Ah yeah. I don't want to risk bringing it on the bike."
"So what will you do?"
"Buy one when I get there; maybe a second hand one in a charity store or something. Or borrow one, if you know anybody who has one that they don't use," I tell her.
"Ok, I will try."
We chat on for a while until Barry sticks his head back in to say he is leaving. Lena and I say our goodbyes a bit too quickly and she blows me a kiss as her image freezes, a comical-looking sight. I take a screen shot to tease her with when I see her.
Barry is waiting for me in the back garden, chatting to my ma who's hanging up washing. He is trying to do keep-ups with my basketball but he's useless at it.
"You shoulda warned me, Paddy," he says.
"Warned you? About what?"
"Your woman. She's a bit of a babe like, pretty exotic! Way too hot for you, mate."
"Pretty exotic?" I repeat, laughing at him.

"I have to hand it to you, she's well cool mate. I can see you staying in Germany. What do you think Bernie?"
My ma laughs her dry smoker's cackle.
"Not on your nelly Barry. He'd miss his oul mammy too much. Can't see Lena washing his dirty boxers for him, can you?"
"Not if she has any sense," he says. "Toxic."

Chapter 29

Bernie Doherty

The home phone rings just as I am about to start into washing a pile of bedclothes. I ignore it for a bit, thinking it is likely another nuisance call; who else phones you on your home phone nowadays. It's definitely not Patrick; he generally calls my mobile, if I am lucky enough to merit contact. But when it keeps ringing I pick it up.
"Hello, can I speak to Maca please?" *Male voice, businesslike.*
"Maca? You mean my Patrick?"
"Is that his name? Patrick? When he plays in bar he's 'Maca'."
"Well he was christened Patrick," *I tell him.*
"Whatever. Can I speak to him?"
I dodge the question. "Sorry, he's not around at the minute."
"And when he will be around? I've been trying his mobile but he's not answering." *A touch of sarcasm and frustration there.*
"Ah right. Well he won't be around for a couple of months, if that is any use to you," *I tell him.*
"How do you mean? Won't be around for a couple of months?"
"Who is this?"
"It's Joe here, from Sailors. I was wanting to talk to him about these gigs this week," *he says; I have a bit of a sinking feeling coming over me.*
"Ah Joe," *I say.* "Well, he is away for the summer you see."
"Away where? He's supposed to be doing three evenings for me here. In the back bar. We talked about it weeks ago. With the Irish Open on in Portstewart there'll be plenty of fans around. I'm sort of relying on him. Any chance you can get in touch and remind him?"

"I can get in touch with him certainly, but it's not going to be easy for him to do it for you. He is on his way to Germany at the minute you see."

"Germany! For the love of...What is he playing at? We had agreed this, months ago, more. Does he not want the work or what?"

"I am sorry Joe. He never said a thing to me about playing this week. He must have forgotten all about it. His head is on other things at the minute," I tell him.

I can sense his annoyance; it is going to be hard to pacify him without any eye to eye contact. He rants on about how is he going to fill this gap at such short notice.

"The thing starts this Thursday. His head must be in cuckoo-land. And he didn't even notice the buzz around the place?"

"He's away since last Wednesday. Cheaper to travel in June, do you see?"

"Good Lord! He coulda had a couple of gigs a night this week, made himself a wee fortune. And you say he's in Germany? What on earth is he doing in Germany?"

"Busking," I tell him.

"Well tell him from me just to stay there and busk to his heart's content for he is no use to me if I can't rely on him!"

Phone slam. Like I am to blame for this?

Patrick McAleese! Just wait 'til I give your ear a good wigging next time you mind to phone home.

I have been texting him every few hours, just to check where he is and if he's made it safe to his Lena. He hasn't always replied, his excuse being that he's been travelling; it seemed to take him days but now that he has reached this Fremdenheim place he might give me a ring. I don't want to be the fussy mother, always phoning him, nevertheless this call from Joe needs to make its way into his forgettery of a brain. So I text him.

> R u ok? Just had Joe on phone mad @u 4 missin gigs u promised 2 do during this golf week? Ring a bell? Txt him XO Mum

'Him and his imaginary musical career!' I say out loud to myself as I hit play on the CD player. Yet again I find myself listening to his recording, for the umpteenth time since he presented me with this going-away-gift, his first CD; well, his and Lena's of-course. He had a whole boxful of them strapped on the pillion seat of his bike when he left. He is so proud of these two songs and so he should be; even the design of the sleeve itself is clever, a graphite sketch of their two faces, very stark but sensitive at the same time. The way it's been done, it seems that the sketches have actually been drawn on the body of a guitar. Apparently Lena did the design and the sketches, based on screenshots they took while FaceTiming each other. He posted this cover picture on Instagram and it's had a bunch of 'Likes' already. The title of the CD, 'MacaLena', is Patrick's idea. How cosy, the two nicknames wrapped around each other like that!

Yeah, him and his Lena. And him and his music!

I had reconciled myself to his choice last year to change from a History course to do Music. I had talked myself into the notion that he is better to be happy and fulfilled in his creative wee bubble than to be studying for a subject that he might be bored with and that, with the best will in the world, could really only lead him into teaching, which I can't really picture him doing, that or journalism or something. Now I am seriously doubting the whole idea.

'Wains! They fry my brain,' I say as I start on the larder spring-clean, several months late of-course.

As I work I listen to his 'Tongue-tied' and 'Angles', over and over again. I have found myself singing along, the tune anyhow. I sit down, exhausted by the wee bit of housework I've done and follow the lyrics more closely. Actually, now I think about it, I have actually forgotten that this is my son singing here, my Patrick, yeah, and his girlfriend. It's a complicated feeling, a mixture of amazement, disbelief and pure pride in how good he is. It's just a pity he is so far away.

My phone pings.

Text from him. Good.

> Chill ma. I left msg for Joe in bar; not my fault he didn't get it. All gud here; closing in on Frankfurt; I'll b with Lena in a few hrs; hot though. U doin ok? X

Yeah, I am doing ok son. I'm doing brilliant on my own here, my daughter sunning herself with her mates in Tenerife and him heading to his Lena in Germany. I'm doing fantastic considering that it is three weeks since my last radio-therapy and I haven't the energy of a dead battery. And I haven't a clue yet whether or not it has worked or if the cancer will come back at me again. I'm grand with the fact that none of the Derry ones even bothered to come over to see *me during the whole business, not even Majella, though she did phone a couple of times. I'm over-the-moon with the thought that I will be back in my dead-end job at the end of this month, witnessing people signing their wills and stuffing meaningless documents in various filing cabinets. I'm totally happy with the fact that I haven't had a man look at me, never mind love me, for the past ten bloody years. Yeah, apart from wondering what this is all for, I'm doing ok son.*

I suppose I have a lot to be thankful for. When you see those poor scared people from the Grenfell Tower and the horror of it written all over their faces. So many lives destroyed forever by that terrible inferno. Yeah, I haven't got much to be complaining about, have I?

Looking back on it, I was proud of myself for how I handled the cancer scare. I had far more courage than I ever imagined I would have in me during those months. It helped me to get through it to have Josie and Patrick to focus on; I had to have a positive attitude for their sakes. I had to give myself a future to be thinking about and planning for, something to have hope about.

Now it is here, that future, and it's a bit more lonely than I had bargained for.

Door-bell and my neighbour Alison beyond it.

"Are ye comin' for a dander while it's dry, Bernie? This dog has been gerning all morning; it near enough has the arms pulled outa me!"

"Aye, I'll come," I say and I go back to get my jacket, Patrick's tune and words running through my head like a drug. 'Light a flame within her darkness, Save her from her mystery.'

Chapter 30

(Patrick McAleese)

How totally embarrassing.
The first thing I say to Lena's parents is completely wrong, I think, and has them looking at each other, (and at Lena), strangely.
I suppose I am trying to make a good impression from the start. I had looked up how to say 'Hello; how are you?' and so on.
Nothing could go wrong with that, right?
Wrong!
The 'Hello' bit is fine, a simple 'Hallo'.
Ok so far.

Then I try something a bit more complicated but doable, in my naive opinion. I try to say, 'How are you Mr Rosenthal, Mrs Rosenthal? It is a pleasure to meet you.'

I had looked this up online and rehearsed it over and over. At this point, however, Google Translate seems to have let me down, or possibly set me up, given the reaction I got.

"*Wie geht es dir, Herr Rosenthal, Frau Rosenthal? Es freut mich, du kennen zu lernen,*" I splutter as I shake their hands.

Lena's hand goes to her mouth, either to hide her embarrassment or to stifle a giggle, I'm not sure. To be fair to her folks, they seem to get over whatever faux pas I have made and welcome me, quite formally I think, into their home.

Later Lena explains that I had used the familiar form of greeting, the intimate 'how are you' rather than the formal one which apparently you should always use when the person you are meeting is a stranger, '*Wie geht es Ihnen?*" In Germany, it seems, you have to be careful what grammar you use when you are talking to a stranger, different words for different contexts. Straight from the start I am cursing my luck for having been put in a French class in school rather than a German one.

Ah well, I hope they will give me the benefit of the doubt. They seem very nice, quite formal and sort of old-fashioned. I had seen them briefly on a FaceTime call to Lena a year back so I kinda know what they look like but it surprises me a bit that they are as old as this, especially the man who could be pushing sixty I would say, certainly well over fifty. Lena's mum is possibly ten years younger, a very elegant lady, tall, still quite blonde and attractive, (for an older woman like), and from first impressions I'd say she is a shy, reserved sort of person. Kinda classy though. The dad is more outgoing, smiles more easily and has reasonable English, which is good, given my hash-up at the start. He is shorter, heavy-set, balding and with a darker complexion than his wife. Having said that, I am struck again by the obvious truth that Lena, the only child in this family, cannot be their natural daughter.

Whatever she is by her biology, she is mine by her choice, overwhelmingly so, and I am well stunned by the warmth of her hug as she greets me. I had arrived late-afternoon on a Saturday after a pretty quick ride down the autobahns from Frankfurt. Unbelievable speeds some of those cars are doing; it's tempting to try to keep up but I played very safe the whole way down.

Google Maps took me right to their door, all so straight-forward. I parked the bike and barely had time to get my helmet off when Lena appeared at the front door and seemed to fly down the steps and into my arms.

"Wow, Lena!" was all I could say as I felt that physical surge of emotion, (and the mad-keen male hormones, of-course), running through me. My leather suit may have protected me well on my journey but this girl's elfin figure burned through it like it was tissue paper. She only broke off from kissing me when her folks arrived beside us and the dad cleared his throat, then, in an instant reversal, it was back to the timid, slightly guilty-looking Lena that I remember from earlier times.

Now we are around the family table for an evening meal before I am to be taken to Gaby's parents' house nearby. It's all quite formal, a strange atmosphere to match the strange food, some kind of fish dish with lots of salad and bread. I am about to tuck in, hungry after not stopping for food since a burger and my first German beer ages ago in an autobahn cafe; thankfully I watch Lena and hold back. I see her bow her head as her father begins to speak in bold-sounding German; suddenly I realise he is saying some sort of prayer before the meal. Don't remember the last time I heard anyone in Ireland say 'grace'; I am taken aback by this but I am sure it is only one of many different customs here in Bavaria. 'Maybe,' I think, 'it is only a custom in this house; after all this man is some sort of clergy, isn't he?'

Silence then reigns at the table. I can't quite work out if this is the norm or if everything is awkward just now because this Irish alien has arrived at their table. Maybe it's considered bad manners here to talk when you are eating? I should have looked that up on Google as well.

Then Herr Rosenthal asks me about my journey.

I tell them the details briefly, remembering to speak slowly and leave space for them to understand.

Followed by silence again.

I decide to make an effort with Lena's mother; she looks so stiff and nervous at the end of the table.

"This is beautiful fish, Frau Rosenthal. I don't think I've had it before. What is it called?"

I can almost see her mind turning this over as she tries to understand me; Lena is watching her too; her husband gives her

time and then speaks to her in German, presumably helping her to translate. Then she begins, her sentence very hesitant.
"The fish...it is *'der Saibling'*. You like to eat it?"
"Yeah, it's tasty. Really good," I say, and it is actually.
That's nice, an appreciative little smile and nod of the head. She speaks to her husband who then takes up the conversation.
"She wants me to tell you that I am catching this fish myself," he tells me.
"Ah brilliant," I say. "Like in a local river or what?"
"No, no. We have some very large lakes here in Bavaria. These ones I have been catching at Kochelsee. I make some special bait for this one; and a small boat."
"Cool," I say. "So you are a bit of a hunter-gatherer?"
Stupid of me to try to be smart at this early stage of the relationship. I watch as he processes this.
"A hunter, ja! I like to do this," he says with a smile and I am briefly relieved. "You also like to catch fishes perhaps?"
"Me fish? Sorry. Never really got into fishing myself, in spite of the fact that I live beside a river and only a few miles from the sea. I wouldn't have the patience. Only fishing I do is in the local fish and chip shop."
Lena is looking at me with that look that says, "Please Patrick, just give over and stop being the funny guy. It's not working."
I know it's not working but I guess I am just nervous and instinctively wanting to make a good impression.
Afterwards I even offer to help with the clearing up and the dishes; this goes down much better with Frau Rosenthal and she gives me that wide smile of hers as I try to insist. Tell you what, she must have been a stunner when she was in her youth, with this figure and a set of such perfect teeth.
"Please to forgive that I am not so good at your language," she says. "I will try to make better if you help me, ja?"
"Of-course," I say, "and please don't apologise. My German is much worse than your English."
Later I follow Lena and the dad as they take me down the street to the Hauser home, Gaby's parents. This time I avoid all potential German language pitfalls, stick to English and the introductions are fine. Again I am struck by the warmth of the welcome, the stereotype of Germans as austere and aloof is being challenged right from these first meetings. I am taken around to the rear of their beautiful alpine-looking house; in their backyard I see a quaint little

wooden building, sort of log-cabin meets garden shed. This is to be my home for the next few months, with any luck. Three rooms inside, a bedroom cum sitting room, a bathroom and a kitchen, all anyone could ever need. They have even left in some cereal, milk, fruit and bread for me.
"This is brilliant," I tell Herr Hauser. "Thank you so much. And would you like me to pay a deposit now or...."
"No, no," he says with excellent English. "That will be fine at the end of each week, if that is ok?"
Lena and I are left together in my new home for a little while. Her father and Herr Hauser talk together in the yard; he is obviously waiting for her but I don't care. I haven't ridden for three days to be with her just to say a quick *'Gute Nacht'* at this stage. We hold each other, leathers-free, and I wonder if it is possible to be happier. Yeah maybe, but that can wait.
"Lena, Lena...I am here."
"Ja, you are here and I can hardly believe this is true."
"I know we need to make plans but right now I just want to hold you."
"Me too," she says.
"Do you have to go back with your dad?"
"How do you mean?"
"Like, can you not stay here with me?"
She pulls away a little and looks up at me. "You must understand my father. He is very strict. So I am not supposed to be here alone with you; that is why he is waiting outside. Please don't be angry with him. It is just how our culture is, and how he is."
"I'm not angry, and I understand. It's just...I have been waiting for sooo long to be with you, you know..."
"Ja, I know. Me too, and we will be together, just us, as soon as we can get an opportunity, I promise. Just be patient Patrick, please."
"Of-course. When do you think we can go to look for a guitar? Need to do that pretty soon so we can work on songs together, right?"
"Monday, I think, we can go to a special shop in Murnau where sometimes they have musical instruments which are not new. My father knows it well. He will take us; it is his day off, after Sunday."
As if he has been listening at the door, Herr Rosenthal knocks and pops his head in; I release Lena. He speaks to her in German, then to me.
"You must be very tired, young man. We will leave you to get some sleep. Tomorrow...", he looks at his daughter and goes back into

German briefly, then, "if you would like to come to church with Lena, we can pick you up at ten thirty, OK?"
Now there's a curveball. A quick look at Lena's expressionless face; I haven't time to process this so I hear myself say, "Great, thanks. I'll see you then."
Her hand slides reluctantly out of mine and she is gone with him.
In a matter of minutes I hit the bed.
Church in the morning? My God, what will Bernie make of this?

Chapter 31

Bernie Doherty

Great; an email from him this evening.

Hi Mum; You ok? Things are good here. Getting used to life. I have a nice wee apartment not far from Lena's. Her folk are dead on; made me stay for Sunday lunch after I went to their church with them; her da is the priest there; (it's not Catholic, something called Neuapostolische Kirche, not a big grand building like you see around here or at home, more of a sort of community centre place); never been to anything like that before; didn't understand a word but the music wasn't bad & Lena sings in a sort of band. Only about 50-60 people, mainly families with kids. Not many of Lena's age so she hasn't any friends there it seems. Probably won't go back but it seemed only manners.
Her mum is nice but can't speak much English.
Got a battered Yamaha acoustic for €75 in a charity shop; It's a good model though and with new strings it sounds fine. Plus I got a couple of T shirts.
We went to Munich Town Hall to enquire about busking permits; had to perform three songs for them before we got a licence but they were happy with us. If we want to sing in Munich we have to go to that office early in the morning to be allocated a pitch; it's all very formal and controlled, typically German. We also contacted an Irish pub, Killian's and left a CD for the manager; no call back yet. Everybody asks why we call

ourselves 'MacaLena'...it seems to be catchy. Need to check with a few more venues. We have our first gig in a cafe here in the village on Fri night. (It is a village too, lovely colourful buildings and an old-style monastery). Lena's father tells me I need to wear Lederhosen if I want to earn any tips. I hope he is joking but he's hard to read. He's different; won't allow Lena to come to my flat on her own which is tight. Early days though; I won't give up on that one!
Hope you are staying good. Say Hi to Josie. Love- Patrick

My son in a Protestant church of a Sunday morning? Of his own free-will? Now I've heard the lot! It's so ironic, isn't it, that I have spent the last half dozen years trying to get him to come to Mass, without any success, of-course; yet one day with his German lassie and she has him getting out of his pit to accompany her to this 'Neuapostolische Kirche', whatever the hell that is.

I've never heard of a 'Neuapostolische' church before. Please God it's not some sort of weird cult that will have him brain-washed and steal him on me. I must look up about it, maybe talk to Father Murphy and see if he has ever heard of such a church. What can you do with these young ones?

For all that, it was good to get such a positive email from him this morning. I was getting frustrated that he'd been three days with her and I hadn't had so much as a text, well, apart from Saturday's 'Arrived safe at Lena's. All good.'

He's a lad, my Patrick. 'I won't give up on that one' indeed. Goes without saying really. The boy is his father's son and there's no helping that. I just hope that he doesn't get hurt, actually that neither of them get hurt.

Oh to be a fly on the wall at this cafe gig. I'd give my eye teeth for the chance.

I re-read the email and, before I leave it, I have to check my emotions and dab a mother's tear from my cheek. He is a long way away after all, my wee boy.

Then I go to check recent Facebook updates. Flicking down through the posts I happen to see 'Eva Cairns was Live on Facebook'. I click on it and watch briefly as this beautiful harp player performs her music in some National Trust mansion somewhere. It gives me an idea and I text Patrick immediately.

> Ta for the email. Ever think of putting ur gigs on Facebook live? Never know, might get you some following & bookings. Love you, Mum

What I didn't say, but what he will read of-course, is that it gives me a chance to see him and her together. I don't have long to wait for his reply.

> Jeez mum ur a genius! Class idea. We'll set up a MacaLena page & do that for gigs, maybe busks as well. & cos it's ur idea u can watch too. XP

Now there's a first. His oul ma is a genius apparently. That's a nice feeling to have at my age, being one ahead of my media-savvy son and being able to give him the benefit of my entrepreneurial creativity. My God, would you listen to yourself, Bernie Doherty. Sure he likely has had this in his plan all along and is only humouring me.
Then I have another idea, just to suss him out. I text him again.

> Thanks, anything I can do to help. You might want to trial the thing out first though; so can I volunteer to be your Guinea pig audience, please? X

A selfish notion I admit but it might make sense to him. Anything to watch this chemistry in action. I hope she is good for him, I really do, but you can't help but wonder how it will all pan out, how it will all end up. Because end it surely must; what's the alternative?
He will be back in Magee in September, she will be in Germany and back in school; no matter how smitten they are with each other at the minute, I know from bitter experience that this kind of infatuation can only lead to pain and possibly disaster in the future. God love them, both of them.

Chapter 32

(Patrick McAleese)

I am sitting beside Frau Rosenthal at the dining room table. Lena is clearing away the plates; her mother has fetched a tattered looking scrapbook from upstairs and sets it gently on the table in front of me. I get the feeling it is like some kind of precious family heirloom, something to be treated with reverence.
"So Magdalena is telling me that you are being interested in the story of my grandfather? Ja?"
"Sure," I say, recalling yesterday's chat about this very subject.
"Ok," she continues, "it is a very special thing to my family, this story, because he was a good, good man. His name was Wilhelm Schultz; this is a photograph of him in his uniform the day in which he is becoming a soldier. It is 1916 and he is also only sixteen."
I stare at the sepia picture; the edges are well scuffed and there is one wrinkle across the middle but it is a striking image. A handsome, smiling lad, full of pride to be going to fight for the Fatherland...just like my Great-grandad, I am thinking. I wonder did they fight anywhere near each other? Strange to think of that, that one might have had the other in the sights of his rifle back a hundred years ago. I don't mention this of-course, but I do ask the question.
"So have you any idea where he fought?"
"Ja, of-course," replies the mother as Lena comes to sit on the other side of me. "You see, this is his account of all the things he saw, the places he was as a soldier. He wrote it in the evenings during battles, and afterwards when he came home."
"This is brilliant," I say. "How come Lena didn't know about this during the trip?"
There is a slightly awkward silence, a quick glance between the two of them which I can't read. I change the subject and read from a rough sketch which he has obviously drawn.
"Peronne, and Bapaume. I think I recognise these names. Lena, were these not towns close to where we were?"
She doesn't seem to know.
"I think these are places close to the Somme," I say. "Maybe he fought in that same area we were in."

"Here it say that he was being a communications officer at that time," Frau Rosenthal translates. "But there is a very interesting story in a later page. I want to tell it to you, Patrick. It is... amazing." She flicks over several pages. I catch quick glimpses of drawings of ruined buildings and forests shelled into a jagged chaos.
"He must have been a bit of an artist," I say.
"Ja, I am thinking this also. Ah, here we are. This is much later in his account. May I try to translate this piece for you? Magdalena, you must help with words please."
"Sure, fire away," I say. ('Fire away', I think! I should try to choose my words a bit more carefully.)
"Ok, he writes this; 'Yesterday (17th August, 1917) when *im rückzug*...What is *rückzug* Magdalena please? Check your dictionary....*rückzug* from the forward line at Langemarck, a shell fell behind me. It lifted my body up and threw it in the air. Pain was in my leg when I came back to the earth. I was almost sick'..."
"*Rückzug* is retreat, mother," Lena confirms.
"Ok. He writes more; 'The English were close behind our places... our positions. I was feeling that my death was coming very near. Suddenly I was being lifted up once more. Not by explosion this time. It was my friend, Jacob. He had come back for me. He put me on his back and ran for his life, for our two lives. My leg was broken. My pain was terrible but together we survived. I will not forget that I owe my life to a Jewish soldier. His name was Jacob Winter, from our nearby village.'"
"That is fantastic," I say. "And do you remember your grandfather?"
"I do, of-course." Frau Rosenthal obviously has warm memories of him too, by her smile. "He was a simple farmer in a village west of here, one hundred kilometres I think. A good Christian man...but you must hear the best part of his story."
"What? There's a better part?"
"Ja, of-course," she tells me. "This part he did not write down...it would have been not a good idea to write down, as you will see. But my mother is telling me this part."
I am curious now. "Your mother was his daughter, I take it?"
"No, no! That is the important point, as you will see. This man was the father of my father, not of my mother. But my father and grandfather were not very close...they were not good friends, because of what had happened."
"It was because of the Third Reich," Lena chips in and I am all the more fascinated now.

"The Third Reich? Hitler and all that?" I say.

"Ja, that is part of the story of my family, not a happy part," Frau Rosenthal says.

"You don't have to tell me about it if you don't want to," I say, all the time hoping that she will continue the story of-course.

"No, you must hear this part," Lena says, taking my hand. "It is very important to hear it. It is why mother is so proud of her grandfather but not her father. It is a little bit like your song."

"You see, after that war...my grandfather Wilhelm got married and had a big family and worked hard on his little farm, but he was not forgetting his friend Jacob. Then the Nazi Party became into power, nineteen thirties, and soon people of Jewish faith were being...how do you say Magdalena? *Verfolgt*?"

I make a guess. "Persecuted maybe?"

"Ok, I think you are understanding. Then the war begins. My grandfather hears of trains taking away hundreds of Jews. He does not know where but he has a bad feeling that this will not be good for Jacob Winter and his small family. He remembers how Jacob did for him. So one night he goes to the next village. He goes to the home of Winter and makes him awake. The mother dresses the two children...I think aged less than ten...and brings some small possessions and food. My grandfather leads them through the forest and high up into the mountain meadows. There he has a barn, you know, full of hay for his cattle. He puts the Winter family in his barn and tells them they must stay quiet at all times. Hiding, no fire, nothing."

"Wow," I say. "And did they survive?"

"Ja, they do survive. He takes them food sometimes at night. It is a two hour journey up to this valley; in the deep snow it is much more, but he does this always. He is afraid he will be caught so many times he is hiding in the hedges all night. But he survives as well."

"Amazing!"

"Tell him about your father," Lena says.

I sense some hesitation, pain even, in Frau Rosenthal.

"My father. This is very difficult. My father was a boy then, perhaps ten, twelve...he was easily pulled...is that how you say?"

"Influenced," Lena helps out.

"Influenced by the people of our town, by the posters and the events of those times. So he joins with the group called the 'Hitler Youth'. My grandfather was not happy but he must pretend that this is ok, you know, so that he does not bring attention to himself or to the family...it might lead to the Winters being discovered. So my grandfather did his life as if he was a supporter of the Nazis, just as most other people in his place, even in his church. Nobody must suspect him. That way he...and my grandmother as well, they helped this Jewish family through the war."

"But that was a huge length of time," I say. "How could they have stayed hidden for like...maybe four years? It's incredible."

"Ja, but later my grandfather was with a resistance organisation...not working with them but helping them, secretly...and so it became possible to....what is *schmuggeln* Lena?"

Again I can guess, just by the sound. "Smuggle," I say.

She smiles. "Ja; you will learn German quickly, Patrick."

"I hope so," says Lena.

"Anyhow, the Winters were smuggled away somehow to Switzerland."

"And did your grandfather ever see them again?"

"He did. After the war they went to America, but before they are leaving they return to their house, and to my grandfather's home and he takes them up to the barn in the mountains. I am sure it was a time of emotion for them, ja?"

"I'm sure it was," I say. "And how did your father feel about that? Did he ever talk about it?"

Again there is that fleeting regret in her eyes. "He must have known then what his father had done. He probably thought that he had been living with a traitor...but he also must have begun to think about the evil that he had been so close to. He was only a boy of-course, and he did not go to fight...but I am sure he would have done this if he had been a little bit older."

"And how did he get on with your grandfather?" Lena asks.

"They were never close after that. Too much guilt. My father had come to be on the wrong side of history, I think, yet his father had been on the right side. It was difficult for them I am guessing."

Too right, it must have been. Incredible, and to be sitting in the home of that hero's grand-daughter and hear such an intimate story from the heart of her family history. I find this just so amazing, a total honour.

What a pity that Lena hadn't known about this before she went on the trip to the Somme; I don't understand why. It would have been a brilliant story to tell in the discussions, the complicated dilemmas of European history, all nut-shelled in one family.

Chapter 33

(Patrick McAleese)

First steps into the big-time world of busking today. Is Munich ready for this? Nerve-wracking for both of us; me because I have no German; Lena because her default persona is a hide-away sort of thing, the exact opposite of what she is going to need to stand in a busy street and sing to attract a crowd. And their Euros.
I am confident enough in my own ability on guitar and singing in public, having cut my teeth in front of skeptical punters in Sailors and various places, but live on the streets of a major European city, no mics or sound system, just my 'exotic' co-star and this beat-up old guitar for company? It is a different ask altogether.
We arrive at the iconic *Neues Rathaus* in Munich city centre. It's 8.00am exactly, according to all the little mechanical characters popping out to do their stuff on the famous Glockenspiel high in the central tower of the building. What a building this is. Gothic-fantasy-iced-cake meets ultimate 3D puzzle. Such a stylish facade to have for your Munich Town-hall.
We've ridden in from Fremdenheim on the bike in just under the hour, Lena perched on the back with the guitar jammed in between our two bodies. It all felt kinda risky; she had to hang on to me and the swaying hard-case at the same time.
We queue in the Municipal Office until a very pleasant official allocates us two different pitches for the day, the first for two hours just off Marienplatz, the second in Odeonsplatz for our afternoon stint. The cost is only €10 for the licence for the day. I ask this lady about playing in other places, beyond the rules. She smiles.
"I can only advise you that it is not legal. You will probably be asked to move on." Then, more quietly, she says, "You probably won't finish up in our prison. Unless you are playing very badly of-course!"
We have time to kill until ten so we have a wander around, guitar in one hand, Lena holding on to my other arm with her two hands. I love it, even if it's just an evidence of her nervousness.
"Let's go and case these joints," I say to her.
"What are you talking about? Casing joints? You have so many things I do not understand."
"Sorry. Don't worry about it. I was trying to sound smart."
"I am afraid, Patrick."

"I know babe. Me too, but we'll be grand."
"But you are so confident. I am not always doing this like you do," she says, hanging on to my jacket, head down.
I set down my guitar and wrap her up in my arms for a second, breathing her hair again.
"Lena, I'm scared shit-less too. This isn't my country. If someone says something to me I won't have a clue."
"Why did I agree to do this?" she says after a little silence.
"Because...because you wanted me to come and be here with you, I suppose. And busking was the only thing I could think of to survive here. Wasn't that what happened?"
"No, I think not. I think I said 'Yes' because the happiest time of my life was singing with you in Ireland, in that pub. That was so good a feeling."
We reach the striking city square called Odeonsplatz. The three imposing arches of what I later learn is called Feldherrnhalle dominate one end of the square, some heroic statues standing on perpetual guard. Beside stands a massive, golden-coloured cathedral. Church and State holding hands, it looks like. Nearby a statue of some ancient King, strutting his stuff on a mighty bronze horse, both green-aged. Imagine playing here in this grand historic site. I want to take a photograph and send it to Mr Donaldson, with some smart comment about how his teaching has so inspired me that now I am busking on the site of Hitler's famous 1923 Beer Hall Putsch, or at least the violent battle which ended it. I am going to be singing peace songs on the very ground that became sacred to the Nazi regime.
Posing on the steps of the Feldherrnhalle, I take a selfie of us, a huge Aslan-like lion statue glowering over my shoulder as if to say, 'If you'd seen what I've seen standing up here for a hundred years you wouldn't be so chirpy'.
We have a set list of ten songs that we prepared yesterday; some better rehearsed than others. I have been amazed at how wide Lena's tastes are. She has been listening to a whole range of stuff, from American songwriter, Sara Siskind, to older artists like Nina Simone and Eva Cassidy. When I asked her about this she blamed her mum.
"Not your dad?" I asked.
"No, my father, no; he is too serious for music and songs. I think he is musical but not a person of broad tastes."
"But your mother is? How come?"

"Ja, she always loves American songs, some British too, I think."
"Does she sing?"
"She can sing, and sometimes she is singing in the house but not when my father is around."
"He wouldn't like it?"
"I don't know. He may not like it but she would always be careful that no one is listening when she sings, even when she plays these great records from her past. She still has a...how do you say? A turntable, a record player, from when she was young. But only if he is out, she plays it; then I hear her singing to a Beatles song or something like that."
"And did you join her? Like, when you were growing up, did you sing with her or what? Otherwise how do you know all these songs from back in the day?"
Lena smiled as she remembered.
"Not with her, but I would sing in my head. I loved these old songs; I learned them in private, you know, my father not knowing what was inside my mind. He is a good man, you know, but he is *altmodisch.*"
I am learning here, and not just some German words. I'm guessing that this one means what it sounds like, outmoded, old-fashioned. More importantly though, I feel I am getting more insight into this girl's psyche and her relationship to her folks.
Anyhow, our set list for today looks like this, a nice mixture of covers and some of my originals;

1. Ed Sheeran's 'Photograph' (PMcA on main vocal)
2. 'Nothing Compares 2 U'- Sinead O'Connor (Lena)
3. 'Tongue-tied' (PMcA)
4. 'Imagine- John Lennon -Eva Cassidy version (Lena)
5. 'One Love'- U2 (PMcA)
6. 'My Baby just cares for me'- Nina Simone (Lena)
7. 'Mystery' (PMcA)
8. 'Falling Stars'- Sara Siskind (Lena)
9. 'Nothing stays the same'- Luke Sital-Singh (Both)
10. Ed Sheeran's 'Galway Girl' (Both)

Back in Marianplatz we find our first pitch in a small covered area not far along from the Apple Store. We take our stand and get organised, guitar case set slightly to our front and side so that people don't have to plough straight into our faces to contribute. I lay a dozen of our CDs against the rim of the case and fix a poster advertising 'MacaLena CD €5.00' to the lid.

This isn't a promising site; people will be rushing past us from one shop to another in this pedestrianised area. But it's what we've been given so we have to make the best of it. We launch into our set.

It's not easy without a PA; I find it difficult to project my voice above the clamour of the city, even at this early time before the majority of the public has arrived in the city centre. And if I find it a problem, how is Lena going to cope with when it's her turn? Not a soul comes anywhere near us during my Ed Sheeran song; not a single coin makes its way into our coffers. Disappointing and worrying. Maybe it's too early. I finish the song.

Now what? Do I speak to the passers-by? Introduce Lena? Or just plough on?

She looks up at me, a small sympathetic smile.

"Ok, your turn," I say. "Go for it. Give it some welly!"

"Welly?"

"Yeah; sing it out like Sinead; nothing to lose."

So she does; she steps forward slightly from me and launches into her song...and soon a few heads start to turn in our direction. That voice! How can such a sweet quality vocal cut through this atmosphere so effectively where mine fell flat on its face? Footsteps begin to slow in front of us, I can see it clearly. Lena can't; she has her eyes closed. Her whole body and soul is being poured into this.

> *'It's been so lonely here like a bird without a song,*
> *Nothing can stop these lonely tears from falling.'*

Pure soul, absolutely gripping right from the start of the song. She has been singing these words in the privacy of her room over the past while, I am guessing. Now they are pushing themselves out into the open for the first time in this very public place. It is the weirdest of feelings, to be on the receiving end of this passionate tsunami of emotion while trying to concentrate on the chords and maintain my street-busker-cool.

The other reaction I have is one somewhere between astonishment and pride. This is the girl who for most of the time I have known her, early on certainly, has been all about timidity, instinctive self-doubt and fearful shyness. Ok, I do recognise the courage she has shown in leaving her folks, at seventeen, to come to cycle in Ireland; plus

the confidence she had to get up in that pub in Dingle to perform with me without a single rehearsal. Now here she is singing to a crowd of strangers on the main street of her capital city.
And we do have an audience, maybe fifteen or twenty strong, growing as I watch. Every eye is on Lena. As we reach the song's end I come to a quick and easy decision; she must go straight into another one of her songs; I am supporting cast here.
She finishes, to a nice warm ripple of applause and about half of the audience move on. As a couple of punters come forward to drop coins into our case I speak to the crowd.
"Thank you ladies and gentlemen; this is Lena Rosenthal, we are MacaLena and our CD is on sale right here and only here. Lena is going to continue with John Lennon's greatest song, 'Imagine'.
She looks a bit alarmed by this so I whisper, "Keep them here babe; you were great," and I start into that unmistakeable intro to the song. She can't refuse; instead she gives me that beautifully happy look of submission and we are off to a flyer.
Two hours later we are exhausted and ready for a break. Half the CDs are gone already. We've been through our set twice, more actually if you include "Eleanor Rigby' and 'Ninety-nine Red Balloons' which we attempt in response to requests, having googled the lyrics. Lovely to see lips moving as people try to join in, in both German and English. I've no idea how much we've made and, to be honest, I don't really care; I would have done this for free, that's how good it feels.
We have a quick lunch in Kearney's Irish pub nearby. The place is overcrowded, mainly with male diners and drinkers. The beer tastes like heaven but then we are both incredibly thirsty. The schnitzel isn't bad either but just to sit for a while and look at Lena is probably what I need most. She is glowing from inside with the joy of it all. I tell her about a new song I've been writing.

> 'Deep inside your heart you are beautiful,
> Underneath the masks that you wear,
> Feels like we're actors in some kinda mystery.'

She just laughs at me. "I am going to the bathroom," she says, "but please don't write a song about that also."
I watch her walk away from me through the crowd of diners. Heads turn after her from some tables. I can understand why; there are girls that walk and there are girls that you notice walking! This girl is

one of those, the queen of them, and here she is with this carrot-headed faker from Coleraine, a duo singing songs in Bavaria. Unbelievable.
"We should move on," she says on her return. "This place is too busy, too much noise."
"Ok," I say, "but we still have an hour to kill."
"Kill an hour?" she says with a shake of the head. "The hour does not deserve to be killed."
"Haha," I laugh. "I mean where do you want to go to spend the next hour, Fräulein Smart-Ass?"
"I want to go somewhere quiet and cool. Come," she says, taking off, "I will show you."
I pay the bill and take the chance to leave a CD and my contact details with the cashier who promises to pass it on to the manager, then I follow her out into the heat of the summer street. She leads the way through the crowds until we reach the front door of what looks like some sort of church or cathedral, gleaming in the sunshine.
"Come inside," she tells me. "It's good in here."
I'm kinda dubious about that claim but I wander in after her reluctantly. We take a seat on the back pew. She snuggles close to me and closes her eyes. It's a very peaceful moment in the middle of what has been a hyper day and we sit there without a word between us for like ten minutes. The building is a massive cavern, arched roof way above us and an imposing High Altar in ornate green and bronze far to the front. So much wealth in these great religious palaces of god. I always find it a staggering contradiction; a stained glass Jesus staring down at his gold-plated church. In my view of things all these riches that have been gathered off the backs of the faithful poor.
"It's a long way from the stable," I whisper, as much to myself as to Lena. She seems to think a bit about this before replying.
"Ja, I always think this as well," she says, then after a bit she adds, "This is St Michael Kirche; Renaissance I think."
"Ridiculous, I think."
"You do not like it here?"
"I like it anywhere I am with you," I tell her.
"Thank you for being here," she whispers, pulling even tighter to me.
This is a specially sacred moment, I am thinking, but are we allowed to be this intimate in a religious building? I doubt it. I sense that we are being observed from high to the side but, when I glance up, all I

can see is a group of scantily-dressed marble angels staring down at us. I nudge Lena.
"We are being watched," I tell her.
She sits up guiltily and looks around.
"Where?"
I point to the statues.
"Up there," I say. "They're jealous, God love them. Look at all that lovely smooth white marble but they are just so cold to each other."
A wry smile.
"You should not say these things in a holy building of God."
"You think he is listening in?" I say.
"Of-course He is listening. He is everywhere, but especially in His churches," she says solemnly.
"You can't be serious?"
"Why not?"
"Well...I just can't imagine your friend Jesus spending too much time among all these riches, not allowed to make a noise or cause a fuss, know what I mean?" I say.
She smiles. "I agree. I think he would like to be out in the street with the people, maybe even busking like us!"
She gets up abruptly and leads me by the hand toward the huge doors.
As we push them open and the sunlight and heat hit us, we are hit by something else...a strange, high-pitched wailing sound, really loud, coming from some sort of amplifier. It takes a minute for me to understand what is happening. I feel Lena's grip on my arm tightening in fear.
"What is this?" I say as the realisation dawns on me that the sound is that of the muezzin, the sound that comes from a mosque to call Muslims to prayer. This is a first for me. I did not expect this, right in the middle of Munich.
"It is a political meeting, I think," Lena says.
She's right too; there is a sort of roped-in area, with a minibus in the centre and speakers on the top. That's where the screeching sound is coming from, so loud people are putting their hands over their ears, some hurrying away. The sound fades down as someone fixes the amplifier controls. We see a guy take a microphone and start to address the people in the platz. I become aware of the posters on the side of the minibus and on the T-shirts of several people inside this cordoned-off area. *'PEGIDA'* seems to be name of the group. Where have I heard of them before? I watch the faces of the

onlookers; some shaking their heads as if in disgust, some controlling anger. I don't see many supporters, but I do see a few *Polizisten* standing nearby, taking a very close interest in the rally; they look well geared up, as if for riot control.

"Let's get out of here," I say.

"No wait," she says. "This makes me so angry."

"Ok, but what good will it do to wait?"

"These people! They come here from other places," she says, "just to stir up trouble. They are not of Munich."

"How do you know?"

"Every person here knows," she says. "They are speaking German from another area, the north of the country. They are not Bavarian."

"What is their issue? What are they about?" I ask.

"They come here to cause trouble. They play loud Muslim prayers, the call to the Mosque. I have never heard this before. We have Mosques and Muslims in all our towns here, yet I have never heard this noise until these strangers come here. They just do it to make conflict and confusion in our people, make fear where there is no fear. And they are supposed to be Christian as well? Why do they think they can do this?"

"Is it to do with an election?" I ask. "Are they a political party?"

"No, I think not a party; but ja, an election in September is coming. Nobody will vote for this but what happens is even more...these people encourage fear and hatred against migrants; they ask people to vote for the *AFD* party; it is against migrants, against Merkel and her good policy to refugees."

As she speaks she seems to get even more upset and angry. This is a revelation to me. I admire her passion; at the same time I want to protect her from this mob. I take her hand again, as if to move on, but she is having none of it. She pulls away and heads straight for the centre of the thing, the roped in area. I am shocked but I follow her, right to one of the T-shirt-wearing guys who is holding out leaflets for people to take. He's a big, well-muscled fellow, probably about forty, sporty moustache. I wouldn't want to rile this dude.

Lena launches into conversation with him, angry, shouting above the noise of the speaker just a few metres away. I have no clue what she is saying, nor what the guy is replying, but I can read a lot from the look on his face. It is a pure sneer; this guy despises her because of her colour, I don't need to be able to understand German to realise this. He can barely look at her without that arrogant hatred seeping out of his pores.

I try to pull Lena back but she shakes me off; the big guy then shouts something at me. Again, despite my ignorance of the actual words, I have no bother understanding his disdain. He repeats the question. I can only guess that he is asking me why I am with this '*migrant*'. The bastard! Lena takes the bait again and gives him the full benefit of her temper, a side to her I haven't seen before. She's sparky, this kid. He just laughs in her face.

"Come on Lena, there's no point," I say. "He's too thick to understand you. Let's go."

The big guy looks at me, working out what I've said. "Ah, you English," he says. "You are good; you have wisdom to get out of EU and close up your borders. We make a bad future for Germany with all migrant trash from every place. Well done English!"

"I am not English," I tell him, "and she is not a migrant. She is as German as you are."

"She is not looking like German to me," he says. "She looks more like Arab or..."

"See what I mean?" I interrupt him. "I look English... but I'm not. She doesn't look German... but she is! You? You don't look like an idiot but...."

I shrug my shoulders and turn away, dragging Lena behind me through the watchers.

We walk towards Odeonsplatz in silence. I sense that she just needs some space before we talk. Eventually she speaks.

"It was very strange," she says thoughtfully. "One minute we are in the peace and quietness of the cathedral. Then..."

"Yeah, the next we were in the middle of that racket. I was thinking the same thing."

"Thank you for speaking for me. You were brave."

"No problem...and by the way, it was you was the brave one. I hardly recognised the new Lena."

"I do not feel much like singing now," she says. "Perhaps you will do most songs this time?"

"Sure," I say, but I am hoping she will change her mind on this when we get started. "What was your conversation all about back there? I only understood one word."

"Which word?"

"Migrant," I tell her. "Seems to be the same in both languages."

"Ja, he tells me I am a migrant. He make me very angry; other people too, because my skin is not pure white like theirs. But I was born here; I am German and I am proud of this place, until I meet people like him. He sees someone of my colour, he think I must be a migrant, a Muslim or a terrorist supporter or something. I tell him I am Christian and he do not believe me. I tell him my father is pastor of a church and he tells me it must be a strange church. He is such a...how do you say?"

"Bigot? Prejudiced, narrow-minded, ignorant."

"Ja, bigot. I hate these type of persons...but I suppose I should not hate him; he is just this way because he has not experience of other people, he has not talked to people from other lands who live here. He only believes what he reads on his leaflets and websites. I pity him."

"Yeah, but at the same time he is dangerous, his views and all. I was scared for you but you were great, kid. Fair play to you for having the balls to confront him."

"The balls? I do not understand...?" she smiles.

"I mean...like, the courage to go and argue with him. We should all be prepared to take on these people."

"Ja, we must," she says. "Do you know this poem? 'First they came for the Socialists, and I did not speak out...Because I was not a Socialist. Then they came for the Trade Unionists, and I did not speak out...Because I was not a Trade Unionist. Then they came for the Jews, and I did not speak out...Because I was not a Jew. Then they came for me...and there was no one left to speak for me.' It is a poem of Neimöller who was a prisoner of the Nazis. I have it on a poster on my bedroom wall."

"Brilliant," I say.

We walk on in silence until we are near our new pitch.

"Talking about your bedroom Lena..." I begin, but stop. She looks up at me; I think there is some strange melancholy in those eyes but I can't interpret this look; it's like you might see in the eyes of your pet dog if it thinks you are disappointed in its behaviour.

"Ja?"

"Do I get to see your bedroom? Like, am I allowed to be there...you know what I mean?"

She walks on silently for a bit.

"My father, you know, he is very strict. You see, it is not permitted in the old custom for you and me to be sleeping in the same house. I have told you this before."

In the same house? Never mind the same room, the same bed!

"Ok sure," I say. "And what about you coming to spend some time with me at my flat, at Gaby's? Is that still out of the question too?"

"Out of the question?"
"Won't your father allow you a wee bit of freedom?" I say.
"Please Patrick. Do not ask any more about this."
"Doesn't he trust you or what? It is kinda natural for us to want to spend time together, isn't it? It's lonely there in the evenings when I go back. I miss you..."
"I know, but please stop this question; you must be patient. I want to be with you, of-course I do, but for now it is only that my father..."
I am a bit frustrated and it probably shows in how I react.
"Jeez, what is it about fathers?" I say, too sharply.
"They are to be respected, do you think so?"
"Oh yeah. Needs to be earned though, in my opinion."
She thinks about this, then twists the question back on me.
"You do not talk of your father to me. Do you not respect him?"
I wince at this and turn away from her.
"Tell me about him," she continues.
I don't answer for a while. She hurries and catches up.
"I don't want to talk about this now Lena, just when we are about to start singing. My father...let's just say I am not about to start singing "Father and Son". Not my favourite person on the planet; he left us for someone else, and for his military career, so...forget about him."
"I'm sorry," she says. "Perhaps later you can tell me about it, please?"
"Maybe, if you want me to."
"Of-course. I want to know all about you. And I am sorry because, in my case, my father has been amazing for me in my life. I am so glad for him, and my mother too."
"That's great," I say, thinking all the time that I still haven't addressed the mystery of how her folks are white Germans while she is anything but. "And you must tell me all about your childhood too. Like...show me your family photographs and all that stuff."
I wasn't being sarcastic at all but she looks at me suspiciously, like she thought I had ulterior motives for this. She doesn't answer.
In Odeonsplatz it is more difficult, stiflingly hot, people less inclined to stop. We do our best until about four fifteen. Then, soaking with perspiration, we start to pack up. As Lena counts the takings my phone buzzes. A number I don't recognise. German. I answer.
"Hi, is this MacaLena?" Irish voice, strong southern accent. I'm confused.
"Who?....Ah...yip, I suppose it is."
"Ah great man. Martin here from Kearney's. You left in your CD?"

"Yip, we did. Hope that was...."
"Are ye free this evening? Tonight like? I have a cancellation."
"Gimme a second," I say and turn to Lena.
"Hey, we have a booking tonight. Can we do it? Kearney's pub."
She smiles and gives me the thumbs up. Then she looks worried and points to her watch.
"Yeah that's great," I tell him. "What time and how long for?"
"Nine till Eleven. Wee ten minute break in the middle. Alright?"
"Sure I say. You gotta PA and all?"
"We have. What's your fee by the way?"
I hesitate. I have no idea what to ask.
"Look, I'll be honest here Martin. This will be our first gig in Munich so I haven't a clue what to ask? What the going rate?"
He hesitates this time.
"Your first gig, eh? So yees are greenhorns to this? Well, you sound pretty good on the CD. Why don't we say...ah, let's see...€120 for the first night and see if you're worth it?"
I have a feeling that's way too low but I don't like to haggle in this circumstance. He could tell me to get lost, so I accept.
"Ok, but if you are happy tonight we will want way more next time."
"Ok," he laughs, "you're a cocky son o' a bitch. We'll see. Be here ready to start at nine, that's nine-German time right?"
"Cheers," I laugh and hang up.
Lena looks up from the guitar case.
"How much?"
"€120," I tell her. "Sound ok?"
"I have no idea," she says, "but we have sold eleven CDs, that's €55, and we have €67.70 as well so I think we did good Patrick."
"Yeah we did, for a first time," I say as we hug and near enough stick to each other's sweat, "but it can get better. We need to think of ways to get a crowd gathered, so they stay with us, you know? They seem to just listen for like 10 or 20 seconds and then move on. That way they get 20 seconds of good music for free and don't feel any moral duty to give us any money, know what I mean?"
"Ja. We need to make them stay more," she says. "I have an idea."
"What's that?" I say, starting to see mischief behind her smile.
"You must play in your boxers only; this will bring a big crowd."
"You're a laugh," I tell her. "Ok, I will if you will."
"But that will not work. I do not have any boxers," she tells me.
"I have a spare set," I say. "You'll look great in them," and she punches me in the ribs.

Chapter 34

(Patrick McAleese)

I am in her bedroom.
It's taken two weeks to get to it but here I am.
Trouble is, I am alone. Lena and her mum have gone off to their weekly pilates, which is a nice thing for a mother-daughter to do of-course but kinda frustrating. I'd been invited round for dinner; then they up and leave.
"Back in one hour only," her mum said. "You are not minding?"
How can I mind? She's a sweet lady and she's starting to treat me as part of the family furniture already, especially this week, I am thinking, when her husband is away in Frankfurt for some church conference. After she'd gone out to the car Lena grabbed my hand and pulled me quickly up the stairs to her bedroom.
"I want you to hear a small recording. I started to make a song...it is not very good but please listen, OK? Don't laugh at me," she says.
"Sure; brilliant," I say as she opens her computer.
She hesitates. "But please close down after...not to look at other..."
"Of-course not; you can trust me."
A quick kiss and she was gone, calling back, "When you hear us come go downstairs please, ok? I do not want mother to know this."
I click play; she sings in German; it sounds great, very pure and naked without any backing music. I have no idea what the lyrics are about until she gets to the second verse; she sings in English.

> *We are the fallen of the world*
> *The hurting people on the street*
> *The shatterings of broken shells*
> *Littered across a golden beach*
> *We wait for you to come along*
> *To gather up the broken bits*
> *To take us to your caring heart*
> *And make us once again complete*

Wow, what class words, I think. The tune too...I love it. Can't wait to put an accompaniment to this. She has some talent hiding inside.
I play the song three times, sensing her pride in it. And I totally get that these clunky lyrics are coming from some needy place very

deep in her psyche. It's such a privilege to be allowed to hear it, even if I haven't a clue why she feels this 'fallenness', as she calls it. Working out the chords to put around the tune is a hell of a lot easier than working out what is going on in Lena's head. There is so much about her that I totally love; we are so meant for each other; we fit into each other like two halves of the jig-saw puzzle hanging on her wall; her Ying to my Yang; yet there are times when I feel I don't really know her, not completely. It's not just that she hasn't seemed to want to make love that's bugging me, (though it is, a bit). It's just this intangible barrier, this veil that she keeps part of herself behind, like she doesn't trust me with a full understanding of who she is or where she's been in her life. Yeah, we are so much closer to it than we have ever been, than we were during those early FaceTime calls, or the first time we really talked in that cafe in Albert. But why am I still trying to solve this girl?

I switch on her radio and lie on her bed; it's on a classical channel; morose Mozart, not designed to lift my mood. This must be his requiem I am listening to. I switch it over to some pop channel and sit on the edge of her bed. It's a cool room this, all very tidy and delicate and pastelly, limes and mauves the main colour theme. A view out over fields and red-roofed farm buildings to the Bavarian Alps in the distance. I study the posters on her walls; not much different to what had been on Josie's walls up until recently when she finally moved out to Belfast, except that it's less over-powering, less male-model orientated and there are a lot more pictures of mountains and forests and rivers here. I pull her pyjamas from under her pillow and breathe them in like they are an oxygen mask. Too exciting, not a good idea.

I go to sit by her desk. The first thing I pick up is a bible, I think; not an old-fashioned black-backed thing that you'd see in the fists of those bible-thumpers on Coleraine's Church Street; this one is packaged up nicely like a fantasy novel. I flick through the pages; all in German of-course, so I put it down quickly, like as if I'm afraid of contamination. Her college files and textbooks are all neatly stacked to the side. This is all a part of her which I don't know and, while I accept that that is inevitable, I do wonder about her life in college, her life with her friends...if she has any. Actually, it does strike me as really rare that she never seems to talk about her friends; she doesn't seem to get many texts; I don't think she uses social media. I don't know about emails; her computer is open but there is no way that I am going to try to spy on her. She trusts me enough for that or she wouldn't have brought me up here.

Should I be leaving something behind for her? Just a whiff of my masculinity, some sort of ethereal presence for her to hold in the night? I don't know; I'm not good at decoding what is going on in the female psyche. In the absence of any other ideas I decide to write her a note and leave it with her pyjamas; nothing too erotic though.

I look around the desk for a sheet of paper. There are a couple of sheets sticking out from a folder two or three down from the top of the pile. I pull the folder out and open it.

It dawns on me that this is Lena's journal, the one she was writing in that night in Albert. I stare at it sort of mesmerised for a second. Maybe I am holding a key to answering some of the questions I was thinking about earlier. But this is her private journal. I shouldn't be looking at it, should I? I put it back on the pile and watch it as if it might give me the thumbs up and say, "Danke buddy!"

But she has left it here on her desk? Her folks can come in here anytime and read it. Which is more than I can do, seeing that it is in German. That consoles me a bit. What harm is there in having a sneak peek, a quick flick through the pages? I won't be able to understand a word. Maybe I'll see my own name in there somewhere..."PATRICK" at the top of every page. Idealised sketches of her hero? Hardly, but I have a look inside anyhow.

As I flick slowly through the pages I don't see very much to massage my ego with. Yeah, there is a splattering of 'Patricks' here and there but, short of getting into translation mode, I am not going to be able to understand what she is saying. I'm curious though.

Then I do see something that I recognise. There is a rough pencil sketch of one of those World War 1 gravestones. At the top is a Star of David. And just below that I read *'Schatten und Geister'*. It is the poem she sent me way back. She has written it out on this drawing of a soldier's gravestone. My eye travels down through it but ofcourse I am not understanding the German, just the odd wee bit of it that I had translated sticks in my mind. It strikes me though that it is different somehow; it seems longer than the version she sent me.

I am curious. I take my phone and do a search in my emails for the one that contained this *'Schatten'*. I find it and sure enough there is a difference.

She had ended her original poem with the line, *'Und die Kälte steigt in mir, -wie ein loderndes Feuer'*, something about 'coldness rising inside her like a fire', if I remember rightly, a very poetic image, I'd thought at the time. But now there is an extra section, one which she hadn't sent me. I am immediately wondering why. It reads like this;

> *Und jetzt schon weiß ich mehr über diesen Soldaten,*
> *Diesen Albert Wolff, Kanonier,*
> *Als ich über meinen eigenen Vater weiß.*
> *Ich kenne seinen Namen.*
> *Ich weiß, dass er ein Kanonier war.*
> *Ich weiß, dass er jüdischen Glaubens war.*
> *Ich weiß, dass er unter diesen Schatten weilt.*
> *Ich weiß, dass er kein namensloser Geist ist!*
> *Ich kann nicht um ihn trauern,*
> *auch wenn mir der stumme Grabstein mehr über ihn erzählt,*
> *als ich über meinen eigenen Vater weiß.*
>
> Magdalena Rosenthal (?) 26/06/16

This is fascinating; these extra couple of verses that she decided not to send to me. Why?
I can't wait to do the translation and get into Google Translate immediately. This is what it tells me.

> *But yet I now know more about this soldier*
> *This Albert Wolff, Kanonier,*
> *Than I know about my own father*
> *I know his name*
> *I know he was a gunner*
> *I know his faith was Jewish*
> *I know he is buried among these shadows*
> *I know that he is not a nameless ghost*
> *I cannot mourn him*
> *Even if the silent tombstone tells me more about him*
> *As I know about my own father*

Oh man!
That question mark after her signature starts to make sense to me now; her introversion starts to make sense; her shyness and self-doubt...her whole enigmatic personality.
"Ah my poor Lena. You don't know who you are," I whisper to myself and I put my head in my hands, my elbows on her desk. Of-course I

have known that she isn't the Rosenthal's natural daughter. Her mum could be from somewhere in Scandinavia, her father a bit more Italian looking. And of-course she must know that she is adopted...but she is searching for an identity, a roots type of realisation of who she is at a far deeper level than her folks have been able to give her.

The euro-trash music on her radio is totally jarring now with how this poem has affected me and I get up to turn it off.

Only then do I see her.

She is standing at the door.

Her hands are at her mouth in a silent scream, her eyes staring.

She yells something at me in German. I open my arms to her but she runs past me and dives on her bed, pulling the pillow over her head. I hear her mother's footsteps on the wooden stairway.

"Lena," I say, "I am sorry...I did not mean to..."

I think this is a massive over-reaction. What is it with this girl? Why has she gone so hysterical about this? It's only her diary; I can't even read it. What have I done here?

Frau Rosenthal looks sort of terrified as she runs into the room. I don't know what she expected to see but the sight of me standing there with my two arms the one length and fully clothed seems to console her a little bit. Her look isn't a condemning one, to give her credit but her English deserts her and she asks me something in German as she goes to sit beside Lena. It's not hard to work out what she is saying though, and I lift the journal to show her that I have been reading Lena's private notes. She nods understandingly and speaks to Lena in very soothing terms. I can only stand and watch, though for a second it does cross my mind that I may have done some irreparable damage to this relationship and I might as well go and pack.

I decide to wait it out; I sit down on the chair again. Lena's mum has a voice like a running stream, musical and consoling. Gradually she begins to touch Lena and takes the pillow from off her head. Eventually Lena turns over on the bed; she still doesn't look at me; her mother talks on; ten minutes of this before I get a single look and it isn't exactly a loving one. It's angry, full of hurt and betrayal and it sticks in me like a thorn. But I won't look away. I will wait for my chance to explain.

She begins to reply to her mum in a soft moaning voice; I haven't a clue what they are discussing and all I can do is hope that it is a healing conversation. I still have to have mine with her; I hope that it is soon. It's starting to get dark outside and even gloomier here in this bedroom. I have an idea to try to break this spell.

"Can I please light one of your candles, Lena?"

There is a long pause before she gives a slight nod of her head.

"Ok, I'll go down for matches," I say.

"No, you stay. I go," says her mum standing up before I can get to the door. Very tactful. She leaves the two of us together. I go to sit beside Lena on her bed.

"I am so sorry Lena."

Nothing.

"I was going to write you a note so you could have something to read when I was gone," I say.

"You are going away?"

There's fear in her voice.

"No, no, no. I am not going away. I mean only when I have gone back to Gaby's tonight. I am not going anywhere."

She just stares at the ceiling.

"Lena, will you listen to me. I love you...right. Please believe me. I love the person you are, OK? It doesn't matter to me that...."

"But you will never know the person I am. There are things about me that you can never find out. I hope you will never...this is why I am not wanting you to see my diary."

"Let me explain what just happened. I opened it...I know it is private and I should have waited to ask you. But I was just flicking through it because...I suppose because I thought it couldn't do any harm, with me not knowing any German. Then I recognised the poem from the cemetery, the one you sent me...'*Schatten und Geister*'. And I saw that there were extra words that you hadn't sent me; I was curious. So I did a quick translation, right?"

"Ja," she whispers.

"I hope that was ok. I didn't read anything else. I'm sorry...you trusted me in your bedroom and I have let you down. But I didn't mean for it to hurt you Lena. I just wanted to know..."

"And now you know that I am not what you think I am. I am not Magdalena Rosenthal, am I? I am some other girl who does not have a name, not Rosenthal, not Magdalena. I am nobody!"

"You are not nobody babe. You are the most incredible person I have ever met. Do you seriously think that just because you don't know who your father was that it makes you any less special as a person?"

"You do not understand," she snaps. "You have your father. You know who you are, from day one. I have no idea about..."
Her mum arrives back with the matches, which must have been well lost, given the time she took; sensitive lady. She lights the candle and I take Lena's hand. She doesn't pull away. Her mum sits opposite us, by the desk. She picks up the journal and asks Lena if she can read the poem, I presume. Lena nods and looks up at me sadly; the candle reflection flickers in the amber pool of her eyes.
"The thing is," I tell her, "yeah, I do know my father but he is a total embarrassment to me. I told you he left us when I was little. That was like ages ago. I've only seen him a few times since. He has another woman. I don't even know if he has any other kids. He is married to being a tough-guy soldier. I despise almost everything about him. So you see, knowing who your biological father is can have its downsides."
"You must not speak of your father like this," she says.
"And you must not imagine that you would have been happier if you had been with your real parents," I tell her. "For a start, Herr Rosenthal is a great dad, from what I can see. And your mum too."
Lena is silent, but I know that what I have said makes sense to her. It has to. Her mother comes to the bed and sits by Lena's head. She strokes her face and speaks to me, carefully.
"We have spoken this to Lena before, that she is adopted; there is much to tell to you Lena, about those days when you were born and all the happenings of then. Your father has promised to speak of these things to you when you are eighteen; so you must wait; your birthday is soon. Then we will speak of the past. Be patient. And," she says as she gives me a smile, "your boy Patrick is right. You have a kind father who loves you. You know this; you know how good he has been to you last year, ja? Now I will go down and leave you for some minutes and then Patrick will go to his place, OK?"
I could hug this woman. She is such a gem of a lady. Lena smiles a little as she leaves and says, "*Danke Mutter.*"
Then she is in my arms and our kisses are long, breath-takingly so.
"Do not leave me Patrick," she says, in between.
"I'm not going anywhere."
After a while we hear her mum call from below.
"Patrick, I think it is time."
"Yip, coming now," I call.
I disentangle myself and stand, pulling Lena up as well.
"What would you like for your birthday?" I ask her.

"I would like you to take me to the mountains," she says.
"Great," I say. "Just us two like?"
"Ja, you and me."
"But your father?"
"I will be eighteen. He will understand and he will be ok because I will tell him that we will be going to see Gaby at his hotel where he is working. It's high up in the Karwendel. And this will be true also."
"What's the Karwendel?"
"A region of very high mountains; it is in Austria but not too far from here. You will love it, even the journey is great for your motor bike. Mountain bends. Bikers come there from all over Europe."
"Brilliant! And...will we be staying with Gaby? Again?"
"Ja, sure. The valley where he is working is so beautiful, and the mountains there. Unbelievable high. It is my favourite place on earth and I want you to be with me there. Please?"
"You try stopping me," I say. "It's a date."

Chapter 35

Bernie Doherty

> Hi mum; u shud watch us this afternoon Live on Facebook; we're playin in a market & in a cafe later, about 7.30. Doing well. Will need more CDs though. U ok? XP

I'm in work son, remember? Actually I am already in the office when I get his text; Mr Johnstone has allowed me a phased return to work until the end of July, so I do five hours a day, 10.30am until 3.30. But I can't miss this opportunity to see Patrick and his girl perform, can I? No way, José.
But what to do? I wonder would the boss let me go if I told him? Naw, don't think so. I think he'd take a right look at me over those half-moon specs and wait long enough for me to withdraw the proposal, especially after him consenting so

magnanimously to these reduced hours. (Like it doesn't seem to dawn on him that I now am trying to do the full day's work in five hours rather than eight.)

'Do you know something?' I say to myself half-way through typing some poor bugger's Last Will and Testament, "I am starting to feel like some sort of headache coming on today. I am afraid I am going to have to go home early, maybe around 2 o'clock when this migraine starts to get really bad."

So that's what I do. Mr Johnstone was so sympathetic, so understandingly generous as usual.

"No problemo, Bernie. Go home. Take some painkillers and get your head down and sure you can maybe make up the hours later in the week. Looks like it's going to be busy with the medical negligence case. You don't want to fall behind."

No, falling behind would never do, would it?

Why am I wasting what's left of my life in this dusty old office? Ah yes, of course...I need to live, don't I?

So I go home, get myself a good strong coffee, just in case I do actually get a headache, go on the tablet and look for MacaLena on Facebook. Sure enough after a bit there they are on my screen, the pair of them. They must have the iPhone clipped on to some sort of stand. I can see bits of them moving around, getting organised. Then Patrick's face appears on screen, looking straight at me out of my own TV; it's a very odd feeling.

"Hi folks. Welcome to MacaLena Live on Facebook, if you're watching; if you're not, you should be, but then you'll never know what you're missing, will you? So why am I talking to you? Anyhow, the rest of you, please stay with us for the next hour or so as we play our songs for you...and for this beautiful town. Let me show you where we are today for this our first live world-wide performance."

The picture starts flying around the place again until it settles and I can see what seems to be a town square surrounded by shops and houses. It's a really idyllic scene, colourful houses like something you'd see in an old-fashioned Christmas card; buildings painted in striking shades of orange, pink, green, red and lemon, a tall clock tower, a fountain, market stalls scattered across cobbled stone streets. It's like a Hans Andersen animation. Patrick is talking over the noise of a chiming church bell and some passing traffic. I am hoping it settles before they start singing.

"So this is a local town called Landsberg am Lech, one of the prettiest places I've seen yet, and watching over us here," as the camera tilts to show us a statue on a tall plinth, "we have the Ever-Blessed Virgin Mary, so we should be alright with her taking care of us. We're not actually sure if we have permission to play on this site, 'cos I wasn't all that clear what the official in the tourist office was trying to say but Lena thinks we are good for a wee gig, right here in the centre of the market. Hope she's right. If they come to complain I'm just going to tell them that I'm playing here because it keeps me off the streets!"

Ha ha, my son; nice one! Did you lie awake long thinking that one up?

Then he looks off screen and calls to her. "Hey Lena, you wanna come and talk to the planet? Please? We need to hear some authentic Bavarian on this stream; even German would do, balance things up."

Lena's face appears on my screen, slightly serious and nervous but looking good. She says a few things in German and gives me a smile...well, gives whoever is watching a smile. Then it's back to the static picture and eventually the action begins.

I have a stupid grin on my face as I watch; they are good together, the harmonies, his guitar which is better than ever and this girl's very unique voice. It all sounds so professional, so good to listen to, even through his phone and this internet connection. He's wearing a lime-coloured T-shirt I haven't seen before; (green so works with his hair colour, I've always thought). Lena is in a white cotton top and lilac shorts, all great at accentuating...I think that is the word that the fashion-writers would use...her skin tone. Patrick looks relaxed, the picture of happiness and, with a sharp wee pang of emotion, I am more proud of him than ever. I wish I'd texted Josie to watch this as well. Maybe he has already though.

As they get stuck into their third song, which turns out to be Simon and Garfunkel's 'Cecelia', (so retro, this 21st century son of mine), I see his phone become genuinely mobile, showing me the audience; Lena must be holding it. I see a good wee crowd gathered around them, happy faces enjoying the show, just ordinary market shoppers, some tourists I'm guessing, quite a few children.

What is happening now, as the picture jumps around showing fuzzy images for a second? Lena seems to be giving out something to some folk in the crowd; a grinning lad of African appearance, a tall blonde lady with a baby in a sling, an older man who looks like an American tourist with his zoom lens camera and someone else I can't quite make out. I can't work out what this is about but suddenly it becomes clear...Lena has given them percussion instruments, maracas, an egg shaker, a tambourine and some sort of wooden blocks...and gradually they are all joining in, adding to the whole rhythm and energy of the song. Some of the crowd start to clap along as Lena leads them, like a spontaneous conductor. It goes very well apparently and at the end the enthusiastic applause is proof of what I am sensing. Now the camera pans around the sea of smiling faces. I am amazed at how the crowd has grown since before; they're a clever pair! This audience participation idea has really generated something.

Now what's he up to, I wonder as Lena focuses on Patrick again? I listen to him addressing the crowd, with interruptions for Lena to translate.

"How many of you have seen the film La La Land? Yes....great, quite a few of you. Brilliant movie wasn't it? Did you like the song 'City of Stars'? My favourite song in the whole show. So would you like to hear our version of 'City of Stars'? No piano here as you can see, just this well-lived-in guitar but we'll have a go at it specially for all the local people in this beautiful city of Landsberg am Lech...ok, it's maybe a town but who cares. 'Ich bin heute ein Landsberger', he says to warm applause.

"Would anyone like to volunteer to film this for us with Lena's phone? Please? Thank you. What's your name? Hannah? Ok, Danke Hannah; we are live on Facebook at the moment you see, so my mum back in Ireland can see. Say 'Hello' to my mum Bernie folks, give her a wave." (*And they do as they are told; this charmer son of mine has a platz-ful of strangers waving to his oul ma from a thousand miles away!*)

"Don't be running off with my phone now," he tells this Hannah volunteer, "and hold it nice and steady, bitte." *Off he goes into the tune, as whoever the new camera-girl is focuses up close on his guitar, then up to his face as he takes the first verse, then to Lena as she joins in with a haunting harmony through verse two.*

Instrumental break and he is talking to them again...can't catch the start of it but looks like he's asking for volunteers again for something. Camera pans around the audience and I see some hilarity going on between the women and their men...can't work out what this is about...until I see one man step forward, looks about fifty actually, quite plump and jolly looking. He approaches Lena who has moved forward towards the crowd as Patrick plays on. What's going on here?

My word, she is going to dance with this guy! There they go, all a bit awkward, neither of them are much good as they try some moves....well actually the wee fat man has style alright and he's spinning Lena around with great gusto. Fair play to them. Lena pulls away and claps him and he does a low bow to great applause. Lena is back into the song for the finale. That went well, a bit of a risk but they pulled it off, the pair of them. I've not seen the movie so I have no idea if they were trying to mimic the moves or just improvising.

It strikes me that my son is very good for this girl; he has always described her as very shy, sad even; she doesn't look too shy now, certainly not sad; either Patrick is bringing her out of herself or she is just so delighted to be with him and so in love that it has switched her light on. I wonder how he has managed that in so short a time? He's only been with her a couple of weeks; must be therapy, musical and/or otherwise...the mind boggles.

Now he's talking to camera again, a kind of moving selfie.

"Danke Hannah. Let's hear it for our volunteer camera girl, yeah. Did a great job. Who wants to be next up? Anyone? Bitte? I need someone to take the phone for this next song because it is a surprise song for my girlfriend and I want the world to see her reaction. She's gonna sit over here..."*(he is manipulating an obviously mystified Lena to sit on the side of the fountain, below the statue of Our Lady)* "... yeah, good, you sit here Lena and, let's see, who can I get to record the song... You, my friend. Great, Danke." *(I can see some young lad come to take the phone)*
"And like I say, this is a surprise, a song I wrote for my stunning girlfriend Lena. Lena is from Bavaria and, as you can probably tell by my obvious lack of lederhosen, I am not. Any guesses as to which country I am from?"

God but isn't he great at working this crowd; he's so magnetic, so enthusiastic and warm. Someone shouts "Schottland!"

"No, not Scotland, but you are close."

"Irland?" *the camera boy says.*

"Ja, Ireland of-course. Germans love Ireland. We have so many people from Germany in Ireland this summer that I didn't expect anyone to be home when I arrived here. And how do you think Lena and I met?"

I watch the faces of the audience; they are hooked on his banter. Lena is translating, but she can barely do it for laughing at him.

"Dating site?" *someone says in English.*

"Good guess but no. Actually what happened was that she saw me on 'Love Island' on TV and started stalking me!"

Lena is laughing as she translates; she tells the crowd something in German and translates to the screen, "He was the one who was stalking me. He even came to my town and arrived at my door to stalk me!"

"Never," *he says,* "Would I do that?"

"Just sing this song," *Lena tells him and he does. It's obviously his own composition and he sings it to her as if she was the only girl on earth. It's really intimate, full of beautifully expressed love, genuine and sincere and personal, yet it's being sung to her in front of maybe fifty German strangers who are hanging on his every word, his every look to his lady.*

I don't catch a quarter of the lyric but I do hear something about 'imagining her dark hair streaming in the wind by the wet Atlantic shore,' and the chorus sticks in my mind in a worrying kind of way.

    My Magdalena, I will never leave you again
    My Magdalena, You're the rainbow in my rain.

And afterwards people are streaming up to throw money in his guitar case and to buy CDs but, while the camera catches some of that as it pans around, what I catch is a quick glimpse of Lena. It is only a fleeting image but I think she has a tissue at her eyes. My God! What has she got to cry about? She's got him and it looks like they're making a living off the back of it!
I must let people know that they are playing later on tonight in this cafe he mentioned. Maybe I'll get a few folks round to watch it with me and have a glass of wine.

Chapter 36

(Patrick McAleese)

21st July, Lena's birthday, so we've decided to forget about busking today. It's been a crazy ride this past few weeks. We've been amazed at how much money we have made; even more amazed at the craic we've had doing it; such a buzz, and she seems to be enjoying it every bit as much as me. But, that said, I've been looking forward to today and just getting to spend some time with her without all the hassles and the adrenaline rush of performing.
Her folks have taken the day off so it doesn't look as if it's ever going to be just the two of us. No worries though; I can wait; we have this trip up into the mountains planned for the middle of next week, after we do a few gigs over the weekend, always the best time for crowds and bar performances. The Irish pubs in Munich have been great for us. It's been crazy, the response from Munich's large Irish contingent, as well as other tourists and local Germans.
All the more reason to chill and enjoy this beautiful Friday.
I am to experience another 'first'; these 'firsts' keep on coming here in Bavaria. We are heading to a nearby lake called Staffelsee and the plan is to go paddle-boarding together. I am just a wee bit nervous about this, not ever having been a great water-freak, but I am assured by Lena that it is straight-forward and very safe. She picked up on my initial split-second hesitation when her dad mentioned the idea and has sort of poked gentle fun at me over it ever since.
Actually, she was dead right. It is so easy and after the first thirty seconds of getting my balance I never once felt anything other than at ease as we skimmed across the water. The surface is

unbelievably calm; not a ripple. It's a huge lake but I'm never quite sure if I am looking at the far bank or at one of its many islands. When we stood by the jetty in Seehausen the clarity of the reflection of the mountains on the lake was like someone's trick photography, an upside-down, colour-enhanced image of idyllic perfection. I find myself taking lots of phone-shots, some of this iconic scenery but most have Lena in the shot, posing in her white bikini on her board like she's a model on a photo-shoot. Instagram is going to crash entirely when I load these up later.

We cross from the jetty to the closest island and have a wander around there. We drink some lemon juice in the shade of the trees, out of the thirty degree heat. Herr Rosenthal takes the opportunity to give me a bit of a history lesson about this place.

"In the ninth century there was a monastery here founded, I have read about this, and it is believed that there is a link to Ireland. A bell of Celtic Christian design was here for many centuries; it came with the monks of Ireland or Scotland. Now it is kept in a nearby church because this monastery is no longer...", and so he continues.

Fascinating, but Lena is holding my hand and leaning into me and the touch of her skin against mine is far more fascinating than the religious heritage of this lake island. If her father is aware of this, or of the vacant glaze over my eyes, he does not say anything.

Or actually maybe he does. He has a brief conversation with his wife in German, or Bavarian, (I can never tell the difference), and then to Lena and me in English.

"Now, Bettina and I will paddle back to Seehausen but you two young people have more energy; you may want to cross the lake, or visit other islands, ja?"

Totally ja, I think and Lena agrees. We leave them and head out west on the oil-smooth water. As we reach the opposite shore half an hour later I am looking down at the flickering reflections of colour and light and it feels like I'm paddling on a horizontal stained-glass window. Beyond the trees that line this lake mountains rise from the plain like layers of grey cathedrals. Clumps of dark cloud have gathered between the highest summits, the colour of plums. The scene is gothically surreal, like a film set for Game of Thrones or something. We bring the boards together and sit on them, facing each other, our feet attracting the attention of shoals of tiny fish below.

"What a day!" I say.

"Ja, but look at the storm clouds in the south. This is a sign of rain coming in the evening. Always it is the same on days like this."
"Really? Even on such brilliant weather?"
"Ja, it is so," she says. "Patrick, I want to ask something of you please?"
"Sure; ask away," I say.
"This evening, my father takes us for dinner somewhere, and then we go home. But I want you to come to my house and stay with me...when he is telling..."
I notice this heaviness falling over her again as I've seen happen in the past, kind of like someone has dropped a dark curtain around her, snuffing out the light in her eyes.
"Sure babe," I say. "What is it? You are sad about something?"
She turns her head away for a minute.
"You know what it is, do you not?" she says. "You know that my father will tell me tonight about...everything. Where I came from and...everything back then."
"Yeah, I know, of-course I know...but he probably doesn't want me to..."
"No! That is not the point. I want you to be there. I need you to be there. No matter what he says, or if he wants you to go, please promise that you will be with me when he is telling me, please Patrick?"
"Of-course babe. Of-course I will be with you."
"I am so scared," she whispers. "I want to know but I do not want to hear it."
She leans forward into my arms and I have to put my feet up over her board to stop it pushing away from under her. Her head is under my chin and I feel a shiver of emotion running through her body. She clings to me and we almost slide off the paddle-boards altogether as my feet can no longer control her board. Instead I grab her as she slips into the water and we somehow finish up lying on my board, her on top of me. Slowly the anxiety seems to drain out of her as I cradle her head. She lifts herself off me a bit and stares down into my eyes; eventually a small smile which gradually turns into an all-out laugh as she realises the absurd position we are in and the fact that her board and both paddles have glided off some distance away.
"What will we do now?" she says.
"I am doing nothing," I tell her. "It was your idea to make love on my board so you can sort out the problem of the paddles."

"I was not making love," she laughs. "I was upset and I needed to be on your board...but you should not have allowed my things to escape."
"With you all over me? You expect me to console you and look after your gear and control all my biological urges with you lying all over me at the same time? That's massive multi-tasking, and I am just a poor Irish boy. You need to go get your board back, and our paddles."
"A poor Irish boy who can not swim! What sort of partner have I got for myself?"
"I can swim; I just don't like getting wet," I tell her and she slips into the water and swims away quickly to her own board. When she is upright again, her paddle in hand, I expect her to try to retrieve mine but she's in a strange game-playing mode and just laughs at me.
"Come on kid, help me out here," I say.
"I want to see you swim," she says; it strikes me that this girl can go from dread and despair to flirtatious laughter in a matter of minutes. I hope tonight isn't too hard for her. Whatever her adoptive father tells her, I want to be there for her as a source of stability, of constancy. I sit down on my board and start splashing towards her using my hands, and too much energy, to the soundtrack of her laughter.

After a lovely meal in a local fish-restaurant we are driving home through a thunder storm. Through the rain-distorted windows we watch the mountains being lit up by huge lightning flashes. The family VW slows as we approach Gaby's folks' house but Lena leans over into the front seat and speaks rapidly to her father. Just as he is about to stop to let me out he hits the accelerator again and the car jerks forward along *Weßobraun Straße*. Lena sits back and gives my hand a little squeeze. We pull into their drive.
I get out of the back seat. It's lashing rain but I still need to wait for an invitation from one of the parents to come in. Lena's mother obliges as her husband stalks quickly away to the front steps. It's almost nine o'clock and there's a stack of talking and listening and questioning and answering to be done before Saturday morning comes around. I follow the family into the living room. Lena disappears upstairs. Her mum lights several candles around the room. They are big into their candles here, and their miniature tin

figurines...farm animals, circus performers, traditional alpine houses and so on. Several family ancestors stare down at us from sepia photographs on the wood panelling. We are as silent as they are. It's a solemn old-fashioned sort of atmosphere as candle essence floats around us.
"Why don't I make some coffee for us?" I suggest. "You guys can sit down and chat."
Coffee at this time of an evening, I think? That was some wise notion, wasn't it. Sure enough, the idea is met with mild derision by the father.
"You want us to be waking all night long?" he says.
"Perhaps tea?" I offer.
"It is ok, Patrick. Relax," coos the mum. "We have a special drink planned for Magdalena at eighteen, her birthday. I am doing this drink now. You sit."
So I do. I sit at the table and stare out at the lightning flashing outside, lighting up the countryside all the way to the mountains. I am feeling very awkward and Herr Rosenthal's silent grump isn't making me feel any more comfortable. He goes into what sounds like a slightly annoyed conversation with his wife and I study the guitar callouses on my fingertips.
As the mother places a glass of orange liquid on the table in front of me I hear Lena running down the stairs again and she reappears in the room in her pyjamas and dressing gown, all very cosy and domestic. Her dad gives her a studied look, then stands up and raises his glass.
"Aperol Spritzer, especially for you Magdalena, our special girl," he says in English, for my benefit and I appreciate it.
"*Alles Gute zum Geburtstag, Magdalena; Lasst uns anstoßen!*" both parents say. I raise my glass and join in, in English.
"Happy birthday Lena."
And that is the last English I hear for a long time. It is understandable but how I wish that tonight, above all nights, I had some basic German. I haven't and so all I can do is watch what happens between child and adoptive parents.
Her dad speaks slowly, gently; I see Frau Rosenthal react emotionally at times and I hear her join in with small qualifications, always very loving in tone. But largely I watch Lena; I try to analyse her every reaction, however tiny. She is incredibly focussed. She asks a question every so often, in the voice of a scared child; her hand goes to her mouth in apparent horror at one point and then

she can't bear to look or to hear, burying her head in her mother's lap until the stroking of her hair seems to bring her some solace and Herr Rosenthal continues.

Apart from the word *München* I don't think I hear a single word that I understand...well maybe one or two, like '*Kirche*' and '*Agentur*' and '*Mutter*'; then I watch as Lena's dad opens an ornate metal box and brings out a couple of objects to show to her. First he hands her a sealed plastic bag which appears to have a lock of hair in it. Lena stares at it almost reverently; she asks her dad something, he nods and she takes the lock of hair in her hands, sniffs it deeply and holds it to her face, an incredibly intense look in her eyes. Instinctively I go to sit with her and put my hand on her shoulder. I feel the surge of emotion from her, crashing like a wave as she breathes, "*Meine Mutter!*"

My God, I think, this is a physical piece of her actual birth mother after all these years, a lock of the woman's hair. But what became of her? Why did she want to give up her baby but want the child to have this macabre memory of her? I am dying to hear the whole story from Lena. But it's not finished yet, obviously.

Her father continues. He holds another small object in his hands and as he speaks I hear repeatedly the phrase '*Maria Magdalena*'. This is mysterious to me and I can barely have the patience to stay quiet. As before, Lena takes from her father what looks like an ornament, a tiny doll or something. I watch her examine it, sniff it and then kiss it, tears streaming silently down her face. I so want to give her some comfort but, apart from the suspicion that this thing, whatever it is, belonged to her mother as well, I haven't a clue what the story is here.

Lena asks a few questions. Both parents answer at times and I can sense the deep empathy in both of them as they explain, I presume, Lena's existence and her adoption into their home. It is a tearful time all round; the tenderness of both father and mother is very touching and I feel privileged to witness it as an outsider. It is a very sacred moment and I do feel more than awkward. In all honesty, but for my love for this girl I would be out of here in a flash.

Just after ten Frau Rosenthal turns to me.

"You are very patient, Patrick. You must be very curious. Lena, would you like to tell Patrick your story or would you like your father to try to tell him in English?"

Lena doesn't know what to say. She can barely talk. In answer she just shrugs her shoulders and leans back into my arms. It's a 'whatever' gesture. I turn to her dad.
"If you don't mind sir, I think Lena is too exhausted by it all; but if you don't want to it can wait until we have a chat later."
He thinks for a bit, then seems to make up his mind.
"Very well, young man; as my wife says, you have been very patient. So I will tell in English...how do you say? The bare bone of the story, ja? Because that is all we know, Bettina and I; we do not have full picture, as you will see."
"Ok, I understand," I say.
"This day eighteen years ago, a small baby was discovered in a box of cardboard. It had been placed inside the door of a church in a part of Munich which I do not know well, east of the Isar river, but...I do not go there. The church was of the Coptic Orthodox tradition; you know this, no? It does not matter to explain this difference to you now, except to say that this church comes originally from Egypt and has members from the Arab community in Munich...that is all I know about it. They have some different theology and practice I think but I..."
I interrupt.
"Why is this important, where the baby was found?"
"It is important. Very important. If the baby was found at a mosque the authorities think that it is a baby of a Muslim girl. If it is found outside a community centre or a shop...no one knows any clues about the baby or its mother, you see? But this baby is found in a place of Christian worship. We must therefore see that the mother is Christian, you understand me?"
"Maybe," I say. "Maybe not."
"Ah, but the baby's mother leaves another clue also. She puts some hair with the child...that is not a clue, but it shows that she wished her child to have some piece of her, ja? The real clue is in the small object which I have given to Magdalena. Show it to him, my dear."
I take in my hands a tiny statue of a red-robed figure, a brown-skinned lady, I note, who is holding some sort of jar, like it is a very precious object. Lena's eyes never leave it.
"This is a religious icon of importance," he goes on. "It is an image of the woman from the Bible known as Maria Magdalena, you see. She is wearing red clothes. She carries a box of ointment for bathing the feet of Jesus in the gospel story."
"Ok," I say, "this is why Lena was given that name, I take it?"

"Ja, but you are jumping ahead," he says. "The lady who was the mother of that baby, our Magdalena, was never found. We do not know what became of her. We only know that she was most probably of Egyptian or other Arab origin. She was almost certainly Coptic Christian in her background. This icon we have had experts to examine; people from the church there in Munich, scholars, I think is your word? They tell me that it is unique to an area of Coptic Christianity in Egypt. It is not a common statue, very rare. So you see, it is a big clue."

"So are you saying that Lena's birth mum came from Egypt?"

"Not exactly. It is possible. These Coptic Christians are being persecuted constantly in Egypt, especially recently but also in the past. She may be a refugee from this but it is impossible to be sure. It is only a clue that this is some part of her identity, you see. She may have been a recent migrant from there, or from any nearby Middle eastern place. Or she may be of earlier migration to Germany, many years ago, we will never know. What we know is that she put the Maria Magdalena icon with her child as a connection to the culture it comes from, a Christian culture of the east."

"And were the authorities not able to trace her? How come she disappeared? Like, this was what? 1999; not long ago. Surely the police...CCTV and all. Somebody must have seen her?"

"The authorities tried. They were not successful. The woman had vanished. Perhaps she perished; the river Isar is nearby. Perhaps the people who were using her had no more use for her. We do not know."

Lena looks up sharply at this.

"What people? Who was using her? What do you mean papa?"

"It is what the authorities were telling us, Magdalena. That the lady was... she was most probably not married...she may have had many men...perhaps employed by a criminal gang."

"How do they know this? They know nothing about her," Lena cries.

"Because, my dear, when you were discovered and taken to the hospital you were very ill; they found that you had some very bad drugs in your bloodstream. You had to be slowly cleaned of these drugs, otherwise you would not be here now. And this is why we were so worried about you, you understand?"

"My mother was a drug addict?"

"So it seems, almost definitely."

"And she needed to make money to buy her drugs?"

"Ja, that is why she became a...how do you have it in English? A 'fallen woman', ja?" Lena's father looks down at his hands.
There is a silence. A 'fallen woman' as your mother! I am thinking that this is so hard for Lena to hear; she starts to cry. It's hard for me to take too. I don't like the term, not one bit, and I tell him this.
"What do you mean, she was 'fallen'? She was a human being, just like the rest of us."
"Ja, of-course she was, Patrick," he tells us. "I suppose it means that she had fallen away from the...the right way of living. She had fallen away from God, turned away from the church, that's all."
"Except that she turned towards the church," I say.
"I do not understand?" He looks confused.
"She took her baby to the church, didn't she? So she had turned back to it, if you think about it," I say, "and so we have Lena."
The parents look at each other and Lena's mum smiles in agreement. I put my arm around Lena and hold her gently until I feel her sobbing begin to subside. "I love you, I love you Lena," is all I can think to whisper into her ear.
"We all love you Magdalena," her mum repeats beside me.
Lena sits forward away from me and turns to her father.
"So you think she wanted to give this statue to tell me that she had been a prostitute, just as Maria Magdalena had been a prostitute?"
"No, I do not think this, my dear. This cannot be. You must not think so. Let me explain you why. First, Maria Magdalena was not prostitute. There is no reference to this in the gospels. Ja, she had seven *Dämonen* cast out from her, she was not a good woman at the beginning but later she was becoming a disciple of Jesus. This box she is carrying in the statue...you see it? It is a jar of ointment, costing much money for a poor woman, and she was using this to wash the feet of her *Meister*. She was a close follower. In the Gospels she is at the important moments in the story, at the cross and the resurrection. It is a myth that she was a...you know."
"Then why is she always shown as a scarlet woman?"
"This was a story created by early leaders of the church in Rome who were male and who were wanting to keep women in their place, not becoming leaders in church life, you understand? So this icon is not about your mother's way of living. It is about her faith, her identity as a person of devotion to Jesus Christ."
Lena looks doubtful about this explanation but I appreciate what Herr Rosenthal is trying to do here, good priest that he is. Anything to give this hurting daughter some hope, some light. At the same

time I am thinking how ludicrous it is in 2017 to be employing a two thousand year old legend about some mythical woman who may or may not have been a whore to try to comfort your adopted daughter. I decide to move the conversation on, away from Mary Magdalene and Lena's poor mother.
"So how did you come to be Lena's parents then?"
The Rosenthals look at each other. The mother takes up the story.
"We had been married for a lot of years and no baby was coming. We talked about adopting a child; we go on a list for this adopting." She looks to her husband to continue.
"Soon after we had registered with the agency we had a call to come to an orphanage in Munich to see this tiny baby girl."
"We fell in love with her from the beginning," continues her mum.
"I totally get this," I say giving Lena a squeeze. "Me too."
"So we discuss her health problems that she has been recovering from in the six months since she was found; the agency is also wanting a family of Christian faith to become her parents."
"Not from this Coptic church though?" I ask.
The parents look at each other.
"It seems that no one from that church had a desire to take care of a new baby; they were asked but no response. So we were delighted, as you can tell, and Magdalena came to be our daughter."
Frau Rosenthal joins in. "The best thing that ever happened to us."
"Me too," Lena adds with her first attempt at a smile since this saga began and they come together in the most incredible hug-in. Not the stereotypical picture of German reserve, I think, but I'm learning. Bizarrely at one point the father breaks out into some kind of prayer; it's not your solemn liturgical monotone church prayer either; this one is spontaneous. He gets pretty excited as he near enough squeezes the life out of his adopted daughter. His wife has to calm him down with some comment about *'die Nachbarn'* which I judge by her look to the window to be 'the neighbours'.
File under 'Weird moments that I have known'.

Later I am walking down the street to my flat. The rain has gone, the thunderstorm having passed on, leaving a lovely clear night with a huge moon resting on the alpine skyline to the south. I have the strongest feeling of isolation, dislocation even. Here I am, well after midnight in a strange and silent Bavarian village, a massively long way from where I live, the place I have always thought I belonged.

Right now I am alone on planet earth staring up at the stars of this foreign sky. What am I doing here? Why have events conspired as they have, so I am here at this point in time? Does any of this matter? How did this come about? Is there any meaning to it all or is the sequence of events that brought me to this specific place at this specific time all just chance happenings? I don't know.

I think back to the lovely coincidence that first brought me into contact with Lena, that strained FaceTime call. Seems like ages ago. How fragile it all was then. And how slowly we grew into each other at the start. At what point did it become love?

What is this 'love' anyhow? Just an intense and irrational set of feelings between two individuals? Two individuals of such randomly diverse backgrounds? Is it simply the emotional connection which is a necessary kick-start to a sexual relationship? Is that what this is all about...biology? About my need to have her in as close a physical relationship as we already enjoy in terms of friendship and emotional intimacy? And if so, what if that never happens, or if the sex is a disaster? Will it all have been pointless, a mirage blown away by the winds of circumstance? And if it does happen, is that any guarantee of meaning, of permanence? It wasn't for my mum!

And how does Lena feel about it all? I did not have much chance to chat any further to her after that family gathering. Yeah, it was a very special honour to be allowed to witness all that happened and I know it was vital to Lena that I was there but I so wanted time to debrief with her afterwards. I wanted to hold her and listen to her heart after those revelations.

It wasn't to be though, as her father insisted that she take no longer than two minutes to say our 'Good-nights' in the hall before I left. I can imagine her now, curled up in her bed, crying through the unanswered questions she must still have, likely being consoled by her lovely adoptive mother but wondering inside herself about the one she never knew.

If I am having my own existential thoughts how much more challenging are Lena's feelings after what she has heard tonight?

One thing I decide as I turn in Hauser's driveway. I will never abandon this girl. Never, no matter what. I have no idea what the implications of this may be, practically speaking, but it's like a light has switched on in my head. And so, as I accept this, I look up to the sky and I say aloud to whoever is listening, "This is it. This is me. This is what I am for, me and her, always."

How ridiculous to be saying this to the moon, I think, as I go inside.

Chapter 37

Bernie Doherty

I haven't heard from him for a day or two. If I mind right last Friday was meant to have been her birthday. I wonder how that went.

Here I am on an Ulsterbus beside Loch Lomond. No, it's not that the driver has taken a wrong turn somewhere around Larne and gotten badly lost; I am on a coach tour to Scotland; I had never imagined that I'd find myself on one of these. Usually if I'm having a holiday away I'd head to the sun, Spain or Portugal or somewhere, but with the Pound so weak against the Euro and with my health issues I thought that this year I should maybe play safe. These tours are dead cheap, we have 2 star accommodation but it's lovely, the food is grand and the craic on the coach is ninety. Actually a few of the passengers seem to be up around the ninety as well but there's a fair few younger ones...you never know who you can meet on these excursions, from what Alison has told me. Looking around at them, I can't see it somehow! Well, that's not exactly fair; there is one man who has been very friendly; he is on his own, like me, and has sat beside me at a couple of the mealtimes. Jim is his first name and that's about all I know of him, that and the fact that he's an electrician from Castlewellan. You never know...this might spark off into something.

The evening entertainment is...'interesting', let's say. It has all those subtle nuances about it that only a Norn Irish person gets. Like when some one asks the accordion player if he can play 'The Londonderry Air'.

"No," he says, "but I'll play you 'Danny Boy'."

He does too, and I have to say he is more than able for it.

The coach driver's jokes are pretty well sanitised too but he did get a laugh with his slightly risky observation about the recent Twelfth of July celebrations. "Some Alliance politician was trying to explain to Theresa May the difference between a working class Unionist and a middle class Unionist. One burns pallets and the other burns pellets," he says.

I looked around the faces at that one; I wasn't the only one doing that either but everybody was in stitches.

"Great that we can get away and have a laugh at ourselves," said Jim across the aisle from me.

Ourselves? Whatever you say say nothing, Bernie.

Anyhow, it's time I heard from this lost son of mine, so I send a wee text.

> Mother calling; anything wrong there? Guitar worn ur fingers down so u can't txt? Any bars about her birthday? You get her something? X

I had tried to get Josie to come with me on this trip, just for company, but she told me in no uncertain terms to go and take a running jump to myself. She had some trip planned for August with a couple of her friends from work. Nice for some. I could have done with her, or with somebody, anybody who understands what I've been through in the past twelve months. I get these times when I seem to lack energy, even wee fits of...well, depression is too strong a word for it but it's somewhere along that spectrum. Just a feeling of pointlessness, yeah and if I'm honest, bouts of feeling lonely and sorry for myself. Which isn't like the Bernie Doherty I used to know and love, that girl who faced down persecution from family and friends in her native Derry and survived, who shook herself loose from an unwise marriage, who brought up two good kids to be proud of all on her own. I look at my phone, waiting for him.

It strikes me that I am kind of living his German love affair vicariously. It's my personal real-life 'Mills and Boon' soap opera, starring my own son. Problem is that it's a bit hard to keep up with the storyline, given his lack of communication. "Here we go now," I think as my phone bleeps.

> Hi. Sorry, ja no finger left on hiis hand so thiis is Lena texting; Ja he buy me engagement ring and necklace. Be happy for me! He is sooo kind! X

My mouth drops open as I read this. Patrick McAleese!!! What are you at? I reply at speed. It comes out all wrong.

> PATRICK!!! Talk to me! U lost ur idiotic mind or what is going on there?

I press send too quickly and then start to realise that the same boy is probably taking the mick. Sure enough, he comes straight back.

> Just kidding. Don't get ur knickers in a twist ma. But I did get her a necklace. Photos on their way. All good but a lot to tell u about the birthday. Busking today in Munich & off on mountain hike 2moro. What's happening with you? XP

That's better. No FaceTime Live performance today though...pity; I'd love to have shown this lot some genuine entertainment live from middle Europe, seeing as we can't afford to go there any more.
Ah well. So he's off up the mountains tomorrow with her. I'm sure that will be some 'high' for him. Pity that all can't be live on FaceBook too. Maybe not though.
I stare out the window at the choppy grey waters of this famous Loch.

Chapter 38

(Patrick McAleese)

So to the Karwendel. And what a place! Awesome is a highly overused word since the Americans got hold of it but it is the only word to described these mountains. Sheer awesome.
The journey into the heart of this Tirolean range was in itself pretty thrilling. I roared up the road known as the *Kesselbergstraße*, swinging around those hairpin bends like a set of over-worked wiper blades. Down left, down right, down left, down-right brilliant...especially with Lena hanging on with her arms tight around my waist, giggling like a kid on a merry-go-round. Up through the forests and along the valley of the Isar river, these head-waters being no more than a weave of shallow streams at this time of year.

Lena instructs me to pull in beside a series of rushing cataracts and waterfalls on the Rissbach river. It is so hot with the leathers and helmet on that I would love to jump into the water but Lena is horrified that I would even think of it. "You will disappear," she tells me. "It is too powerful." She's probably right, not worth the risk but I do bathe my feet and splash a lot of water around both of us.
We eat a picnic lunch which Frau Rosenthal has insisted we bring with us, cold sausage, crusty rolls, some bananas. The constant roar of the river is our soundtrack, the air full of alpine flowers.
"What did my father say to you before we were leaving?" Lena asks.
I'd hoped she wouldn't ask this question. I can't answer it, not truthfully, not fully.
"He talked about how much you mean to him and your mum," I say.
"What did he say about me?"
"That he loved you, that's all," I lie. "Actually, it was more me that he wanted to talk about."
"How do you mean?"
"Just that he is enjoying getting to know me; stuff like that. He wanted to know about my background, my folks and all."
There was an element of truth in that alright; it had felt at times a bit like an interrogation on behalf of the 'Historical Enquiries Team." What was my father's background? My mother's? Why had my parents split up? Was the fact of their different religions an issue? Was my mother a practising Catholic? What about me myself? And had I had many girlfriends?
But this had only been a mild intro to the main point he had wanted to talk about of-course.
What were my intentions with Magdalena? (Dear God!)
I can't quite remember how I answered that one. I spluttered something that, whatever my involvement with his daughter, it would always and only be motivated by my love and respect for her. It must have come out alright, (and indeed I was not bluffing him in any way,) because he moved on to explain.
"Let me tell you why I have a big concern for her," he had begun. I'd been about to say, "Look, I understand; she has been through a lot in the last couple of days, finding out about her mother and all," but he preempted me.
"You see, it is not only these things which we have spoken about on Friday night. These things do affect her. But there are other much more serious things which have happened in her life which make

Magdalena a girl of complicated character; you must understand that; you must try to forgive her and be a rock for her."

I'd been a bit flabbergasted by this; I wasn't quite sure how to react so I had just said something like, "But of-course, I want to be someone she can depend on, of-course I do so please don't...."

"You see," he had continued, "Magdalena tried to build her house upon sand. She trusted in...let me just say that she believed a lie. We did not know at the time. Her whole house came tumbling down and almost destroyed her."

The clergyman had been speaking in English but he might as well have been talking in double-Bavarian as far as I was concerned. 'Houses built on sand'? Was this some kind of spiritual metaphor that had escaped me in my inattentive rebellion during RE classes? What was this lie she had believed in? Was it to do with her birth-mother? Had Lena been expecting her to be a saintly Mother Theresa type who had had a modern immaculate conception?

Whatever it was, listening now to some of the things her father was saying I started to wonder if I really knew my girlfriend at all. I had tried to express a kind of bland empathy about the situation but it must have showed that I was totally in guess-land here.

"Look," I'd said, "whatever she has been imagining or whatever she has been through...we can work it out together, her and me. I will listen to her stories and try to be as wise as I can with her, alright?"

"I am doubting very much if she will tell you. You see, she wants you to continue to love her so..."

Whaaat? This had sounded like some kind of slur on his daughter's character. What sort of issue could be serious enough for him to be saying a thing like that about Lena, his girl? I couldn't have this.

"Herr Rosenthal, there is nothing Lena, or yourself, for that matter, can tell me that will affect my love for her, trust me."

He'd jumped straight back at me. "And can I trust you, young man, can I trust you to...ah, to stay away from her tonight when you are alone in the mountains together? I speak of...how do you say in English...the sins of the flesh, you understand?"

This had taken me by surprise and I found myself saying, "Of-course, but we are not alone; Gaby will be around I think."

"Gaby may or may not be around but I must have your promise on this?" he had said with that intense look he can muster, like I saw when he was preaching to his flock on my first Sunday here.

"Yes of-course," I said.

At that point I was crossing my fingers all the way up to my elbows, figuratively speaking. He had reached out to shake hands. I did but inside my head I was screaming, "Your daughter is eighteen sir! She can make up her own mind about what we do together."

Now as she and I eat lunch in silence it has become a barrier between the two of us. I cannot very well say, "So what is this sand you have been building your house on Lena? Your father tells me that there are things you don't want me to know in case you lose me; what would they be?"

I make a conscious decision to put this from my head, to continue as we have been and to enjoy this couple of days in the Karwendel that I have been so looking forward to.

I notice that she is wearing the birthday gift I bought her beneath her Irish T-shirt. I pull her over to me so her head lays on my lap and my hands play with the pendant.

"My little Irish colleen," I say. "Irish, Bavarian, German..."

"Perhaps also Egyptian," she says. There's no irony or regret in her tone, I am glad to hear.

"Yeah, well wherever," I say. "Whoever dreamt you up and stirred your DNA together did a fantastic job. You look just beautiful, babe."

"I do not agree but I am glad you think so," she says.

We spend a while throwing stones into the cascading water before getting back on the bike.

"In a few kilometres we are in Austria," she tells me. "It is only half an hour to the hotel where Gaby is working. Then we climb, ok?"

"Of-course ok," I say, "you are the tour guide," and we set off again, south along the river valley. It is a beautiful ride. We climb higher into the mountains, past meadows of amazing flowers and magnificent old trees. We pass a few isolated wooden huts, scattered randomly on the mountain sides. I am wondering what they are so I point and do the inquisitive hand sign to Lena behind.

"These are for farmers, to store hay," she yells. "Like the barn where those Jewish people were being hidden, you know...in mother's story about her grandfather. It was just like this, I think."

People seem to have a thing around here about setting up little towers of stones in the river beds...they are everywhere. Actually people are everywhere too, stacks of them; I probably shouldn't be surprised by the numbers of them. This is Munich's playground after all, the Alps and the lakes.

We reach the Gasthaus where Gaby works, park the bike and go inside to look for him. There he is behind a bar, all smiles to see us

both. And yes, of-course he is planning to come with us on our hike up to the head of the valley, after he finishes work in an hour or two. He tells us that he has already booked his stay in something called '*Falkenhütte*', a refuge hut of the Alpine Club.
"You are staying there too?" he asks.
"Nein, we are hoping to borrow your tent," Lena says. "We brought two sleeping bags with us."
"Ok, you may have my tent of-course but I think it will be cold; we are above 1900 metres there."
"I think we will be ok," Lena tells him with a tiny smile.
We leave him to his duties and head out into the heat again. It's hard to believe he was warning us about cold later tonight. It must be over thirty degrees here. The gear makes it worse of-course, as we wander the rough path between the river and the meadows.
"This water is too tempting," she says.
"I was thinking that too."
"Come," she says. "We go this way."
She turns off the main track to follow a tributary stream towards a deep-looking gully in the rock face.
'What has she got in her head now?' I am wondering. "Do you know where you are going?" I ask.
"Ja, I have been before."
I start to hear the sound of gushing water from above. We clamber over piles of scree and dead trees, presumably victims of past avalanches. Soon we reach a spot where this stream tumbles over a tall barrier of rock in a stunning waterfall. It must be about half a dozen metres high and it has carved out an idyllic pool in the rocks.
"Wow, this is beautiful," I say.
"Ja, perfect for us to cool down." She starts to peel off her gear.
I don't need a second invitation. I watch her, wondering where she is going to stop. Soon we are standing hand in hand beside each other in nothing but our underwear.
"You done this before?" I ask.
She shakes her head. "I think it will be very cold so be careful; do not jump straight in. Also watch out for the sharp rocks underneath."
We lower ourselves into the water and, if the sight of Lena's gorgeous brown figure didn't take my breath away already, this ice-cold water does. I'm gasping within seconds. The pool is only a metre or so deep, certainly at the sides, so it's less about swimming and more about splashing around to try to generate some motion heat. Lena swims away from me towards the centre where the

surface is being churned up by the fall of water. I'm not sure this is a good idea. How would I be able to help her if she gets cramp?

"Hey come back here," I shout. "Stay beside me."

"Always," she grins as she swims back into my arms.

"Who needs a Coors Lite?" I joke through chattering teeth. "This is absolutely freezing!"

"Of-course; it is coming from the melting glacier above."

I am not really thinking about melting glaciers as the smoothness of her body slides all over me. I am experiencing conflicting instincts in my own body; it's a kind of argument between survival and arousal. Literally two minutes after we've gone down into this water I have had enough. I am not sure that, even if I get out right now, certain parts of me will ever function again; more likely just break off.

"Come on girl, let's get out of here," I say but she's enjoying this, grinning at me as she pins me down in the water.

"You are too cold, my poor little one?" she mocks. "Don't you have cold water in Ireland too?"

"Maybe, but I generally walk around it," I say as I swing her over so that she is underneath me. I dunk her head below the water.

"I baptise you, Magdalena McAleese, in the name of..."

Her head pops up and she seems annoyed.

"Patrick, do not mock this," she says.

"Sorry babe; let's get out. I am frozen from head to toe. There's bits of me may never thaw again."

"I have noticed this," she teases.

We climb out to the bank and I try to open my rucksack but my fingers have lost all feeling and power. Lena has to do it for me; she pulls out our bath towel and wraps herself in it, laughing at the shape of me, barely able to protest at her selfishness. Then she opens the towel wide and I join her inside. We hold each other until our bodies warm each other up again. It's a very special and a very long, slow reenergising moment.

"When you pushed me under the water just now...did you call me Magdalena McAleese?" she asks.

"Yeah, I got confused; it must have been a brain-freeze," I tell her.

"I liked it," she says; then as my hands start to explore around her hips and thighs inside our towel-tent she reacts abruptly and pulls away. "But I do not like this Patrick!"

I stop of-course, and my puzzlement with this girl grows. She opens the towel to release me.

"Sorry," I say, "but you give me all the wrong signals and then you chicken out, Lena. What am I to make of you? We are holding each other like lovers and you can sense my..my desire for you...then you pull away. I don't get it. I'm sorry if I have annoyed you; I am just..."
"You are impatient, like all boys," she says. "You want to make love to me before you know me, before you can really understand me; that is all. It does not mean I don't love you Patrick."
I shrug my shoulders in defeat. I watch her as she starts to dress again. I am starting to shiver again, missing her warmth.
"How do I not understand you? I have known you for what, over a year now. I think I know you pretty well. I think you know me too, and I think you love me as much as I love you; you make me the happiest person in the world, Lena."
"Thank you," she says, softly, shyly.
"So how much more of you is there that I do not understand yet?"
She dresses, mechanically, not looking at me, her mind far away.
"It's like you are an onion; I peel away one layer, and then there is another. I think I've gotten to the bottom of you but I discover there's more layers. They seem to go on and on and I'm starting to fear that I may never get to the real you. Believe me babe, it is the real you that I love and that I want but, these mysteries...I don't know."
She turns back towards me and stands there, her head down but I can see the tears tripping down her face and falling on the grass, her own mini waterfall. She looks so pathetic, so broken.
I go to her, still in only my boxers, and hold her as she sobs. Eventually she whimpers into my ear.
"Patrick, I do not want to lose you. I would make love to you now if it meant I would never lose you, I would. But you will go away."
"I am not going anywhere. Trust me. Let me love you, completely."
"I want to. But..."
"But what babe?"
"I am scared. There are things which have happened. You do not know...and I am afraid that if you have me and then find more things about me later...that you will run away from me."
"Lena, nothing will make me run away from you. That is the truth. It's like the song I was making for you when we were in that Irish pub in Munich. I finished it the night of your birthday."
"What song?"
"Did I not tell you those lyrics?"
"No, you did not. Do you remember them?"
"Yeah, I think so."

"I want to hear them."
"Ok," I say and I start to recite the words as I can recall them.
"No," she says, "sing them please."
"Sing them? But..."
"Please? Just hold me and sing to me."
"Ok, but I'm shivering here; help me dress first."
So she does; and then I sing to her.

> *Nothing I can say, nothing I can do*
> *Can help you understand the way I feel for you*
> *It's not just how you look, it's not just what you wear*
> *It's not your smiling eyes or the way you do your hair*
> *Deep inside your heart you are perfect*
> *Underneath the mask that you wear*
> *Lord only knows I don't deserve this*
> *Lord only knows how much I care*
>
> *Something in your life, something in your past*
> *Has undermined the truth that love can really last*
> *I can feel your pain, your mother went away*
> *But please believe me girl when I say I'm here to stay*
> *Deep inside your heart you are perfect*
> *Prettiest girl I've ever seen*
> *Lord only knows I don't deserve this*
> *Lord only knows just what you mean*
>
> *Deep inside your heart you are perfect*
> *Prettiest girl I ever knew*
> *Lord only knows I don't deserve this*
> *There's nothing I can say, there's nothing I can do*

"That is so lovely, Patrick," she says. "But I am not the beautiful person you think."
"Yeah you are; don't argue. I see you from the outside and I think I know you on the inside."
"No you do not," she says, "but it feels like you already know more about the inside me than I have been realising. The words about something in my past...how did you say?"
"Undermining?"
"Ja; this word I do not know but I think it is right. I was in a fake world for some time. Nothing was what I imagined it was. I was too

naive, too stupid. I made a bad mistake. Now I find it hard to love. I do not find it hard to love you, but I find it hard to love you like you want, like you deserve."
"Ok, and can you tell me about it, whatever it was?"
She thinks about this for a bit. 'Don't disappear into your guilt trip again,' I am thinking. She sighs heavily.
"I will try. Can you wait until Gaby is with us? He can help explain it."
"Gaby knows about it?" I am shocked.
"He was my only friend through all my trouble. Yes he knows; he has been my only supporter...until I meet you," she says with a sweet little smile.
We leave the pool behind us and descend to the valley floor again, but I think I will not forget it's chilling water nor the closeness it produced between me and my girl.

It is quite a climb up the main Rissbachthal to the high saddle between two ridges of jagged peaks; we leave the valley floor and hike through thick coniferous forests until we come out above the tree line. The views are as magnificent as I have been told and I find myself taking shot after shot on my phone, not least some brief videos of Lena and Gaby walking through herds of cattle, their bells ringing loud across the otherwise silent landscape.
Above us we see occasional eagles soar close to the cliff edges, riding the thermal currents and looking for their next meal. I've been told to look out for deer but I see nothing. Lena climbs the steep rocky path ahead of me seemingly with little effort as she chats with Gaby. They have such energy but I am struggling; the air is thin and the rucksack and tent don't get any lighter. It is wild and lonely up here on top of the world. At one point Lena is a good fifty metres ahead of me; she turns and waits until I catch up.
"Have you seen any wild life?"
"Yeah, I've been following a couple of mountain goats for the last hour. I'm guessing the one with the beard is 'Billy'," I tell her.
"And the one without?" she asks.
"She's hot," I say. "So hot she could start a forest fire here all by herself."
"Ha ha," she says. "You are too funny."
"Can we stop and eat soon?"

"Only another half hour until we are at Falkenhütte," Gaby tells me.
"And there we can make hot coffee," Lena says, "and use their facilities before we set up our tent."
"Our tent? You sure you don't want to sleep inside with Gaby?" I say, with just a hint of the green-eyed dragon in my query.
She gives me a funny look and ignores the question. Instead she slips her hand under my arm and puts her face against my shoulder.
"Will my Irish boy please stop being silly?" she says. "And also will he stop being a big strong stubborn male and allow me to carry the rucksack for the last part of this climb?"
"Thought you'd never ask," I say and hand it over to her.
"I did ask, if you have forgotten but you wanted to show off to Gaby that you were so tough."
"Gaby? Why would I want to show off to him?"
"Ah boys," she says smiling. "You know how boys are. My muscle is bigger than yours."
Later, after a pretty sparse meal of dark brown bread, chunks of hard cheese and strips of smoked ham, we are sitting on a couple of logs outside our tent, she and I with one sleeping bag wrapped around our shoulders and Gaby cuddled up opposite in the other. We have descended from the very exposed site of the mountain lodge to pitch our tent in a more secluded little valley between rocky outcrops, with a few scraggy trees and bushes for company. The temperature has already fallen dramatically and must be close to freezing point, even though the sun is still just above the horizon.
We sit in the silence of expectation, Lena with her head down, leaning tightly into my shoulder. I don't want to say anything. I suspect she has talked to Gaby on the climb up about whatever it is she feels she has to tell me but obviously it is not his place to start the whole saga. So it is down to Lena really, if she wants to talk through this what is hopefully the last layer of the onion. But I do understand it is very difficult for her.
I try to think of anything I would find difficult to tell her about. There is nothing. Family matters, my father...all that I have already shared with her. There haven't been any other girlfriends, at least not serious ones that I have been in a going-out relationship with; yeah there was Madison but she was just a fantasy type of thing.
"Patrick?" she says, out of the blue.
"Yeah babe?"
"You will not be my first boy."

Good, well...good that she has started, but that's a bit of a stark beginning. I wait. Gaby is examining a pine cone very closely.

"Ok," I say. "So what? You had another boyfriend."

"Don't be...what is your word? Flippant?"

"I wasn't being flippant. I just mean that it's no big deal."

"It is...a very very big deal."

"Ok why?"

She looks at Gaby and speaks to him in German. From his body language I am guessing that he's not going to be much of a help to her in this. She's on her own, poor girl.

"Please Lena, it's ok," I say as I sense her little body shake with feeling beside me.

"I wish it were ok."

More silence. This is slow conversation. The priest would have left the confessional by now. I'm hanging in there.

She appeals to Gaby again. He is reluctant but to be fair to him he sits forward and becomes her advocate, a very gentle one too.

"Ok," he begins. "This is difficult Patrick; you see, when Lena was fifteen she became involved...I think that is how you say it, ja?...involved with a gang of boys from another town, not of our school...and it was a bad experience for her."

Lena is shivering beside me now, clinging to me.

"It's ok, babe," I tell her.

"It is very hard for her to talk about, you can see. But I do not know all the details; it was abusive; Lena was a victim and she suffered much pain, physical but also mental."

Oh my God, I am thinking; how could any such thing happen to this beautiful girl, to my Lena? What sort of world? What sort of guys would... She begins to speak for the first time in a while.

"It began as a relationship through Facebook. I met a boy online. I thought this boy was fifteen also. But he was older. I did not know in time."

"I'm so, so sorry," I say. "You don't have to say anymore Lena. It's ok."

"No, you must know."

"Yeah, please just listen to her story Patrick," Gaby tells me.

She takes a slug from the bottle of wine we have brought and resumes.

"The first boy, he came for me after school one day. I should have suspected...he was driving, so he was older, perhaps twenty something. I went in his car. He gave me alcohol and maybe there were other drugs inside it. I was not able to remember much. I was away from home for the whole night. There were many boys at the house. Some other girls too. I do not know how many of these boys had me. It seemed like many. I could not think...I could not do anything." She fights back her tears again and I feel her pain like a fire in my head.

"You poor kid! How did you get away, like get back home?" I ask.

"I did not escape. I was too...dizzy. My father, next day he took Gaby and searched for me but they were not finding me. So they went to the police. Through my Facebook page they were able to tell who the boy was and they tracked him down. The police made a raid on the place. Some boys were arrested. I was questioned too, then I was taken to hospital, to check everything and do some procedures...even that was horrible."

"Jeez Lena, that is a terrible story," I say. "But you were alright, after the hospital checks like?"

She looks at Gaby for help.

"Not really alright," he says. "It has taken a long time for her to make this recovery that you see now. She was...Lena was very low afterwards, depressed, some self-harming, not eating and quite sick. Our school was a big help; Herr Fischer especially. He insisted that she be allowed to go on the History trip to the Somme."

"Thank God for Herr Fischer," I say and Lena responds with a squeeze.

"Ja, he and Gaby saved me; these two and God," she says. "Nobody else wanted to be near me. Herr Fischer is the one who used music to try to reach inside me. It was not only about my singing. He also played me so much beautiful classical music; hours and hours of it. And I think it helped to sort my mind and to calm my emotions. He is a lovely man."

"And Gaby too," I add.

"Gaby is my best friend in all the world," she says, "except for you, of-course. But he has been so kind. I always feel safe with him. He wants nothing from me. I always like friends like Gaby who are gay because they have this kind spirit, not taking advantage of me."

Not like me, I am thinking as I hang my head. I could barely wait to get into her pants; what a selfish idiot I feel now. I think Gaby reads me, because he switches the subject in my direction.

"It is not like that," he says. "I enjoy your company as much as you enjoy mine, Lena. And the other thing that has helped you to recover is that you found this Irish boy to love."

"But he only loved me because he did not know me," she mumbles. "Now he must want to leave me and find someone who is pure."
"I have already found someone who is pure," I tell her. "She is sharing a sleeping bag with me at the minute and she is pure. Pure magic as well as everything else."
She just cuddles closer. "I was so scared you would walk away from me Patrick. You can not believe how scared I was. Even now I can hardly understand that you want to stay with me."
"What happened those guys, by the way? Were they charged?"
"Ja, they were," Gaby answers. "Their gang was broken up. Two are in prison. I think. And some were sent to a special school...I think you say it is to re-make their character. It was an important case in our courts."
"Gaby came every day when I spoke...my evidence," Lena says. "Everybody else in school thought I was a *Schlampe*...what word is it in English?"
I can't answer that but I can make a good guess.
"My father said this word. A 'fallen woman'? A slut, do you say? It was a bad time in school but...but now I am so happy for you two, my only true friends. I thank God for both of you; and I say thank you to both of you for being with me. I love you both, in different ways of-course."
I'm thinking back to when she sang 'Imagine' in front of all those school-mates who knew her back-story. Wow! How brave she was to do that.
"My parents were good too. My father said that God had forgiven me but that I also should forgive myself. But that is difficult. I feel so stupid, so dirty. Today, when you held me in that freezing cold water with you, Patrick, I felt that I can begin to forgive myself."
"That's great babe," I say.
Gaby starts to struggle to his feet. "It is time for me to get in from this cold," he says. "You two will be ok together tonight, I think, ja? Or would you like me to stay?"
I look from his wide grin to Lena's coy smile; no need to reply, so I struggle to my feet and I give him the warmest hug I've ever given another guy; Lena joins in and it is a special moment.
Not quite as special as the long, gentle intimacy I have with Lena all through this wonderful night in the freezer that is the Karwendel. I will probably never be so cold again in my entire life, nor so happy. We lie entwined inside both sleeping bags, fully-clothed and clinging

onto each other for heat; we giggled, kissed, sang and eventually slept...slept for a long time.

Without realising it, we had camped in such a position that the early morning sun, rising above the rim of the eastern mountain range, shines directly into this valley and pours heat on the side of our tent. I feel Lena stir beside me; she seems to be struggling with her jeans.

"Come, my Patrick," she says.

"Come where babe?" I say, sitting up, thinking she means breakfast.

"No, no, you stupid boy. You need me to explain? You have healed me. I feel so...so happy, so new, you know? So clean."

"Yeah?"

"Yeah. And now...I want you...come on, Patrick! Love me."

So...I'm sorry, Herr Rosenthal, but there is no way your daughter was going to let me keep that rash promise I made to you.

There are no words, so I will not attempt to put any around it; just to say that now I know that I am alive, really alive and, more importantly, I know what being alive is all about...it's about love, pure and simple.

Afterwards, as we climb to the Falkenhütte to try to catch some late breakfast with Gaby, the song in my head is that great Dire Straits classic,

Juliet, when we made love you used to cry
I said I love you like the stars above
Gonna love you till I die

Chapter 39

Bernie Doherty

Josie was with me when I got his latest email. She's back a day or two from Venice and full of chat about it, especially after getting caught up in a spot of bother with a few local residents protesting about their ancient city being taken over by tourists.

This summer it would seem that 'tourist phobia' has been appearing all over Europe. No sign of it in Norn Ireland though, unless you count a wee evangelist standing outside the Titanic Centre, (appropriately), with a sandwich board

warning visitors that 'The End is Nigh'. Maybe that was just a cartoon I saw somewhere.

Peculiar, the situations my wains find themselves in. Patrick living on the streets of Munich but making a packet, from what he tells me, and herself debating human rights with angry Italians on the streets of Venice. Ok, the canals of Venice. Still, as she says herself, it could have been worse.

'We'd thought of going to Barcelona. Thank God we didn't; we'd have been there when that madman drove his van into all those pedestrians. You're hardly safe anywhere these days. It's just pot luck."

So what was Patrick's news this month?

Not much different from last; still loving it and even more in love than ever, if I am reading right between the lines.

Hi Mum; You doing ok? Things are pretty good here. We've been having a heat-wave so it's not too comfortable to be singing out in the baking sun. We've done really well during August. Even this past couple of weeks we made good money most days; a lot of happy faces in our audiences, which makes it worthwhile. Mostly they're looking at Lena, to be fair; she's such a different girl to what she was like way back, happy and totally confident in her performance, soulful & gutsy. She's even taken to wearing a T-shirt in support of the Charlottesville civil rights people in US; that raises a few eyebrows from some here, the far-right AFD types, but she doesn't give a hoot. And we are doing a couple of new protest songs I wrote. 'Dylanesque' her teacher told me! Her singing now is unbelievable. More and more I am just her accompanying guitarist, and songwriter of-course.

Oh yeah, meant to tell you about Lena's teacher. Herrn Fischer, Otto; I met him when we were on that trip together last year. He's the one who persuaded Lena to start singing in public. Cool guy, for a teacher like.

Anyhow, he'd seen our Facebook posts and got in touch with Lena; he came to a gig we were doing in a local town and loved it. So he's getting us a few gigs in venues where he has contacts. He's even lent me his own guitar, a Guild, way better than the old Yamaha I been using. I can sell it now.

We went with him to a classical concert last week; didn't expect to enjoy it but it was some show; full orchestra and choir in one of Munich's massive cathedrals, doing Haydn's something or other. Lena looked like an Egyptian princess in her black dress...I stole your nickname for her and called her 'Cleopatra' for the night. Had to borrow some proper dress-up gear of Gaby's myself. He is still away working but his folks have been great to me, very nice people.

It's a different world, that whole classical culture. It was cool to see it from inside, rather than on TV like. I did enjoy it, despite myself. Mrs Kelly would be proud of me, and likely a bit astonished. I noticed she has tuned in to some of our live performances; she made a couple of nice comments. We've had quite a few likes from old school friends. Plus I've run out of CDs twice and had to get more burned, a good sign.

Next weekend Otto has got us tickets to hear one of his favourite bands, I forget the name but they are a sort of fusion band, world music type of stuff. It's in some club in Munich. It's kinda nice that he's taken us under his wing and is promoting us. He's been very good to Lena in the past when she had some problems.

How did Josie get on in Vienna? She wasn't all that far away from me when she was there; we're pretty close to the Austrian border here. Is she enjoying her job? I'm glad you got the chance of a wee break in Scotland.

Look forward to catching up when I get home on Sept 23rd. I start back at Magee on Mon 25th so that gives me a couple of days to get organised. It's going to be tough leaving Lena but she'll come over to me whenever she gets a break from college, maybe even Christmas. You'll love her mum.

Bye for now, Px

My goodness, this boy has it bad!
They are so young, the pair of them. How on earth is this all going to pan out? I hope neither of them get hurt in the process.
He says he will be home on the 23rd? That's the Saturday, for God's sake. He will have been travelling for the guts of three days; he'll be shattered and will probably sleep all that Sunday before he wakes up in real life again and remembers who and what he is.
It is going to be so difficult for him to readjust to being the ordinary wee student in Derry again. No more the glamorous life of the international performer, with people buying his album and girls falling at his feet, (as I am quite sure they do, despite his claim that it is Lena who has become the star of the show.) How is he going to cope with some scrawny lecturer who has never cut it in the music world himself and who wouldn't know a good authentic performance if it jumped up and bit him on the bum...and now telling Patrick

about 'stage presence' and 'vocal projection' and all that other jargon I see in his file? Patrick could buy and sell some of them after this summer's experience.

And maybe worst of all, how is he going to feel about his cold journeys back and forward to Derry without his girlfriend on the pillion seat warming his back? Life is just about to get very lonely for my Patrick and there is not a thing I can do about it.

I doubt very much if it will be of any consolation to him that a certain Jim Devlin has been texting me every couple of days since we came back from that Scottish tour and wants to meet up when he 'happens' to be up on the north coast for a golfing weekend. Lord knows I've waited long enough for somebody to show any sort of interest in me, let alone fake a golfing weekend to be anywhere near my vicinity.

'Vienna'! Patrick never did listen much.

Chapter 40

(Patrick McAleese)

We take the train into Munich for the fusion gig in *Weltmusikclub;* the venue is a disused church, now transformed into an arts facility. You don't want to be trying to ride home through this city on a motor bike after midnight; better to be able to have a few drinks and relax. Actually that is only part of the reason. The real reason? I will be leaving Germany in three days time. I will be leaving Lena in three days time!!! This will be our last chance to spend a night with each other so, despite her father's objections, I have organised a room in a hotel not far from the venue. Makes all the sense in the world; even Lena's mum saw that and sort of took our side in the family discussion.

"Nein Anton," she told her husband. *"So a Schmarrn! Du wearst do net middn in da Nacht nach Minga fahrn und de hoin!"."*

Lena translated for me afterwards. "This is a typical Bavarian sentence," she told me. "It is not usually written in our country; it means, 'It is silly for you to drive into Munich at that time of night to bring them home.'"

Too right Frau Rosenthal. She is much more understanding and more modern in her outlook than her husband. I have the feeling that, whereas he won't be devastated to see the back of me, the mother might even miss me around the place. Certainly she has been more than warm in her chats since we had those birthday celebrations, and those revelations about Lena's beginnings, back in July. At one point, when we had gone to Lena's college for her annual results and were waiting for her in the car outside, Frau Rosenthal spoke very openly to me. In her faltering English she said that she had liked having me around and that it had been very good for Lena.

"You are not knowing how much it is that you have done. Our daughter is a different girl since you have come to us, Patrick. Please, you must know this...and my thanks, my husband also, but he is not saying this...yet he is glad. You have made Lena to open up...like a flower, you know? And now we can see she is more happy inside."

"Danke," I said.

"She has made her problems, I mean her mistakes, ja? Now they are past, I am sure. I do not know how you do this, but thank you."

"No problem," I said. "I think those mistakes got washed away in a waterfall in Karwendel."

"She told you of them?"

"Yeah, she told me all that happened."

"Ah good. It was a bad time."

She examined her fingernails for a bit, then, "We were afraid that we were losing her then. She was changing so much in that year; not like our little girl anymore. It was much more trouble than when we told her she was adopted. She became like a stranger to us. But it was a phase only, thank God."

"Yeah, we all go through phases."

"And what is this waterfall please?" she asked.

I laughed at the memory.

"We had a bit of a swim in a mountain stream," I told her. I mock-shivered at the memory. "It was cold but magic at the same time."

She smiled and looked at the students streaming in and out of the college.

"I am sure that you were very happy in the mountains," she said.

"Absolutely."

"Do you think that she will want to go to you in Ireland?"

This was a bit awkward at the time because Lena and I had chatted about her coming over to me, but I was guessing that she hadn't run it past her folks. She was hesitant to do this because she had already had a sort of 'trip of a lifetime' to Ireland with Gaby earlier this year. Even though she had made a stack of money with me over the summer she didn't fancy asking her parents about making yet another journey. I played safe.

"Well, we have talked about it," I told her, "but we haven't decided anything definite. I would love her to, of-course."

"Ja, this I know Patrick," she laughed as we watched Lena come across the car park, "and I think she also would love to go to you. But you will come back, ja?"

"I will come back for sure," I told her.

"And you will be welcome," she said, "but you must be learning German."

I was sensing though that this was not a condition of me returning.

"German or Bavarian?" I asked.

"Both of-course."

"I have learned a little German," I told her.

"Ja, I am knowing this," she said. "I heard you one evening tell Lena '*Ich liebe dich*'."

"That's not fair. Eavesdropping on us!"

"I do not know this word," she said laughing.

It was a lovely conversation and once again I felt that she was a very sound person, always very positive. I saw it too when she congratulated Lena on her exam grades; her results were good enough that she can go into the final year of her course without having to repeat any units, like some of her friends apparently. Actually I had thought that Lena would be over the moon about her results but she didn't seem to be; she just appeared a bit withdrawn, in that dreamy kind of way that she sometimes has. Maybe it's just the thought of the two of us separating soon.

So now Lena and I are in Munich and we are trying to find this former church building where tonight's gig is. It's a part of the city we have never been to before. Munich is generally a classy looking city but this sector is just a bit on the seedy side. We've checked into the hotel and asked for directions but no one seemed to know anything about it. So we wander along various streets until we stumble on it, a tired-looking red-brick building, patchily discoloured and well-weathered, with boarded-up windows. I am no expert on Gothic or Baroque styles of churches but this one doesn't look too old, maybe 1800s. I'm guessing that it's not been in use as a church for a generation. The building may have survived the American bombing during World War Two but it has not survived the process of secularisation in Munich like everywhere else. So here it stands after its conversion and refurbishment, ready to host a concert of world music from many diverse places. The original founders and devotees, whatever their brand of religion, will be turning in their graves at such a desecration tonight.

Lena seems to be looking forward to the thing; there's a vibrancy about her as she bounces up the steps ahead of me. She turns to wait, eyes bright, hand outstretched for me. I'm guessing that the fact that her musical mentor is the one who enthused about the gig and bought us the tickets is behind her curiosity. Myself, I can't admit to any great anticipation. Maybe it is because I don't know what to expect. I am really only here to be with Lena; every second together is doubly precious now that we are about to be separated.

We enter, a semi-dark, fusty environment with a whiff of marijuana, joss-sticks and scented candles in the air. If there was a DeLorean car somewhere around I'd swear we had just time travelled back to sometime in the Sixties. As our eyes get accustomed to the dull light a couple of laughing figures approach Lena and some prolonged hugging follows. I wait for introductions; turns out they are college friends. One is a tall guy called Julius; he's obviously African by origin. The other, Karim, tells me in excellent English that he is from Morocco. They are full of chat to Lena, all in German though, and it looks like they have latched on to her for the duration of the gig. That's fine by me but it's not like I had much say in the matter.

As I queue for beers I watch as they laugh together; it strikes me that Lena is obviously a lot more popular with her peers in this new college than she was with her school mates back during last year's Somme visit. In this short space of time she has done more chatting and joking around than she did in the whole of that trip. I'm pleased to see this, of-course, and they seem like nice guys.

I look past their conversation and examine the surroundings; there are chairs around the walls of the place but the floor has been left free for dancing or just standing around. My focus turns to the stage; it has a very impressive back-line of gear. Behind half a dozen mics and monitors there's a whole range of amplifiers, percussion instruments, keyboards and various guitars. Wow, it must be brilliant to have such a set-up behind you when you go onstage, I think. Hanging from the false ceiling there are glass globes of planet earth with various coloured lights inside them, one of which is a sort of flickering strobe, not good if you are epileptic. The stage backdrop is a collage of world flags. I instinctively look for the Irish one...but Karim is speaking to me.

"So are you Northern Irish or the Republic?"

"Northern," I say.

"Ah ha, you will no longer be a European soon I think," he tells me. Well informed, this guy.

"Well, the good news is that even after this whole Brexit thing happens," I say, "I will still be a European because I have an Irish passport."

"Ah yes, that is good. But strange too, because you are a citizen of the United Kingdom as well? I think this is national schizophrenia you have in your country?"

I laugh, but I am well impressed by this fellow's grasp of our distant politics. "You are not far wrong," I tell him. "We do suffer from a whole bunch of delusions in Northern Ireland, that's for sure."

"And you? Do you have a problem with these identities?"

I am a bit surprised by this query; it's not one anyone has ever asked me before. I play for time.

"How do you mean like?"

"Well...British? European? Irish? World citizen? Perhaps this is why you are at a *Weltmusik* event?"

I evade with an embarrassed laugh. "I'm just me," I tell him.

"Nobody is 'just me'," he says.

I am about to say that Bavaria has similar issues of identity but he asks another question. He's like a dog with a bone, this guy. "Ok, let me ask...do you think your politicians will be able to solve these complications in Northern Ireland, this question about how your border should be?"

"Not a hope," I tell him. "The British Government would wash their hands of us tomorrow and our local politicians can't even agree on what to call a Fisheries Protection Boat."

He smiles and turns back to Lena; maybe I'd gotten too detail-specific for him or perhaps it's just that she looks a whole lot better than me. Either way it doesn't matter because the announcer has just taken the stage and is delivering safety and evacuation announcements, which I understand zilch of. Nor do I understand his introductions. He gives way to the band emerging from backstage.

I count ten of them.

Three girls out front on main vocals, one holding a violin and another holding maracas, a Japanese-looking percussionist with a Jamaican drummer complete with dreadlocks and national T-shirt, a tall blond bassist who could be from anywhere in Northern Europe, a couple of Latin-looking brass players, a cellist in her *Dirndl,* the

Bavarian national dress and a guy in Lederhosen with an accordion hanging from his shoulder. Some line-up! I feel the first tingle of anticipation; let's hear how they sound.

They sound...ah, let's just say they sound 'full-on'. It's a big sound, for the first number anyhow. Everyone is giving it everything and the sound guy is struggling with feedback and an overpowering bass guitar. It takes him half the song before you could really start to distinguish the instruments and work out what they were trying to do. I find that first number a bit of an assault on the ears. If you were to ask me to describe the genre I could not give you a definitive answer. Alright, benefit of the doubt to them; maybe that's what world music is all about, blurring the edges.

The second song? Edges still blurred. I hear a bit of Bavarian Oompah-Pah, a lot of Italian jazz over the top of it from the two guys on trumpet and horn, a fantastic accordion solo, (if only I could hear it above the cacophony of noise), and pretty strong vocal harmonies from the three out front. I look at Lena and her mates; they seem to be well wrapped up in it all, faces glowing. What am I missing here? Am I just a boring, big-headed, overly cynical critic looking for ways to pull this show apart? Maybe I am. I'll try harder.

The third tune features the percussionists and the bassist. All three are brilliant exponents of their craft and I can't help but admire their technique...and their stamina, as the 'tune' goes into its tenth minute. Lena is bopping up and down like a pogo dancer; it's great to see her so happy but ten minutes of percussion and bass? Not my cuppa tea.

After that it becomes a matter of survival for me. The whole performance turns into a bit of a soundscape blur; one song is pretty much the same as the previous one, (I'm tempted to say 'only worse'). I start thinking to myself that I wish they'd chill for a minute and maybe let two of them play some sweet tune from say Cuba or Finland or Korea or anywhere. It strikes me that it is the misplaced urge to fuse these traditions at the expense of their individual spirit that lies behind this disaster of a show. I've heard it in albums back home; some record producer takes a perfectly good Irish trad band and sticks computer-generated Indian tabla percussion on to every track, maybe with some jazz saxophone and it just jars the beauty out of the thing. I have no doubt that fusion can be done; Paul Simon was a master of it in albums like 'Graceland' and 'Spirit Voices"...but this smudge of music is driving me up the walls. I am all for multi-cultural mixing but this show is making as much sense as a zoo at feeding time.

I don't want to be a dampener on Lena's enjoyment of it, that's for sure, so I have to keep pretending that I'm cool with what's going on; at the same time my head is starting to hurt. There's probably another hour of this to go. I could slip out to the loo, or outside for a breath of fresh air; she wouldn't mind that, I think; she's safe with these guys anyhow. I grab her affectionately and pull her close so I can whisper-shout in her ear.

"Babe, I'm gonna slip out for a minute, alright? I'll be back."

"Are you ok?" she asks, smiling her exuberant smile up into my weary eyes; she's not been reading my body language during the show, that's for sure.

"Yeah, I'm ok. Just a bit of a headache; I'll get some air for a minute. back soon. *Ich liebe dich,*" I say.

"*Ja, ich liebe dich auch,*" she says with a quick kiss.

I make my way out through the dancers towards the rear doors. Some guy steps into my path and asks me something in German. I haven't a clue so I just say, "English". "Ah, English," he says. "You need some gear?" Oh right, he's trying to sell me drugs, I realise. "No thanks, I'm cool," I tell him and squeeze on out through the crowd. As I push past a few smokers just outside and start to go down the steps I sort of bump into another guy coming the other way. I notice him because he isn't really watching where he is going, his head covered by a hoodie, a rucksack on his back; he seems to be arguing with someone on his phone, someone called 'Ali', his voice rising as he talks.

I reach the pavement and look up and down the street. It's a poorly lit part of the city; there aren't many people about. Should I walk...

Suddenly I have a terrible thought.

That guy wasn't arguing with 'Ali'!

"Allahu Akbar! Allahu Akbar!"

That's what he was chanting to himself!

The realisation hits me like a hammer.

Lena is inside there. What if he is a ....

My heart is thumping in my chest.

I make a mad dash back up the steps.

Through the smokers to the door.

As I reach to push it open there is an almighty crash of sound and the door basically comes at me, lifts me like I was a doll, drives me back through the air and I feel searing pain as it pins me against a solid stone column for a moment before I slide to the broken tiles. My last conscious sensation is of heat and smell...and a growing darkness as I lose the light.

𝄞

open eye ~ it's fuzzy ~ drunk? me? ~ two faces at me ~ I am sore head hurts ~ Jesus, what is the noise? ~can't see much ~ bad picture ~ i t i s buffering, must be~ bloody ringing in my ears ~and stinking ~can't seem to move much ~ fierce head on me ~ buffering is too slow ~ it's too dizzy ~ go asleep again ~. fading. ~ blue in-out lights ~ on off on off -on off ~ way too bright ~ black people at me ~ can't hear what they want, faces in close ~ see their lips in thick glass ~ d o n ' t know a word ~ "Ok" I say ~ 'sure' ~ it's in E minor I think, no? ~red flashing sounds ~ is it sirens are they? ~ dull noise like underwear... underwater I think I said~ naustyus ~ what the hell is this? ~ people running, every place ~ eyes not focusing ~ uniforms running, at bent over angles ~must be bad connection ~ gonna be sick...... booouugk ~ vomit on my front here clean ~ it is cold in me ~I should get up yeah ~ can I get legs below - stagger a bit on wall ~ wile sore head like -hands on ears ~ standing sideways leaning now to pillar ~ what the devil am I doing so sore? ~ bloodly fingers I see ~ no idea ~ need to get away from it ~ bent-over, get up system straight ~ walk, walk. ~fall down steps ~no idea what ~ g e t away from here ~ walk away walk away walk away ~ run across road benting over ~I hear you horn ~stop ~ fuzzy faces staring ~ crying at me ~ no I am crying ~ w a l k on away ~ who the frick am I now? ~ b i g white ambulances flying ~ no idea, just walk away ~

ringing in this head ears of mine ~ where is this place? see a bridge here, a river ~ walk beside dark Guinness river ~ people holding me talking ~ stupid words, don't get it~ pull away, blood on hand too ~head sore ~ no idea no idea no idea just walk away ~ didn't mean to fall over ~ sweet mother o' mine pray for us slimmers now haha, lol ~. 'my name' policegirl says....'Patrick' ~what am I doing here? 'Highway to hell ~. So help me please, please help me, help me ~oh god no idea ~ why so confused Maca? ~ no feckin' notion. ~

Chapter 41

Bernie Doherty

We have a lovely meal in the Old Coast Inn, Jim and me. He's on the sirloin and I have salmon; a bottle of red and a bottle of white. There's a fellow tinkling out some old classics on an electric keyboard and above his head two rugby teams are battering hell out of each other on a silent big-screen TV.

The chat is grand. It's always a risk when you've met somebody in a vacation setting to get together afterwards, I feel; not, mind you, that there was any heady holiday-romance type of thing happening when we were in Scotland, nothing of the sort. It had all been just chat, many degrees south of flirtation. I'd have smelt that a mile away and would probably have given him short shift. No, it hadn't been like that. Not until I began to realise that I was looking forward to his next text. How I had slipped from friendly neighbour chat on the coach to responding so coyly to the blatant chat-up lines in his texts I do not know, but slipped I had.

Now over our first dinner we have actually approached the subject of our marriages. He raised the matter first and in doing so probably realised that he was raising the stakes in the relationship as well.

"I was married for twenty years," he told me. "Lisa was a chiropodist in Newry; then one day she never came back from work."

"What happened?"

"A load came off a lorry just as she was driving past. She never stood a chance."

"So sorry Jim."

"Yeah well...it was just the luck of the draw I suppose. A second either way..."

I had wondered why a man like this was on a coach tour in Scotland rather than flying off to somewhere a bit more exciting; he tells me now that since his wife's death he has developed some strange phobias, including a fear of flying. I am sympathetic to this kind of problem, having had various mental health issues of my own after my marriage broke up.

"What about kids?" I ask after a silence.

"Yeah, two girls, both away in England now. Yourself?"

So I tell my story, trying not to be too hard on Robbie. "It was just one of those things," I tell him. "Opposites attract, like they say... but incompatible at the end up."

"And you say you have two as well?"

So I tell him all about my pair; Josie first and then Patrick. He seems fascinated by what my boy is up to in Munich.

"Would always have loved a son," he says, "but after we lost a couple of babies I couldn't put Lisa through it all again. I suppose it's too late for me now."

I laugh and take the bait on that one. "You never know your luck," I tell him. "Sure you might meet some healthy thirty year old just dying to help out."

"You think I might get that lucky, do you? Some poor girl with a white stick and a labrador maybe."

We have a good laugh at that and he drains his glass of Merlot. Mind you, looking at him, she would be blind to miss the fact that he has a great physique and has looked after himself very well; very handsome for a man of fifty, in my book anyway.

I find the courage to tell him about my cancer scare, holding my emotions together pretty successfully, but I see some pain in his eyes as I talk. Then he tells me that he has lost an older sister to the exact same thing. It's a strangely awkward moment in the conversation; these common life experiences should be something that bring us together but maybe we don't know each other well enough yet and the stories seem to collide and bounce us briefly into our own private areas of pain.

He goes out to the toilet and I check social media on my phone. At the same time I am wondering what his intentions are, and how he thinks this evening is going to end. I hope he is not too pushy. I want to take this real slow and get to know him before we get too close. I was stung once in my life and there is no way I am intending to become a serial victim. Yeah, it is nice to have someone feel you are special enough to take out for a meal, and I am flattered by his attentions, but small steps and slow Bernie, remember!

The piano player seems to have packed in his act for the time being as Jim returns and takes his seat opposite me.
"Did Ulster hold on?" he asks.
"What?"
"The rugby match. Did Ulster hold on?"
"No idea. Is it over?" I say.
"Yeah," he tells me looking over my shoulder at the TV. "The news is coming on."
"Sorry; I couldn't see it from here," I say. "I would hardly know anyway. Sport wouldn't be my thing; certainly not rugby. Patrick hated it at school. He is a football sort of guy. What about yourself...?"
I notice that I have lost him; his eyes are on the TV and he's not really paying attention to me. 'Manners', I think, as I watch him, miles away.
"Bernie," he says, "where did you say your son is at the minute?"
"Munich. Why?"
"Oh dear," he says. "There's been some sort of a terrorist incident."
I spin in the seat.
The Breaking News banner across the bottom of the screen reads,

"Munich; suicide bomber attacks concert goers."

My heart lurches in my chest and I feel like I am going to faint. Jim notices;
"Hey Bernie," he says, "it's a massive city. He won't be within miles of it."
"He's at that concert. I bet he is at that concert! I know he is!" I cry.
"Nonsense; don't be worrying yourself. There's dozens of concerts going on on a Friday night in a place that size. Calm yourself."
"Get the barman to turn up the sound," I shout at him, eyes glued to pictures of ambulances and the flashing blue neon of police cars. Jim hurries to the bar and soon I hear the announcer.
".....feared that there are a significant number of injuries and unconfirmed reports speak of fatalities within the church building. The concert has been organised by the Weltmusikclub, the Munich branch of the World Music Club, and at present it is unclear as to whether this event has been targeted by Islamic extremists, as was the Bataclan in Paris and the Ariana Grande concert in Manchester, or indeed by a Neo-Nazi anti-immigration organisation as a statement against the celebration of multi-cultural identity....."
"That is it!" I scream at Jim. "That is the concert he was going to, I swear it. Look..." I go as quickly as my frantic fingers will allow me to emails on my phone and find Patrick's last communication. I read it aloud.

"Next weekend Otto has got us tickets to hear one of his favourite bands, I forget the name but they are a sort of fusion band, world music type of stuff. It's in some club in a suburb of Munich."

"There you are! He's at it. I know he is."
"Not at all, calm yourself Bernie. Like I say, there's bound to be dozens of gigs in a place the size of Munich," he tells me.
"Listen," I say. "'World Music type of stuff'! That's what the TV just said. 'The Munich branch of the World Music Club'. It's the one he is at, him and her."
"My God, you could be right," he says. "But don't worry Bernie, he's probably OK. Why don't you ring him...that will put your mind at ease."
"Yeah, right," I say, then, "but what if he doesn't answer? I'll be in a worse position."
"Yeah, I know but all you can do from here is try. Go on, ring him."
I fumble so much with my phone that I am amazed I can actually use it and hear his phone ringing. It rings, on and on. No answer. My God...this is every mother's worst nightmare and it's happening to me, right now, right in front of this stranger that I am trying to make an impression on.
"Try again," the stranger tells me.
"What?" I say.
"Go again, try his number again. Are you sure you got it right?"
"Of-course I got it right," I shout. "There's only one bloody Patrick on my phone."
People are staring at us; the barman is signalling to us. "What's wrong there? Keep it down folks please."
"It's alright," I hear somebody saying. "She thinks her son might be caught up in...."
The phone is ringing again. I listen and listen and pray.
'Please God let him answer the phone. Please Patrick! Please!'
No answer. I start to howl. Jim takes the phone off me and sits me down.
"Get her a cup of strong tea, with sugar!" I hear him shout from inside my cocoon. I sit, head in my hands. A couple of women approach us. One reaches for my hand. I don't know her at all but she is trying to pacify me. "It will be alright dear, just wait and be patient. God will look after him."
The other woman rubs the back of my neck, my shoulders. Where has Jim gone? Oh, I want to be sick, I think. I get up quickly. "Take me to the toilet. I'm gonna throw up," I say. They get me up and out just as the barman arrives with tea.
"Thanks," I say. "In a minute."
I make it to the bowl in time and retch up the dinner I have just enjoyed. 'Patrick!' 'Patrick!' 'Patrick!' between each retch.
I am getting cleaned up at the sink between these two strangers when the door burst open and Jim rushes to me. He's holding out my phone.

"I think it's him," he says. "I kept trying and this person answered. I just can't make much sense of him."
I grab the phone from him.
"Patrick? Is that you Patrick?"
Silence. I look at the screen; yes, it's still an active call. I try again.
"Is that you Patrick? Can you hear me? It's your mother?"
More silence...then...
"Mum?"
His voice!
Oh my God, I have never in all my born days been so glad to hear anything as I am now to hear "Mum". It's an unbelievable cocktail, a rush of adrenaline and relief.
"Are you ok Patrick?"
Another bout of silence. Maybe it's the distance.
"Patrick? Can you still hear me? Are you alright?"
A very hesitant voice speaks to me; it sounds kinda choking, like he is finding it difficult to speak, like something is stuck in his throat.
"Yeah... I think so," he says.
"Were you at the concert, were you?"
"I don't know," he whispers. "No, I don't think so....It's not yet. We are going to a concert I think...someday soon."
Oh Jesus, there is something not quite right here.
"Patrick, were you at the world music concert tonight in Munich?"
Very slow to reply.
"No... it's next week maybe... I think anyway."
"Are you ok, Patrick? Are you sore anywhere?"
"Yeah, sore head," he says after a few seconds.
Oh my God! He is hurt. He was at the concert. He's been hurt, maybe hit on the head. What can we do here?
"Patrick," I say. "Is Lena with you at the minute?"
"Lena?" he says.
"Yeah, Lena, your girlfriend? Remember? Where is she at the minute?"
"I don't know. Maybe home."
"Where exactly are you at the minute, Patrick?" I ask.
"Where am I? I don't know....Hang on," he says. I hear him mumbling in the background. Is he asking somebody where he is or what's going on? I also seem to hear the wailing of sirens in the distance.
"Patrick, are you in Munich at the minute? Do you know?"
"They say it's in Munich. Why?"
"Why? For God's sake Patrick...because there has been a bomb at the concert that you were at. It's on the news here in Ireland. A bomb! You must have been in the concert and you have been hurt. Where are you sore? Are you in the street or what is going on?"

"Keep it simple for him," Jim advises me. "Short questions Bernie."
"Yeah ok," I say. "Do you understand that Patrick? A bomb? At the gig?"
"I don't know....can't remember," he says. There's something very funny about his voice. It's like he's half cut or something.
"What about Lena? Is she with you son?"
"No...no Lena. She's not here."
"Was she at the concert?"
"I don't know. Yeah maybe, maybe not. I don't remember.... She's looking forward to it anyway."
"Patrick, are you still in the concert place, some church or other?"
He seems to be checking where he is.
"No.... it's a cafe place. There's tables and stuff."
"Ok, and you are safe?"
'Yeah, I'm ok. Something has happened 'cause there's police everywhere."
"Thank God for that," I tell him. "Are you on your own or are there people with you?"
"Both."
"What?"
"I'm on my own, but there's people in the cafe with me like."
"But what about Lena?"
"I don't know," he says. "She's not here."
James advises me from behind. "Get him to try and tell you the last thing he remembers."
Good idea.
"Patrick," I say, "what is the last thing you remember? Can you tell me?"
"Not really."
"We're you at Lena's house today?"
"I think so, yeah."
"And how did you get to Munich? Were you on your bike?"
"Let me think ma...a minute...I remember now...that bit. We left the bike behind, I think so anyway. Maybe Lena's father...I don't know."
"We? So Lena was with you?"
"Don't know mum. Yeah, I guess."
"So when is the last time you saw her?"
That seems to have him confused. He doesn't reply for a while.
"Patrick? Lena....when did you see her last?"
"I don't know. At her house maybe. Why?"
"Why? Because you have survived a bomb at the concert and she is not with you so where is she?"
There is silence...then I hear him sort of muttering, spluttering too.
"Patrick, are you ok?"
"I don't know where she is," he says. I sense him starting to cry. I've got to keep him engaged here.

"Can you phone her?"
"Yeah ok, I can try that," he says.
"Good, you do that. I'll call you back in a wee while."
"Yeah."
"Patrick hang on. Do you have a number for her folks?"
"For who?"
"Lena's parents?"
"Don't think so mum."
"Ok but can you remember what their town is called? And what Lena's second name is?"
"She is Rosenthal."
"And the town they live in?"
"Agh mum, no idea...hang on. It's...Frem-something. Let me think a minute. Fremden...something....something like that, yeah. Why?"
"'Cause I am going to try to get in touch with them and see if they know anything about her."
"No way mum, don't do that. Her da will not be too happy. I am meant to be looking after her...Oh mum, I don't know where she is!" Again I think he is crying.
"Look Patrick, calm down. You should try to phone her. She is likely alright, wherever she is. Ok, I'll call you back."
"Ok, bye."
"Bye. Love you son!"
And as I come off the phone the mother in me kicks in again and takes over from the calm counsellor I have been trying to be and I bawl my eyes out for a while. Jim has held his ground in the female toilet, despite a few strange looks from ladies putting their heads in the door. Now he leads me out to the corridor and holds me tightly, the strangest of circumstances for our first intimacy.
"It's ok Bernie. He's alive. He's a survivor."
"Yeah, thanks be to God!" I blubber.
"Let's see if we can contact an international directory and get a phone number for this girl's parents," he says.
"Hang on," I tell him. "I have an idea. Her father is some kind of clergyman in a church I have never heard of...but I can find it's name in my emails. Give me a minute."
I have it in seconds.
"Google this for me," I tell him. "'The Neuapostolische Kirche of Fremdenheim'. If you can find that there might be a phone number for him. Rosenthal is his name."
I wait as this stranger does the search...stranger before tonight but I have a feeling that he knows me better after this first date than many a bloke after six months of courtship. How would I have coped with this trauma without him?
"Got it," he tells me. "Pastor A Rosenthal, Neuapostolische Kirche, Fremdenheim; and there's a number for him. Bingo."
I call it immediately. The strange ringtone sounds for ages but is suddenly interrupted.

"*Ja, Rosenthal*".
The voice sounds tired, irritated; it is nearly midnight there, I remember.
"Hi, this is Bernie Doherty phoning from Northern Ireland," I say. "I am Patrick's mother."
"Oh, yes. I am sorry. We are in our beds now but it is ok. Is everything alright?"
"No, I am afraid not. I have been talking just now to Patrick in Munich. Do you understand me? Yeah? There has been some sort of terrorist attack at the concert. Patrick is hurt but he has survived; he seems to be concussed....you understand, his head is damaged, his memory, but he is ok."
He takes a second to process this, my Derry accent maybe getting in the way of the English, despite my best efforts.
"You say a terrorist attack? We have not heard any news here. Let me put on our television."
I hear him speak very abruptly to his wife and hear her cry, '*Magdalena!*'.
"You say Patrick is ok but you do not tell me Magdalena is ok? What does he say about her? Is she not with him?" he asks me.
"I do not know anything about Lena. That is why I am calling you. Patrick has lost his memory...it is a head injury I think, going on his conversation with me. He had even forgotten he was at the concert. So this is why I am calling you sir. You need to get to Munich and try to find your daughter...and if you can, please also find my son and make sure he is alright."
"*Ja, ja*, I understand. This is a big shock. Do you know what part of Munich we must go to? Where is your son?"
"No, I don't know Munich you see, but if you look at the television reports you will hear where it is. The concert was in some old church, that is all I know."
"Very well, my wife and I shall go now to the city and try to find her, and Patrick."
"I am so sorry."
"*Ja*, I am also sorry. He should be with Lena, but if he has hurt his head as you say perhaps this is the reason..."
"Look sir, can I give you Patrick's phone number, just in case you need it to contact him?"
"Please," he says. "I may have this already but please..."
I read it off to him from memory.
"Thank you...and your number please also?"
"Good idea." I give him my number and he is gone.
"What now?" I ask the new man in my life.
"A taxi to wherever you live Bernie...and if you like I will come with you, it's your call."
"Please," I say. "Just to help me get through this night."

Chapter 42

(Patrick McAleese)

My phone feels dull and stone-heavy in my hands. Everything feels like it's in slow-mo at the minute, like I am in wifi but with a terrible slow speed. The coffee that some kind person gave me is thick and dragging and too sweet but I drain the last of it. There's no answer anyway from whoever it was I was phoning. I can't seem to get who that was...or why I was to phone them.
"You feeling any better mate?"
"Yeah, I'm good thanks."
"Look me in the eyes for a second. Follow this finger ok? Can you follow it? What day is it?"
I am confused. Why is this man doing this to me? Who is he?
"Do I know you?"
"No, but you staggered in here an hour ago and you were all over the place. I heard you mumbling away in English and being a Scouser myself I tried to understand what you were talking about. I'm afraid it didn't make much sense."
"Why not?"
"Well, at the start I thought you were on a bad trip but then you were feeling your head a lot and when I checked I saw a huge bump back there, so I'm guessing you fell and hit your head or something. There's some sort of terror alert on the other side of the river, unless you got hurt somehow to do with that. But you were definitely out of it for a while there. Then you got that phone call and that seemed to bring you back."
He is not making a lot of sense to me.
"A phone call?"
"Yeah. Not remember?"
"Who was it phoning me?"
"You were on the call, not me mate, sorry. Sounded like your mum though."
"Who was I calling just now?"
"No idea. Here let me see your phone...we can try the number again. Let me see....recent calls...you know someone called Lena?"
"Yeah, Lena. She was calling me?"
"No mate, you were calling her. Look. Want me to try her again?"
"Sure."

"She your girlfriend?"
"Yip."
"Nice. What's she like? This her on your screen-saver?"
"Yip. She's good, why?"
"No reason. Just trying to get you thinking, talking."
"Ok...she's cool. Best girl I ever..."
Oh dear. I'm back in sob-mode. What's wrong with me?
"Steady on mate. I was just asking. Anyway, she's not answering here. Is there anybody else I can try for you?"
"Don't think so. Thanks."
I have the phone back in my hands and it feels different, squarer, like it's heavier than before. What has he done to it, this guy? He is away to the bar again, to those lights that are way too bright. And why is that music so loud in here? Where is this anyway?
English he said. Scouser? What the hell is Scouser? Where is Lena? Mum phoned. This feels dire, this feeling in my brain, like I'm having to think in thick sticky treacle stuff, with slow steps, like I'm climbing a sandhill but not getting any higher. Did I do drugs tonight? My head is still hurting at the back. Blood? No...I check again. So fuzzy in this place tonight, wherever it is. That feeling of hopeless buffering again, like I just can't connect with something.
There's something I have to do, somewhere to go. I wish I could get it. It's just outside my head. It's like a bird, a swallow diving past me on the green outside our house...too fast to get it into focus. I can't get what it is. But it's there, bits of it, like it's in behind the glass of an old-fashioned beer mug and moving slow...slow until I want to catch on to it, then it's fast like a fly on a window pane. I can't grab hold of it. Flittering about on the other side of the glass.
These ads on the wall are not in English. Is that because I am in...ah yeah, I am here of-course. I am so pathetic. I forget everything nowadays. But I still am good at lyrics. I still remember the lyrics of every song I've ever written and that must be dozens. Even the covers we do. She is so good. My Lena.
What is this I am to do? Why is she not talking to me? I feel like a dizzy fool for forgetting everything but it won't talk back to me. Not at the minute. It is so frustrating. I am sooo drunk I think...but yet I don't remember drinking a lot. Drugs? Did I take some tablets or some sort of dope? I don't think so. It is not like me to be so out...
My phone is going. Who is this? Not a contact number anyhow. I answer.
"Yes?"

"Is this Patrick?"
"It's me ok." I don't know who this voice belongs to I think.
"Patrick, it is Magdalena's father here. Are you ok?"
"Magdalena's father? Oh no, no, no..." I start to cry again. I have no idea why I am crying. I sob like a baby as he chitters away in my ear. The English guys comes back to me across from the counter. I see him sideways, my head down on the table. He takes my phone. His back to me, I hear him talking to the man on the phone, who is...Herr...what's-his-name? Lena's father, I think it is. Did he say that? Maybe.
I catch some words.
'Alright' - 'Concussion' - 'Bomb' - 'No-one else' - 'Medical care' - 'Wound' - 'Safe' - 'Stay' - 'Bruno's Cafe' - 'Something-complicated-*Straße*' - 'Twenty minutes' - 'Sure' - '*Auf Wiedersehen*'.
I take the phone back.
"So that man is worried about you and your friend Magdalena, ok? And so he is coming here to pick you up and make sure you are alright, if you need medical help or whatever. And to try to find your girl, ok? So you hang in there mate, put your head down and rest yourself till he gets here. You want another coffee? No? Ok."
"Cheers," I hear myself tell him, like it's from another body, another voice, not mine. The lights are flashing past outside of the window. That frickin' noise!

I wake up, because someone is shaking my shoulder. My head hurts again...so much.
I wish it would stop. I wish the shaking person would stop and let me sleep. No way.
"Patrick. Wake up. It is Rosenthal, Magdalena's father. Ok? Remember?"
"Yeah," I mutter. My mouth tastes like a sewer. I need a drink. I try to get up. No way again. Sit. I sign for a drink, the internationally recognised sign for "Get me a drink NOW!"
The Englishman is back in a flash with water. Great. Lena's mother comes to me. She has tears on her face I think, in her blue eyes too, I notice. She takes my head in her arms, very nice...ah that hurts...I pull away quick and she is mortified, hands to her mouth, eyes wide and tearful.
"Is your head very sore Patrick?"

"Yeah", I say. Just what you'd know. She examines it and speaks in German to her husband.
"Ok, but first we must ask about Magdalena, then we will get medical attention for his head," he says.
"Lena," I say, and blubber again.
"Can you remember what happens Patrick?"
"Not really. It's all a bit of a haze," I say.
"Well, can you remember what was the last time that you saw Lena? Please try to remember where you were when you saw her last."
I shake my head. Aaah! I say, "I am sorry. I can't think."
Frau Rosenthal sits down opposite me and takes my hand. It's very sweet. She looks at me like a mother would. My mother?...she was talking to me on the phone I think? Ok, I hope she is good.
"Patrick, we will do this in small steps, one at a time, like learning as a baby to walk, ja?"
"Ok."
"You walked with Magdalena to the train? Ja? In Fremdenheim? From our house? Do you remember that?"
"Not really. I guess I did."
She goes to the counter and speaks in German to someone there. I have no idea what but the euro-pop music suddenly stops blaring. That's better.
"Thank you," I tell her.
"This will be better for you," she says.
I don't get what she means, but then I hear some gentle classical tune come from the speakers. I must show some curiosity on my face because she smiles at me.
"Please, you must just relax and let this music come into your mind. Just accept it, let it wash over you. Close your eyes. Don't think about anything for a moment. Ok?"
"Ok." I do as she says for a while, don't know how long. It's good. Then I hear her again, outside of me.
"Do you remember leaving our house with Magdalena earlier today Patrick? You were joking with her, taking her bag, holding her hand?"
"I think so, maybe. Just about."
"Then you get to the station, ja? The train...it was fast, you sat beside Magdalena? Held her hand again?"
I think really hard about this. Did I hold her hand?
"Was she happy?"

"Yeah, I remember now. She was so excited. This gig we were to go to. Fusion music, she said. Otto told us about it."
Frau Rosenthal looks quickly up to her standing husband. He is trying to be patient, one foot to the other foot. The Englishman tries to pull him away to give the lady and myself some peace. It's a good idea too, I think. I need space to wipe this dirty glass clean. Put the torn strips of paper back together so I can read it all, the bits of facts from whatever has gone on.
"So the train...it comes to Munich, to the Hauptbahnhof. You and Magdalena get off together. Is she holding your hand still? What do you do then? Do you remember?"
I struggle about the hand-holding. I'm fairly sure we held hands at some point but what I do seem to see is the U-Bahn doors opening for us and we jump inside. So I tell her this. She seems happy.
"Then what?"
No idea. Not for a long time...until she gives me the clue. The hotel! Yeah we went to our hotel first, checked in. I think as hard as I can about this. It's still hazy but I have a feeling we had a small beer at the bar before we went walking, walking somewhere...somewhere new.
"So you walked? Remember anything about the walk?"
No, not really. It's fuzzy now. Misty, like beside a river. Yeah, we walked by a river, we did. I remember that. We couldn't find the place. The church we were supposed to go to. It was closed so we went to another place....no? No, I don't think we did do that. I can't get past this point. Can't remember what way we found it. What was it we were to find?
"Music?" Frau Rosenthal says.
"Music? Yeah music...I remember that much. 'Cause it was shit! Sorry, Frau Rosenthal...I mean it wasn't what I would call great music. It was all going off, too many drums, pure chaos. It really wasn't my scene...and Lena was talking to..."
Goodness, things have come back to me, I suddenly realise. But I feel so tired.
"Well done, Patrick, well done. Now just relax, let your brain rest a bit. Have some more coke. Close you eyes, rest your mind."
Her husband speaks impatiently. She answers sharply. I hear but I do not see. My head is down but I think he is put in his place. His wife is in charge here, for once. I doze off in no time. It feels good. I actually hear myself snoring but it sort of pleases me. Jeez what a strange feeling, caught somewhere in between consciousness and

dreamland. And I think of Lena in this half-lit world. My unbelievably beautifully cool babe. What has happened to her?
I sit bolt upright. "Lena?" I say. "Where is Lena?"
"That is what we want you to remember Patrick," says her father.
"At the concert. She was talking, ja? Who to?" Frau Rosenthal says.
"I don't know, actually I don't know them. One was a big guy, he was black; the other guy....I don't know. I think he talked to me about something...maybe music? I don't know. It's like this is all coming and going, like. I'm trying to focus binoculars," I say.
"Yes, I understand. And what happened then? She was talking? Was there anything else you remember? Were you happy together? Was she dancing?"
"Yeah, dancing. You know how she is. Bouncing about....she was so happy."
"And you Patrick? Were you happy?"
"No, like I say, it wasn't for me, that music...I got a sore head with it."
"So what did you do?"
"I don't know. Maybe just closed my ears. I can't remember."
"This is wasting time Patrick," Herr Rosenthal interrupts. "Come with us, we go to the police."
"Just a few more minutes, Anton," she says. "Rest again, dear Patrick."
I put my head down. This is exhausting. My brain is back in shut-down-get-the-hell-out-of-my-face mode. My eyes close. I feel a hand on my head, fingers running through my hair, caressingly. I hear like an incantation coming from Frau Rosenthal, soothingly, solemnly. It's sounds as if it is some sort of prayer and it washes over me like a cool shower. For some reason it takes me back to the mountains; I start to think back to that wonderful experience with Lena...pure nirvana. Will I ever see it again? Where is she now? Why is she not here with me?
This music...it is so sweet, calming. It's like somebody has thrown a huge stone into the middle of a pond but now we wait and the music is calming down the ripples until you can hardly see them any more...the surface goes back to what it had been and you can see the reflection of the trees and the sky again. It is all becoming....but then, just as I am about to see things clearly and remember, it gets all murky again.
"What is it, Patrick?"
"I don't know where Lena is," I say.
"Why not?"

"In the concert. I was with her in the concert, I remember that. Then it goes dark again. I don't know why she isn't here."

"It says on the news that a bomb exploded in the concert. Were you in the building then? Were you with Magdalena then?" Frau Rosenthal sounds very desperate now.

"I don't remember...sorry. I don't know where I was. I don't know where Lena was. I just can't see it."

"You were not with her when the bomb..." Her father sounds pretty disgusted.

"Maybe I came out...before the bomb. I don't know. Yeah, I remember that there was a bang.... a huge crash; that's all I can recall. I must have hurt my head."

The parents look at each other.

"So perhaps you were not with Lena at that moment, when the explosion came?"

"I don't know. Maybe."

"Thank you Patrick," says Frau Rosenthal. "You did so good."

"Better to stay with my daughter though," says her husband, "but now we must get to the hospitals to search for her."

"I am coming with you," I say.

"Ja, you are," her father says.

As we get up to leave the Englishman speaks from the counter. "Can we go back to some real music now?"

I stumble over to him. He raises his head from his tablet and gives me a rueful smile.

"Looks like you were one of the lucky ones...I mean, if you were at that gig and survived," he says. "Lots of casualties, according to Euronews."

I give him a limp smile.

"Thanks."

"No problem mate. Take care. Hope you find your girl."

"Me too," I say over my shoulder and follow the Rosenthals into the night streets of a depressed Munich.

Chapter 43

Bernie Doherty

First date and here he is, back in my place. Never imagined I'd hear myself admit to something like this; it's just not me.
He's gotten a taxi for us from the hotel; then when we arrive at my house he just kinda follows me in. It isn't like I have invited him or anything, but I don't object either. It just seems the natural thing to do.
Once we are in the kitchen he starts to make me a cup of tea. I watch from the table. Patrick! My poor son, caught up in this. Still, it could have been so much worse. What about his girl? I wish he would phone me back with some news.
Jim brings the tea.
"Bernie," he begins. "Look, don't misunderstand me here. It's just...I don't feel I can abandon you tonight, after all that's happened. I don't have to stay; like, I will get a taxi back to my hotel if you want me to."
"It's ok," *I hear myself saying.*
"Are you sure?"
"Yeah, you've been very understanding and I appreciate that you were there. Here too. I don't know how I would have coped with tonight if I had been on my own."
After a pause he says, "You've been too long on your own."
"Maybe."
"Listen, if you want me to stay just say...like, have you a spare room I can sleep in? Or a couch? If not I can disappear."
I slurp my tea, embarrassingly, as I process this. It doesn't exactly sound like some kind of indecent proposal, does it?
"That would be grand," *I say.* "Yeah, Patrick's room is free. If you don't mind being a teenager again?"
"I don't mind at all," *he smiles.* "So he is still a teenager, is he? He's having a fairly adventurous youth."
"He's still a teenager but only just. He turns twenty next week. Imagine! My wee boy twenty! And he might never have seen it if he'd been close to that bomb."
"Too right. You never know the day or the hour. Lisa left for work one morning as usual and never came back."
I say nothing, eyes down into my tea.
"Sorry," *he says.* "That was bad timing. I should have kept my mouth shut."
"It's ok," *I tell him.* "We can talk more about that sometime if you like."

"Sure, of-course. Thanks."

We sit in silence, the silence of memories and regrets...and of a mother's worries.

"I wish he would phone me back. What time is it in Germany now?"

"It's nearly one o'clock here so it must be coming two over there. Do you want me to phone him again?"

"Would you? Please. Try it anyway."

So he does. No luck. It just keeps ringing. Maybe his battery has gone. What a time this would be for that to happen. How would we get in touch? Maybe he's just out of coverage.

"No joy at the minute," Jim tells me.

We have exhausted the chat, and it's not the only thing is exhausted. I yawn through the silences between us now.

"Look, it's getting very late Bernie. You should get some sleep."

"Yeah, you're right. Don't know if I'll sleep much but I'd have a better chance if I was lying down, wouldn't I?"

"Absolutely. Right, come on," he says, standing up and holding out his hand to me.

Oops...don't misunderstand this gesture, I tell myself as I take his hand briefly and he pulls me up. I disconnect from him to put the cups in the sink and then lead the way up the stairs, my heart fluttering like a butterfly. When is the last time a man has followed me up the stairs, and in my own house, and after one in the morning? What is he thinking behind me? What is he looking at behind me?

We reach the landing and he cuts the tension with the obvious question. "So where's his room then?"

I am relieved but I still manage to sound dry-mouthed as I say, "This is his place here. I have the sheets washed fresh for him coming home. Hope it's alright."

"It'll be grand. Thanks."

"You might find a pair of his pyjamas in the cupboard but...maybe not," I say, looking at his fifteen stone frame.

"Hardly fit me, would they?"

"Likely not," I laugh.

We look at each other across the narrow landing...just a brief glance but it's loaded. I turn quickly to my room, the whiff of his aftershave in my nostrils.

"Goodnight; sleep well," he says behind me.

"Yeah, nite; you too."

It's not easy to sleep. I am so tired but my mind can't switch off. Where is Patrick now? How is he feeling? What about his head? Is he still confused or has he come round any? Where is his poor girlfriend and how did they ever get separated...like they have been joined at the hip for the last few months so what happened to split them up tonight?

I feel so far away. It's a mother's worst nightmare, or at least it could have been, but for that brief phone contact. How on earth would I have coped if we hadn't been able to talk? Jim has been very good tonight. I owe him big-time.

Jim!

Where is this relationship going, if anywhere? These awful circumstances have thrown us together in a way that nobody could have predicted and in a way that has given me the chance to see him performing in a crisis. Thankfully not performing in any other role, not yet anyhow. I am not ready for that. At the same time, I like what I have seen of Jim tonight. He has been calm, and he has shown me care and consideration. I hope these events don't drive him away from me once he has gotten past the obligation to do the decent thing. I would hate to lose his friendship after such a short time.

I must have started to drift off but suddenly I am sitting bolt upright. My phone is ringing. I hit the light and fumble for it on the bedside table.

Is it Patrick? No such luck. It's a number I don't recognise. I press accept and wait for a slow sounding connection. As I do my bedroom door is pushed open and Jim comes in wearing nothing but his boxers. My God!

"Hello," I hear. "This is Anton Rosenthal speaking."

"Ah right. Hello Mister Ros...Herr Rosenthal. What news?"

"What news? Ja, there is some news which I thought I should tell you."

"Good. Thank you for phoning."

James sits on my bed facing me. I am in a serious conversation here and all I can see is his big muscly chest, hairy as a bear, four feet away from me.

"Well, we have found your son. Patrick is well. He has a bang on his head and is still a little confusing but he is improving all the time."

"That's brilliant. Yeah, he's confusing alright," I smile. "But what about your daughter? Have you found her yet?"

"I am sorry to say..." I seem to lose him briefly. Silence.

"Go on, I can still hear you. Is she alright?"

"Magdalena is missing still. We have no trace of her...is that how you say? We can not find her."

"Oh dear, I am so sorry. Has Patrick no idea where she might be? He was with her, wasn't he, at the concert like?"

"Ja, I think so. Ja! But he can have no memory of what happened to her. He does not know why they are separate at the concert. His memory is missing. Now she is missing also."

"I am so sorry. Can I speak to Patrick please? Is he there with you?"
"For sure he is, yes. Patrick!"
"Hi mum," I hear his voice.
I well up again and Jim pats my knee through the quilt. These bizarre little moments keep happening tonight.
Patrick consoles me that he is fine, that his memory of the night is slowly coming back to him, wee details of the journey, people they talked to at the gig and so on but he still cannot work out why he survived and she is missing, at least she was not with him afterwards.
"Where had she gone?" I ask him. "If you were in the venue, this old church place and she disappeared. How come?"
"Maybe it was me who was gone," he says. "It must be that. I must have left her but why would I do that?"
"I don't know. Maybe you will never know. Some people who get concussed lose those few minutes of their lives forever."
"Maybe. I hope not."
"So where have you been to look for her?" I ask.
"We went to the concert place first but it is all taped off. We talked...or Lena's dad talked to some police officials but no way we're we getting through. He begged them."
"And what did you see happening?"
"Still some ambulances and fire vehicles in there but we were a good way back from it so I couldn't see very much. Nothing but flashing lights."
"So have you been to any hospitals or..."
"Yeah, just one hospital. The main one. It's all so chaotic though. They are so busy helping injured people and stuff. They haven't time to talk to you. Lena's dad had pictures of her on his phone but nobody had time to look. I think that will have to be sorted out later, when they get organised. I just hope she is in one of the hospitals... but I don't know. Mum...they say there are some people dead."
"I know son but..."
I hear him gasping and I know he is in some kind of terror or shock. Oh Lord, I would give my right arm to be with him now.
"Patrick....hey son! Listen to me! Don't you start thinking the worst. Lena will be fine. You will find her. It will all be alright, you'll see," I tell him but I know I am lying to myself. How do I know what the outcome will be?
"I hope so," he whispers and I hear the anguish in his small voice. "I can't see me living without her mum, I honestly can't. If she is dead..."

"Don't talk like that Patrick. You've got to have hope! You've got to believe that she'll be ok. It's just a matter of being patient and helping her folks to find her. Look son, you've got to be strong for them, right? They must be going through hell at the minute, so don't show them your worries on top of their own. Lena would want you to be strong for them, you hear me."

"You're sounding like you know she's dead," he says. "'Lena would want you to be strong for them.'"

"If it sounded like that I did not mean it like that," I tell him. "Now where are yous staying? Will you be able to get some sleep? Have you had any more medical advice?"

"Here, I'll put you back to Herr Rosenthal. Bye."

"Bye son. Love you."

But Herr Rosenthal isn't there when I speak to him. I think they must have hung up by mistake. I have had some questions answered but I am left with other ones. Not least the one sitting on the edge of my bed.

"He's very worried," I say.

"That's understandable Bernie. It is just a waiting game now, and there's nothing harder."

"I want to go to him."

"I understand that. Who wouldn't?"

"Do you think I should?"

"I think you should get some sleep if you can. In the morning we can talk about that and we will make a better decision then, ok?"

'We'? I think. 'This is a 'we' matter now, is it?'

"Yeah, you are probably right."

He is still sitting on my bed.

"What time is it?" I ask.

"Twenty to three," he says standing up. "Time you were asleep."

"Yeah."

"I'll go. Goodnight again."

I just look at him. There's something in my eyes that he reads. He reads it well and sits down again.

"A hug Bernie...and that's all."

"A hug would be lovely."

"Come here."

I do and he's gone from my room less than a minute later.

Chapter 44

(Patrick McAleese)

This has to be one of the most traumatic mornings of my entire life. For a start, a few of the details of what happened last night have been on the radio news as we drive around the city; Lena's father has been translating for me and what he has told me has been jogging my memory. I have a misty vision now of a shadowy figure pushing past me on the steps of that church and hearing his fanatical mutterings.

We have driven to four different hospitals; Munich seems to have dozens of clinics and medical facilities; we have visited the main ones, looking for any news of Lena, but no joy. We have been phoning emergency numbers, or at least Herr Rosenthal has, but again nobody seems to have a clue about what has happened to her. We have given her details and description to the police but they haven't come back to us yet with anything concrete. It's like she has been vaporised off the face of the earth.

What I find totally frustrating is that all these conversations are going on in German and I cannot follow any of it. Even after another fruitless phone call Lena's parents are frantically gabbling away and I haven't a clue if there has been any trace yet. They seem to have forgotten that I am not understanding any of this. I feel extremely isolated. Stuck in the back of the car, all I can do is observe and try to pick up clues. I can sense the negativity from her dad; I can hear the two of them arguing away in their exasperation, their fear that their daughter may be dead. I don't need to be able to understand the lingo to see the dejection in his posture when he has finished inquiring at yet another hospital desk.

Presumably Lena didn't have anything on her which could be used to identify her.

'Identify her!!!'

The very term has me shuddering.

How is this going to feel if I find myself in the next few hours staring at a small figure beneath a white sheet on some cold mortuary slab? A scene from 'Silent Witness', except that as the sheet is pulled down I find myself staring at the face of the girl who has come to mean all the world to me. It's a nightmare image; it horrifies me and

I find it hard to shift as we drive to our fifth hospital, a smaller one in the west of the city, well away from the location of the bomb.

I tend to doubt that she will be here, it seems such a drive but, according to Lena's mum who turns to explain to me, someone at the University hospital has suggested to them that a few patients may have been taken out to this place as the other facilities filled up with casualties.

"It is a small chance," she explains. "It is our last hope. We must pray that she is there and she is safe."

Yeah, pray lady, pray. It can't do any harm, can it? I will pray myself, although I will never admit to anyone afterwards that I did. I don't believe; I can't bring myself to believe in a god who lets something like this happen. I can't for the life of me understand why anyone believes strongly enough in their god to actually carry out an atrocity like this, and in that god's name too!

'Allahu Akbar! God is Great!'

God is greatly over-rated if this is the kind of thing he inspires, if this is the kind of carnage he takes delight in. I don't believe in any god who would get himself mixed up in such idiocy and chaos. I don't believe, but still I will pray that god, if there is such a being... if there is a god who likes humankind and who doesn't like to see the people he is supposed to love die or get hurt for some evil cause. I will pray to any loving god who will help my Lena and help us to find her, if possible in the next hour or two before I go clean raving mad.

So I hear myself, inside myself, softly going over the words of the Lord's Prayer, choking a bit at the words 'your will be done on earth as it is in heaven,' and then stopping short at 'deliver us from evil'...while I think about the evil that happened last night, and the fact that I survived it, while others didn't, the 'others' possibly including Lena. Lena, who has just really found herself in the last few weeks, now lost again. In my head my prayer turns into a song, the one I wrote for her a while back.

My Magdalena, I will never leave you again

It becomes part of my prayer, like it or not. If it is answered I kinda make that mental pledge; 'I will never leave you again'.

All this while we are sitting in an endless traffic jam. Munich's efficient road systems seem to be as under stress as the rest of the city today. It seems to take ages before Herr Rosenthal eventually finds this 'Something-or-other-Clinic', a huge ice-cube looking construction, and parks the Passat in a rose-lined car-park. We approach the ultra-modern building, the sun dazzling our eyes as it reflects off its glass frontage. Inside the atmosphere is much less frenetic than the other hospitals we have visited; there are far fewer people in the foyer; the whole atmosphere actually feels quite cold and clinical, which I suppose isn't a bad thing for a hospital in normal circumstances but on this occasion gives me the creeps.

As we reach the main Information Desk I ask Lena's mother to try to translate the conversation for me.

"I really want to understand what they tell us," I say.

"I will try of-course but it is difficult."

I have to wait a while for her to start, after her husband talks to several officials. I watch as he shows a photograph but I can watch no longer. I join in the discussion and show them my screen-saver shot, a recent and very clear close-up of Lena's face. I start asking questions, regardless that they seem a bit taken aback to be having to switch so abruptly to English.

"This is a recent picture of her. Have you any way of telling if she is in this hospital? Can you show us which ward to go to to look for her?"

The main lady stares down at me. She is crazily tall and dressed in an arctic-blue trouser suit with matching eye-shadow; all about power, this one. She takes my phone, looks at the picture and turns her back to me to talk to her colleagues; if I am reading their body language properly this is a crucial moment. I don't like their serious silence as they look at my picture and then at each other.

"Please talk to me! Tell me what you are thinking," I plead. "Is she here? Have you any idea? Is she alive or..."

The lady slowly turns back to me and her expression does not give me a whole pile of joy.

"Who are you please?"

"I am Patrick; I am her partner," I hear myself tell her in a small voice. "Do you have any info about her?"

"We are not certain, you understand...but we think she may have been brought here. We must take some time to confirm this please, if you can take a seat and wait. I must contact the...the ah...various departments."

"Ok, but can you be as quick as possible please," I ask.

"Of-course, young man, but we have procedures to follow; we must not make any mistakes here, or raise any false hopes. So if you don't mind sitting over here in this private room. I will personally go down to *der Keller,* how do you say in English... I forget. I will make some checks. Would you mind if I take your phone with me? It may help in the identification."

"Of-course," I say.

She speaks in German to Lena's parents; I feel a cold draught go through the place as I watch their reaction to whatever she has told them. They hug each other immediately, the mother shakes with some instant shock.

Oh my God...please don't let this be bad news! Please don't let her be lying in some metal locker in a morgue!

"What have you told them?" I ask her. "Tell me please."

"I am unable to give you any information yet, because I do not know for sure, you understand."

"What is *'der Keller'*?"

"The basement," Herr Rosenthal says through a dry throat.

"The basement? But...why the basement? Are you saying that she is in the mortuary or what?"

"No, I am not saying anything, not yet. I only ask you to be patient and to be prepared for any kind of news."

"Ok, but please hurry," I tell her.

"Of-course."

She closes the door and leaves behind her an absolutely tense silence. None of the three of us wants to speak; each of us knows exactly what we are thinking, dreading. Herr Rosenthal sits with his head in his hands in utter despair, his breathing slow, deep and deliberate, like he is trying to keep himself from an outburst of some kind. His wife weeps gently beside him. Neither of them look at me or offer me any relief from my own fears. We sit like this for fifteen minutes. The only words spoken are in German, and they are few. I start to feel sort of naked without my phone; I want it back, not least to look at Lena but also to contact my mum. I need to hear her voice just now. My head starts to throb again and I hold it tightly at the sides.

These minutes drip like the slow melt of an icicle. How am I going to take this news? Feelings from my childhood echo back to me, feelings that are so difficult to put words around, feelings I endured as nightly torture while my parents fought and which climaxed on that ghastly night when my father left home for good. Back then I often experienced a sickly taste in my mouth; I always associate this kind of nausea with fear, like when I'm dreading something, and right now I am having a physical flashback to it, that taste!

The door opens. Three heads stare, animal intensity in our eyes.

It's just a random girl offering us coffee.
Deflation, relief and exasperation swirl together as we look at each other for the first time in ten minutes.
"I do not think so. Danke."
The catering girl leaves us to ourselves again, to our intimate disconnection. Actually I would have loved a strong coffee to try to shift this oral sourness.
Why are words so hard to come by in a situation like this where normally you are tripping over them? My brain feels like it has been sterilised; any thoughts I have are brittle, freeze-dried, without consequence. That is why there is nothing to say.
Footsteps. Purposeful footsteps across the tiled foyer.
Through the frosted glass panel I see the strobed flash of distorted blue, the gangly image of our news-bearer. She enters with more assurance than she had left us; she has news I think.
She speaks in German to the wide-eyed parents, then translates some for me, which I really appreciate.
"You will please come with me," she says. 'Sure I will,' I think as she gives me back my phone.
We scurry after her across the foyer to the lift. I watch her hand, closely. She ignores the 'E', the lowest button, and presses '5'.
Up we go. I try to read her face but she's the mistress of inscrutability. Not a clue. At least we are going up, not down. A good omen, I hope. Unless of-course...
Out of the elevator and along a quiet corridor. How come this place is so silent and calm while the other hospitals are chaotic today? I try not to be reading doom into every clue but I am failing miserably. We enter a side office and a white-coated doctor with a bent nose rises to meet us, shaking hands and introducing himself as Jan Badenhorst. Again I am hoping that the dialogue will be in English but I am disappointed. I have to listen to an endless introduction, trying to read between the lines, the clues in the body language of this doctor, of the Rosenthals, especially the mum. It's a mixed message from what I see, initial smiles and a hugging of her husband's arm, followed by concern.
"She is here and she is alive," Lena's mother tells me through a twisted smile, "but she is very ill."
"Fantastic," I say. "How ill? What is wrong with her?"
"Wait," she says and resumes listening.
To his credit the doctor turns to me and speaks in what sounds like a South African accent.

"Ah, you are the friend who doesn't speak German? I'm sorry; let me fill you in on your girlfriend. She was brought here by ambulance from the scene of the attack, quite late actually, after most casualties had been recovered and taken to emergency facilities nearby. I have been informed that initially it was thought that she was a fatality as well; she was actually found underneath such a body, that of a very large chap. It would seem that she was partially shielded by his bulk. He may have saved her life."
"Wow," I say. "Yeah, I remember there was some big guy with us. Is she badly hurt? She will recover, won't she?"
"It is too early to say. You must be patient. We have induced a coma, short acting sedatives and ventilation. That is standard procedure for anyone brought in who has a suspected brain injury. The next twenty four hours are the most important; let her brain and her vital organs settle. If we get her through that period she has a chance of making it."
"And what exactly are her injuries?"
"Well, given that she's been in an explosion she has been fortunate; few signs of serious external injury, a laceration on her lower leg...we took some shrapnel from there. An area of significant bruising on the back of her head; she has taken a forceable blow there, some abrasion and bleeding, though the skull seems to be intact. Still, you must understand that she was unconscious when she arrived here. In terms of head injury, as yet we do not know conclusively if there is damage to the brain. We will be conducting further scans today. The torso appears to be alright but our initial assessments can be difficult with an unconscious patient, so we will be monitoring lung function and all the internal organs, liver, kidneys, the gastrointestinal tract and so on. But for that one shrapnel wound the limbs seem to have been miraculously protected, given her proximity to the actual explosion and compared to some of the injuries we have seen in other victims. So it's just a matter of time...it is early yet, you understand? But you all can be very thankful for her miraculous survival thus far. Fingers crossed she will make a recovery but you must be prepared for any scenario."
"Can we see her?"
"Yes, of-course; she is in Intensive Care... so only from a distance."
I have never known that you could be so ecstatic and so distressed at the same time. Now I do. It is really difficult to describe these

conflicting feelings. As the Rosenthals resume their conversation with this doctor I send a quick text to my mum, just the basics.

I am absolutely desperate to see Lena for myself. I know she is not conscious, I know she is totally out of it and will not be able to see me or hear me but I just want to somehow communicate with her that she is going to make it through this...that she has to make it through this. I need to say some things to her, like that I love her, that I am going to stay here with her and be with her on this journey, that I am sorry I abandoned her in the gig. Actually it strikes me that if I hadn't come outside when I did I might not be here now; I certainly might not be in a position to be finding Lena, to be promising to take care of her. It is a freaky thought and, although it doesn't make any rational sense, I am sort of thankful that events worked out as they have. It could have been so much worse, like if both of us had been dancing together in that church and this fanatic had walked in and blew himself up right beside us. Heavens above! That would have been it for both of us. Goodnight! But I was out of it and escaped with only a bump to the head. She has survived, so far, because her little body was somehow protected by her friend, whatever his name was. It is all so random, so unreal.

"Can you follow me please," I hear the doctor say. "I am taking Magdalena's parents to see her now if you want to come; just a brief visit at this time because she will be taken for her full body scan in a few minutes."

I leap into line behind them and head towards the IC unit.

Chapter 45

Bernie Doherty

I have been very patient, waiting for him to phone all morning. I have waited long enough. It's nearly four o'clock and all I've had was the brief text from him saying that they had found Lena, injured but alive in some hospital.

I am on my own again. Jim has gone to his golf match. He promises to be back for tea and to see how everything is in Germany. I have shopping to do before that. Steak, red wine, the usual. No...actually the unusual.

Patrick answers my call straight away.

"What news son?"

"Well, I've seen her anyway."

"And how is she?"

"She's unconscious mum," he says. I can sense from this distance how distraught he is, despite his best efforts to keep himself under control.

"Yeah but that's to be expected," I tell him. *"That is to give her body time to heal, to adjust...that's what they do."*

"But it's terrible...like, she looks dead in the bed. I got a real shock. She's so pale, white as a ghost. Not a movement out of her; you can hardly see the sheet rising and falling as she breathes. She's all wired up to monitors and drips, tubes everywhere...it's unreal, like something out of a sci-fi movie. I feel like she has slipped so far away from me, from herself even."

"The poor girl. But at least she's not in pain."

"God sake mum! That's what people say when somebody has died."

"Yeah, sorry. I didn't mean it like that. I mean she is not suffering and that's the best you can say for now. Please God she makes it through. They can do amazing things in medicine nowadays."

"Yeah, but what if she doesn't? What am I ...how am I meant to....?"

"Patrick, for goodness sake get a grip of yourself. You have to stay positive son. Don't think about her not making it through. You keep thinking positive thoughts for her, say your prayers for her. I am going to Mass tomorrow with Jim and we are going to light a candle and get the priest to say a prayer for her. I've put it on Facebook too. Dozens of people are thinking about her."

It is strange, isn't it? I have never met his girl and yet I have half the country saying prayers for her like she was my own daughter.

"Jim? Jim who?"

"What?"

"You said Jim?"

"Oh yeah...sorry. I meant to tell you that I have this friend staying with me...."

'What am I saying?' I think. 'Staying with me!'

"I don't mean staying with me here at the house like. I mean he is playing golf in Portstewart and he came to see me."

Silence.

"I think he spoke to you on the phone last night, do you remember? Just before you spoke to me? You were still pretty dazed at that stage. Are you feeling any better today?"

"Jim who?"

"Jim...ah...God but his name has just gone clean outa my head for a minute. Devlin. Jim Devlin. He's from County Down."
"How come he's in the picture?"
"We met on the coach-tour to Scotland. He's been very kind to me, especially during all that happened last night. You'll like him Patrick, I know you will."
"Right....well, I'd better go here."
"Hang on, hang on Patrick. Don't go yet. You haven't told me anything about how you are."
I hear nothing for a while.
"Patrick? You still there?"
"When were you going to tell me about this Jim?"
"I was going to tell you. Sure you'll be home next week. I was going to tell you about it all when you get home."
Silence...then...
"I won't be home next week ma."
"What do you mean you won't be home? 'Course you'll be home. You have to start Uni on the Monday morning."
"I won't be home. I have to be with Lena."
"She'll be getting over it by then Patrick. She has good parents. You don't have to stay and hold her hand like."
"Well, I am staying with her anyway. Uni will understand. I have been in a terrorist bomb. There will be some way. Whatever, I'm staying with Lena."
I can't argue with him when he is in this emotional state, I know that. Best just to let him take his head."
"Ok," I say. "That's a big decision to be making when you are so upset son, but I understand. Would you not come..."
"I am staying mum," he interrupts.
"But next week is your birthday."
"Who cares? It's only a birthday."
"How long for, do you think?"
"No idea. As long as it takes."
"Ok. Would you want me to come over? I have never even met..."
"No, you stay with Jim there. I'll be alright. Bye."
"Patrick," I say...but he has gone.
This isn't good. Why has he taken this Jim thing so badly? It's my fault for dropping it into the conversation out of the blue; probably just shocked him, hence the reaction. Not good though. He needs me at the minute, more than for a long time, and there he is hanging up on me, cutting the communication.

I phone him back but no answer. Typical. I send him a long text.

> Love you son; so sorry I have annoyed u; I meant 2 tell u all about Jim but this crisis happened on our 1st nite out. He was a big help too. I will support whatever u decide about staying. Do u want me 2 contact Magee & explain? I am so sorry about Lena & I want to meet her. Seriously I will come if u want me 2. XMum

He comes back almost immediately.

> No prob. Just chill mum, don't be coming over. I need space 2 think this out & b with Lena. Will let u no later what the scan shows. XP

Isn't it just the strangest thing that he and I, who have been so close and so dependent on each other for years, are finding ourselves being wedged apart by these new relationships? All the more so, in that I have never met his Lena and he has never even heard of Jim. Maybe it always was inevitable that we would be divided like this, that he would be increasingly torn away from me by his lover, that I would find someone else to fill the void. But if so, it is something I haven't seen coming. And so abruptly! Maybe I've been in denial about it for yonks but today it has crept up on me and punched me between the eyes, punched me into the reality that life moves on as surely as the clock keeps ticking.

I just hope his head isn't totally ruled by his heart; life is a long haul and he needs to make good decisions now, otherwise he is throwing away his education and his future. I wish I could be with him and talk to him.

I'm going to look at flights to Munich, just a look, just to see.

Chapter 46

(Patrick McAleese)

We are back in Dr Badenhorst's office, the three of us facing him across his desk. It's late afternoon, verdict time.
The conversation is in German with English subtitles, at least that's how it feels. He talks at length to the Rosenthals, then throws me a very quick summary, his clipped Afrikaner accent matching the brevity of his staccato comments. I might feel marginalised, hurt, except that my focus is entirely on what is being said.
"The scans show no impairment of brain function at this point."
Brilliant! She is going to be ok. The fear that she would be brain-damaged and have to spend the rest of her life like a vegetable had been huge in my mind, especially after that stark image of her lying so pale and still on her bed.
Back to German for a bit...then..."All vital stats are good, Patrick."
"Fantastic," I hear myself respond to her mum. "Thank God."
A bit later I hear the doctor switch briefly to English. "Respiratory system seems largely unaffected, no rib fractures, lungs are fine."
Then German again, at length. The parents start to relax in their seats, still holding hands as they have been since they walked down the corridor to hear the verdict. I am pleased for them. I am pleased for myself, massively relieved by this news. Inside my head I start to hear Ed Sheeran's 'Perfect'.

> *'Well I found a woman, stronger than anyone I know*
> *She shares my dreams*
> *I hope that someday I'll share her home*
> *I found a love....'*

Then suddenly everything changes.
Everything!
Frau Rosenthal sits forward in her chair, urgently, her hand at her mouth...what have I just heard her say?
"*Das Baby? Welches Baby?*"
The doctor looks from one Rosenthal to the other, then to me. Lena's dad joins him. It is a stare of confusion, of question. In Herr Rosenthal's case there is an element of horror in the stare as well.
"Did you say 'baby'?" I ask.

"Ja, 'baby'," she repeats.

For a split second I think, Ah she's speaking in German of-course. I wonder what this 'baby' means in English. How does it translate? Funny that it sounds so similar to our word for a...for a baby like! Baby?

I am about to ask when the doctor speaks to me.

"I have just told them the good news that Magdalena's baby seems to be perfectly ok," he says. "You will be happy to hear...actually you seem very....perhaps you were not aware that your partner is pregnant?"

Oh my God! Baby!!!

What the hell...?

I want to run, run and hide. I need space right now! I get up and head to the door.

"Stop, young man! Stop there!" Lena's dad shouts. "You are not going away! Sit down!"

"No I need...just give me a minute on my own. I'm not going anywhere...just outside here," I say. And I do. Into the corridor. It can't be. Down the corridor. She can't be pregnant! Half-running, stumbling. No way can this be happening! A couple of nurses separate to let me run through between them, stare at me like I'm mad! She can't be; the only time we didn't use protection was that morning in the mountains. God, what was I thinking? Her as well...

Someone calls after me but I run on. Oh my good Lord!

I reach her ward. Push the door. There's a nurse on a chair, filling in a form on a clipboard. She stares at me. I stand by Lena's bed. I am sort of shivering. The blue monitor screens flash and bleep at me in synchronised mockery.

The nurse says something in German, very quietly. I hold a finger to my lips, look at Lena. Still so ghostly, almost translucent, like even her skin colour has been drained out of her. Whiter than white! But so peaceful. How can she be pregnant? She's lying there like a marble statue of the Blessed Virgin. Jesus Christ, how can she be pregnant?

"Lena," I whisper. "I love you. It's going to be alright babe."

Babe...yeah! Babe and baby!

"It's going to be alright."

The nurse has me by the arm, gently. She is pulling me back, back towards the door. I look back over my shoulder, half-expecting Lena to have sat up. This nurse is strong and not taking no for an answer. Out to the corridor.

"You can not do this," she says to me.
"I know. I'm sorry," I say. "I just had to see her. I didn't know..."
"Didn't know what?"
"That she was pregnant."
"Ah, I see. Still, you must not disturb her please. She must remain very still for now, you understand. You must wait in the other room."
"No problem," I say, backing away up the corridor. "Look after her."
"Of-course," she says with a smile. "I was, before you..."
I turn and, as I do, I am looking at my reflection in the glass panel of a door. This isn't me though. This is some magnolia-faced guy with blood-shot eyes and really messed up ginger hair, and he looks like he's just seen a ghost. A pathetically stupid looking bugger he is too.
I stumble slowly back to the office. By the time I've gotten there I have thought of several different options, none of which make any sense to me. The first problem though is to face up to these parents. It's gonna test me. And them!
They don't look at me as I re-enter the office. The doctor is talking but stops and waits for me to sit; the atmosphere is taut, like an over-tight guitar string about to snap.
"Look," I say. "I had no idea. Neither did Lena. I am sorry..."
"You should be sorry," the father says, not making any effort to soften his anger. His wife takes his hand and speaks softly to him. It doesn't change his course or tone. "I warned you and you promised to me that you would not do this. You promised before you went to the mountains."
"I know sir. I am sorry. It was...unavoidable."
"I do not know this word but it was a sin, a filthy sin against my daughter."
I shake my head but sit quiet at this piece of stupidity. There is no point in telling him that at that moment when we made love for the first time Lena and I both felt that we were in our purest, most sacred, most alive moment.
"What have you to say for this?"
"Only this sir. That what had happened to Lena in the past, when she was abused by those guys...that was a sin, yeah! She had just told me about it that night up in the Karwendel. She wanted me to know. But when we slept together up there, that was not a sin, as you call it...because we are in love, so it was the most natural thing in the world. The best thing I ever did."
The doctor slipped sensitively out of his office, leaving us to argue this out.

"Ja, and the most natural thing in the world is for the girl to fall pregnant as a consequence. You will not suffer. She will."
"Fall pregnant?" I say. "Why 'fall', like it is a terrible sin? I thought god is supposed to be the life-giver, is he not? With all due respect sir, this pregnancy thing is his idea, so how can it be a 'fall'?"
"You presume to argue with me about God, young man?" he fumes.
Again Frau Rosenthal comes to my help. "Anton, Patrick is right. We should not be having argument now. We should be celebrating that Magdalena is alive. Also to pray that she may recover. We should be thanking God that the baby she is carrying inside is also going to survive, not arguing this about right or wrong."
He sulks in silence for a while, then, "Ja, but we must consider what to do also. Should Magdalena have this baby or not? And if she does, should it be put for adoption, like she was?"
"Hang on sir," I say. "Surely this is not your decision? It is Lena's decision. You can advise and all that but Lena...Lena and me actually, we make the call."
"How do you mean? She is a child! You are a boy. A boy from Ireland. You will disappear and leave her with the consequences of your lust."
"Sorry, Herr Rosenthal, but you need to understand that I am not going anywhere. Lena and I are together. We were before and now there is all the more reason to be together...whatever she decides about the baby."
Frau Rosenthal comes to me, pulling her chair over to face me. "You mean that you will not run away Patrick?"
"Of-course I will not run away."
"But you have studies. You have a life in Ireland. Your mother. You are so young. You cannot take care of our daughter," she says.
"I can try my best to take care of your daughter, and my daughter, if it turns out to be a girl," I tell her. "It's not the first time in history this has happened like."
"But your own family...?" she says.
"Put it this way. I have had years of experience of learning how not to be a father. Or a husband. Lena and I will work this all out."
"Ja, but she is so young. Perhaps she must have this, how do you say in English....? Ending pregnancy?"
"Abortion, you mean? Yeah, well, maybe....but it's up to Lena, isn't it?"
Now horrified expression crosses her face.

"Nein, nein, what is this I am saying," she says, looking more and more confused and distraught. "She can not do this. It is a terrible thing to think of. Oh Magdalena! What are you to do?"
Herr Rosenthal has been sitting head in hands. Now he starts a whole lament. When he finishes his wife explains to me.
"He speaks about how we are trying to rear Lena, how we have struggled as parents of a baby adopted who is of colour, how we nearly lost our marriage when she was losing her way at that terrible time. It is too sad."
"What is to become of her?" he cries in English. "She has learned nothing from us, nothing from our church. She has turned her back on her faith. She has shamed us over and over. Now if she has this baby she will be a child who is an unmarried mother, like her own mother was."
"It is very different. Lena has me," I say.
"You? And how do you think you can support her? Your songs? Your street singing?"
"Yeah, maybe that," I say, "but I can get a job as well."
"What job? You don't even have our language. You may think you can support her at the moment but you are young and you will lose your interest; you will grow tired of her wildness and her wilfulness. You will leave her. She may end up on the streets. This is not a good society for such young girls who have lost their way."
His wife stops him again, speaking to him quite forcefully in German. When she finishes I add my own 'wisdom'.
"Herr Rosenthal, my mother taught me not to lose hope. Face up to difficulties, keep the faith."
"What faith? You have no faith, I think. You are outside of church."
"Maybe, but I have faith in Lena, and in myself."
"That is not enough for living, young man. I fear for you both."
"Well don't. Look, you must have faith in whatever you believe in...but please don't sow your doubts into our lives."
There is a long silent pause as he thinks about this. Eventually it is broken by Lena's mum.
"You have spoken so well, Patrick."
After maybe five minutes of quietness her husband gets up.
"Now we should go to see Magdalena, together," he says and out of the blue he stretches out his arm to shake hands with me.
It's a nice gesture. I am amazed at this generosity in the middle of his shock and anger. We shake, a first sign of hope and Lena's mum smiles her approval through sad eyes.

Later I sit with Lena through the night. The parents have gone to a hotel, which I am glad of. There was no way they were going to persuade me to leave her; when they saw that they seemed content to trust me to be with her.
I fall asleep on the chair but only after I have sent my mum an email, sort of to explain everything that's happened, the baby and so on. It's going to be some crazy bit of news for her. Granny Bernie!
In the morning the door opens and Gaby comes in; he gives me a hugely warm hug. Thoughtfully he has brought the guitar.
"I am so sorry," he whispers. "Poor Lena."
"Thanks for coming," I say as he stares down at her.
"Is she going to be alright?"
"We hope so. Today they will begin to take her off the drugs that have her in this coma; then we will see what happens."
"I brought your guitar so you can sing, you know...to bring her back to you. All those songs you wrote for her."
"It's a risk though," I tell him. "Might send her the other way!"
"I don't think so, my friend," he laughs. "She needs your therapy more than ever now."
"You know about the baby?"
"Yeah. Just now. Met her folks in the restaurant."
"How were they about it?"
"Somewhere between annoyed and resigned," he tells me. "They do think a lot of the baby's father though...I should tell you that. They think that if she recovers from this and decides to have the baby you will be a good father."
"Jeez...really?" I say.
"Yeah, really."
"That's cool," I say. I am well surprised.
"But Patrick, I have been thinking about my little friend Lena. She is just a girl to me, not much more than a child. Because of this, because she is so young..."
"Yeah, what?"
"It is difficult to say...may I ask if you are thinking it is best to stop the pregnancy? She is so...unfortunate, don't you think?"
"It's an option, I suppose..... but it will be her call."
"Of-course, but you are the father, so you have an opinion as well?"

"To be honest Gaby, I am kinda shell-shocked. At the minute I could agree to anything. I need time to think it all out, the consequences, the practicalities."

"The practicalities are easier, in the circumstances. She is only what...six, seven weeks pregnant, ja?"

"How'd you work that out? You her personal sexual guru like?"

He laughs. "No, but I was in the mountains that night as well."

"Ah yeah. Good guess."

"What I am trying to say is this. Lena is not 'very' pregnant; she has just had a massive physical trauma. She is in a coma. And she is already in hospital. To end it now is easy; it is understandable too because it gives Lena a better chance of recovery, don't you think?"

"I don't know what to think. Yeah, I see your point. But it will be her call, and whatever she decides I will back her."

"Me too, if that's any comfort. But then I will not be the one changing dirty nappies at four o'clock in the morning!"

"Ah Gaby, I was relying on you. That's the least you could do after leaving the two of us alone in that tent," I tell him. "It's all your fault."

"No, no," he laughs. "It's just a pity you aren't gay; then this would never have happened."

Chapter 47

(Patrick McAleese)

It's been a very long day.

Lena had her drip and ventilator tube removed around mid-day, although she is still wired up to all sorts of 'bleeping' monitors. Dr Badenhorst has told us that this is the crucial stage; if and when she wakes up she will be very drowsy for a while, she may have perception difficulties, personality change, some loss of normal function. He cannot be sure. Nor does he know how long she may still be unconscious. It could be hours, days even.

We take it in turns to sit with her, but, having said that, I find it impossible to disengage with what is happening back in the ward when I am out walking around the hospital campus in the warm September air. The whole thing has this surreal feeling about it.

I visit a nearby store to stock up on a sandwich and some comfort food. The newspaper headlines blare out at me. I can't read the German but it is easy to read the figures and the pictures. How lucky Lena and I have been, given the number of casualties. I watch people's faces as they scan the headlines or buy a paper. Maybe it's just my imagination but I think I see a new bleakness in their eyes, a sort of dazed fear where usually it's a sophisticated indifference. Knowing that terror has come to their city isn't easy to process.

My phone bleeps and I see an email from my mum. This is going to be interesting.

Hi Patrick, Well you don't half know how to turn a story into a blockbuster. I am still in shock. My good God son! I had slept in this morning after a late night. Jim ringing the doorbell woke me for Mass, so I never got your email until after we got back home. There we all were, listening to Father Murphy saying prayers for poor Lena and her lying in a critical condition; it's maybe just as well he didn't know about the other condition or he might have been less inclined. Agh no, he's a sound priest.

So my wee boy has managed to turn himself into a father, and me into a granny, please God...that's if everything goes well of-course and Lena makes it through this. It gives me very complicated feelings and thoughts. I am not going to condemn you, Patrick. How could I do that with my history? But when you get home I might get you some material to read about contraception. Do you know how far gone she is?

Have you contacted the uni yet to ask for time out? Even a couple of weeks should be do-able according to Jim. His daughter had to take a break from Queens when her mother was killed. Jim sends his best wishes, by the way, and is looking forward to meeting you. He has been more than kind; he couldn't have arrived into my life at a better time.

Everybody is asking about you and sending best wishes, even some of your old school teachers. You probably haven't had time to keep up to speed with all the Facebook posts and comments but your story is known far and wide now. I wish I could be with you. Talking about it on the phone is no substitute and texts are hopeless to say what I am feeling. Neither can this email. I would love to know, for example, how Lena's folks are taking all this. I am sure you are not flavour of the month. Don't let it get you down, alright. Stay strong. You are the strongest 20 year old I know and the best son I could ever have asked for. You'll come through this so hang in there. Love you, Mumxxx

Thanks mum; I am trying to do my best, but sitting out here on this immaculately tidy lawn with my back against a sturdy lime tree I am feeling very alone. I am disconnected from my folks at home, from all the securities of the old Academy, from my college mates and now from this girl who has so totally invaded and taken me over.

The evening traffic roars past on the nearby autobahn; Bavarians listening to their radios, already moving on from the tragedy of Friday night in their city and wondering what is new news in the world; Münchners with their own little lives to be leading, their own private thoughts in their own particular language, each isolated from each other by braking distances. And I am isolated in my own thought-cocoon, in this moment of not knowing who I am or what the hell I am doing in my life. Yes, I know who I was, or at least I thought I did; I know what I was aiming for; I know when I was at my best...generally with a guitar and a set of ideas and words to be crafting into a song.

Now? Now I don't know very much. Not of the big picture anyhow. Yeah I know I am smelling the scent of fresh-cut grass and it isn't any different to the grass in Coleraine; I know, as I scratch my back against it's sinewy bark, that this tree has been here for maybe a couple of hundred years and will outlive me by the same again, unless it decides to fall over on me and end it for both of us.

These are weird thoughts, but not any weirder than the thought that I nearly lost the first girl I have ever truly been in love with, may still lose her! Not any weirder than the idea that in a few months time I may be a dad, nor the notion that the straight-forward life I had expected to live on our wee western island may have to be chucked in favour of a future in the middle of mainland Europe.

If I could relive the past couple of years would I change any of it though? If I could have foreseen the future back during that "Find the Fallen" trip would I have chickened out of it, any of it? I would change last Friday night, yes of-course; I would stay well away from world music gigs in Munich! I sit too long pondering all this. It's not that I am depressed, far from it. I'm just challenged to look into my own inner mind and try to put a bit of order on the avalanche of emotions that have crashed over me in the last couple of days.

I find myself thinking of lyrics for a song, or maybe just lines for a poem. Usually with me it's the guitar chords and the tune that comes first; right now the words are sprouting up like mushrooms from mental spores deep inside. This is different; these ideas don't seem to need to hang on to a tune structure; they shoot up towards the light and I cannot hold them back. And the words are strange to me, almost alien...like my head has been taken over by someone from a different century. I scribble frenetically on the inside of my sandwich wrapper, listing ideas, scoring out words.

If I had known when I saw you first,
your perfect beauty darkening my screen,
the hidden girl behind those fallen eyes,
the sorrow and the pain of where you'd been.
If I had read some trusted horoscope
or heard a warning bell of coming fire...

My phone vibrates in my pocket as a message arrives

> Where are you Patrick? Please come back at once to be with Magdalena. She is still in coma but we need to leave for evening church. AR

Sorry; of-course you do Herr Rosenthal. I have just been seduced by the muse yet again and lost track of reality. These words will wait for me though. Lena may not. I start jogging back to her.

It's just the two of us. Lena lies there, same as before. I can see no change, apart from the obvious... the web of tubes and wires that surrounded her has thinned out a bit during the day. Ten hours since they reversed the induced coma. No sign of consciousness yet. 'Oh God,' I am thinking, 'I hope she is not brain-damaged or something. 'I know the tests say she's not but I don't see any change in her from earlier. "Come back to me babe," I keep breathing into her ear.

They tell me that she can probably hear me; according to some site I read people in comas often return to consciousness with stories of lucid dreams and tell of their awareness of things around them when they are apparently dead to the world. So I keep talking to her. "Do you remember when..." and I tell her some of my best memories of the bizarre things that have happened in our short lives together.

I keep telling her that I am sorry I left her alone in the concert, that if she wakes up I will never do anything like that again. I talk about the time I found her in that pub in Dingle; how that decision to go look for her changed the course of my life, and how glad I am that I returned from my doubts in 'The South Pole Inn'. I talk about that first night we spent together in the mountains. I wonder should I tell her about the baby? Maybe not yet, it wouldn't be fair if, by any chance, she is hearing and understanding me and can't express any distress she might feel about being pregnant. Actually, I start to wonder...perhaps she even knows already. She must have missed her last period, maybe two. She never gave a hint to me if she did. Unless that is why she has been a bit withdrawn lately, quiet and not her usual self. I'd been wondering if it was down to my leaving soon.

I play Otto's guitar to her. Thank you Gaby for bringing it, a brilliant thought. I play every tune I've ever written, every song, though I don't always project my voice above a whisper. I play into the late evening, hours on end, until the tips of my fingers hurt. It's like a busking marathon in *sotto voce*.

I am half-way through '*My Magdalena*' for the second time when I suddenly begin to suspect that... I am being watched!

I flick a look to Lena. Her eyes are slightly open. Her head is still in the same fixed position but she seems to be trying to squint at me.

"Lena, can you hear me?"

The eyes close again. Maybe it was just my imagination. I watch her intensely, wondering if I should call a nurse or someone. For about half a minute it is back to the usual stillness, then, as I keep repeating her name, her eyes open again. Thank you God! I can hardly keep from some outburst of relief.

"Lena babe, can you hear me? It's Patrick. Are you able to speak?"

No answer, just the sideways glance. There's no recognition in her eyes. I decide to just wait and see, so I take her hand and sit beside her on the bed, gently stroking her hair. I am watching her eyes intently for any sign of question, of pain or of understanding. They are focused on me for a while, as if trying to figure out who I am; then they start to swivel around the room, very slowly at first. I can see some sort of query in there but then she shuts them again and goes back into drowsiness.

I press the 'attention' switch and a nurse puts her head in the door with a questioning "Ja?"

"She has just wakened up, just a little bit. She looked at me," I say.

"Good. I call doctor now."

When she's gone I ask, "Lena, can you hear me? You are in hospital. There was a bomb but you are alright now."

The eyes open again, half-open I should say. She stares up at me, so innocent, so vacant. I want to fill her up with the old Lena again, transfuse some joy and life into her.

"Should I play some more music?" I ask, for want of a better idea.

"*Bitte.*" It's softer than a whisper, more like a breath of air that's tired from carrying this feather of a word.

Fantastic! She is ok. I start to finger-pick "Imagine" and I swear she gives me the faintest of a smile. It's hard to know though, and the moment is disturbed by the entry of Dr Badenhorst.

I watch and listen as he speaks in gentle German to Lena. She just stares at him and listens without response, then I see her eyes wander off to the side and her head make a tiny turn. Her face wince in pain though and she stops, just the eyes roving. It strikes me that she is looking for me, the familiar face; it's a great feeling to realise this...recognition, memory, so I step forward into her line of vision and she locks on to me like I am magnetic.

"You remember Patrick, ja?" the doc asks her.

"Ja," she whispers. Simple but it is the best thing I think I've ever heard.

Monday evening, three days after the terrorist attack.

Our own terror has evaporated spectacularly over the past twenty-four hours as Lena has returned to us. Earlier today I had a period alone with her in her private recovery ward. It was a special time, both of us just so thankful to still be here, alive and in one piece and, above all, with each other. We didn't say much; she was still very tired and dozed off just when I was getting the courage worked up to tell her about the baby. Probably the meds.

Now her folks are here too, gathered around her bed. I don't have a clue how they are going to approach the subject of the pregnancy and more and more I wish I had managed to talk to her about it first. Now it's too late. I am just hoping Herr Rosenthal doesn't throw some sort of fit. Lena doesn't need that right now. Despite her smiles and her warmth to me she hasn't actually said a lot. It's as if there is some part of her that I can't reach again. Maybe it's only a reaction to the trauma she's been through but it feels as if she is not quite as sure and secure with me as she had been before.

The chat is general for a long while, too long a while. Eventually her father takes the bull by the horns and speaks to her; it's all in their own language of-course, and makes me regret all the more my own hesitation earlier. Thankfully though, he sounds gentle, sympathetic even. I watch Lena's face for an emotional reaction. Nothing. She just looks up at the blank screen of the television opposite. Her dad keeps talking; he appears to have asked her some questions and is waiting for an answer.

Lena doesn't respond. She seems locked away again, unemotional and detached. I can stand this silence no longer. I get up from my chair and go to sit beside her on the bed. I try to put my arm around her but she feels stiff, resistant. I whisper into her ear.

"Lena, please don't go away from me again. Whatever you are thinking please tell me. I need to know."

The only response I get from her is that I feel her shoulders start to shake; she begins to weep, her head buried against me.

"Just give me some minutes alone with her," I ask the parents and they disappear without complaint, apart from her father's upturned hands.

"Are you worried about the baby, the pregnancy?" I ask.

She nods and, through her sobs, I hear her whisper, "I am so scared Patrick."

"Don't be scared babe. I will be..."

"How can I be not scared? It is...terrible."

"I know babe," I say. "It's a massive shock. What I mean to say is, try not to worry about it too much at the minute. Whatever happens, I will be here for you."

Slowly she settles down a bit. "How will you be here with me? You go back to your mother, to your course. You are leaving... next week? I am alone," she whispers through her tears.

"No, no way. I am here. I am staying with you, until..."

Until? Until what I don't know. After a bit she turns away and speaks. "You want me to get rid of it?"

"No I don't want you to get rid of it, not unless you want to."

"But you want me to, don't you?" She speaks very slowly. "So you can be free to go back to Ireland and be alone, as before. This has

all been a fairytale summer, Hansel and Gretel, but the fairytale is over. I am left here with a baby inside. I did not want this."
"Lena, please stop and listen."
"No Patrick. You must listen. When I did not have my period I feared I was pregnant. I did not want to tell you, so that you could go home and I could work out what to do. Maybe an abortion. Or maybe I would do what my mother did...leave my parents, have the baby and give it away to some person who could look after it and give it a better future. I did not know what to do, I could not tell you. I tried to be happy so that you would not notice. And you did not notice; you were happy and you were going home again. So now you must go home. Like this had not ever happened. This is all my fault. It cannot spoil your life."
I am well shocked by this outburst. I have to hang in there with her and get her through this.
"It is never your fault, Lena...and nothing is spoiling my life. You are the best thing ever to happen to me. I am not leaving you."
"But you must. You must complete your study."
I shake my head, but I can't think what to say to her.
"Do you want me to have an abortion Patrick?"
"No, I don't Lena. I want you to make the decision."
"But it is your baby too. You must tell me what to do."
"I can't do that babe. That's not fair. Look, when we made love it was a mutual thing, wasn't it? It wasn't one sided. We talked about it; we both wanted it. It was a totally together thing. So this decision should be the same, right?"
"Yes," she says, "but you are not telling me what you want to do?"
"I am, but you are not listening!"
"What? I am listening."
"Did you hear me say I was going back to Ireland, to my studies, to my mum? Did you hear that? Because that is not what I said, is it?"
"No."
"I said I was going to be with you. That is what I meant. I am not going away Lena."
"But how can you stay? What will you do?"
"What have we been doing? Making music together. We can still do this, sometimes. Maybe record more songs, sell them."
"I don't think that this will be enough."
"Yeah but there are plenty of chances to work around here. Maybe in the Irish bar, you know. I can learn German. Maybe I can take a music course here too. It might count towards my degree."

"Maybe. But what will you tell your mother, and your college?"
"I have already told my mum. She knows I am staying."
"You told her? She knows about the baby?"
"Yip, and I will be emailing my tutor to tell him the situation, ask for a year's leave from study. I can go back next year and pick it up."
"Ja, you see? You will go back. You will leave me next year and..."
"No I won't babe. You will be with me. You and the baby, right? That's if you want to have the baby. You haven't told me yet. This is all coming from me. You haven't said anything."
"I know. I do not know what to say."
"What is your instinct? You are so young; that was Gaby's opinion."
"You have discussed this with Gaby? Not first with me?"
"Lena, for God's sake," I say, exasperated. "At that stage we hadn't a clue if you were going to make it out of your coma."
"Ok, but God did bring me from the coma, you know this, ja?"
"Whatever. Anyhow, you were going to keep it from me that you were pregnant, so that's us even, yeah? And you still haven't told me how you feel about having the baby or not."
"I know. It's difficult."
"Try me. At least you understand now that I am going to be with you whatever. Does that help?"
"Of course," she says, then pauses to think what to tell me. She takes the little Maria Magdalena statue which her folks have placed on her bedside locker. Holding it up, she stares at it intently. Eventually she says, "My mother was in this same circumstance, except that she was abused and she was on dope, and she didn't have someone like you to love her. But she still gave me life, yes?"
"Too right. If she only knew how happy I am for that choice," I tell her. "And if she only knew what a cool girl her daughter turned out to be; I think you've done her proud, and the Rosenthals of-course."
"'Done her proud?' I do not understand this."
She stops me as I begin to explain.
"But also, I want to see this baby of ours," she tells me. "I want to see how its ginger hair will look on top of its brown face. It will be a Celtic-Egypt mixture."
I laugh with her.
"And I want to know if it will play music," she adds.
"Do you wonder if it is a boy or a girl?"
"Of-course," she says, "but I hope a boy; then if you ever go away I will have this boy to remember you by...your songs too, of-course."

"But that won't be necessary," I insist, "because I am not going away. This is one Northern Irish boy who is going to stay in Europe."
"Until he leaves," she teases.
"And if he leaves he will be bringing his wife and his little girl with him to Ireland, you better believe it, Magdalena Rosenthal."
"'His wife? And his little girl'?" she smiles. "It will be a boy! And who said I was ever going to marry you, Patrick McALeese?"
"Nobody, but you will have to though, won't you?"
"Why will I have to?"
"I can think of dozens of reasons."
"Tell me these reasons."
"'Cause you love me, 'Cause I am the father of your baby. 'Cause I am the only one who can write the songs for us."
"Ha, ha," she says. "I do not think this one is a good reason."
"Well, here's a good reason. After Brexit you won't be allowed to come to live in Norn Ireland with me, 'cause you're an EU citizen. You'll need a wedding certificate to say that you're married to me."
"Oh, I see," she laughs, "so it is just a...how do you say? A marriage of convenience? A wedding after blackmail?"
"Maybe," I say. "I'm your ticket to the future."
"You have a high opinion of yourself."
"And why wouldn't I? I have the most beautiful girl on the planet and we are going to be together from now on, married or whatever."
"Ok," she says, "but not 'whatever'. We can be married I think. Perhaps. Eventually."
"Great," I say, sitting forward to hold her. We've only just begun when her parents open the door. Lena pushes me off, half-kissed.
"But first you must ask my father and mother."
Cheeky smile.
"Ask what?" her father says as he takes her hand.
I hesitate, looking at the laughter in Lena's dark eyes.
"Please go on," she says. "I cannot wait to hear this."

Chapter 48

Bernie Doherty

And so I lost my Patrick. Lost him to Europe, 'as part of the Brexit negotiations'...that's what I told Mr Johnstone in work. I think he sort of half believed me too; either that or he just thinks I'm as mad as he always suspected.
"Oh right," he said, as if he expected me to go on to outline the new Irish border arrangements next.
And I have had my first conversation with the mother-to-be of my first grandchild; Patrick FaceTimed me from Lena's hospital bed, literally, and we chatted. A nice girl, like he always told me. Still very pale, despite her ethnic colouring, like a cup of coffee that somebody had poured far too much milk into. Not much more than a child and yet she's carrying his baby, God love her. What I liked about her though was that she just seemed so sincere and warm as a person, even in these unbelievably difficult circumstances that she's in.
"Patrick has told me so much about you; it is all good too," she said. "He is very proud of his mum."
That was nice now, wasn't it? And of-course I was telling her that she must come soon to Coleraine and meet us all, all two of us, three if you include Jim...which, increasingly, I do.
"How about you come here for Christmas, the pair of you?" I asked. "We even have a big Continental Christmas market in Belfast to make you feel at home. Frankfurters and wheat beer."
"If I am with Patrick I will feel at home," she said, giving him her shy smile, the warm glow in her brown-sugar eyes enough to melt him.
God but isn't she the wee romantic. Seems like she's got the waffle-virus, no doubt straight from the lips of my smooth-tongued son.
"But you'll come, won't you?" I asked.
"Lena will be five months pregnant by then," Patrick told me. "Are you allowed to fly at that stage like?"
"Listen to you! It's a bit late to be starting to follow rules and take precautions," I told him.
"Whatever mum," he said with a reluctant half-smile.
"Of-course she can fly. It will give her and me the chance to get to know each other, before the baby like."
"Yeah, I know all that, but money...don't know if we'll be able to afford it then."
"You know what, Patrick, leave all that to me. Promise me you'll come."

"Ok, promise...if you're paying. Thanks."
"I didn't say I was paying," I told him.
"Well...what then? You said to leave it to you."
"Yeah, I did. Leave it to me. I'll phone yer man in Sailors and get you gigs every night of the week; that will help your money situation, alright?"
A sideways smile from him at the mention of work.
"But...I thought you wanted us home so you could get to chat to Lena?"
"Exactly son. And as I am chatting to Lena you'll be out earning your bread, singing your songs, leaving the two of us in peace to get to know each other."
"Jeez mum!" he said. "I'm starting to regret the promise already."
Lena popped her head back in front of the screen, smiling.
"Ja! This is good. I think I need to learn how you are talking to Patrick, controlling him like this," she said. "You will teach me please?"
"Of-course Lena," I told her. "Us women have to stick together, right?"
"I think so, yes," she said and she snuggled into him on the hospital bed.

Acknowledgements

In the process of writing this story I have very much appreciated help and advice from the following;

Tassilo, Marille and Sophia Mueller, generous and patient Bavarian friends who have not only provided translation advice but have allowed me the privilege of seeing their beautiful country and its local culture through their insightful eyes;

Hannah Polityck, a very able German student who was involved in the 'My Adopted Student' Project and who provided perceptive editorial and translation comments;

A number of friends and family who contributed to the writing and editing process, including Stephen Steger-Hoey, Connor Richmond, Dr Gareth Jones and my own children.

Sara Marques who generously (and bravely) allowed a total stranger to take the phone-pic which became the foundation image when I was designing the front and back covers of the book.

The talented David Moore who collaborated with me in writing and performing several of Patrick's songs for upload to Internet platforms. (These may be listened to on Soundcloud, on the accounts of 'DavidMoore', 'dadunlop' or 'Patrick McAleese'. My own Vimeo account also contains video presentations of some of the songs.)

Finally, deepest gratitude to my wife Mary whose painstaking reading of the text has as ever been invaluable.

Author's note

'We, The Fallen' is a work of fiction. While I was inspired to write the story during my recent involvement with the 'My Adopted Soldier' Project, the characters and events portrayed in this novel are entirely products of my imagination and bear no relationship to any persons or happenings involved in that or any other project.
Anyone interested in the work of the actual project can access information at www.myadoptedsoldier.com
This has a link to RTE Nationwide's programme about the project.

ABOUT THE AUTHOR

David Dunlop was born and raised in north Antrim, N Ireland. He spent many years in education, both as a teacher and as a school leader; in those roles he exercised his passion to bring together young people from across N Ireland's various divides so as to encourage a shared understanding of history and culture. To that end he wrote and directed several stage musicals with historical and cross-cultural themes and which drew on his experience of various musical genre.
David's first two novels, 'Oileán na Márbh' and 'The Broken Fiddle', were works of historical fiction, both set in the north-west region of Ireland. 'We, The Fallen' is his first novel to have a contemporary setting and theme. All three are available from the usual online websites.

email- dadunlop50@gmail.com

Printed in Great Britain
by Amazon